WITHDRAWN

Say it Was

The Way It Was

By the same author

Bowie
Pilgrims
Sophisticated Ladies

A beginning, a middle
and an end (24 poems)

The Way It Was

Gerard Mac

ROBERT HALE · LONDON

ISBN 978-0-7090-8645-1

Robert Hale Limited
Clerkenwell House
Clerkenwell Green
London EC1R 0HT

www.halebooks.com

2 4 6 8 10 9 7 5 3 1

Typeset in 10½/13pt Sabon
by Derek Doyle & Associates, Shaw Heath
Printed and bound in Great Britain
by Biddles Limited, King's Lynn

To Jack, Jessica, Angus
Harry and Sally

'We didn't want to fight, Dad. It
was just the way it was.

Tom Blanchard to his father,
Boston 1782

ONE

THERE was a sudden hush in the crowded hall as the man on the stage repeated his allegation. 'And for anyone who didn't quite catch what I said or maybe can't believe his ears, I'll say it again. All redcoats, officers and men, are thieves and rapists.'

A slightly built man of about fifty in a powdered wig and with frills at his wrists rose meekly to protest. 'Surely, sir, such robust language in the presence of ladies. . . .'

The man on the stage, powdered with nothing more than the dust of a day in the saddle, smiled down at his timorous heckler and replied with exaggerated contrition. 'I am so sorry, madam, I have no wish to offend you.'

At the back of the hall someone laughed. There was a scraping of chair legs and Ben Withers, with a sidelong glance at his two friends, Tom and Hank Blanchard, stifled a chuckle and they, too, struggled to contain their mirth.

The stout figure of a Mrs Hegarty stood up. Mrs Hegarty, who feared no man. 'You may think you are clever, coming here with your offensive remarks, Colonel Morgan, if that's what they call you, but you have no business making fun of decent people.'

The man in the powdered wig smiled uneasily to express his appreciation but Mrs Hegarty had something to say to him, too. 'And you have no right to prevent him from telling what he knows, John Hawkins.'

She turned back to the stage. 'You are making some very serious charges here, Colonel, but we want to hear the truth. If you have proof of what you are saying, then let us hear it.'

Deciding it was time to leave, one of the ladies present stood up and made her way to the end of her row. Others followed, some shepherding out disgruntled daughters and children who sensed they were about to be deprived of the chance to witness a rare old row.

Colonel Morgan waited until his audience had settled down then he noted how attentive they all were, as if they were eager to be entertained by some new and preferably salacious gossip. A tough, wiry man in his fifties, he had been through many wars. A professional soldier, he had been in the British Army, driving a supply wagon, in the Seven Years' War with France. He had been wounded in the mouth in that war and he had lost most of the teeth in his lower jaw, a tale he never tired of telling. He liked to boast, too, that he had once been flogged for striking an English officer – and he had the scars to prove it.

But, despite his shortcomings and though a daunting figure at first sight, Dan Morgan inspired a rare loyalty and admiration in those who served under him. Racked now by rheumatism and a nagging sciatica that gave him a noticeable limp, he was still prepared to come out of retirement to recruit and to lead men in the rebel cause. He turned to his adjutant and, with a curt nod, stood back.

The adjutant, a lieutenant of no more than twenty years of age, stepped forward to face the hushed audience. 'Ladies and gentlemen of Boston,' he began, 'it is our intention this evening to show you the depths of depravity and inhumanity to which these so-called "soldiers" of the British Army are prepared to sink. We call upon you good people to hear and to take note of what ill fate has befallen so many of our womenfolk at the hands of these . . . these animals.'

A line of Morgan's men stood at the back of the stage. They were dressed in everyday farming clothes, none wore a uniform but each carried a rifle. Slightly to one side of them stood three disconsolate young women. The presence of these young women had affronted more than one gentleman in the audience and almost all of the older ladies. Who were they? Why were they here? They looked like camp followers in need of a good bath.

The young officer beckoned to one of the girls to step forward. 'Tell these good people your name.'

'Ella Frost,' the girl said. 'Ma name is Ella Frost.'

'And you have a story to tell, Ella.'

The girl nodded and the lieutenant smiled in encouragement. 'Please,' he said. 'Proceed – and speak up.'

The audience by now was mostly male and intimidating. The girl looked at the blur of faces then down at her interlocked fingers. 'Ah lived with ma pappy and ma sister and ma sister's baby in ma pappy's house near a place called Graves End.'

'An' where might that be?' a red-faced man in the second row demanded. He was a meat wholesaler, dependent for much of his business on the local Army barracks and from the look in his eye he was ready to challenge everything the girl said.

'That's out on Long Island, sir,' the lieutenant said.

'Where 'bouts on Long Island?'

Colonel Morgan stepped forward. 'Will you shut your great fat mouth and listen?'

The butcher sank back in his seat as, gently and in a totally different tone of voice, Morgan turned to the girl. 'Miss Ella, if you please.'

The girl looked down at her hands. 'We were in the house when those bloodybacks come crashing in with their bayonets pointing. They ast ma pappy if he was loyal to the King of England. And ma pappy, he says, "Ah'm an American." They ast him again, "Do you support those rebels, sir?" And ma pappy says again, "Ah'm an American." So they shot him dead.'

There was a gasp from the audience.

'They shot him dead and he died right there in ma sister's arms.'

She had gripped the attention of the audience now and Colonel Morgan was pleased. 'Go on, Miss Ella,' he urged. 'Tell them what happened next.'

'They started running about the house, pulling open the cupboards and drawers and things, taking what they want and then they went and raided our food store. They stole our milk and pappy's whisky. Then two of them come for me. They drag me out back. Two more was holding ma sister down and ma sister was fighting to get to her baby. But they started in throwing that poor little baby up in the air and they stood in a ring and ma sister run from side to side to get him back but they just kept throwing him up in the air like he was a rag dolly.'

Ella paused, her head bowed, then she looked up and stared out at the rapt faces of her audience. 'Was then the most awful thing of all happened. Ah can still hear ma sister's screams.' She faltered, looked back at Colonel Morgan then went on, 'One of those men throwed ma sister's little baby high up in the air. And they dropped him. Right on

9

his head. And they just laughed. But he was dead.'

Several of the ladies who had remained pressed lace handkerchieves to their mouths. The young lieutenant looked at Colonel Morgan to ascertain if this was enough but Ella made the decision for them. Dry-eyed and defiant, she went on, 'And then they dragged ma sister to the barn and three of them dragged me back in the house.' She held her head high. 'And they tore off all ma clothes.'

There were open mouths now and the audience was in shock, but one lady whispered to her husband and, a little embarrassed, he half rose from his seat to ask, 'What happened? I mean, how did you escape? Did they just leave you?'

Ella shook her head. 'A sergeant came and ordered those men away. Then he did what they done.' She hesitated, as if reluctant to go on, but then she stared defiantly at the man who asked the question. 'And after that he dragged me to the barn and showed me where ma sister lay dead. He told me that's what would happen to me if I didn't go with him and be his comfort.'

At this point Colonel Morgan intervened. 'Miss Ella was forced to travel with the British for some time. She was forced to submit to the demands of this . . . this animal who calls himself a sergeant. And she is only one of our young womenfolk who has suffered in this way.'

But most of the men present were not yet ready to leave the question of Miss Ella and one, a portly man in the front row, asked in a faintly sceptical way, 'So how *did* you escape?'

'Ah crept away one night when he was asleep and ah hid in the wood 'til they left. Then some of Colonel Dan's men found me and ah was scared o' them, too, at first. But there was no need being scared of them. They fed me and found me some decent clothes and helped me get myself aright.'

'Thank you, Miss Ella,' Dan Morgan said and his lieutenant brought forward a second girl.

She was shorter than the first girl, round and plump where the other girl was thin. She had thick dark hair and a moon face that reddened as she spoke. 'Ah was out at the river with ma momma,' she began. 'Ah was helping with the wash when those bloodybacks come riding by. Then they sort of turned about and came back. They took ma momma off in the wood. Ah could hear her screamin' and fightin' but there was nothing she could do.'

'They raped your momma?' a man with bulging eyes asked.

'Yessir,' the girl responded, 'then they stripped off ma . . .'

'I reckon that's about enough,' Colonel Morgan said, stepping forward. He bowed to Ella and the other girl. 'Thank you, girls. Thank you very much.' And in a louder voice he announced, 'I think we can stop right there. Seems to me some of you old goats is beginnin' to enjoy this.'

There were embarrassed grunts from the older men, wide grins from some of the younger fellows present and a haughty restlessness bristled the ladies who had stayed.

'Purpose of this meeting,' the colonel went on, 'is to address you young fellows. We want you young fellows, as many as can, to come and join us. This is your land. It don't belong to some puffed up high and mighty across the ocean. He ain't your King and this ain't his country. It's your country. Yours and mine and every Americans. But we're gonna have to fight for it. We want you to come out and join the fight. Protect our womenfolk, our children, our homes. Take what's rightfully ours and save our country. That's what we ask of you tonight.'

There were short bursts of applause here and there and three young brothers from a family of farm hands climbed up on the stage. Several other young men joined them.

Tom Blanchard looked at his brother and Ben Withers. 'What do you think?'

But at that moment one of the town's leading citizens, a Mr Percival, became the centre of attention. He was a man whose opinion, publicly at least, was much respected and as he came to his feet the commotion in the hall gradually died away. Dan Morgan, sensing that people wanted to hear this man, held up his hands.

'You wish to speak, sir?'

Mr Percival nodded courteously. 'That I do, Colonel Morgan. Thank you.'

'Quiet now!' Morgan ordered and a respectful silence ensued.

'I am a reasonable man, Colonel,' Mr Percival began, 'and I have no reason to doubt that you are, too.' He looked around, as if directing a question at the audience. 'But I feel I must ask myself: Why should these . . . *ladies* be believed? Was anyone witness to these alleged events?' He was measuring his words with care. 'It could well be, and I am not saying that it is so, but it could well be that these ladies have been primed to tell of these outrageous occurrences. To *invent* them, perhaps, to assist in the recruitment of impressionable young men.'

One of Morgan's aides stepped forward. 'What you sayin', sir? God damn you!'

'Say it plain!' insisted another.

'I am saying,' Percival went on, 'that for all we know these young women may be no better than common whores, paid to make a spectacle of themselves in this degrading manner.'

The man who had first challenged him leapt from the stage, startling Percival with the ferocity of his reaction. 'Why, I'll kill you, you pot-bellied. . . .'

Arms and bodies came between the man and Mr Percival as Dan Morgan imposed his authority from the stage. In a calm, commanding voice he ordered, 'Gentlemen, please, we are not here to fight – not yet.'

To Mr Percival he said, 'You choose your words unwisely, sir. One of the young ladies brave enough to stand here and relive the dreadful ordeals she suffered at the hands of the British is now the devoted wife of the young gentleman who attacked you. His fury at your words is understandable, is it not? I trust, therefore, you will make due allowance for his sudden though not unwarranted outburst.'

The young man had barely reached him, only slightly bruising his cheek with a glancing blow before being restrained. And now, as much taken aback by the colonel's disclosure as by the attack itself, Mr Percival looked shaken. Though not unaware of the hint of sarcasm in the colonel's quiet rebuke he turned to the young man who was still being held by two others from the stage. 'I didn't know,' he said. 'I am so sorry. I apologize to you and to your good lady. I apologize unreservedly.'

The young man shrugged the others off and climbed back on the stage. Quietly and carefully, Colonel Morgan picked up Mr Percival's words. 'You didn't know. You didn't know – and that, sir, is precisely why we are here. You and good people like you simply do not know. Well, we are here tonight to tell you. The British, the 'bloodybacks' as we call them in their repulsive red coats, are roaming our land, destroying our property, robbing us of our possessions, and yes, as we have heard here tonight, defiling our womenfolk at every opportunity.

'We are here to offer our young men the chance to fight back. Why not join us? Join with us now and we will rid our land of this evil scum! Or, if you are unable to join us now, for whatever reason, pledge your support for our cause and join us in the future. This is our country and we must make that plain, not just to the British but to the whole world!'

Cheers broke out as many of the young men present, spurred on by Dan Morgan's cries of 'Come now! Come join our fight for freedom!' climbed up on the stage.

Filled with a sense of foreboding, Tom Blanchard knew that the world, *his* world, was about to change forever.

TWO

T HE anger that simmered that night at the meeting of townsfolk and recruiting rebels had boiled up and spewed out on to the moonlit street. Minor skirmishes had become commonplace at that turbulent time but the real trouble began when a small crowd, fired up by rebel propaganda, converged on the nearest easy target. It was the openly ostentatious home of a senior Customs official, a much disliked man who displayed a fawning loyalty to the British crown.

At first it was just a few disgruntled and unruly young men pelting the man's home with lumps of clay and small stones. But the crowd grew and there were those present who were happy to encourage and incite the rioters to further excess.

The night was cold but bright with stars and the large wood-frame house, no more than a dozen yards back from the road, was a black silhouette against the dark-blue sky. The first few missiles brought no response, as if the house was unoccupied, but as the second barrage rained down a shattering of glass was heard and a yellow light moved in a downstairs window.

The Customs official was mid-forties, a balding, corpulent man with a heavy black moustache and dark disdainful eyes. He seemed to relish his job of enforcing the imposition of taxes on his fellow men and this, together with his loyalty to the British and his unfortunate manner, had not endeared him to many of those who knew him. He was married to a local girl, half his age, and they had two small children.

'Get out here!' someone screamed and the stick-wielding mob moved closer.

On the fringe of the crowd Tom and his brother craned their necks for a better view. To their left a small group of girls, more excited at being out on the street unchaperoned at such a late hour than by what was happening at the house, were laughing in their direction. They were girls who attended Miss Healey's school for young ladies, led as usual by Imelda Harvie, the daughter of one of the richest men in Boston. Missing from the group was Melanie Stokes, a tall, slim, willowy girl with a mischievous smile. Already Melanie had gone off with Tom's friend, Ben Withers.

Melanie and Ben had hurried away into the darkest shadows as they did at every opportunity. It was known throughout the town or, at least, throughout their wide circle of friends and acquaintances that these two had eyes for no one else. No one could remember exactly when it started, not even Melanie or Ben, but it seemed as if they had always been close and their loyalty to each other had never for a moment diminished.

Imelda Harvie, whose interest in young men was as wide as Melanie's was narrow, professed to be Tom's brother Hank's intended, but Hank was in turn captivated and exasperated by her often flighty and inconstant behaviour. 'I wouldn't worry your head about her,' Tom told him with all the authority of a twenty year old. 'Let her have her fling. She'll always come back to you.' To which Hank replied, 'That's what worries me.'

Tonight, now that Melanie had left, Imelda was with three other girls, two of whom Tom recognized. The third was a girl he didn't know. He had never seen her before and he was curious to know who she was. But his attention was claimed by the sudden forward rush of the mob.

Some of the men in the forefront were carrying lighted torches and threatening to set the house on fire. Imelda's brother Edmund, a plump young man who resembled his sister in many ways but was not nearly as pretty, gripped Tom's arm. 'We've got to stop them!' he cried. 'The family are still in there.'

The rioters were throwing torches at the house but to little effect. Then one of the men ran forward to throw one through the broken window into the living room. The Customs official appeared in the porchway almost at once and was greeted by a chorus of jeers. He was holding a rifle, levelled now at those in the front line.

'Go on,' someone shouted. 'Fire if you dare!'

'Lynch him!' cried another.

But he stood his ground and as they closed in he didn't flinch, his

15

rifle trained on the nearest man.

'Get him!' was the cry and, as the crowd rushed forward, the rifle was pushed skyward and a shot rent the night air.

Behind him the house had caught fire and flames from the inside licked the window frames. Again the crowd surged forward and, as the Customs official fell beneath their feet, there were screams from the women in the roadway who could see at an upstairs window the white, terrified faces of the man's wife and their two small children. Tom and Hank joined in the rush to alert those at the front and turn the attack into a rescue.

On his knees now the Customs official realized what was happening. He looked up at the window, saw the flames and the billowing smoke and without hesitation ran inside. A few of the men went to help but they were beaten back by the scorching heat. Tom and Hank rushed forward with similar intent but they, too, were stopped in their tracks as a great whooshing sound swept the ground floor, the flames erupted and the upper floor collapsed.

It was well into the night before the flames died away and the next morning only a smouldering ruin remained. The bodies of the young wife and her two children were found beneath a pile of rubble and charred beams. The Customs official's blackened remains lay, barely recognizable, on the twisted stairway.

Two nights later Tom and Hank were invited to a soirée, an evening for young people from the 'right' families. Their mother was, as always, anxious that her two boys should move in the best social circles. She cherished the hope that both her boys would marry well and, as she frequently told her husband, there was no reason why they should not. There were several nice girls from good families and both her boys were handsome, upright young men. Mr Blanchard merely replied, as always, 'Who they marry and *if* they marry is entirely up to them.'

It was as they were about to leave for the party, spruced up with hair brushed and in best suits, that Mr Blanchard took them aside. 'You both know Max Harvie,' he said, with reference to Imelda's inordinately rich father. 'If he's putting on an evening At home, then he must have a motive. I reckon he might want to talk to you and the other young fellows about the Loyalist cause. He's got it in for these rebels and my guess is that what happened the other night has given him a real fright. If I were you I'd stay out of it, try not to get involved either way.'

The boys shuffled uneasily, glancing at each other, aware their father didn't know they had gone along to hear Dan Morgan.

Mr Blanchard smiled, thinking they were simply anxious to get off to the party. 'I suggest you listen politely to what he has to say. But don't commit yourselves to anything.'

'What do you think about the old man?' Hank asked as soon as they were out of the front door. 'I mean, who do you reckon he's for?'

It was a difficult question. The townsfolk were being forced by circumstance to take sides. Loyalist or rebel. They were going to have to make up their minds, show their true colours. People were saying that things were coming to a head. But all this had been going on for a while now.

Tom could remember a hot summer's day a few years back when, as a small boy, he had watched a furious mob march on the home of the state governor, Thomas Hutchinson. The mob had completely wrecked the governor's home, hurling furniture and paintings and family effects into the street, stealing whatever they could eat or drink or turn into cash. It was said that the governor was lucky to escape with his life that day. And now, just two nights ago, a government official, his poor wife and their two children had died as a result of a mindless and unforgivable act of arson.

'I think he's like most people,' Tom said. 'He doesn't like the rioting and destruction of people's homes. But he thinks the rebels have a case. How can the British expect to tax us and tell us what to do from three thousand miles away?'

'Is that what you think?'

'I'm not sure what I think. But this Dan Morgan, *Colonel* Morgan, is not someone we can just shrug off. If half of what his people are saying is true we are going to have to do something about it.'

'We?'

'We Americans, Hank.'

Tom came to a halt in the carriageway of the Harvies' house. For a few moments he stood quite still, listening to the lilting music of a military two-step, his brother Hank by his side. From the darkness they watched together as the chosen ones made elegant shapes in the golden glow of the windows. He was young. His brother Hank was young. And they were unattached. Their lives stretched ahead of them like wide tracts of untrodden snow. For no apparent reason a tear pricked his eye. Hank glanced at him curiously.

'Better go in,' Tom said gruffly. 'I need a drink.'

Imelda was at the door to greet them as Alfred, the Harvies' manservant, drew it open. 'Hank Blanchard and brother Tom. I thought you two were never coming,' she reproached them. 'Why is it you are always late, I'd like to know? I suppose you are so vain you believe nothing could possibly happen until you arrive.'

Tom smiled. 'Well, has it? Anything happened?'

'You are just so . . . so. . . .'

'Imelda,' Hank said, 'shut up, will you? For once in your life put those lips together and keep them there.'

'And why should I do that, Mister Henry Blanchard? Are you going to kiss me?'

Hank made a face. 'If you don't mind we need a drink.'

Tom's eyes were scanning the room.

'It's no good you looking for what I think you're looking for, Tom Blanchard,' Imelda told him. 'My cousin Sarah has a full card already. It's the early bird catches the worm.'

'We'll tell your cousin you called her a worm,' Hank said.

Imelda was indignant. 'I did not!'

Hank made a gesture with his hand as if holding an invisible glass. 'Drink. We'd like a drink.'

'You can help yourself at the punch bowl,' she said, her chin rising, and as a parting shot she added, 'You can drown in it for all I care.'

They crossed the room, free for a moment of Imelda, to where punch bowls and ladles and tumblers were set out. But when the two willowy daughters of a British Army colonel engaged them in conversation Imelda was quick to rejoin them.

'There's someone I'd like you to meet,' she said, smiling sweetly at the two sisters as she skilfully steered Tom and Hank away.

Imelda's cousin was surrounded by young men, at least four of them waiting to mark her dance card. Tom and Hank hovered on the fringe until a girl stopped by and waved her card under their noses. Imelda said Hank would catch her later. 'We were about to do this one.'

Hank said he couldn't do a reel or whatever it was the trio in the corner were playing, but Imelda ignored his protestations and Tom was left alone with the girl.

'I'd love to, Marie,' he said as she thrust her card at him, 'but I'm already down for most dances and I can't stay late.'

His excuses sound feeble even to him and the girl gave him a sad little smile of resignation. 'Sorry,' he said.

'So am I,' she replied and turned away.

Apart from Ben Withers who was dancing with Melanie, Tom was probably the tallest of the young men present and over the heads of her would-be partners he could see Imelda's cousin. She smiled at him shyly and he wanted to return her smile but he could only stare back at her, captivated.

So her name was Sarah. But who was she? Where did she come from? Well, to begin with, she was Imelda Harvie's first cousin. He knew that much. She was, he understood, from over Roxbury way. Her father was a farmer, not too fond of Mr Harvie by all accounts because he supported neither loyalists nor rebels and refused to be drawn into what he called Max Harvie's 'politicking'.

Sarah's mother and Imelda's mother were sisters and from time to time, mostly on social occasions, the two girls had been brought together. These occasional meetings had been going on since they were small children but, though they liked each other and got along reasonably well, they were not alike. Most of this Tom had learned from his brother Hank who was, whenever the fancy took her, Miss Imelda's intended.

Imelda was all right, Tom would concede if pressed. But he had long suspected she was more than slightly mad, apt to do the craziest things out of boredom or devilment or both. Sarah seemed, if not exactly serious, more *sane*. She also had an effect on the people around her that seemed to Tom quite extraordinary. Aloof without being cold, wary without being unapproachable, for Tom she had an irresistible air of mystery.

Finding the right approach was what troubled him. He wanted to go over, introduce himself but, as he would be the first to acknowledge, he wasn't great with girls – at least, at the outset – and he didn't want to make a mess of it.

The music seemed to speed up, the dancers reeled with increasing abandon. Tom took a large gulp at his tumbler of punch. He had been trying to look suave and self-possessed but the fruity mixture went up his nose and he coughed and spluttered, losing his composure. When he looked again Sarah was with a tall, broad-shouldered young man named John Foster.

19

Slim with smooth dark hair, Sarah was carefully groomed for the evening as were most of the young ladies present. But what made her so striking was her eyes. She had the most compelling eyes Tom had ever seen. There were grey green eyes and bluish green eyes but these eyes were like bright emeralds, set as they were in a beautifully sculptured face that was flushed pink right now with the excitement of the party.

Imelda danced by with Hank and noticed that Tom was alone and looking less than comfortable. Hank explained that Tom had a crush on her cousin but was probably too shy to go over and get acquainted. 'Well, we'll just have to do that for him,' Imelda said and she dragged Hank with her.

'Tom Blanchard,' she declared. 'I'm ashamed of you.'

'And why is that?' Tom asked sadly.

'Because you are too scared to go out and get what you want,' she told him. 'I'm going to introduce you to Sarah right now, you great loon.'

Tom scowled at Hank as if Hank was in some way responsible for not controlling his interfering girlfriend. 'No, no,' he said anxiously. 'I can do that myself.'

'Go on then,' she insisted and Tom found himself with little choice but to make his way to Sarah's side.

He hovered awkwardly, awaiting his opportunity, but Sarah was still in conversation with John Foster. Then suddenly, surprising even himself, he blurted out his name, his face a bright red. 'I'm Tom Blanchard.'

John Foster, who had known Tom since junior school, glanced at him sidelong and said sardonically, 'Is that a fact?'

The green eyes regarded Tom with only the barest hint of amusement and if she was affronted by his intrusion she didn't show it. Encouraged he rushed on, 'I . . . I understand you are Miss Harvie's cousin.'

John Foster was beginning to bristle when Imelda stepped in to draw him away. 'My card says you are next, John Foster.'

So Tom and Sarah were left alone. 'I'm sorry,' Tom said.

Sarah gave him a smile that made him catch his breath. 'For what?' she asked.

'For barging in like that. I don't usually go around barging in on people.'

She laughed. 'I'm glad to hear it, Mr Blanchard.'

'Please,' he said at once, 'you must call me Tom.'

She laid a hand lightly on his arm. 'I would love to dance with you, Tom, but my card is full. I wish you had come over earlier.'

'I don't want to dance with you,' he said quickly.

'Oh?' Sarah looked puzzled.

'No,' he said. 'I want to talk to you.'

'What about?'

'About us. About what we're going to do. I mean, now that we've met.'

Sarah laughed in surprise. 'Is there something in the air around these parts? You are just as mad as my cousin Imelda.'

Her partner for the next dance was at her side and she led the way to fulfil the promise on her card.

Tom pounded his fist into the palm of his hand and, much to the amusement of those nearby, cried, 'I'm going to marry you, Sarah,' though he was not sure that she heard him as she wheeled away.

But he was still alone when Hank and Imelda caught up with him. 'Can't be helped,' he said lamely. 'She has a full card.'

'You don't have to follow these old things,' Imelda told him, though they both knew that you did. 'I didn't have John Foster down just now but he couldn't very well refuse me. If a lady says she has his name on her card a gentleman can scarcely refuse to dance with her.' She smiled conspiratorially at Tom. 'I'll get Sarah to say you're next. Or wait. I have a better idea.'

The music came to a halt and Sarah's escort brought her back to where she had been standing and where Imelda and the boys were waiting. He hovered, not wanting to leave, but Imelda said, 'Your brother is looking for you. I think he's in the garden.'

Only half believing her, the young man bowed to Sarah and moved away.

'You are cruel, Imelda Harvie,' Tom said. 'Do you know that?'

'And you are slow,' she told him. She asked to see Sarah's dance card. Every dance was taken. 'This won't do,' she said. 'You two have no time to waste.'

Tom and Sarah glanced at each other wide-eyed but both were curious to know what she planned to do and neither raised any objection. Imelda pushed Sarah's card into Hank's pocket and went over to where the trio were about to start the next dance.

It was her house or, rather, her father's house, and in a way she was the hostess. She asked the elderly violinist to call for quiet as she wished to make an announcement. He tapped his music stand with his bow, but Imelda was not satisfied. She took the bow from him and tapped so loudly he became concerned for its welfare.

'Ladies and gentlemen, I have a small announcement to make,' Imelda told the quietened gathering. 'I am afraid the dance card of my dear cousin Sarah has been misplaced and a new one must be substituted. The card was full and only gentlemen who have a legitimate claim to dance with Sarah should come forward.'

There was a movement towards Sarah but Imelda threw up her hands in mock horror. 'Gentlemen, please. I will bring a new card in just a moment and if you will come to me we can save Sarah further embarrassment. Thank you. So sorry for this interruption, please proceed.' She waved a hand and the trio began to play.

'The trouble with Imelda,' Tom said, 'is she doesn't know what's true and what isn't.'

'Worse than that,' Hank said. 'She doesn't care.'

Sarah laughed. 'Do you dance, Tom?'

'With difficulty and a great deal of help.'

She slid an arm through his. 'Perhaps you will allow me to help you around the garden.'

They had almost reached the terrace windows when a new announcement gave them pause. Mr Harvie had taken a lead from his daughter. He promised to be brief. 'I had hoped to address the young gentlemen present this evening at a short meeting in the annexe, but Imelda informs me I must not spoil the party.' A portly man with a ruddy complexion, he smiled benevolently. 'I have some important news to impart and I would deem it a favour – a personal favour to me – if as many of you young men as can will meet with me here at three tomorrow. I assure you, gentlemen, this is a matter requiring your urgent and most serious consideration. Your future and the future of our country is at stake. Tomorrow afternoon then, if you please. I trust and hope sincerely you will all find the time to come. Thank you.'

THREE

THAT Sunday most of the young men who had been present at the Harvies' house the previous evening returned as requested. Tom wanted to go for one reason only: to see Sarah again. But Mr Blanchard had said more than once that it was not wise to get too involved with Max Harvie. In Mr Blanchard's experience anything Max Harvie did he did for himself. Tom accepted what his father was saying but he attended the meeting anyway and his brother Hank went with him.

About twenty of the town's most eligible young men were already gathered in the Harvies' rear garden as Tom and Hank arrived. But there was no sign of any girls. Mr Harvie had given strict instructions that there were to be no distractions, no ladies present and no punch. All that was on offer was the apple juice served up at a side table by the Harvies' black maid Vanessa.

'I want to start by thanking you boys for coming,' Harvie began solemnly. 'Gather round now. Gather round.'

The young men faced him in a semi-circle.

'I called you here today,' he went on, 'for you to hear me out then go away and do what you believe is right. But I sincerely hope you will listen, one and all, and give fair consideration to what I am trying to say.'

'I wish he'd get on with it,' someone muttered.

'What *are* you trying to say, Mr Harvie?' Ben Withers asked, giving voice to the shuffling and unease that was beginning to take hold.

'Well, as I was about to say, it's time for us all to decide where we stand. Now we may be Americans through and through, but we do owe a certain loyalty to the King, His Majesty the King of England.'

Glances were exchanged as the unease set in again.

23

'Now this . . . this trouble we are having all started because the British saw fit to levy a duty on us, their so-called stamp duty. Well, as I see it, at least, the way it was put to me, the British are obliged to maintain an army here, an army of trained men, soldiers who can protect us from the incursions of the French or . . . or the uprisings of certain renegade Indian tribes or anyone else who thinks they can give us trouble. Well now, such armies have to be paid for and as the British soldier is here to protect us and our property it would seem only fair that we should pay something towards the cost of keeping him in our country.'

There was no rumble of agreement, no general assent, just a shuffling of feet, until one young man ventured, 'My gran'pa reckons we shouldn't need no army to protect us. We should be able to protect ourselves. He reckons we should have an army of our own.'

'Is that so?' Max Harvie said sarcastically. 'Is that what your grandpa reckons?'

The young man looked embarrassed. It was well known that his grandfather, a joke in some quarters, had a drink problem.

'The old man could be right, Mr Harvie,' said the youngest boy there. 'Lots of people don't like the British. Down on the bridge, Medford way, there's a big sign says *British go home*!'

'How old are you, Davy?' Harvie asked.

The boy called Davy looked down at his boots.

'Fourteen?'

'I'll be fifteen next month,' Davy told him.

'Well boy, I don't know what you are doing here,' Harvie said. 'You're pretty young to be getting into grown-ups talk. Were you here last night, at my house? Were you invited here today?'

Tom Blanchard came to the boy's rescue, diverting Harvie's attention. 'Most of us were at the meeting addressed by Colonel Morgan, Mr Harvie. He told us of some of the things the British are doing to people, our people and our womenfolk in particular.'

'Dan Morgan? That old reprobate? Why, he was in the British Army himself one time. That's how he got to look so ugly. Got all his teeth knocked out.' Max Harvie laughed but no one joined in.

'I don't think I'd call him ugly to his face, Mr Harvie,' Tom said.

'He's no good, I tell you. He's just a drifter, a . . . a nothing.'

'Well, sir,' John Foster said. 'I have to say he sure was convincing the other night. He was telling us what the British do to women.

Seems no woman is safe.'

'Scare talk,' Harvie said dismissively. 'He doesn't mean our women. He means *loose* women. A soldier is a soldier anywhere. Now come on, boys. We all know what goes on when a gang of young fellows go out on the town and have a little too much to drink. Lots of fellows have been up to the Indian camp Friday nights. Nothing new about that. Ask your daddies. Or your gran'daddies come to that.'

'Colonel Morgan was talking about Bloodybacks breaking into farms and robbing things and raping respectable American girls, Mr Harvie,' Hank Blanchard insisted.

'There are always stories . . .'

'These were not just stories,' someone said. 'He produced the girls to prove it.'

Max Harvie was losing his patience. He didn't want to talk about the transgressions, true or otherwise, of the lower ranks of his protectors. The clear and simple message he had hoped to put across had been distorted by interruptions. Angrily, he felt he had lost his grip on the meeting. 'If you boys want this country to be run by rabble rousers like Dan Morgan,' he said, his voice shaking, 'go ahead. Support them if you must. But I am telling you, here and now, our wisest course of action for the future is to remain loyal to our sovereign, the King of England. That way we can play our full part in world trade and bring peace and prosperity to this land. Our interests are protected and we are a part of the most powerful nation on earth.

'Now,' he said, calming a little, 'I called you young men here today to try to guide you in the right and proper direction. You represent the cream of our city. You are the sons of our most successful men. If we are to maintain our true place in society we must protect our families and our way of life and the best way to do that – indeed, the *only* way to do that – is to remain loyal to our king.'

He had regained a degree of control now and his voice had stopped shaking. 'The position, gentlemen, is this. Any one of you who wishes to join the British Army should apply to me personally. I will see to it that you join as a fully commissioned officer. You will serve for a period of three years at the end of which you will be free to retain your commission or take a substantial gratuity. Think about it, boys, at the end of those three years these rebels will be crushed and you will be free to pursue whatever line of business you favour, a much respected, privileged former officer of His Majesty.'

25

He surveyed the young men arranged before him. 'Well,' he said, his red face breaking into a smile, 'do I have a volunteer?'

'I think I might be interested, Mr Harvie,' one young man ventured. 'But I'd need to speak to my father first.'

'Your father knows,' Harvie told him. 'If you are prepared to serve then he has no objection.' He looked for his own son. 'See here, my boy Edward has aready volunteered. He will be joining his company Friday next.'

Imelda's brother shrugged his shoulders at Tom and Hank as if to suggest he'd had little option.

'How about you, Ben Withers?' Harvie asked lightly. 'You'd make a fine-looking officer.'

Ben looked him in the eye and said quietly, 'I don't know yet, Mr Harvie. I don't know what I'll do.'

'Tom Blanchard? Henry?'

'We must speak to our father first,' Hank said.

'Well!' Harvie's manner was expansive now, genial even. 'If you boys will let Alfred have your names – just to express an interest at this stage, of course – then we can proceed to the conservatory where Mrs Harvie and Imelda have laid on some light refreshment as only they know how.'

He was smiling broadly as if his little recruiting rally had been a great success. Alfred, his manservant, in tailcoat and wig, stood by Vanessa's table, offering a quill to those young men who waited in line to sign their names.

That spring, in the weeks that followed their first meeting, Tom Blanchard and Sarah Dowling saw each other often. Their romance had blossomed and Sarah had spent as much time as she reasonably could at the Harvies' house where her Aunt Mary was happy to have her, if only as a steadying influence on Imelda. But time was running out for Tom and Sarah and a period of separation loomed.

More and more of Tom's contemporaries had taken sides. Most of his friends and acquaintances from college had joined the British Army and, under Max Harvie's patronage, had been granted instant commissions. Others had left home quietly and the general, though mainly unspoken, assumption was that they had left to join the rebels. Tom and Hank, along with Ben, discussed the alternatives often well into the night.

Reports were coming in now of frequent skirmishes and confrontations between British soldiers and bands of rebels. At a gathering on Lexington Green to hear a farmer turned rebel named John Parker, the crowd was beginning to disperse when a large contingent of British soldiers suddenly bore down on the surprised assembly.

The soldiers were led by three officers on horseback. With cries of 'Lay down your arms or you're dead!' they charged the largely unarmed crowd and one of the British officers fired a pistol. Many ran for the cover of a tavern as troops discharged their muskets. Eight of those running away were killed and at least another ten were injured. The rebel farmer, John Parker, was shot in the leg.'

In Concord a second skirmish soon followed. One of the rebels fired a shot and the British soldiers responded. But unlike the rebels in Lexington, the men in Concord, calling themselves the Concord militia, did not disperse. They were better prepared and they stood their ground, firing back *en masse*. By the end of that first concentrated volley four British officers were wounded and three soldiers lay dead.

Hundreds of rebels were gathering in Concord now and there were rumours that some of these men had scalped wounded soldiers and were behaving in a way that was not expected of even the most savage of the Indian tribes. To add credibility to the story was the fact that a Concord youth had killed a British soldier with a blow from a tomahawk.

The British now attempted to stem the tide of support for the rebels in the countryside with a full scale show of strength. But the planned operation, which they had hoped to keep secret, became common knowledge and as soon as they set off two horsemen rode ahead of them to alert the waiting rebels. The British made an ill-disciplined and undignified retreat.

It was clear after this that the rebels were armed, well-organised and well capable of rallying popular support. Even as the British returned to their camps near Boston they were fired upon from behind walls and hedgerows. The rebel strategy, at this stage, was to lie in wait as the soldiers marched by then fire upon them from the rear.

This then was the beginning. The iniquitous legislation of the past few years had finally sparked the bonfire of anti-British feeling and the revolution was under way.

Tom Blanchard, his brother Hank and Ben Withers spent many of those April evenings on the porch at Melanie Stokes' house, quietly discussing the war and the part they should play in it. Max Harvie wanted all of what he called the 'better class' young men to don the uniform of the British officer. It was their duty, he said, to protect the way of life their forefathers had strived so gallantly to establish. To protect *him* and *his* way of life, Ben scoffed.

The army paid a good pension to officers, according to Harvie and eventually, when they made the obligatory trip to London, officers of the rank of captain and above were presented at Court. A British Army commission could open many doors, not just in England but throughout Europe and later, too, when a man returned to make his way in the world of business. A colonel or even a major on the board of a company added a touch of class to that enterprise, Harvie pointed out, and the holders of such titles would always be in demand.

But the call of the rebels was difficult to ignore. Though it was claimed that these marauding bands were made up of rogues and vagabonds who roamed the countryside treating the situation as an invitation to plunder, Colonel Morgan and his men had been very persuasive. Ben Withers for one had little time for the British. He was an American, he said. And he was nobody's 'subject', loyal or otherwise. He refused to be ruled by some pompous 'king' with delusions of grandeur.

So far, of their circle of friends and acquaintances, only Edward Harvie, Imelda's brother, had taken up a commission. He was at the Induction School for newly recruited officers on North Street. It came as a considerable surprise and shock then to the brothers when they arrived at Melanie Stokes's house one evening to hear that Ben had joined the British Army.

'Ben?' Tom couldn't believe it.

'The British Army?' Hank was equally incredulous.

Melanie's eyes were dark-ringed. 'I didn't want him to go,' she said tearfully, 'but he just wouldn't listen.'

FOUR

'ID he say why?' Tom asked.
Melanie shook her head.

'We could go to North Street and ask him,' he suggested.

'I don't think so,' Hank said with a laugh. 'They might drag us inside, sign us up.'

'But was there a reason? I mean. . . .'

'Yes, Tom.' Melanie looked over her shoulder and lowered her voice. 'He says he has to join the British. There's something he has to do. You know how he is. He'd made up his mind. There was nothing I could say or do to stop him. I told him I'll wait for him and I will. I'll be here when he gets back. He knows that.'

Tom and Hank looked at each other. The same thought had occurred to them both. Maybe Ben had been recruited as a spy for the rebels.

'He said he realized you'd be surprised, shocked even. But I was to tell you that one day you would understand.'

A couple of girls and a young man ambled into the yard and Melanie greeted them with a smile, but Tom sensed that she was only going through the motions. It was pretty obvious that now, with Ben gone, parties and gatherings on the Stokes's back porch would soon become a thing of the past.

Tom turned to Hank. 'I won't believe it,' he said, 'until I see him in a red coat.'

They said they had to go and Melanie seemed to understand but just as they were about to leave Imelda Harvie arrived on the arm of John Foster, the tall young man who had danced with Sarah.

'Where have you been, Henry Blanchard?' Imelda demanded. 'You

29

were supposed to come to my house.'

Hank looked embarrassed. He had forgotten he'd arranged to meet Imelda at the Harvies'. Tom grinned at Imelda and said cheerfully, 'Well, you soon found an escort, Imelda. You don't need Hank.'

Imelda squeezed her escort's arm. 'John is joining the army in the morning,' she announced proudly. 'My father has arranged for him to receive his commission at once.'

'Old Max get to you, John?' Hank suggested with a grin.

John Foster frowned. 'I'm joining the British Army because I want to. It's the right thing to do.'

'My father is so pleased with John,' Imelda announced smugly. 'My father says all the best young men are proving loyal to the Crown. My own brother has already gone and I do believe our own Ben Withers went just this morning. I'm sure Melanie will miss him terribly but it has to be done. This rebel nonsense has to be nipped in the bud or we will all suffer for it. Now how about you two? Isn't it time to nail *your* colours to the mast?'

'You think we should join the navy?' Tom asked innocently.

Imelda faced him squarely. 'You know full well what I mean, Tom Blanchard, and there's no escape. It's time to do your duty, time to stand up and be counted. It's time for you and Hank to accept your responsibilities like men.'

She had relaxed her grip on her escort, her hand now resting on Hank's arm. 'You'd look so smart in a red coat, Henry. So handsome and so . . . so upright.'

Tom and John Foster stifled the laughter in their throats and turned away. 'Imelda,' Hank said calmly. 'Shut up.'

'Why, Hank? Why?' Tom was still agonizing over Ben's decision. It went against all that Ben had said about the British – and Tom was a little hurt, too, that Ben had left without any explanation. 'He practically said he was going to join Dan Morgan.'

'Maybe he has,' Hank offered, 'and they've made him a spy.'

'I think he would have told us.'

'Thing is,' Hank said, 'What are *we* going to do?'

'Well, I expect you're going to be a redcoat like your lady friend says,' Tom answered with a sardonic grin. 'Yessir, Mr Harvie. I'm yo' man.'

'Imelda is not my lady friend. She just uses me when she has no one else. You saw her just now, hanging on to John Foster.'

'You, my dear brother, are Imelda Harvie's insurance. She'll keep you dangling until she's tried all the others. Then, if she's still not taken, she'll settle for you.'

Hank threw a half-hearted punch and Tom stepped back, with a laugh. 'Think you're funny, don't you? Well, I'll tell you, when Imelda comes looking for me next time I just might not be here.'

Tom laughed again and Hank chased him up the path to their own house where they sat down on the steps to the front porch. It was decision time. And they both knew it. Redcoat or rebel. They were going to have to decide one way or the other.

With the declared aim of surrounding Boston, rebel groups were forming all over Massachusetts. After the defeat at Concord and the ignominious retreat that followed, the British had arrived, chastened by events at a place called Bunker Hill. It was on the Charlestown peninsular, just north of the city.

The British had lost over 250 men and they were increasingly under siege. In the hills all around there were fires late at night, like red eyes keeping watch from the camps of the rebel soldiers. Day by day the number of rebels increased and by the end of April at least 10,000 men were ready and poised to pounce.

Mrs Blanchard saw her boys on the porch and told them their father wished to speak with them. He was in the field out back.

'Your ma's worried sick about all this war-mongering,' he said, when they caught up with him. 'Doesn't want you to get involved.'

'We have to do something, Dad,' Hank said.

'I know that, Son, and I suppose you ought to take the King's commission Max Harvie reckons he can fix.'

Tom looked questioningly at his father. 'But?' For the first time in his life Mr Blanchard didn't know how to advise them. 'But you're not sure, are you, Dad?'

'No, Tom,' he said. 'I'm not. There's an argument for both sides. The British say we need their protection. But we must pay for it. And we do. We pay for it by letting them run things their way, control the ports and the passage of goods. And there's taxes. If they hadn't been so heavy-handed with their damned-fool stamp duties things might have been different. Thing is, we can raise our own taxes. And as for protection, we don't need 'em. We can take good care of ourselves –

31

as I suspect they're about to find out.

'On the other hand, if the rebels are guilty of half the things they are being accused of then we don't want anything to do with them. Oh, I know the British are capable of some pretty despicable stuff but – I don't know. What we're hearing about some of these rebel mobs – scalping people and such, cutting off ears, burning homes to the ground – we need to know the truth.'

'So what do we do?' Hank asked.

'You could just stay home. Your mother would love that.'

'We can't, Dad,' Tom said. 'You know we can't.'

They were walking back to the house. 'Well . . .' Mr Blanchard came to a halt and faced his sons. 'I don't know too much about politics. Never took much notice. Too busy working for all that stuff. But what I do know is that this country is ours. It's called America and it's for Americans. The British can't hold back progress and I believe their best people know that. I reckon they're getting ready to fight a war they already lost.'

'Ma thinks if we do anything at all we should take up Mr Harvie's offer,' Tom ventured.

'Your mother thinks Hank should marry Imelda,' Mr Blanchard said with a smile, 'but I wouldn't advise it.'

At supper that evening the Blanchards' maid brought news that rebel troops had raided Roxbury. Tom thought at once of Sarah.

Early next morning a delivery boy came with papers for Thomas Bradford Blanchard and Henry Bradford Blanchard inviting them to present themselves within seven days at the British Army office, North Street, where a Colonel Bowater would be pleased to assess their suitability to receive a service commission in the army of His Majesty King George III.

Tom told Hank he was going to Roxbury.

It was a bright sunlit morning with that feeling of dryness in the nose that presages a hot day ahead. Mr Blanchard had told Tom he could take the dray if he would bring back some fence staves from the wood-cutter who used only good quality pine at his yard behind the main street in Roxbury. Well aware of the dangers his brother might face, Hank had insisted on accompanying him. The hills and roads all around were said to be swarming with rebels.

Along the main coach route they saw no one until they crossed the causeway known as Boston Neck where they saw a solitary figure slumped by the wayside.

'Pull up,' Tom said.

'Why?' Hank was holding the reins lightly. 'He's just a Negra kid.'

'He looks tired.'

The young Negro watched them warily as the cart trundled by then the yellowish whites of his eyes rolled back as, deferentially, he averted his gaze.

'Pull up!' Tom insisted.

Hank shook his head but did as his brother asked.

Tom turned on his seat to look back. 'Need a lift?'

The young Negro looked around as if to make certain Tom was talking to him. 'It's all right, sah. Ah jes takin' a li'l res'. Thank you. Thank you, sah.'

They were out on the open road and still some distance from Roxbury. 'Come on, if you're coming,' Tom told him. 'I'm sure you'd rather ride.'

The young Negro drew himself up and hoisted the heavy pack at his feet on to his shoulder.

'Stick it on the cart,' Tom said.

He swung the pack on to the empty cart and jumped up to a sitting position beside it.

Tom moved sideways on the driver's board forcing Hank to move along. 'Come on up here,' he invited. 'Can't talk to you back there.'

Nervous now, the young Negro climbed up beside him, trying to take up as little space as possible.

'What do they call you?' Tom asked.

'Jimmy, sah.'

'Jimmy, huh?' Tom put out a hand. 'Well, my name's Tom and this is my brother Hank.'

Jimmy took Tom's hand, surprised by the gesture. Hank nodded at him over his brother's shoulder, wondering what Tom was up to.

'Please' to meet you, gentlemen,' Jimmy said, uncomfortable now up front beside Tom and Hank when every convention decreed that his place was behind on the cart.

'You going to Roxbury, Jimmy?' Tom asked.

'Yeah. Ah mean, yes sah.'

'No need for any of that stuff. I told you my name's Tom and this is Hank.'

33

'Yessah, Missah Tom.'

Tom raised his eyes skywards.

'Leave it, Tom,' Hank said. 'It's just a habit with fellows like Jimmy. You know that.'

'What are you doing out here, Jimmy?' Tom asked.

'Jes' working ah guess,' Jimmy said, then he felt obliged to explain. 'Ah works on Mister Mabbut's place back there and ah gotta take this stuff in to Rox. It's a firebox needs fixing.'

'Doesn't Mr Mabbut have a cart? He can't expect you to carry that weight.'

'Ah'm all right,' Jimmy said. 'Long as ah'm taking them rests.'

'So,' Tom said. 'Seen any rebels in these parts?'

The young negro was immediately back on the defensive. 'No, sah. Ah ain't seen nothing.'

'Come on, Jimmy,' Tom said. 'You must have seen something. We hear the rebels have taken Roxbury.'

Jimmy shook his head. 'Few strangers passing through but ah don't know if they was rebels.'

'What about soldiers? Redcoats?'

'They all pulled out about a week back.'

'Anyone want a drink?' Tom took a small canteen from behind the backboard, removed the stopper and offered it to Hank. Still gripping the reins as the horse kept up a steady trot, Hank threw back his head and took a good swig at the water. Then Tom took back the canteen and handed it to the young Negro.

Jimmy looked at the canteen, then at Tom. Was this some kind of trick? Was the white boy about to humiliate him in some way? It wasn't done to drink from a white man's canteen.

'Go on,' Tom said. 'Take it.'

Jimmy's throat was dry as old parchment. He looked at the canteen, hesitating, wanting it.

Tom thrust it at him. 'Take it.'

He took it and drank a deep draught of the cool water, carefully wiping the mouth of the canteen before handing it back. 'Thank you. Thank you, sah.'

Tom took a good long drink from the canteen himself, wiped the mouth, replaced the stopper and stowed it behind the board.

'Ever hear of a family named Dowling?' he asked.

Jimmy nodded. 'Ah knows Mister Dowling.'

'You know Mister Dowling?'

'Mister Mabbut knows Mister Dowling.'

'Well, that's where we're heading. To the Dowlings.'

Jimmy threw him a curious glance.

'Jimmy?' Tom queried.

'Well, ah don't know if you know, sah, Mister Dowling's place got burned down.'

'When was this?'

'Just last week. Saturday, ah guess.'

Saturday! That was the day Sarah went home.

'Gang o' them rebels went in and sorta took over for a few days. Then when they was ready to move on . . .' Jimmy's voice trailed.

'What? What happened?'

'They killed Mister Dowling. Ah heard they killed all the family.'

Tom's hand went out to Hank and Hank brought the cart to a halt. 'You sure about this?'

'Oh yeah. Yes, sah. Ain't nothing up there now, Mister Tom. Just a burned out wreck.'

'All the family?' Hank asked. 'Are you sure?'

'Well, that's what ah heard. Mister Mabbut had one of his own men go up there with the wagon. There was five bodies come down.'

'Five bodies?' Hank was aghast.

'Do you know who they were?' Tom asked, dreading the answer.

'Just the family, ah guess. The only survived was just one person. And that was the little help boy. They say he saw what was happening and he ran away.'

'Why were they killed, Jimmy? Was Mr Dowling a Loyalist? Did he support the British?'

Jimmy shrugged warily. 'Ah don't know, sah. They say the men was drinking and they just wanted the women.'

'The women?'

Jimmy averted his eyes as if he felt he had overstepped the mark and regretted it at once.

'What are you saying?' Hank demanded, taking over from his brother who looked too shocked to ask.

'They say the men who did it did some bad things to those ladies before . . . before they killed them.'

Tom gripped the young Negro's threadbare shirt at the neck. 'How do you know this? Who told you?'

35

'Leave him,' Hank said. 'He's only telling what he's heard.'

Tom relaxed his grip and smoothed Jimmy's shirt front. 'Yes. Of course. I'm sorry, Jimmy.'

Jimmy kept his head down, not sure what to say or do.

'And you think these were rebels?' Hank asked.

'That's what they say, sah,' Jimmy said, as if he didn't believe it.

'What do you mean?'

Jimmy frowned, afraid he had again overstepped the mark.

'Look, Jimmy,' Tom said. 'Just say what you mean. We want to know what happened.'

'Well,' Jimmy began, cautiously, 'folks was kinda surprised when they said it was the rebel soldiers done it. There ain't been no trouble with the rebels round here. The only trouble is when they fight the British or they spring an ambush or some such. Most of the trouble is with the British soldiers.'

'What kind of trouble?'

'Ah don't know if ah should say, Mister Tom. Ah don't wanna get in no. . . .'

'You're just telling us what people around here think.'

'It won't get you into any trouble, Jimmy,' Hank assured him. 'Not with us anyhow.'

'Well, what ah heard was that folks round here blame the British. They go around breaking into folks' homes, taking food and things and attacking the womenfolk and stealing the livestock. Not the the rebels. They don't do that and that's why most folk around these parts support the rebels.'

For the remainder of the journey Tom sat with his head in his hands. He couldn't bear to think what might have happened to Sarah and he didn't want to know the truth because he feared the worst.

On the fringe of town Jimmy told Hank he would like to step down. Hank pulled up and Tom raised his head. Jimmy lifted his pack from the cart and thanked them profusely, glad now to be off the front seat. He'd been more than a little apprehensive at the prospect of riding along the main street up front beside the two white boys. There were plenty of folk in Roxbury who would take exception.

The cart trundled into the town square on the stroke of noon. It was a fine warm day and the people of Roxbury were going about their business as usual, throwing strong black shadows on the dusty road. Tom and Hank left the cart at the woodcutter's yard and arranged to pick it up later.

'Where are we going?' Hank demanded, hurrying after his brother down the unmade street.

'To the church,' Tom said.

Hank looked up, saw the outline of the white wood church and its cross beyond the cluster of buildings ahead and followed in silence, aware that Tom's mood precluded further questions.

The church, less than five years old, had been paid for by local subscription and the generosity of one or two well-off benefactors. Consecrated by a visiting Anglican bishop, it had become a focal point for family life and already there were several headstones under the maple trees in the section of the gardens set aside as a burial ground.

'What are we doing here?' Hank asked.

'Sarah's family were church people,' Tom said. 'Her father helped build this place.'

He went on through the open door and stood for a moment in silence, looking towards the altar, taking in the stillness. Hank stood behind him, cap in hand.

There was a movement in the transept to the right and a young man in clerical garb came to greet them. He smiled pleasantly, welcoming them in, filled with a youthful enthusiasm as if new to the job and anxious to make a good impression.

'Hello there!' he said cheerfully, his hand extended, and in a quieter tone, in deference to his surroundings, 'Welcome to the House of God.'

Tom shuffled uneasily. He was not a great believer. He only attended his own church at his mother's insistence and Hank was the same. They shook hands in turn with the young minister.

'Tom Blanchard. My brother Hank. We're from Boston.'

'Good, good, pleased to meet you. I'm Pastor John.'

'We were wondering if the Dowling family were among your parishioners.'

'They were.' He frowned. 'Terrible business.'

'We only just heard what happened,' Hank said.

'Are we too late for the funerals?' Tom asked.

'I'm afraid so,' Pastor John said. 'Very sad. Dreadful. It was

Thursday. They were buried here on Thursday. No stone yet, of course, but I can show you where.'

He beckoned and, stooping to pass through a narrow postern door, they followed him out of the semi-darkness to the burial ground where the midday sun gave a golden sheen to the newly cut grass and enhanced the colours of the freshly laid flowers.

A temporary wooden cross marked the spot and Tom's heart was heavy at the thought of Sarah lying there. 'It's a new grave,' the young pastor said, 'a family grave and, sadly, it's full.'

'Full?' Hank queried.

'The most we lay to rest in any one grave, even where a large family is involved, is five. *Full* means five interments.'

'There would be Mr and Mrs Dowling, Sarah's sister, her little brother and . . .' Hank broke off, not wanting to add Sarah's name to the list.

'You knew the family?'

'Sarah,' Tom said, with difficulty. 'I knew Sarah.'

'Sarah had a sister and a little brother,' Hank offered.

Pastor John nodded sadly. 'That would make five.'

'Killed by rebels,' Hank said.

'So I understand.' The young cleric's tone suggested he was not entirely convinced.

'You have reason to believe otherwise?' Tom demanded.

'No,' Pastor John admitted tentatively. 'It's just that we have been *told* rebels were responsible. I'm afraid it's easy right now for people to do bad things and blame it on the rebels. But most of the rebels and their supporters I've met are good honest folk. They feel they have genuine grievances against the British. And if you boys are Loyalists, I'm sorry. I can only speak as I find.'

Tom and Hank nodded in acceptance. 'Sure,' Tom said. 'That's fine by us. We're not Loyalists anyway. We are not anything yet.'

A couple of paths away a tall skeletal Negro, bent by the years, was standing in the shade of an overhanging maple. He was dressed in threadbare work clothes, a single bloom in his hand.

'I believe that's Joseph,' Pastor John said quietly. 'I understand he was Mr Dowling's manservant.'

Tom was already striding off towards him. Guiltily, Joseph straightened up as if he'd been caught trespassing.

'Hello there,' Tom said. 'My name's Tom Blanchard. I'm making a few enquiries about the Dowling family.'

'Yessah.' Joseph lowered his head and looked worried.

'You worked for Mr Dowling?'

'Yessah. That's right, sah.'

Hank and the pastor had caught up with Tom and the three young men confronting Joseph seemed to him to form some kind of tribunal.

'Ah didn't do nothing wrong, sah,' he said, his pale watery eyes appealing to the young pastor.

'No, no, of course not,' Pastor John assured him.

'I'm sure you won't mind answering a few questions,' Tom said. Again Joseph lowered his head and looked worrried.

'What happened that day, Joseph?' Tom coaxed him gently. 'Can you tell us?'

'Ah don't truly know, sah. Y'see, sah, ah wasn't there or maybe ah'd be lying dead, too.'

'You liked Mr Dowling?' Hank asked. 'He must have been a good master or you wouldn't be here bringing flowers.'

'Mister Dowling was a good man, sah. Good to me, anyways. But ah bring the flowers for Miss Pansy.'

'Miss Pansy?'

'Miss Pansy was Missus Dowling's maid and she was killed with the rest of the family.'

'Miss Pansy is buried here?' Tom queried.

'Yessah,' Joseph told him. 'Miss Sarah, she insisted.'

'Miss Sarah?'

'Yessah.'

'What are you saying?' Hank demanded. 'That Sarah isn't here? She isn't dead?'

'Oh no, sah.' Joseph looked shocked. 'Miss Sarah ain't dead.'

Tom was speechless and he could only listen as the pastor gently coaxed Joseph into telling his story. Apparently, on Mr Dowling's instructions, Joseph had met Sarah at the coach stop and taken her home in the trap only to find her family dead and the house burned down.

'Miss Sarah,' Joseph told them, 'was took to the Aunt's house. She was kinda shocked and not herself, sah. She got took to a place up country where they take care of ladies who. . . .'

His voice trailed and Tom gripped his arm. 'What are you saying? They think she's lost her mind, is that it?'

'Steady now,' the pastor said. 'Joseph is only trying ro tell us what he knows. Miss Sarah must have suffered a terrible shock. All her family – murdered. Her aunt probably thought she'd be better off away from here for a little while.'

'That's right, sah,' Joseph added. 'Ah hear tell Miss Sarah was not well enough to go to the burying.'

'My God!' Tom muttered, trying to contain his anger. 'I'd like to kill those people.' Then: 'I want to know who did this.'

'In the Good Book,' the pastor said quietly, 'revenge is wrong.'

'An eye for an eye,' Tom told him.

Hank laid a restraining hand on his brother's arm. 'Easy, Tom. We'll probably never know who did it.'

But Tom remembered that Jimmy, the young Negro, had mentioned a little boy who was said to have seen it all.

FIVE

Sarah's Aunt Alice was friendly enough when Tom and Hank arrived at her front door. Visitors were invariably welcome. But when she heard the reason for their visit she was suddenly cool and unhelpful.

'I just want to know what happened to her, ma'am,' Tom said.

'Why? Why do you want to know?'

'Well . . . we sort of became friends.'

'How? When?'

'When Sarah came to Miss Imelda Harvie's party. We talked and . . . and danced.'

'Have you not spoken to Imelda or her mother?'

'No, ma'am. We thought. . . .'

'There's no use pursuing my niece, young man. She is not, well, she is not herself. Naturally the ordeal she went through affected her deeply.'

'Affected her mind?' Hank asked tentatively.

Aunt Alice threw Hank a look of disdain for asking, but Tom would not be deterred. 'Where is she?'

'I can't tell you where she is. I have sworn not to have her disturbed under any circumstances. It will take time – a long time – and she may one day begin to recover. But not yet. There is a slender chance she may get over this terrible business – though the scars will remain – but she needs peace and tranquillity and she is with people who will make certain she gets it.'

'Who?' Tom demanded. 'Who are these people?'

'You saying she's in a hospital somewhere? Hank asked.

'I am not saying anything, young man.' She turned to Tom. 'I think you had better put Sarah out of your mind. I'm sure there is no shortage

41

of suitable young ladies in Boston.'

Back at the woodcutter's yard the cart had been loaded with staves as promised. Tom paid the man and they set off for home, but when they came to the sign for Mabbut's Farm Tom turned the cart up the rough approach road. According to the Dowlings' manservant the little boy Buzz had been taken on by Mr Mabbut.

'You sure this is a good idea?' Hank asked.

'No, but I want to ask this boy Buzz a few questions.'

A surly-looking man in his late fifties was watching two Negroes dig a drainage trench by the gateway to his land.

'Good day to you, sir,' Tom said pleasantly as he slid from the driving seat. 'I'm looking for Mr Mabbut.'

'You're looking at him,' Mabbut said coolly.

'Tom Blanchard, sir, from Boston. And this is my brother Hank.'

Mabbut nodded. 'You boys are way off your track.'

'We're friends of the Dowling family,' Tom told him.

'That so?'

'At least, friends of Miss Sarah Dowling.'

Mabbut looked them up and down. 'Why ain't you boys in the army?'

'We got our papers just this morning, sir,' Hank said. 'We're to report in seven days.'

Mabbut frowned. 'Should think so, too. My boy volunteered right away. Soon as these people started gettin' outa hand.'

Tom nodded and smiled approvingly.

'So what can I do for you?' Mabbut asked.

'We're interested in what happened at the Dowling place and who was responsible.'

'Common knowledge what happened up there. Damned near whole family wiped out by those vermin.'

There was little doubt which side Mabbut was on.

'We hear you have a little boy called Buzz working for you,' Tom said tentatively.

'What about him?'

'We hear he saw what happened back there and we thought we'd like to talk to him, if you don't mind.'

'Nothing to talk about. The boy saw it all. These people went on the rampage, killing and such, and he hid himself away 'til they were done.' Mabbut's expression hardened. 'They killed his mother – Mrs

Dowling's housemaid – and I don't want things stirring up for the boy. He's a good little worker. So I'll be obliged if you leave things be and go on your way.'

'We just want to talk to him.'

'I said no.' Mabbut stepped nearer with a hint of aggression. The two Negroes stopped digging. 'Just go on your way. Join the King's army as you are meant to and help rid us of this rabble. Let 'em see we mean business.'

'Look, Mr Mabbut,' Tom said apologetically. 'We just want to see Buzz. We want to ask him. . . .'

'I said no!' Mabbut picked up a spade. 'You will not set foot on my land. So you'd better go. Now!'

Tom gripped the noseband and turned the horse and cart. He looked back at Mabbut, nodded then climbed aboard beside his brother. The cart rumbled down the dirt track but before they reached the main highway Tom pulled up again. Jimmy, the young man they had given a lift earlier, was coming towards them. Jimmy's face lit up in a brilliant smile of recognition.

'Looking for me, sah?' he asked, aware this was most unlikely.

'What would we want with a no good loafer like you?' Hank replied with a good-natured grin.

'We've been to see your boss,' Tom told him. 'We wanted to talk to this kid Buzz, the boy who worked for the Dowlings, but old Mabbut wouldn't let us.'

'Yeah?' Jimmy looked surprised. 'What do you wanna know?'

'We heard it was this Buzz who said rebels were responsible for what happened.'

'That's right,' Jimmy confirmed.

'Would he know a rebel from a British soldier?' Hank asked.

'He's only a little kid but he sure knows a rebel from a Redcoat.'

'We'd like to talk to him, Jimmy,' Tom said.

Hank shook his head. 'Don't let's involve Jimmy in this. He could get in trouble with Mabbut.'

Jimmy shrugged. 'Ah been in trouble before and ah'm thinking of leaving this place anyways.'

'Oh?' Tom said with genuine interest. 'Where would you go?'

'South, maybe. Ah don't know yet. But ah hear a man can get himself a nice piece of land down there.'

Both Tom and Hank looked doubtful.

'Ah been told there's Negras with there own land.'

'I hope so, Jimmy,' Tom said.

'Let me see if ah can find young Buzz,' he offered. 'Ah guess he'll be up by the hen patch right now – where he is most days about this time. Ah can take you up there on foot but we needs to hide the horse and cart.'

'Fine,' Tom said.

'There's a good place down the road and a shady spot for the horse, about a quarter mile back.'

'Right,' Tom said. 'Let's go.'

Hank was still doubtful but, for Tom's sake, he went along with the plan and soon they had hidden the horse and cart from view in a pleasantly shaded copse. Jimmy led them back up a narrow track to the boundary of Mabbut's farm.

Wielding a long-handled broom a small black boy, his mouth open and his eyes vacant, was cleaning out a chicken hut with measured mechanical strokes. Crouching low, the Blanchard brothers followed Jimmy then stayed back as he raised a hand. Alone, Jimmy crept forward in the undergrowth, calling softly, 'Buzz! Buzz, over here!'

The boy looked scared then he saw Jimmy. 'Hey, Jimmy!' he cried, wth a gap-toothed grin. 'What you doin' there?'

Jimmy held a finger to his lips and beckoned and Buzz did as he was bid. As soon as he was within reach Jimmy grabbed him and drew him down into the long grass.

'Don't look so scared,' Jimmy told him when Tom and Hank appeared. 'These gentlemen just wanna ask you some questions.'

Buzz froze and his startled eyes were all that moved, darting from Tom to Hank and back to Jimmy.

'It's all right,' Tom assured him. 'We're not going to hurt you. We just have a few questions, that's all.'

Jimmy looked anxious, peering around for any sign of Mabbut's men. 'Better hurry.'

'You were at Mr Dowling's place when they burned it down,' Tom said quietly.

Buzz looked at Jimmy, terrified.

'It's all right,' Hank said. 'We don't blame you for anything. We just want to know what happened.'

Buzz looked again at Jimmy who nodded in encouragement.

'That place got burned down and Missah Dowling got killed and

Missus Dowling and . . . and ma mamma. . . .'

'Who did it, Buzz?' Tom asked gently.

'Missah Mabbut said it was the rebels.'

'Mr Mabbut said?'

'Yessum.' Buzz nodded vigorously. 'Those bad men came and they killed everyone 'cept me.'

'And Mr Mabbut said they were rebels?'

'Yessum.'

'And you told the sheriff they were rebels?'

'No, sah. The sheriff knew they was rebels anyways.'

'How did he know?'

'Ah don' know, sah. He just said this is the work o' them rebels.'

'You got a good look at these rebels?'

'Yessum. There was a lot o' them, about twenty, maybe more.'

'And what were they like? How were they dressed?'

'Waal. . . .' The boy hesitated uneasily.

'Buzz?' Jimmy prompted.

'They was wearing them red coats.'

'They wore red coats?' Hank exclaimed.

'Yessum. That's right.'

'But redcoats are British soldiers, Buzz,' Tom said quietly. 'They are not rebels.'

'That's what ah thought,' Buzz said. 'But Missah Mabbut and the sheriff, they say ah gotta forget that cos those men was definite rebels.'

Ben Withers had no doubt where his loyalty lay. In time he would join the rebels. But there was something he had to do first. And that entailed joining the British Army. He had explained it all to Melanie and she had understood. She had not wanted him to do what he planned to do but, knowing him as she did, she knew there was nothing she could say or do to dissuade him.

Melanie had known Ben Withers since they were infants. They were schoolfriends, members of the same group throughout their adolescent years and then they were lovers. She was seventeen that first time and it was Ben's eighteenth birthday. Ben had often joked since that it was the best birthday present he ever had.

It was a hot June night and they had slipped away from the party in Ben's backyard. They had gone down to the banks of the Charles River where the moon and the stars and the dark outline of the trees and the shrubs were reflected in the slow moving water. There was barely a sound, a stillness in the warm night air, and there was no delay, no hesitation. They had come here to do what they wanted to do and they did it. And for a time it was as if they were the only two people alive.

Young as they were, they were ready for each other. Melanie had welcomed Ben with an all-consuming warmth on that first heedless occasion. But they had put things on a more sensible plane since then. That first time had been out of their control and they had been worried about the outcome until the end of the month.

Now, after almost five years, they were still totally committed to each other and all that deterred them from getting married was the lack of accommodation. Ben planned to build a house out by the river but he hadn't made much progress because there was some delay in releasing the land. The British consul had ruled he should pay tax on the transfer of the five acres bequeathed to him by his father's late brother and he was as yet unable to raise the money.

For a while their plans had to be shelved. There was a war to be fought. Small skirmishes would give way to all out warfare. Young men had to play their part or be branded cowards and many of these young men were the early casualties. Ben wanted the war out of the way before he and Melanie brought children into the world and Melanie knew and understood this. But this other thing had baffled and worried her until she had made him explain and though he knew it would equally baffle his friends, especially his best friend Tom Blanchard, he had made Melanie promise not to tell a soul why he was joining the British.

After a long and quietly passionate evening alone in a room above his aunt's shop they had said a goodbye tinged with the despair and anxiety of time slipping away. They had then walked down the empty lane to Melanie's house in the chill April air as they listened to the baying of the wolves in the hills up country.

'Don't let them get you, Ben,' Melanie said, not wanting to cry, not wanting to make his departure any more difficult than it was, but with a tell-tale catch in her throat. 'Don't let *anything* get you.'

'I'll be all right,' Ben said.

'And I'll be waiting,' she promised.

At dawn he was packed up and ready to go, though his appointment with the army board was scheduled for nine o'clock. He said goodbye to the aunt who had cared for him since his mother and then his father had died, her eyes dimmed as she watched his tall athletic figure turn and raise a hand at the end of the boardwalk.

He was early and he was deliberately so in order to linger as he passed by Melanie's house. He didn't want to wake or surprise her. He just wanted to pass close by before going on his way. But when he turned the corner to the lane she was at her gate. She came running towards him and he dropped his bag and swung her round as she was swept up into his arms.

Melanie was breathless, her hair tangled across her face. 'I wanted to catch you before you left.'

Ben held her close with one arm as he drew the strands aside. 'I thought we did all this last night.'

Arms around his neck, Melanie clung to him as if she would never let go. 'And I wanted to do it all again this morning.'

He arrived late at North Street but fortunately the interviews were running late.

A powdered and bewigged colonel was sitting between two officers of lesser rank behind what looked like a refectory table. Ben faced them, standing to attention.

'Benjamin George Withers,' the colonel said, stressing the name 'George' as if this in itself was reassuring evidence of Ben's loyalty. In fact it was the name of his father's brother, the one who had bequeathed him the land on which the King or his representatives were now, in Ben's eyes, demanding a ransom and calling it 'tax'.

'Yes, sir,' Ben said.

'Father was a merchant, I understand. And mother was an Allerton, no less.' The colonel was impressed.

'My father's family were good people, too, sir,' Ben said evenly. 'They came from Virginia.'

'Yes, of course.' The colonel's manner was expansive. 'Fine old English families. Sound Loyalist stock. And now Mr Max Harvie has recommended that we offer you a commission in His Majesty's Army. Great honour for any young man.'

Ben nodded.

'An officer of the British Army is first and foremost a gentleman. He is loyal to the Crown and he is ready and willing at all times to lay down his life in the service of his King and country.'

Ben nodded again, thinking: this *is* my country but I have no king.

47

'Now when a young man is put forward in this way and is found to be suitable and from suitable stock, he is sent for a month's training in the ways of the military and the conduct required of an officer. If he survives this course of induction – and not every young man does – then he is assigned to one of His Majesty's regiments.'

One of the lieutenants leaned closer to the colonel and a brief whispered conversation ensued.

'Ah!' The colonel smiled up at Ben. 'I can confirm that as of yesterday and in view of certain ... er ... developments the period of officer training has been reduced to two weeks. You should be able to see some action rather sooner than might have been expected.'

The colonel offered this as if it was a stroke of good fortune and he expected the news to be received with enthusiasm. But Ben didn't respond. 'Was there something, Mr Withers?'

'I don't want to be a commissioned officer, sir,' Ben said.

All three frowned up at him.

The colonel eyed him coldly. 'And why is that, may I ask?'

'I want to be a foot soldier.'

'A foot soldier?' the colonel echoed in disbelief. 'You want to join the infantry?'

'Yes, sir.'

'A private soldier? In the ranks?'

It was clear the colonel and his lieutenants had little respect for the men under their command.

'Cannon fodder,' muttered a lieutenant.

'Why on earth,' the colonel asked, 'would you want to enlist in the ranks?'

'I'm willing to serve, sir,' Ben said. 'I would just like to do it my way, if you don't mind, as a common soldier. That way I might see this action at first hand.'

'An officer of the British Army leads from the front, sir,' one of the lieutenants said indignantly.

But Ben insisted. 'I would like to join the ranks.'

The colonel looked perplexed. 'You are sure about this?'

'Absolutely, sir. I was present, as a boy, when Captain Preston of the 29th faced a raging mob outside the Custom House. The way those men conducted themselves on that occasion left a lasting impression on me. I would like to join the 29th – as a common soldier.'

The three officers were nonplussed. There had been nothing but trouble with the 29th in Boston. They were thoroughly disliked and distrusted by the people. Work was scarce yet in their off-duty time, in order to boost their meagre service pay, soldiers of the 29th had done menial jobs for less than the going rate and this had inevitably upset and alienated the locals. They were also rough and ill-mannered, given to drunkenness and lewd behaviour, and there was frequently friction over the way they pestered and sometimes even molested local women.

'Mr Withers,' the colonel said with an air of resignation, 'you are absolutely certain you do not wish to accept the offer of a commission in His Majesty's Army?'

'With no disrespect, sir,' Ben said, 'yes.'

The colonel glanced at the others. 'Well,' he said, 'it seems a pity to lose such a fine-looking young man, but if that is your wish . . .' He turned to one of his lieutenants. 'Where are the 29th?'

'Boston Neck, sir.'

'Oh, well. That shouldn't be a problem. Wait outside, Withers, and we'll . . . er . . . see what we can do.'

Ben sat down in the dingy corridor where others were waiting to be interviewed and ten minutes later a short, stocky sergeant called his name. Ben stood up, towering over the sergeant, and the time-served veteran eyed him coldly.

'Turn down a commission, eh?' the sergeant said. 'Follow me.'

SIX

IT began six years before. Ben and Tom were fourteen years old. Hank and Melanie were twelve. It was early March and there had been a heavy fall of snow. The four had been to the pond down Bay Street to see if it was frozen enough to take their weight. It wasn't and Hank had got his feet wet.

They were on their way back, laughing at Hank's discomfort, when they came across a crowd outside the Custom House. There had been a running battle between the redcoats of the British Army's 29th regiment and a large gang of local youths who had started the trouble by throwing snowballs with stones wrapped inside. The disturbance had been curbed somewhat by the intervention of three officers who had called their troops to order. The four youngsters climbed on to an empty market stall to get a better view.

The soldiers had withdrawn as directed but the growing crowd was not satisfied. There were shouts of 'Kill the rascals!' and 'Lousy lobster sons of bitches!' Fire bells were ringing and fire engines were being pushed across the street to create a barrier. Apprentice boys ran through the snow, hurling insults and their loaded snowballs at the British and one youth made an obscene gesture and an insulting remark to a uniformed officer.

A British soldier, standing guard in a sentry box by the Custom House, stepped forward and hit the youth on the head with his musket. The crowd responded by pelting the sentry with snowballs and lumps of ice and the sentry fixed his bayonet and loaded his musket. The crowd jeered and chanted, 'Fire, damn you! Fire, you coward! Fire, if you dare!'

A squad of soldiers, hastily summoned, came running at the double through the moonlit streets. They were led by the duty officer, an

Irishman, a Captain Preston. At the Custom House Preston ordered his men to halt and load their muskets. The soldiers then formed up and faced the crowd.

'You can't kill us all!' someone shouted and the rest took up the chant. 'You can't kill us all! You can't kill us all!'

An elderly man walked up to the army captain at this point and said calmly, 'You do not intend to fire on these people?'

'Of course not,' Preston replied.

But then one of the soldiers was knocked to the ground by a heavy wooden bar thrown by two youths. When he recovered the soldier raised his musket and urged on by his comrades fired into the crowd. At once the others began firing with him though, it was established later, Captain Preston had not given the order.

Three people fell and more followed before Preston jumped in front of his men, knocking up their muskets and screaming for them to stop. The soldiers did as they were bid and some members of the fleeing, panic-stricken crowd returned to tend the dying and the wounded. Three men had been killed and seven injured, two of whom died later.

Clinging to the swaying supports the four children saw most of what happened until youths began ripping wood from the stall and the flimsy structure collapsed.

The day of the funerals was a memorable occasion and the dead were seen as martyrs to the rebel cause. All over Boston church bells tolled and shops and stores and schools closed as a mark of respect. Ben Withers along with Tom, Hank, and Melanie lined the route with the thousand or more mourners as the open horse-drawn hearses rolled slowly by.

Captain Preston and several of his men were tried for murder. Tried separately, as the officer in charge, Preston was found not guilty. There was no evidence to suggest he had ordered his men to open fire. All but two of the soldiers were also acquitted. The two who were convicted were found not guilty of murder but guilty of manslaughter – their punishment was to have the letter M branded on their thumbs – and soon they were permitted to rejoin their regiment.

Bowing to the pressure of public opinion, sustained by a well-orchestrated campaign in the *Boston Gazette*, the 29th regiment was removed from the city. The incident became known as the Boston

Massacre, further enshrining those who died as martyrs.

Ben Withers had reasons of his own to remember the occasion. He had seen at close quarters the man who had fired the first of the fatal shots, one of the men subsequently branded, and he had remembered the face, the cruel uncaring eyes and the scarred lip. He had seen that face before, on his thirteenth birthday in fact. It was a face, he had vowed then, that he would never forget and now he was older, a man in his own right, it was a face he was ready and eager to confront.

He was twenty-one now, he told himself. Or almost. And there was something he had to do. It was not going to be easy but, as he followed the gloating little sergeant to be kitted out in black breeches and a red coat, he was not discouraged. He had been enlisted, as he had requested, in the 29th and that was a good start. He knew, too, from the reports of the trial in the *Gazette* of seven years earlier, that the man's name was Duckett. Private William Duckett.

Tom and Hank returned home convinced it was not the rebels who had burned down the Dowlings' place. The redcoats of the British Army were responsible but, for reasons of their own, there were people who wanted to blame the rebels. This was in line with what Colonel Morgan claimed at the public meeting and the boys had been inclined to believe him. Now they were certain that what he said was true.

Their father believed his country did not need the British and that, in the long term, the British could not possibly maintain control. But he had not said so and he had never once tried to influence his sons' decisions. He had left it to them to make up their own minds about which side they should join.

Tom and Hank told him they were not interested in taking up the offer of a commission with the British. They were going off to join Dan Morgan's rebels. There would be questions, they said, and they hoped this would not cause trouble for the family. Quietly pleased, their father reassured them. He would simply say they had gone and he had no idea where. Which was partly true, he added with a smile.

Mr Blanchard embraced them in turn, wished them well and told them, as he always had, to fight for what is right. 'Right is on your side,' he said. 'The rebels are in the right. This is their country, our country, and we have no place for a king.'

Their mother, he said, would not be happy at their departure – obviously. But consoling her was his responsibility. They should leave, he suggested, as if they were taking up the commissions offered by Max Harvie. He would explain things to her later.

Tom spent his last evening at home composing a letter to Sarah. He wrote that though they had known each other for only a very short time he was not in any doubt that he wanted to spend the rest of his life with her. There was no one else and there never would be. He would search for her until he found her. Then he would ask for her hand in marriage. The problem was where to send it.

Hank spent his last evening at home avoiding Imelda. She had assumed that Hank and Tom would take up the commissions her father had arranged for them. Hank didn't want to deceive her and so he didn't want to discuss his plans. But Imelda arrived at the Blanchards' house in a closed horse-drawn carriage with a footman at the reins and Hank was obliged to join her.

As soon as they were alone in the dark carriage Imelda threw herself on him, pressing her lips on his. 'Oh, you're such a baby!' she complained when he hesitated. 'You're a soldier going off to war, Henry Blanchard. You might never return! Do you realize that? If you were a real man you would carry me out to the barn and have your way with me.'

All he could say was, 'Imelda, please. The recruiting office is only down the road. I expect I'll be staying in Boston for a while. I'll probably see you tomorrow.'

'Then you could have your way with me again tomorrow,' she told him. 'John Foster tried to have his way with me and he isn't even my beau.' Her eyes glazed over in the moonlit carriage. 'He looked so grand in his uniform.'

'You've seen him?'

'He came by yesterday,' Imelda said, searching in vain for a hint of jealousy in Hank's eyes. 'He's a full lieutenant already.'

'I thought he had to go away for training.'

'Well, he does. But not right away. He has his officer's uniform though. He bought it yesterday morning and he came right over to show it to me. He looked wonderful.'

'He probably thought it might help him to have his way with you.'

'Well, it nearly did,' Imelda confessed, then she smiled sweetly. 'Why, I do believe you're jealous, Henry Blanchard.'

'Am I?' Hank asked, innocently.

Hank and Imelda were almost the same age but in many ways he

53

was so much younger. He'd been up country a couple of times to the Indian camp but nothing much had happened. He'd gone with Tom and two of their friends and an old squaw had served them Indian liquor. Hank had simply fallen asleep and on each of these occasions, when he woke up, he was lying in the back of the cart, his head throbbing and all he remembered was the throwing up.

Tom had warned him not to drink the stuff. You had to buy it. That was part of the deal. But you didn't have to drink it. Most of the boys poured it away when the old squaw wasn't watching. Yet even on the second visit Hank was so nervous when she brought in the girls he took a good long swig from the bottle and again he was sick and only half conscious all the way home.

The others, including Tom, said they'd had a girl but Hank was not all that convinced. He'd asked Tom what it was like, but Tom could only say it was 'funny', a sort of funny feeling he couldn't describe. He would have to try it for himself, Tom said. But not with Imelda. Not unless he wanted to be tied to the Harvies for the rest of his life.

The morning they were due for interview at North Street Tom and Hank said goodbye to their parents, and their mother was unable to hold back her tears.

'I hope you don't get into any trouble because of us,' Tom said quietly to his father.

'Don't you worry about us, Son,' his father said. 'What you are doing is right. Just take good care of each other. That's all I ask. Try to stay together and come home safe.'

The rebel forces were gaining both in strength and credibility. It was May, 1775, and news had emerged that a party of forty rebels led by a wealthy merchant named Benedict Arnold had joined forces with a band of farmers from the Appalachian Mountains to take a British fort at a place called Ticonderoga. The British soldiers, 150 miles from Boston and believing themselves far from any battle zone, had been surprised and easily overcome. They were rounded up, rowed across Lake George and marched to Hartford in Connecticut. The rebels thus acquired over a hundred cannon and several mortars and these were taken south for the use of the growing and increasingly confident rebel army.

*

The officers' quarters at the British Army barracks at Boston Neck were barely basic. The bunkhouses allocated to other ranks were even worse. The building of the compound that housed the 29th regiment had been started by a French Army ordnance unit some years earlier but was never finished. Yet it was occupied now by more men than it was intended for in the first place.

Ben Withers surveyed the barracks with a mixture of dismay and disgust. As instructed he had reported to the duty officer who took his name and newly issued service number and told him to find a bunk in number three.

The bunkhouse had the airless odour of stewed cabbage, of unwashed bodies and urine. The occupants, sullen and unkempt, sat or lay on the rough wooden bunks awaiting orders. Ben's tall wiry frame filled the doorway, blocking out the sunlight, and several heads turned towards him.

'What have we here?' someone asked.

A large, bloated man with watery, fish-like eyes, a dirty vest and army breeches raised himself from his bunk. 'Lookin' for a bed, are ye? There's one here.'

There was an empty lower bunk. Ben went towards it then saw a large hole in the wall at its head. A small, slightly-built Irishman was sitting cross-legged, like a leprechaun, on the upper bunk. 'Sure an' there's a gale blows through most nights, so it does.'

It was the only bunk that was not occupied. Ben put his small sack of belongings on the bed with his army issue bedroll. Then he went outside to survey the gaping hole. About twenty yards away was a derelict hut. Ben went to inspect it, found what he wanted and prised away a large square of wood. He set this over the hole then rolled a couple of small boulders forward to hold it in place. Next he piled rocks and stones on top until the cover could no longer be seen and using a flat piece of wood as a spade he filled the gaps with mud. Then he went back inside.

'Now why didn't I think o' doing that?' the little Irishman asked of no one in particular.

The big man was sitting on Ben's bunk and with two others, fawning lackeys by the look of it, was examining the contents of Ben's sack.

'Put that down,' Ben said quietly.

The big man was holding a small picture frame. It contained a portrait a travelling artist had painted of Melanie when she was just sixteen.

Ben was angry now. 'I said put that down.'

The man stood up and held the portrait high for all to see. 'We'd form an orderly queue fer 'er, wouldn't we, lads?' he leered and he rubbed the picture against his crotch.

Ben was about to lunge at him but he held up his hands and carefully placed the portrait on Ben's bed. 'I'll fight yer for it.'

The others moved away to create a space as he squared up to Ben with confidence as if to say he would soon dispose of this country boy. But Ben did not back down and the Irishman's eyes lit up, his arms clasped tight about his legs. This young fellow was about to take on the bully Bastin, by God! Sure and it was time someone taught the man a lesson.

Ben came to the bunk and removed his jerkin.

'Watch 'im, son,' the Irishman whispered. 'He's a dirty fighter.'

'I say we should do this outside,' Bastin said reasonably. 'Don't want t' damage our l'il home now, do we?'

Ben nodded and turned to go outside and, as he passed, Bastin hit him hard behind the ear. Ben staggered against the door frame then fell out on to the rough ground and for a moment lay there, Bastin circling him, fists rotating at the ready.

A crowd formed to chants of 'Fight! Fight!'

'Get up, powder puff,' Bastin taunted.

Ben drew himself up to his full height, stretched his neck to ease the pain behind his ear and coolly awaited Bastin's charge.

'Come on!' Bastin cried.

Ben smiled. 'No, fat man. You come on.'

Bastin was incensed. He charged bull-like at Ben but Ben stood his ground, saw his opening and placed a solid punch into Bastin's thick neck. Bastin spluttered and went down on one knee.

'Kill him!' was the cry. 'You've got 'im!'

Clearly there was a store of resentment against the big man and most of those watching wanted Ben to finish him off. Bastin was still down on one knee and Ben knew he could choose his spot. He could have knocked him out with ease but he didn't. He stepped closer, looked down at his immobilized opponent and, fearfully, Bastin's watery eyes looked up at him, expecting the *coup de grâce*.

His eyes friendly, Ben was smiling, but in a low voice that only Bastin could hear he said, 'Touch anything of mine again, fat man, and I'll kill you.'

Ben drew him to his feet and, putting one of Bastin's arms about his shoulder, helped him back inside. The watchers were disappointed but their respect for the newcomer visibly increased. He'd had the man exactly where he wanted him and yet he'd let him get up. He'd actually *helped* him get up.

The little Irishman, who had raced outside to watch with the others, was back on his upper bunk, his crumpled face even more creased, his legs crossed as he rocked with silent glee. Ben picked up his sack and recovered his belongings, the portrait of Melanie unharmed.

'You!' The duty sergeant appeared in the doorway.

Ben looked over his shoulder.

'Yes, you. What was your name again?'

'Withers, Sergeant.'

'You're on a charge, Withers.'

' 'Tis not fair,' the Irishman protested.

'Shut up, Paddy,' the sergeant warned, 'or you'll join him.'

That night Ben lay awake, watching Bastin's bulky mound in the bed across the aisle. 'Tis all right,' the little Irishman whispered, 'I'll watch him. You get some sleep.'

Towards noon Ben was brought before his company commander. 'Fighting amongst ourselves is frankly rather ridiculous, don't you think? Huh? And should be severely dealt with. Eh? However, in view of the fact that several witnesses have come forward to say you were merely defending yourself I have decided to let you go this time with a warning. Any more trouble and I will show no mercy. Understand? I will also warn the other man involved.'

The captain leaned across the makeshift desk and in a quieter, less censorious voice, asked, 'What on earth are you doing here, Withers? I mean, as a ranker. I don't understand.'

'I want to earn my stripes as a foot soldier, sir.'

Far from being impressed the captain looked at Ben as though his choice was both foolish and incomprehensible. 'Getting into fist fights,' he said tartly, 'is not going to win any stripes. Return to your unit now. And remember, no more trouble. Oh and Withers, it's not a good idea to make enemies in your own billet. Sometimes in battle accidents happen. A soldier can get a bullet in the back.'

'Yes, sir.' Ben stepped back a pace, saluted smartly and turned, and as the sergeant marched him out and through the orderly room he caught a glimpse of John Foster, resplendent in his new lieutenant's uniform. John had just arrived to take up his first posting. He paused momentarily, surprised to see Ben, and their eyes met. But neither spoke. They were on different sides of the social barrier now.

SEVEN

Tom and Hank Blanchard took the early morning coach to Roxbury and made their way to the church where they sought out the young minister. Pastor John promised, if the opportunity came his way, to pass on Tom's letter to Sarah. He asked if they had decided what they were going to do and they told him they were going now to join the rebels. One should remember, he told them, that there are good men and bad on both sides. He wished them well in the coming conflict and said he would pray for them. Tom and Hank shook hands with him, walked a short distance out of town then crossed a field for the cover of the trees and undergrowth at the foot of the hills that were said to house units of the rebel army.

Ahead of them in the dappled sunlight they saw the young Negro, Jimmy, who worked for the farmer Mabbut. 'Hey, Jimmy!' Tom cried. 'What are you doing here?'

'Ah been trailing you,' Jimmy said with a huge grin. 'Ah saw you going in to town and ah was wondering what two big city gents like you was doing out here.'

They laughed and Hank said, 'Shouldn't you be hard at work for Mr Mabbut?'

'No, sah, Mister Hank,' Jimmy said with mock servility. 'Ah'm sick and tired of Mister Mabbut and his donkey and his goat and the rest of that uppity family.'

They laughed again then seriously Jimmy asked, 'Where you going anyways? What you doing out here?'

'We're going to join up,' Hank told him.

'We're going to join Colonel Dan Morgan's rebels,' Tom said.

Jimmy's eyes lit up. 'That so? Then supposin' . . .' His expression of enthusiasm faded. 'No, ah guess not.'

'Supposing what?' Hank asked.

Jimmy shook his head as if he'd decided what he had in mind was out of the question.

'You thinking of joining us?' Tom asked gently. 'Is that it?'

Jimmy smiled sadly. 'If ah thought they'd have me ah'd go there right now. Just the way ah is. Ah ain't got no belongings anyways.'

'Well come with us,' Hank said.

'Yes,' Tom said. 'Why not? What's to stop you?'

Jimmy rubbed his bare arm. 'This. This'll stop me.'

The boys looked at him, genuinely puzzled.

'The colour of ma skin. Ah expect them rebels don't take no Negras.'

'Why do you say that?' Hank asked.

'They don't take Negras no place else.'

'The British have black men,' Hank told him.

Tom frowned. 'I don't think I've ever seen one.'

Hank nodded with conviction. 'I saw a black drummer once.'

Jimmy was not convinced. 'There ain't no place for Negras in the British Army. There ain't no place for Negras in the world, 'cept for working and slaving and such. Mister Mabbut treats his old dogs better than he treats us.'

'Well,' Tom said, 'Mabbut is a Loyalist. He has the superior ways of the British. You know what I mean? There's British and British. The ordinary British soldier is treated like a no account slave. He's of no importance, except as cannon fodder. Then there are the officers and gentlemen with their airs and graces. They treat everyone else as if they were something messy they just stepped in.'

'You don't like 'em,' Jimmy said.

'We don't care about them either way,' Hank said. 'They're nothing to us. We just want them out of our country.'

'We're going to win this war, Jimmy,' Tom said, 'and things are going to be different. We're Americans. We don't need some fancy king from thousands of miles away telling us what we can and can't do.'

Jimmy shrugged. 'And where does this leave me?'

'You're an American,' Hank said. 'You were born here, weren't you? This is your country, too.'

60

'Ma gran'daddy was kidnapped from some place in Africa. They put chains on him and those chains are still there.'

'Our grandfather came from England,' Tom said, 'but we're not English. Not any more. We're Americans and so are you.'

'If you want to come with us,' Hank told him, 'that's fine. But you'll have to forget all this black stuff.'

They had walked a little way through a wood, the leaves of the trees shielding them from the scorching sun, but when they came to a clearing the sun beat down fiercely making them smile and luxuriate in its warmth.

'You're Jimmy, that's all,' Hank said exuberantly. 'No different to the rest of us.'

Even to Hank this sounded patronizing. Tom threw him a look and asked, 'What's your other name, Jimmy?'

Jimmy shrugged again. 'Ah don't know. Ah guess we just take our massah's name.' He screwed up his nose. 'Jimmy Mabbut.'

'Jimmy Mabbut,' Hank repeated.

'Ah don't wanna be Jimmy Mabbut,' he blurted out. 'No, sah! Ah don't want nothin' to do with that ol' slave driver.' He laughed and, happy at the prospect of escape, he spun round, holding his arms up to the sky. 'Ah ain't no Mabbut.'

'What would you like to be called, Jimmy?' Tom asked, charmed like his brother by Jimmy's spontaneous display of *joie de vivre*.

Jimmy looked up at the sun. 'Sunshine!'

'Sunshine?' Tom and Hank queried together.

'Jimmy Sunshine. Ah wanna be Jimmy Sunshine.'

'Well, that's it,' Hank said. 'Jimmy Sunshine it is.'

Tom grinned. 'And if you're coming along, Mr Sunshine, we'd better get going.'

Jimmy laid a hand on Tom's arm. 'Ah don't want to get you boys in no trouble. When old Mabbut knows ah'm gone he'll have his boys out searching for me and when they come they come with dogs.'

'Once we join Colonel Dan, that's it, Jimmy,' Tom assured him. 'They'll not get you then. You'll have your own musket. And you'll have us. Hank and me.'

'Sure,' Hank agreed at once. 'You'll have us.'

Jimmy's eyes shone, filled with hope. But already Tom and Hank were wondering just what lay ahead for him.

*

'Wivvers!'

'Private Withers, Sergeant.' Ben's response was smart and correct, but his clear enunciation of his surname sounded like a reproof.

Pressing his taut, straining face close to Ben's and having to stand on tiptoe to do so, the drill instructor fixed him with narrowed eyes and the threat of repercussions to come. 'All right, Wivvers. Report to the orderly officer. Now! At the double!'

The orderly officer was John Foster. 'Ben!' he exclaimed when they were alone, his hand extended. 'Come in. Sit down.'

They shook hands and Ben found a chair in the small, cluttered shed used as an orderly room. John Foster, resplendent in the finery of a lieutenant, faced him from behind a desk that served to mark the gulf that had opened up between them.

'What on earth are you doing in that outfit?' Foster asked.

'It's what they issue us private soldiers with, sir,' Ben said in a humble voice and with the hint of a smile.

There had never been any doubt in John Foster's mind that Ben Withers was his own man and nobody's fool. High marks in most subjects at school. Good at games. A crack shot with a rifle. A strong oarsman. And also, though many of the girls were attracted to him he was not a womanizer. He was a one-girl man. Since they were children no one had dared to flirt with Melanie Stokes. She was Ben's girl. All this and a good family background made his present situation totally incomprehensible. Ben was no private soldier. He was first-rate officer material.

Foster was intrigued. Maybe Ben was on a special assignment, an undercover brief to report back on the mood of the men. 'I don't want to embarrass you, Ben. I was thinking maybe you are working as a ranker on some secret mission. So I won't ask.'

'Ask away,' Ben said. 'I have nothing to hide.'

'Then why? Why did you turn down your commission?' Foster asked. 'Everyone was amazed. Mr Harvie couldn't believe it.'

Ben needed help and John Foster was in a position to help him. 'John,' he said seriously, 'there is something I must do. I can't tell you what it is right now. It's sort of personal. But if you will, I think you can help me.'

'You think I can help you but you're not going to tell me how?'

Ben leaned forward and said quietly, 'I have no right to ask and if you don't want to be involved all you have to say is no.'

'So what is it?'

'There's something I need to know. I want to trace someone. A soldier. I think, as an officer, you might be able to help.'

'You could have been an officer. You could have helped yourself.'

Ben nodded patiently. 'The thing is, when I find this . . . this person I want to be a ranker same as him.'

'You've lost me, Ben, but go on. How can I help?'

'I'm looking for a man who took part that night in the massacre.'

'The massacre?'

'Yes,' Ben said. 'You were there. We all were. If you remember three people died and several more were wounded when the Army opened fire on the mob. An Irishman, a Captain Preston, was in charge. Some say he gave the order to fire, some say he didn't. But it was two of his men who did fire and that set off the whole thing. They were all charged with murder. . . .'

'. . . and acquitted,' Foster said.

'True. But two were charged with manslaughter. They were found guilty and branded. It's one of these two I'm looking for.'

'Why? Who did he kill? A relative or someone?'

'Not exactly.' It was clear that Ben was not going to elaborate.

'We'd have to go back to the record of the trial to find his name.'

'I know his name. It's Duckett. Private Duckett.'

John Foster saw how serious Ben was about this and he reacted accordingly. 'It must be four, five years ago now. Anything could have happened. He could have been at Concord or Lexington. He could be dead. He could have been sent back to England.'

'This is what I hoped you might find out for me, John.'

If he was honest John Foster would have to admit his first couple of weeks in uniform had been boring. His senior officers appeared to have little time to spare and he had not yet been told what his duties were. The senior NCOs seemed to patronize new and inexperienced commissioned officers and it was no good taking them to task because there were so many ways in which a raw lieutenant needed their help. Ben's curious request might prove a welcome diversion.

'Promise me something in return,' he said, 'and I'll see what I can do.'

'Go on.'

'Promise me that if you find this Private Duckett and you do whatever it is you want to do you will reapply for a commission.'

Ben smiled. 'I promise you I'll serve my country to the best of my ability.'

John Foster stood up and they shook hands once more. 'Take care, Ben.'

'You, too,' Ben said.

'Private Duckett.' John Foster repeated the name with an air of puzzled amusement. 'Find Private Duckett. Whoever *he* is.'

Tom, Hank and Jimmy had walked what seemed like several miles in the hills beyond the town without meeting a single rebel soldier. The only human they had seen so far was a solitary Indian who was cooking something over a small fire but at their approach he had fled for cover. They were hungry but they did not take over the meal he was preparing and went on their way. Tom and Hank had rations for two, barely sufficient when shared with Jimmy, and they knew they would have to make contact soon or start foraging for food.

Towards the end of that long afternoon, as a bee-loud haze settled on the hillsides, they at last came to what looked like an encampment. Hank had gone on ahead and reached the crest of a rise. Tom and Jimmy, bringing up the rear, hurried to his side when they heard his call. 'Down there,' he told them and when they looked they saw a cluster of tents.

They were not wigwams. They were military in style, long and low. Tom scanned the valley for redcoats. 'They may be British.'

'No,' Hank said. 'They're rebels. They must be.'

'Just look at all those horses,' Jimmy enthused. A corral to the left of the camp fenced in at least a hundred. 'Must be rebels,' he went on. 'Them British is short on horses. Leastways, old Mabbut reckon so.'

There was a rustling sound behind them and a thick-set bearded man emerged from a thicket, his rifle levelled. All three of them turned in surprise as four other men broke cover, rifles raised.

'Hello there!' Tom said going forward, his hand outstretched.

'Get back,' the bearded man ordered, 'or I'll blow your head off.'

'No need for that,' Tom said. 'Colonel Morgan wouldn't like it.'

'What do you know about Colonel Morgan?' the man demanded.

'We are on our way to join him,' Tom said, 'at his invitation.'

'We want to fight the British,' Hank added.

'You want to fight the British.'

'Until the only ones left on our land,' Hank said, 'are dead ones.'

'If you are rebel soldiers,' Tom told him, 'we've come to join you.'

Their calm, confident demeanour disconcerted the bearded man and he was not sure how he should treat them.

'Who's he?' one of the others asked with a nod in Jimmy's direction.

'We ain't allowed to bring our servants,' said another, in an attempt to mock the Blanchards' accents, and his companions sniggererd.

'He's with us,' Tom said, unsmiling, and the look in his eyes dared them to question this.

In the camp in the valley the boys were given food and drink and held in a tent with a dozen or so others who had come to join the rebels. A few militiamen, Tom noticed, were kitted out but there was a shortage of uniforms and most volunteers were still wearing the homespun clothing they arrived in.

A young lieutenant, whose badge of rank was an armband, was questioning them one by one. Where were they from and what experience did they have? Were they tradesmen? What skills did they have?

Tom told him that he and his brother had declined an offer of a commission in the British Army. They had listened to Colonel Morgan and they hoped eventually to join him. The lieutenant said they were short of junior officers. He would arrange for them to see 'the chief'. The chief was a stocky, fatherly man from Long Island named Colonel Putnam.

The colonel questioned the brothers together. He wanted to know all about them. Who their father was, where they were educated, why they were offered commissions, and he nodded at the mention of Max Harvie. He apparently knew Harvie or knew *of* him but his expression suggested he hadn't much respect for the man.

'We heard Colonel Morgan when he came to town, sir,' Tom told him, 'and we wanted to join him. We're not British subjects, we don't want to be and we'd welcome the opportunity to prove it.'

Colonel Putnam nodded again. 'You might also be spies.'

'There's nothing we can say to that,' Tom said, facing the colonel's searching stare. 'Except that we're not.'

'We just want to help set our country free,' Hank said.

'Well, in my outfit everyone has to prove himself. Unlike the British, we don't make a man an officer until we see what he's made of. If you boys want to join me you start in the ranks.'

'Yes, sir,' Tom said and Hank nodded in agreement.

'And if Colonel Morgan's men come by we can see about you join-ing them, if that's what you want.' He laughed and his shiny red cheeks glistened in the glow from his table lamp.

'But I can tell you this, you might find you're far better off with my lot. Colonel Morgan has what he calls his 'elite' force now with a crazy German drilling them night and day.'

Colonel Putnam stood up to signify the interview was over. 'There is one thing we need to sort out,' he said seriously.

Tom and Hank waited, standing to attention before his desk.

'You can't join us with your personal servant in tow,' he told them. 'You'll have to send him home. I hope you realize that.'

'Of course, sir,' Tom said. 'But Jimmy – the black boy – is not our servant. He's a friend.'

'He feels the way we do,' Hank added, 'about our country. He wants a new and independent America, same as us.'

The colonel raised his eyebrows. 'That's a very naïve thing to say, young man, and you know it.'

'Why?' Hank argued. 'Why shouldn't he feel that way? He was poorly treated by his Loyalist master and he's had enough.'

'He was born here,' Tom said. 'Just like us.'

The colonel shook his head. 'There are people on our side who feel the same as the British about Negras. You know that.'

'But not you, sir?' Tom pressed him.

The question bordered on the impertinent but the colonel merely smiled. 'I always treated my servants well, son. That way I got a good day's work out of them. But when all's said and done, a Negra is a Negra.'

'Jimmy is a good shot and a good horseman,' Tom said, though he didn't know if either claim was true. 'I'd rather have Jimmy at my back than some of the so-called *soldiers* I've seen. He just wants the same chance as everyone else to fight for his country.'

'I like you, Blanchard,' the colonel told him. 'You're so damned innocent. You both are. All right. So we give him a chance. But it's up to you to see he doesn't get into any trouble with the rest of the boys.'

'Yes, sir,' they both said.

'What's his name?'

'Er . . . Sunshine, sir,' Tom said.

'Jimmy Sunshine,' Hank said.

Colonel Putnam looked at them obliquely, his eyebrows raised, then he wrote the name on the pad before him. 'Jimmy Sunshine!' he said.

EIGHT

B<small>EN</small> Withers had only been in the army three weeks when he was back in the orderly room. He had been promoted sergeant and awarded three stripes before he had finished basic training and it was not what he had planned.

The duty officer was a dour-looking Scot. 'Ye better see the lieutenant,' he said. 'It was 'im put you up for this.'

John Foster was away that day, summoned to headquarters in Boston. When he returned Ben asked to see him at once.

'I'm grateful, John,' he said. 'But I didn't want this. In fact, it's the last thing I want. Is there some way you can get it rescinded? Give the stripes to someone else?'

John Foster held up his hands. 'Hold on.'

'I didn't ask . . .'

'Ben,' Foster said sternly. 'Private Withers. Stand to attention and shut up.'

Ben stood to attention, aware that John Foster could have him chained if necessary.

'Now listen to me,' Foster said. 'You don't put your stripes up yet. You don't put your stripes up until you're posted. Do you understand?'

'I'm to be posted?'

'I told the colonel you were wasted in the ranks. I suggested we should make you up to sergeant and post you out of here.'

'But why?' Ben reacted angrily. 'I don't want . . .'

'Will you listen? Please? I haven't found this Duckett fellow yet but I will. I don't know where he is but he hasn't gone back to England. That much I do know. He was due back but he didn't want to go and

68

he asked to be kept on for a further term. Now he's not dead or, at least, he's not listed as dead or missing. So all I have to do is find out where he is. What regiment he's with and, if I can, get you posted there.'

'I didn't have to be promoted.'

'Ah, but you did. They don't move other ranks around except in whole battalions. You can't apply for a transfer if you're a ranker. It's officers and senior NCO's only.'

Ben's attitude softened.

'From what I hear,' Foster went on, 'this Duckett is a nasty piece of work. He was transferred from the 29th soon after his trial. Seems they wanted him as far from Boston as possible.'

'Sorry for the outburst, John.'

'That's all right. But if you want a posting you have to take the stripes. Simple as that.'

Ben nodded.

'Now the promotion is from the date of the transfer. When I find where this man is I'll do my best to get you posted there.'

'You're a good man, John Foster.'

'I know,' Foster said with a laugh, 'and I'll probably get myself cashiered if anyone finds out what I'm doing.' He was obviously in good spirits and in a mood to talk. 'Can I ask you, Ben, man to man, what do you think of Imelda? Imelda Harvie.'

'Nice girl,' Ben said spontaneously. 'Bit spoiled by her old man, but a good sort at heart. Even if she is crazy.'

Foster laughed again. 'I've asked her to marry me.'

Ben was taken aback. 'I thought she was Hank Blanchard's girl.'

'Well, she was. Sort of.' Foster shrugged. 'But Hank should have made his intentions plain, don't you think?'

'He's known Imelda since they were kids.'

'Well, I reckon Hank Blanchard and his brother are off Imelda's guest list right now. Did you hear about those two, what they did?'

Ben shook his head. 'What did they do?'

'They didn't take up their commissions and after Mr Harvie had gone to the trouble of smoothing their paths.'

'I didn't take up mine,' Ben said.

'Ah, but that's different. At least you joined the army. They say the Blanchards have defected. They've joined the rebels.'

*

69

The commander of the British Army in Boston, General Gage, had more than 5,000 men at his disposal. Yet he and his army were besieged in the city by a force widely described as 'a band of peasants'. The British Government felt the commander was not up to the job and despatched three generals to help him out. Generals Clinton, Howe and Burgoyne arrived towards the end of May 1775. In Boston harbour their declared aim was to sort out these rebellious colonials once and for all. But they soon found these so-called peasants were well organized and, in the surrounding countryside, very well situated.

The countryside around Boston was covered with woods and stone-wall enclosures, an uneven terrain crossed by gullies and ravines. The new generals decided an attack must be made on Cambridge across the Charles River as soon as possible as this was where the rebel force was concentrated. Throughout one night, in order to block the army's projected path, more than a thousand militiamen built a high wall fortification above the small almost deserted borough of Charlestown.

By first light these new defences were completed and the crew of a British warship lying at anchor offshore were astonished at the overnight transformation. A broadside was fired at once at the new defences, but the cannon balls merely hit the mounds of earth and rolled back down the slopes.

There was much discussion now amongst the British generals on how best to proceed. General Gage, who still considered himself the senior commander, disregarded the newcomers and decided on a full frontal attack. In the early afternoon of 17 June British soldiers were marched down to the landing craft in their winter uniforms of thick scarlet cloth carrying three days' rations in their heavy packs and rolled blankets on their backs.

Watched by huge crowds on the surrounding hills and from the rooftops of Boston, the first wave of troops were rowed across the water. The cannon on Copp's Hill and the guns of the British Navy kept up a covering barrage of deafening intensity and the landing went unopposed. Twenty-eight barges bumped and scraped ashore. The troops were landed, the barges pushed off again and the sailors rowed back fast for the second wave.

As the soldiers ran up the beach and hillside to establish their position the rebels fell back. Behind them on Bunker Hill another thousand rebels had assembled. Reinforcements were on the way from Cambridge and the arrival of a regiment of New Hampshire volunteers gave fresh heart to the tired men who had built the battlements.

The British, three red lines of heavily laden soldiers, advanced up the slope through the long grass and clay pits and the twisted branches of wild-growing apple trees. To their left they were under heavy fire, plagued by snipers in the otherwise empty buildings of Charlestown until red-hot shot was despatched to set the wood-frame houses and the whole town alight, the wooden church steeples reaching out of the flames like blazing torches.

Shots from the British fleet thudded around the rebels, sending up clouds of dust, but the rebels had been ordered to hold their fire. Ammunition and powder were in short supply and they had strict instructions that not a single shot should be wasted. The men from New Hampshire were not to open fire until a stake their commander had driven into the ground was reached by the British. The rebels on their right had been told to wait for the order to fire then aim for 'the fancy vests of the British officers'.

When they did open fire the effect was devastating and scores of British soldiers fell. At the second volley, again fired in unison, many more were killed or wounded and the British lines broke up in retreat despite the drawn swords, the thrusting bayonets and the screamed threats of the officers attempting to halt them.

The British general, John Burgoyne, wrote later that this was *'one of the greatest scenes of war that can be conceived . . . to the left the enemy pouring in fresh troops by the thousand . . . our ships cannonading before them . . . a noble town in one great blaze . . . the hills round the county covered with spectators in anxious suspense . . . and a reflection that a defeat was perhaps the loss of the British Empire in America.'*

But the British were determined. Beaten back twice with dreadful losses, the generals regrouped their men to launch a third attack and this time they broke through. The British advanced, shouting and screaming with bayonets fixed as they stepped over the bodies of their dead comrades. The rebels, almost out of ammunition, turned and ran.

The retreat was orderly, without panic, but as they reached Bunker Hill and joined those who had stayed back and dodged the fighting in the front line, an unseemly flight ensued and over 400 rebels were killed or wounded. But the British had lost far more. At least sixty of their officers had been wounded and twenty-seven had been killed. Of the men in the ranks over 200 died and more than 800 were wounded, almost half their total strength.

The British held the battlefield and thereby claimed the victory. But it was not a victory to celebrate. They had suffered too many casualties and their depleted army was totally exhausted. There was concern, too, at the disorder and indiscipline in their ranks in the face of battle. But the most significant outcome of all this was the realization that the rebel army was a genuine force to be reckoned with and not the disorganized rabble many supposed.

It was soon after he told Ben Withers of his intentions that John Foster returned to Boston to see Imelda Harvie. Imelda had promised to give him an answer and her warm, reassuring manner at their previous meeting had given him good reason to believe she would accept his proposal of marriage. But Imelda was far from sure this was what she wanted. She enjoyed the role she was playing far too much to give it up just yet.

The centre of all the intrigue and romance in her circle of friends, she was the fixer not the fixed, the matchmaker not the matched. She enjoyed mild flirtations with most of the personable young men she came across, even those among the workhands at her father's plant where she revelled in the glances and the appreciative stares she drew whenever she went by. But she was always careful not to get too involved.

From an early age Imelda had noticed and been drawn to the Blanchard boys. Tom Blanchard was friendly and courteous but he was clearly not interested in her in any amorous way. Imelda had accepted this though later when Tom was obviously smitten by her cousin Sarah she was somewhat miffed. Sarah was pretty enough and she had these startlingly green eyes. But apart from that, she thought, Sarah is no better looking than me. And she doesn't have my worldly charm.

But Tom had never been in her reckoning as a possible suitor, she told herself. Not really. His younger brother, Henry, was another matter. Henry and Imelda had known each other since they were children but it was only when he had come to the house with Tom for her sixteenth birthday party that he'd been surprised and totally dazzled. He was only fifteen at the time, just a few months younger than Imelda, and he was captivated by the unexpected poise and air of sophistication surrounding their elegant young hostess.

Now, when a girl named Anna Burnside announced with great solemnity to an inner circle of confidantes that she had lost her virginity and Imelda and her friends were consumed with envy, Imelda thought of Henry Blanchard. It was generally deemed outrageous for this to happen out of wedlock but among these privileged young ladies it was viewed with scandalized awe and it conferred a special status on the confessor.

It was like floating on a pure white cloud in a clear blue sky, Anna proclaimed when pressed in what seemed a laughable and utterly fatuous account of the experience thus casting doubt on whether it had happened at all. The seducer, she told them in a loud stage whisper as they sat in a crinolined group under the oak tree in the Harvies' rose garden, was this tall dark stranger, a gentleman gambler, a business acqaintance of her father. He was just passing through on his way to purchase a coral island in the Caribbean Sea. Pressed for details Anna's imagination ran wild and, as she contradicted several of her earlier statements, those who had originally doubted her story doubted it even more.

Imelda was one of the more bluntly outspoken. 'A tall dark stranger?' she scoffed. 'What would such a man want with you?'

'He said if he left me with child he would come right back and marry me,' Anna claimed.

'How would he know if you were with child,' someone asked, 'if he's gone south?'

'If he found out,' someone else said, 'I guess he'd go even further south.'

The whole discussion had swiftly dissolved into ribaldry and laughter and poor Anna had been left to sulk. But the thought had stayed with Imelda. She was the leader, she believed, of this group and it was surely up to her to be the first. And so to this end she arranged to be alone with Henry Blanchard just before he left to go to war.

It was early one afternoon and there was no one else in the house. Her father was out at business. Her mother was at a meeting of the school board. The cook, Vanessa, was asleep on the back porch and her mother's housemaid had gone to the store to order provisions. Imelda sent the houseboy to inform Hank she must see him at once. It was extremely important and he must come right away.

Hank came at once as requested. He was leaving next morning and he supposed he ought to bid Imelda some sort of formal farewell. She was not really his girl as he repeatedly told his brother, but he couldn't deny they had this special relationship.

He knocked at the front door and got no response. He went round to the yard and the back porch. Vanessa was asleep. She was breathing deeply in a sonorous snore on the gently swaying sun chair, and he knew she would not thank him for waking her. He went through the kitchen, looked in the morning room but there was no one about. He wandered as far as the front hall. 'Hello?' he called, a little concerned now that he might be trespassing. 'Imelda?'

At the foot of the sweeping stairway, scene of so many social gatherings but deserted now, he paused.

'Henry, darling.' Imelda's mellifluous voice floated down from the wide landing in a loud whisper. 'Come up here. I have something to show you.'

Hank looked around doubtfully.

'Come on,' she urged, more strident now. 'Come upstairs.'

Hank walked slowly up the stairs like a condemned man mounting the scaffold and Imelda couldn't wait to draw him along the landing and into her bedroom.

For a moment he stood just inside the doorway and gazed in wonder at the indulgently furnished room of dolls and cushions and mirrors and in the centre of it all Imelda's plush bed with its cream-coloured silken coverlet. He knew he shouldn't be here and, as always with Imelda, he wondered what she was up to.

'Come over here, you big loon.' Imelda pulled him to a place beside her on the bed.

'What?' Hank was scared that someone, her father, anyone, might appear in the doorway. 'What do you want, Imelda?'

Imelda smiled at him in such a way that anyone less flustered would have had no doubt what she wanted. She puckered her lips, pushed him lightly back on to the silky coverlet, straddled his tense body and planted a lascivious kiss on his open mouth.

Hank struggled to come up for air. 'Imelda!'

'Get these off!' she ordered and she began to unbuckle one of his boots.

'No!' he protested. 'I'm not stopping!'

'Oh, but you are,' she informed him voluptuously, and she pushed him back on the bed to pull off the boot.

Hank tried to get up but his red face was pressed against her bulging bosom. 'Why must I take my boots off?'

'So's I can pull off your breeches is why,' she informed him and it was then that he panicked.

Her tongue between her lips, her eyes alight, Imelda gave a gentle tug to the lace bow that held her in check and the pink plumpness of her breasts spilled out against his burning cheek.

He struggled to escape but the more he struggled the more she succeeded in pulling down his breeches. 'What are you doing?'

Melodramatically, Imelda narrowed her eyes. 'I'm a girl,' she breathed, 'and I want to be a woman.'

'What?' he asked, genuinely mystified, and he found to his alarm that she had taken him in hand. 'Imelda!'

'What's the matter with you?' she complained and she began to knead him, like a piece if dough, her knuckles in his groin.

'Ow!' he cried. 'That hurts!'

Imelda was astride him now but just as his resistance was beginning to recede Vanessa's voice came bellowing up the stairway. 'You up there, Miss 'melda? Your momma's home.'

They leapt from the bed and Hank struggled with one foot in his fallen breeches as she pushed him towards the window.

'Go!' she whispered hoarsely. 'Go now!'

He opened the window and looked down on what seemed quite a drop. But Imelda was pushing him out and there was no way back. He pulled up his breeches, climbed out and lowered himself to cling to the ledge, his arms out as far as they would go, then he dropped to the garden below. Imelda picked up his boots and threw them down after him, narrowly missing his head. Smiling weakly at the elderly gardener who was looking on, bemused by this unconventional exit, Hank picked up his boots and made his escape.

Imelda was still intact then when John Foster asked her to marry him. She liked John. He was good-looking, popular, a bit of a ladies' man and he was from a good family. He was not, though, someone she could boss the way she bossed Henry Blanchard. But he was a young man of whom her father would almost certainly approve and probably prefer to Hank. Her father, she knew, was slightly wary of the Blanchard boys. He hadn't always been on good terms with their father.

Joe Blanchard was a strong-minded independent horse breeder

who didn't readily follow fashionable causes or fall in with the mood of the day and he sometimes appeared to make fun of Imelda's father. In Imelda's view this was unfair. Her father could be pompous and self-important sometimes, but he was a good man with the good of the community at heart and she knew it would make him happy if she married John Foster. But Imelda couldn't decide. The truth was, she wasn't yet ready for marriage. When she told John Foster that she loved him she meant it. She did love him. She loved all her male friends and she was having too good a time to give all that up just yet.

As arranged John Foster had come by to hear her decision and she had delivered her carefully rehearsed response. 'John, darling, I love you. You know I do. But marriage . . . I don't know that I'm ready yet. It's a big step. I need time. Just give me a little longer.'

'I may not have much longer to give, Imelda.' John appeared to have matured overnight or at least since donning his officer's uniform. Much of his easy-going, bantering way had gone and he wanted a decision. 'In a war,' he said, 'not everyone survives.'

But she had asked him again to be patient, pleaded with him, begged him in her most theatrical manner to give her another week. As a gentleman, he told her, he could only accede to her request. That same evening word had come that all officers must return to their units by midnight. John bade Imelda 'farewell for now' and rode back to his base at Boston Neck.

The next morning Lieutenant John Foster and a company of marksmen were despatched as reinforcements to the troops preparing for the attack on Charlestown and the hills beyond. When they arrived the first wave of troops had already stormed the barricade and been repulsed. The second wave were being rowed across the water. John Foster's company lined up with the third wave for the attack that was finally to succeed.

As the rebel force before him disintegrated this new young officer, John Foster, was jubilant. Fearlessly he flourished his newly acquired sword as the rebels turned and ran. Tall and resplendent in his highly coloured officer's garb, he led his men forward in the rout of the enemy. Even the bodies of those fallen underfoot did not give him pause, nor dim his youthful enthusiasm. If this was war he was enjoying it. His first taste of battle, his first campaign, was an all-conquering success and the feeling was one of great exhiliaration as he turned, sword held high, to exhort the stragglers to catch up. Then a wayward ball from his own artillery struck him full in the face and took off his head.

NINE

A s raw recruits Tom, Hank and Jimmy had remained behind with other newcomers to guard the rebel camp to the west of Roxbury. Colonel Putnam had sent his best organized troops to join the rebels at Bunker Hill. Many of those remaining were disappointed at not getting into the action but the hoary old time-served ex-army captain left in charge told them, 'You'll get plenty of action soon enough.'

The camp midway between Roxbury and Cambridge was close to the Charles River. There was the corral for the horses and a number of supply wagons were tied up nearby. A series of large tents bordered a central parade ground. Two of these were the 'admin' offices, one was a sick bay and the fourth was the cook house. 'Nice 'n' handy,' the wags would say. 'It's outa here (the cookhouse) an' inta here (the sick bay)'. Meals were taken in an open area behind the cookhouse, either sitting on the sparse grass or standing up.

The volunteers came in many shapes and sizes. Tall, short, fat, thin, town boys, country boys, farmhands, fishermen, college boys, clerks, army deserters, retired professional soldiers, dedicated patriots, aimlesss drifters and vagrants looking for the next meal. From the well dressed to the ragged, most wore the clothing in which they arrived. Few uniforms were available and none was promised.

The days were long, warm and pleasant that June and after the early morning drill and the firearms training that followed there was little to do but wait. Wait for orders. Wait for news. Wait for news of the fierce battle raging across the bay at Charlestown. Wait for something to happen.

Tom and Hank had been separated from Jimmy one morning in a drill exercise down by the river and their platoon was late returning for the midday meal. As they waited in line they saw that Jimmy was sitting alone on the grass, a little distance from the others, and though it was common practice to sit wherever there was space it looked to Tom and Hank as if by choice no one wanted to sit near him. Tom and Hank exchanged glances, aware that something must have happened that morning and curious to know what.

They took their bowls of beef stew and made a show of greeting him loudly and sitting down on either side of him.

'What's wrong, Mr Sunshine?' Hank asked quietly. 'Clouds got you covered?'

'Ah'm all right,' Jimmy said, though he clearly wasn't.

'Hey!' someone called from a group of men a few yards away. 'Fella! Over here.'

The man was looking at Tom. Four or five of the men Jimmy had been drilling with were sitting around, some still eating. Tom strolled across.

'How'd you git to bring your slave with ya?' the man asked.

Tom was standing over him, looking down, still holding his bowl of stew. 'I beg your pardon?'

Several of the watchers were amused by Tom's polite respnse and one wriggled effeminately and mimicked his reply.

'The Negra boy,' the first man said. 'Why d'ya bring him?'

'He is not my slave,' Tom said calmly, 'and I didn't bring him. He's my friend and he came because he's an American just like you. And like you he doesn't want to be ruled by the British.'

'He ain't like me,' the man snarled. 'Not in *any* way.'

Tom nodded. 'No. I guess you're right. He isn't like you. Not in *any* way.'

Someone sniggered but someone else said, 'Clean ya boots, does 'e?' And another asked. 'Do ya washin?'

Then one went a step too far. 'Keep ya nice an' warm nights in ya l'il bed?'

Tom turned on the man, yanked him to his feet and poured the bowl of stew over his head. At once the others were on their feet. Hank and Jim came to Tom's aid and fists flew wildly for several seconds. A single shot in the air brought them to a halt.

The drill sergeant trained his pistol on the brawlers. 'Don' nobody move 'til ah says so.'

The captain emerged, stern-faced, from his tent. 'What's going on here, Sergeant?'

'Nothin', sir,' the sergeant told him. 'Just a little disagreement is all. We got things under control.'

The captain looked at the dishevelled men, at the man with stew in his hair and on his face. Then he turned to the sergeant and nodded curtly. 'Carry on, Sergeant. And make sure there are no more little disagreements.'

'Sah!' the sergeant responded smartly and the captain went back into his tent. 'Settle down,' the sergeant ordered. 'Now! Si' down!'

The men sat down on the grassy bank. The man with stew on his face wiped it away and glared at Tom Blanchard. Tom picked up his empty bowl and sat down with the rest.

'I don't know what you were fightin' about. I don't want to know,' the sergeant said. 'But we're here to fight the enemy not each other.'

Calm had been restored but the resentment remained and the sergeant sensed it. 'Anybody, and I mean anybody, steps out o' line from now on,' he warned, 'he'll have me to deal with.'

There was a silence all round as the sergeant went back to the main tent. Then the man Tom had emptied his bowl over called across, 'Ah'll be watching you, fella.'

Tom went back and crouched down before the group of men who had started it all. They were sprawled or sitting on the grass and they sat up and stiffened now, ready for more trouble. But Tom said quietly, 'I don't know what it is with you fellows. Jimmy Sunshine is a good man. He's a good friend and he's a good shot. Take it from me, boys. You'll be glad to have him on your side – not against you.'

'He's a Negra,' one said reasonably.

'Negras ain't supposed to have no firearms,' said another.

'He's a soldier,' Tom said.

'Where ah come from Negras know their place,' said a third, 'and ah'd like to keep it that way, smart boy.'

'Then maybe you're in the wrong army,' Tom told him.

He went over to the cookhouse to rinse his bowl and get a refill but the servers had gone and the lids were on the pots.

'This was about me, wasn't it?' Jimmy asked.

'It was nothing,' Tom said. 'Forget it.'

'Ah shouldn't a come,' Jimmy said quietly, his head still down. 'Ah ain't welcome here.'

'Now you listen to me,' Tom told him. 'You're with us now. We stick together. The three of us. No matter what. That right, Hank?'

Hank punched Jimmy affectionately in the shoulder. 'No matter what, soldier. No matter what.'

Imelda Harvie had promised Tom Blanchard she would do all in her power to find out what had happened to her cousin Sarah since that dreadful day at the Dowlings' farm. Imelda's mother had wanted to take care of Sarah. She was welcome to stay with them, she said, for just as long as she wanted. But the Dowling family had plans of their own for Sarah. Mrs Harvie's sister had married John Dowling and John's sister, Sarah's Aunt Alice, was adamant that Sarah must stay with them. Sarah was a Dowling not a Harvie, and she would remain a Dowling. None of them had acknowledged the fact that Sarah was eighteen years old and might have views of her own on the subject.

That first few days Sarah had stayed with her Aunt Alice then the family doctor and her aunt's husband had arranged for her to go to a convent hospital in Philadelphia. It was a place where the sick could go to recuperate, or in a separate annexe join a retreat, a form of religious isolation where penitents and others could rest and pray and reassess their lives. Sarah saw it as a way out of the well-meaning but claustrophobic care of her Aunt Alice and the rest of the Dowlings. She wrote Imelda that she was happy to go.

Imelda had heard nothing more from Sarah but just then other matters were claiming Imelda's attention. News had come through a bulletin posted in the window of the North Street print-shop her father owned that twenty-seven officers of the British Army had been killed in the battle of Bunker Hill and sixty-three had been wounded. There was no mention of the 226 British soldiers killed and over 800 wounded. Listed among the dead was Lieutenant John Foster of Boston.

The small crowd that gathered around the print-shop window included several of Imelda's friends and acquaintances and they were shocked to read of John's death. John had only been in the army a matter of weeks and already he was dead, a casualty of war. The news was swiftly relayed to Imelda who threw up her hands in horror and ran in search of her mother.

Mrs Harvie was in the living-room with her husband and her husband's physician, a Dr Smithson. Mr Harvie had not been well. The uncertainty of the past few weeks had taken its toll.

'Oh, Mother!' Imelda wailed. 'It's John. John Foster. He's dead.'

81

Mrs Harvie gathered her daughter in her arms. Imelda had told her mother of John's proposal and she knew her husband would have been well pleased with such a fine son-in-law. She also knew Imelda was more than likely to have turned John down.

'He asked me to marry him.'

'I know, dear,' her mother said. 'I know.'

'What's this?' her father asked. 'John Foster?'

The doctor looked anxiously at Mr Harvie.

'He's dead!' Imelda sobbed accusingly, as if her father was to blame. 'He asked me to marry him.' The tears flowed. 'And I told him I would accept if he had your approval.'

'Why, he's a . . . he was a fine young fellow,' her father said, perplexed. 'Of course, of course I would have agreed.'

'It's no good now,' Imelda told him. 'It's too late. Why did you have to send him to this stupid war?'

'Imelda!' Her mother was angry now. 'Your father did not send John anywhere. John was a volunteer.'

'Daddy arranged his commission.'

'It was John's wish,' her mother said sternly.

'And now he's dead.'

'This is what happens in a war,' Harvie said quietly, conscious that he had also arranged a commission for his own son. 'People get killed.'

'He asked me to marry him,' Imelda repeated.

The doctor was embarrassed. This was a purely family matter.

'I want John!' Imelda cried hysterically. 'I want him back!'

Max Harvie looked at the doctor helplessly but Imelda's mother remained calm, suspecting Imelda was enjoying the histrionics.

'Go and lie down, Imelda,' she said firmly. 'I'll come up and see you shortly. Dr Smithson is here to see your father.'

'Oh no,' the doctor responded. 'You mustn't mind me, ma'am. I . . . I was just going.'

Imelda turned with a sob and ran up the wide stairway to her bedroom, knowing she could fool her father but not her mother.

'This is dreadful,' Max Harvie said, 'and a damned shame. Fine boy like John Foster. Excellent young man. Poor Imelda.' He turned to Dr Smithson. 'Perhaps she needs a little something to calm her down, help her sleep.'

Mrs Harvie shook her head. 'I'll see to Imelda,' she said. 'You mustn't worry about her. I'm sure she'll be all right.'

Max Harvie accompanied the doctor to the door, their meeting cut short. The doctor had not only come to the Harvie house in his professional capacity, he was there also as a representative of a group of Loyalists who were considering, at Harvie's instigation, contacting the chieftains of some of the Indian tribes to the north of Boston and, with inducements, enlisting their support against the rebels. They would meet again, they decided, in the morning.

Imelda lay on her bed, her round pretty face blotched and stained with tears that were not wholly genuine. She was saddened, but she knew that nothing had changed. She'd had no intention of marrying John Foster and now, perversely, she wished she had accepted his proposal publicly. She could then have put on a performance of high drama, dressed in black and played the leading role in some sombre interment ceremony. She even wished she had allowed John to have his way with her when he had so obviously wanted her. He had promised he would not make her pregnant and now she would be 'in the know', ahead of all her friends with the probable exception of Melanie Stokes.

Still, for Imelda, all was not lost. She could hint that she was now a complete woman. She knew the answer to one of the great mysteries of their young lives. And she could still cut a tragic figure. She was the girl who had lost her beau to the war. She could hold her head high, save her tears for the privacy of her bedroom and be a credit to the soldier she had loved and lost. Imelda Harvie was totally and irredeemably shallow. But she was not a malicious girl, she was just silly and her love of life was infectious. Those who knew her well knew that her role as a great tragedienne would soon begin to pall.

Apart from her mother, if there was anyone who could not be fooled by Imelda it was Melanie Stokes. Imelda had spotted Melanie at the clothing store earlier that week and had hurried over to tell her that Ben was all right. John Foster had seen him. He was one of John's men, Imelda had said. He was only a private and, of course, as an officer John could not spend much time with him. But she had asked John, she said, to 'look out for him'.

Melanie had smiled sweetly. She could have risen to Imelda's unwittingly patronizing bait and said that Ben was a private soldier because he wanted it that way. He had turned down a commission. But Melanie knew Imelda, knew her capacity for making fatuous and often insensitive comments. She knew, too, that Imelda was the spoiled daughter of an over indulgent father, a silly girl who was, for all that, basically kind, generous and fun to be with. She simply allowed Imelda to prattle on. But she did worry about Ben. Melanie knew that Ben could take care of himself and would not need John Foster or anyone else to look out for him. Ben would survive army life, even as a lowly private. But the news of John Foster's death had frightened her and she prayed that Ben would be sent to some place where the war was not raging, some place where there was little danger. She prayed he would find the man he was looking for and that the war would soon be over.

Those who could read gathered round the bulletin board at the camp near Boston Neck. Ben, taller than most, stood on the fringe and ran his eye down the list of officers. Lieutenant J.B. Foster, he read. He inched his way closer to the board. The list was headed: KILLED IN ACTION. Then the line: *The following officers* . . . The names of the twenty-seven officers killed in action were listed. Second from the last was Lieutenant J.B. Foster.

So John was dead. Just one battle had proved one battle too many. A young fellow like John Foster with all his life ahead of him, all that life unlived. Gone. Lost forever. He hadn't disliked John, Ben told himself truthfully. What he had disliked was the scheming ambition bred in him by his family background. Or was that fair? Tom and Hank were from a similar background but they were neither scheming nor especially ambitious.

John had wanted to make a good marriage, set up connections, good connections. That was the way some people lived. Everything aimed at personal advancement. Well, good connections couldn't help him now. In truth, the good connections were responsible for his death. If it wasn't for Max Harvie, John Foster might not have rushed into the army. And if he had survived the war he might well have married the crazy Imelda. Ben shook his head philosophically. Whichever way you looked at it, poor old John was doomed. But then perhaps he and Imelda deserved each other.

Ben turned away from the board, retracting this last thought at once. Imelda was a good sort at heart. And John was not a bad fellow. Easy to get along with. Just . . . well, a little too obviously ambitious. But maybe that was how it should be, Ben reflected. Maybe it was *he* who was out of step with the rest of the world. He smiled to himself.

He'd suspected this for some time.

John's death meant that the official enquiries about Duckett would come to an end. At least John had tried. The business of the three stripes proved that. The trouble was that without John quietly overseeing the course of events Ben might now get posted to some Godforsaken outpost with no news of his prey. All he wanted was to find this man Duckett. That was all he wanted from the British Army. But without John's help it might not be possible.

Two days later he was summoned to the orderly room where he was marched into the presence of John Foster's replacement. The new lieutenant was an anxious-looking, pink-cheeked young man who looked as though he had come straight from school. Facing Ben, whom he took to be an experienced soldier, the young officer seemed embarrassed and not sure how to behave.

'I ... er ... I've taken over from Lieutenant Foster,' he said hesitantly, as if apologizing for being there.

Ben felt a rush of sympathy towards him. Poor kid would probably get killed the first time he stuck his neck out.

'There's something here I don't quite follow,' the young lieutenant went on.

Standing to attention, Ben waited patiently.

'You are Private Withers?'

'Yes, sir,' Ben said.

'Well, there's a note here from Lieutenant Foster. You know that Lieutenant Foster died heroically at Bunker Hill?'

'Yes, sir,' Ben said gravely.

'Well, I don't quite know what your connection is ... er ... was with Lieutenant Foster. . . .'

'Perhaps you will allow me to explain, sir,' Ben suggested.

This soldier was unlike any of the rankers the young lieutenant had come across so far. He was clean, courteous, well-spoken. 'Please,' he said. 'Please do.'

'I knew Lieutenant Foster before we enlisted. We were at the same school. We both lived in Boston. We knew the same people.'

'You were not offered a commission?' The young lieutenant reddened, wondering if he had stumbled across some scandal he ought to have known about. 'I mean. . . .'

'I was, as a matter of fact. Through a Mr Harvie, Max Harvie.'

The lieutenant brightened. 'Same as me.'

'Yes,' Ben said. 'But I wanted to see army life as it is in the ranks. I wanted to experience the war as a private.'

'I see,' the lieutenant said, though he clearly didn't.

'Also, I asked Lieutenant Foster for help in tracing a man I wish to contact, a Sergeant Duckett.'

'Ah!' The young lieutenant's face lit up. 'That's it. That's what this is all about.' He picked up a paper from his desk. 'Lieutenant Foster left a note before he was sent to Bunker Hill. It just says: *Memo to Private Ben Withers. Sergeant William Duckett is with the British Legion, a regiment of light cavalry and foot soldiers.*'

Ben was delighted. 'Thank you,' he said, remembering to add 'sir'. 'I really am grateful.'

The British Legion it turned out, was stationed in New Jersey, somewhere along the Delaware River. The lieutenant promised to put in a request to the commanding officer that Ben should join them as soon as possible. It didn't occur to him to ask why Ben wanted to find the man or even to ask whether it was official business or a purely private matter. He was just happy, it seemed, to have solved the mystery of the note on his desk.

Two weeks later a more senior officer wanted to know why Ben had asked to join the Legion. Was he not proud of his regiment?

'It isn't personal, sir,' Ben lied. 'I am to deliver a message to a certain person. A person who is serving with the Legion, sir.'

The officer looked sceptical. 'And what is this message?'

'I'm afraid I'm not at liberty to say, sir.'

The officer was aware that Ben had turned down a commission, choosing instead to join the ranks. Was there more to this, he wondered, than meets the eye? Perhaps he was working for some higher authority. Espionage, perhaps. Undercover work.

Ben noted the hesitation. 'I promised that if anything happened to Lieutenant Foster I would do my utmost to deliver the message on his behalf.'

'Why didn't Lieutenant Foster deliver this message himself?'

'I understand he was refused permisssion to join the Legion, sir,' Ben lied again. 'Rankers and NCOs, he said, can be spared. But the regiment is reluctant to part with its officers and, in any case, he didn't want to leave the 29th.'

'And you can't tell me what this message is?'

Ben shook his head. 'I'm sorry, sir. But I gave my word.'

The officer eyed him for a moment then said curtly, 'Dismiss.'

Ben believed that was the end of that and began at once to plan his desertion, but a few days later a posting came through. He was to travel to Trenton, New Jersey, to join the British Legion with the rank of sergeant under the command of a Colonel Tarleton.

TEN

GAMBLING and women were two of the biggest problems for the rebel army. The young men who had been left behind in the camp were getting stronger, fitter, more organized, more like members of a disciplined fighting force. They were training well, drilling every morning and, among other things, having horse-riding and firearms tuition every afternoon. The difficulty for their commanding officer, Colonel Putnam, was to keep them out of trouble when they were off duty. They played games, one in particular that was very popular, a game with sticks and a small piece of wood. The wood, which was sharpened to a point at both ends, was chipped up into the air and despatched as far as possible with a stick. This and other less skilful games they played for money.

Colonel Putnam, as all officers did, frowned on the gambling and issued orders that it was to cease forthwith. Anyone caught playing for money would be dealt with severely. The games were then played for straws – which were later exchanged for cash. The colonel knew this, of course, but no punishments were carried out and the gambling went on. A sergeant, who had once served in the British Army, had discussed the problem with the colonel and they had agreed that to turn a blind eye was probably the best solution – unless, the colonel said, the stakes get out of hand. 'I dunno, sir,' the sergeant said. 'Some o' these fellers would bet on two flies crawling up a donkey's ass. We could never stop 'em.'

The problem of women was even more acute. Their leaders had ordered that under no circumstances must a member of the rebel forces molest or in any way insult a local female. The strictest of proprieties must at all times be observed. Lewd behaviour, sexual assault and rape, the rebels were told, were hallmarks of the British.

The good reputation and image of the rebels as patriots and liberators, Colonel Putnam ordered, must not be tarnished in any way. A rebel soldier accused and found guilty of rape would be shot. This had been made clear to all ranks. But the colonel had to keep the lid on the simmering cauldron of 300 lusty young men. They wanted women. They *needed* women.

'You must remember what it was like, sir,' the sergeant teased him gently. 'It's like walking around on three legs.'

'I am not so far gone that you need to jog my memory, Sergeant,' the colonel said tartly. But common sense told him the sergeant was right. Something had to be done.

A few days after the sergeant's *cri de coeur* two large tents were erected beyond the corral and a well-known local madam was duly invited to staff them. The arrangement soon proved inadequate as long queues quickly formed every evening at the first tent where several young and some not so young women awaited selection. Now, with stretches of canvas draped across taut ropes to form partitions, the tents were divided into sections. 'Cus'omers', as the girls called the waiting soldiers, selected a partner and as a section became vacant together they moved in.

But the demand became so great that the selection process was abandoned and the 'cus'omers' were obliged to take whichever girl was next in line. The madam, a large fat lady known as Auntie Moll, sat on a stool between the two tents, collecting the money in her widespread lap and allocating the girls.

Each couple were allowed only ten minutes, sometimes even less, before Auntie Moll called a number. 'Five! Get the hell outa there. Now!' And frequently she would need to add such irate reproaches as 'Number Two! I will not tell you again!' Occasionally she would need to send in a couple of the armed guards who were there to protect her and her girls and they would prise some frantic young bull from the, usually, bored recipient of his ardour.

Hank Blanchard saw this as an opportunity to join the ranks of the initiated, the men of the world. He would be able to tell Imelda truthfully if she approached him again, 'No, this is not my first time.'

Friday night was the busiest night for Friday was the day the rebel soldiers received their meagre pay. There were those who condemned the whole business as 'degrading, unholy and soul-destroying'. Those of a religious bent were appalled and openly criticized the colonel. But

Colonel Putnam was responsible for a large concentration of men with time on their hands and he knew what was important and what was not. His brief was to keep them out of mischief as they awaited the call to arms and he knew of no better way. When a delegation of church elders asked to speak with him he was ready for them. 'Men are men,' he told them, 'Would you rather I turned them loose on the town on Friday nights?'

Hank was excited. 'You coming, Tom? I could stuff a grizzly bear.'

'From the look o' some o' them women,' someone said, 'you'd be better off with a grizzly bear.'

'You want me to hold your hand,' Tom said. 'Is that it?'

'You're no expert,' Hank said, aggrieved. 'You haven't done it all that often yourself.'

Jimmy Sunshine was lying on his hunk.

'How about you, Jimmy?' Tom asked. 'You coming?'

'Ah don't think so,' Jimmy said.

'Come on,' Tom urged him. 'It doesn't mean anything. It's just something a man needs to do now and again.'

'Come on!' Hank hauled Jimmy from his bunk and reluctantly Jimmy followed them outside.

They set off around the corral, Hank dancing on his toes. 'All right, clever,' he said, addressing his brother. 'So how many times *have* you done it?'

'Dozens of times,' Tom said with a grin.

'No, you haven't,' Hank challenged him. 'Twice, maybe. At the Indian Camp.'

Actually it was once. The first time Tom's enthusiasm deserted him and he was as limp as a dead fish. The second time he had succeeded but he'd been scared, too, because the tough little Indian girl had clamped her bare legs so tight around his backside he had been unable to withdraw in time. The last thing he wanted was some little half-breed calling him 'Father' and he still worried about the possibility from time to time.

'What about you, Jimmy?' he asked to halt Hank's interrogation.

Jimmy shook his head. 'Tell you the truth ah think maybe this is not such a good idea. Ah mean, it's supposed to be somethin' special, ain't it? Somethin' you do in private with the person you is fond of.'

'Well, ye-es,' Tom said tentatively and he thought of Sarah and what

she might think of him if she saw him standing here in line. 'I suppose
it is. But if you've never done it before maybe this is how you can learn
to do it well. Then, when the time comes, with the right girl . . . well,
you sort of know what the hell you're doing.'

The queue seemed to be moving fairly fast. Two soldiers at Auntie
Moll's knee were claiming they hadn't had their full ten minutes but
the guards moved them on and soon it was Hank's turn. There seemed
to be only three girls on duty so they stayed in their own section of the
tent and Auntie Moll directed the men to them. She took Hank's
money, looked him up and down and said, 'Number three, and don't
look so scared. She won't bite.'

Hank went into the tent and lifted the flap on number one, catching a glimpse of puny arms and legs spreadeagled beneath a huge
heavyweight soldier.

'Number *three*, dumb head!' Auntie Moll screamed and Hank
dropped the flap as if he'd been scalded.

From her stool Auntie Moll, her composure instantly restored,
looked at Jimmy. She shook her head and made a noise in her throat
that clearly meant, 'No. Out of the question.'

'Why not?' Tom demanded.

She stared at him haughtily. 'Ma girls don't take no Negras.'

'Then they don't take me,' Tom said.

Auntie Moll merely shrugged. 'Next!'

Tom opened his mouth to protest but Jimmy had already turned on
his heel and hurried away. Tom ran after him.

'Jimmy!'

'Don't worry about it,' Jimmy said as Tom caught up.

'I'm going to see the colonel about that woman.' Tom was furious.
'I'll get the old hag banned from the camp.'

'Tom, please. It was nothing. Ah shoulda known.'

In the tent Hank had found the girl in number three. A couple of army
blankets covered the grassy ground but there were no other refine-
ments. The girl was waiting, bare-legged and shoeless, her arms folded
across a short, greyish shift. She was no great beauty but, despite a
slight cast in her right eye or perhaps because of it, she was not
unattractive. As Hank entered she no more than glanced at him. She
simply lay back on the blankets and drew the short shift up to around
her waist to reveal she was naked underneath. Hank swallowed.

'Come on then,' she said, opening her legs wide.

Grunts and a variety of noises could he heard coming from other sections. Hank knelt down carefully then spread himself over the girl. But he was not sure how to proceed.

The bored girl uttered an oath and unfastened his breeches. Expertly she guided him and at once he began a frantic thrusting, moaning loudly. The girl fended him off.

'What?' Hank paused in mid-act.

'You got toothache or somethin'?'

A reference to his agonized moans. Tom had told him that was what you did. You moaned. It was that brother of his and his so-called sense of humour.

'Number Three!' Auntie Moll's voice boomed out. 'Time's up!'

'But I haven't finished,' Hank protested.

The girl pushed him away gently, looking down. 'Ah think you'll find you have, soldier boy.'

Sarah Dowling stayed at the convent near Philadelphia for the full three weeks of her retreat. But at the end of that time she was ready to leave and she resented any attempt to make her stay. The mother superior prayed that Sarah would see her way to becoming a novice and in due course take the necessary vows. But Sarah had no wish to become a nun.

At the end of her enforced isolation from the outside world two letters awaited her. One was from her cousin Imelda. The other, to her great delight, was from Tom Blanchard. She took the letters to her room to read them in private. Tom's letter, she decided, she would leave until last, a joy to come. But as she read the letter from Imelda she frowned.

Tom Blanchard, Imelda wrote, had come in search of her. No one could or would tell him where she was and he had begged Imelda to help him find her. But by the time Imelda's mother had heard from Sarah's aunt, Tom and Henry Blanchard had gone missing. Missing! thought Sarah. What on earth could she mean?

Imelda's letter went on to explain.

When I say 'missing', I mean they didn't take up their commissions in the army. They were expected at the barracks on North Street on the Friday morning but they didn't arrive. No one seems to know where they are or what has happened to them. Even Mr Blanchard says he doesn't know. Some say they have gone off to join these rebels, but I don't believe they would do a thing like that. Not when Daddy went to such trouble to arrange their commissions. But then some strange things are happening in these tumultuous times.

For example, what do you think of Ben Withers? He arrived all right and joined the army, but he actually turned down his commission! He said if he was going to serve it would be as an ordinary soldier. Can you imagine that? But Ben Withers has always been sort of unpredictable. I feel sorry for my friend Melanie. An ordinary soldier for her intended! Saddest news of all is that my dear friend and beau John Foster has been killed in action. A real hero! Fighting for King and country, as Daddy says. Even sadder, before he went into battle, John actually asked me to marry him!

Imelda didn't dwell on this even though it was true. She knew that Sarah was sceptical of what she claimed. Not in an unkind way, but sceptical.

Still, she wrote, *you barely know any of these boys. Although I do believe that one day you will come to know Tom Blanchard better than any of us. Tom has never had a one true love in all the years I have known him, but I just know he is totally smitten with you. When I saw him last he was desperate to know where you were and what had happened to you. Mother says you will probably stay there at the convent as that is what everyone thinks is best for you. Write and tell me they are all wrong.*
Your loving cousin, Imelda.
P.S. I do hope you hear from Tom soon and if I see him or Henry I will be sure to give them your address.

John Foster dead. Sarah remembered him as a tall, fair-haired, good-looking young man who more than once had tried to catch her eye at Uncle Max's get-together evening. This now was the stark truth. People were dying in this wicked war. We must pray for these poor souls, the mother superior said every morning at prayers. But praying wouldn't change anything. It wouldn't stop the war and the senseless killing.

John Foster was dead now and there would be many, many more.
Tom! Sarah clutched the second letter, then tore it open.

My dearest Sarah
I have searched for you without success. Imelda has promised to
inform me of your whereabouts as soon as she knows where they
have taken you. But my brother and I are moving on and we will
not, may never, see Imelda again. I am entrusting this letter to the
priest, Pastor John, at your home church in Roxbury. Pastor John
says he will do his best to get it to you and I believe him. I must
tell you, Sarah, that Hank and I have not joined the British. For
reasons which, when I find you, I will explain in full, we have
taken a different path. If you are in a place of safety, and I trust
that you are, then please, I beg you, remain there. Remain there
until these conflicts are resolved and I can come to claim you as
my bride. I wish to marry you, Sarah, and I only wish I had told
you this sooner. I want to marry you and spend the rest of my life
taking care of you as I am certain no other man could. I know
that we have not known each other long enough or well enough
for me to make such a claim but I believe you feel as I do. It was
in your eyes the night we met and I will never believe otherwise
unless I hear it from your own lips. Please be safe and wait until
I come for you wherever you are.
All my love, Tom.

The rebel forces assembled and entrenched in the countryside
around the city were well supplied with horses. The British Army in
Boston had desperately few. Only trained horsemen were allowed
their own mounts, the rest had to soldier on foot. When Ben Withers
asked for a horse to take him south to join his new regiment his
request entailed a further delay. A cavalry officer tested his riding
ability and was favourably impressed. His report was positive but
there was still no horse. Then one morning Ben received orders to
report to an encampment by the river, close to the outskirts of the
city where he would be allocated a horse. He would be personally
responsible for the feeding and well-being of the animal. If it was
lost or stolen he would be ordered to pay the cost of a replacement.
It was to be his means of transport to his new posting and his mount
for the remainder of his service – until the war was over or until he

was dead, whichever came first.

Ben's little Irish friend seemed genuinely sorry to see Ben go. An odd-shaped leprechaun of a man he had found his way into the British Army by default. Arriving penniless in London from his home in County Cork he had heard that the British Army was offering bounties to volunteers. At the recruitment centre in Haymarket he found the requirement for the infantry that no recruit should be less than five feet six inches tall and physically fit had been relaxed. Even so he had to stretch himself to the limit to make the new minimum of five three, declare in a pugilistic, if comic, pose that he was fit to fight any man present and promise to pay the recruiting sergeant eleven pence if accepted which was all the money he had.

Ben said goodbye and the Irishman watched as he made his way downhill on foot to the camp by the river. There was a corral at the camp and about 200 horses. Ben reported to the adjutant and a groom took him out to the stables. But there was not much to choose from. Most of the horses were old, worn-out, ready for the knacker. Ben's eyes wandered to a group in a small enclosure. He couldn't have one of those, he was told. Those were the best, specially set aside for officers. But he was travelling south to join the cavalry of the British Legion, he explained. Makes no difference, he was told. It was one of the old nags or nothing. Make your way by coach.

A pen of about thirty horses caught his eye. They looked good at first glance and he went to the fence to investigate. On the flanks of two or three he saw the brand BLA. It was the brand of the Blanchard stock and Ben was puzzled. Mr Blanchard was not a known Loyalist. In fact, many suspected his sympathies were with the rebels. He was unlikely to sell stock to the British.

'Where did these come from?' Ben asked the groom.

'Don' know. On'y come in today. Ain't bin written up yet.'

'So these are available?'

The groom frowned. 'Don' know 'bout that.'

'They look like local horses to me. Does the army buy local?'

The groom looked at him sidelong. 'Not buy exactly. We goes in an' we takes what we want.'

'Isn't that stealing?'

'Oh no,' the groom said. 'We always leave an IOU.'

Ben was inside the pen, amongst the jostling stock. He chose a reddish brown bay, roped her in firmly but gently and led her towards the gate.

'I don' know if yer can 'ave 'er. I mean . . .'

'Half a guinea,' Ben said.

The groom gulped. 'Well, I s'pose if yer was in a hurry an' yer went on yer way right now then maybe . . .'

'I'll go now,' Ben said and he looked disparagingly at the army issue saddles piled in a heap. 'I can take her into town and buy a saddle.'

The groom couldn't resist. He'd have Ben's permit, that is the authority to take a horse and saddle, and to dispose of he'd have the unwanted saddle with half a guinea thrown in. It was too good an offer to miss. 'Better go then,' he said. 'Right away.'

He gave Ben a blanket and a new rope and, Indian fashion, Ben rode away, down the hillside to where he could cross the river and ride up into the city.

ELEVEN

Tom was concerned now about Jimmy's morale. Although he said he was 'all right' he seemed more than usually withdrawn.

A tall thin man who called himself 'the regimental drummer', Tom noted, was the only other Negro in the entire camp. He was a friendly, genial fellow with a long thin face and gleaming white teeth. Tom drew him aside one morning and asked him if he'd ever been to the tents.

The drummer had seen Tom around and was aware of Tom and Hank's friendship with Jimmy. He had never been to the tents, he said, not because he didn't want to but because 'old Moll don't take no Negras.' He laughed uproariously and added, 'An' ah'll tell you somethin' else. Ah don't know no Negras who would take old Moll!'

'But what do you do for women?' Tom asked.

'Not much, ah guess.'

Tom was serious. 'Where do you go?'

'There's this place in Cambridge,' the drummer told him. 'It's a place for black men only.'

'I don't think Jimmy would go to Cambridge. You know how he is. Too damned proud.'

'Being proud don't solve nothin'.'

'So what do we do?'

'Why should you care?'

'Jimmy's my friend.'

The drummer pushed his bandsman's hat forward, scratched his head and looked Tom in the eye. 'Is that right?'

'Jimmy's my friend. I'd like to help him out. That's all.'

'Ask the colonel,' the drummer suggested. 'He's a reasonable fella. He might persuade old Moll to bring in some black gals.'

The suggestion appealed to Tom and his opportunity to ask came sooner than he expected. The following afternoon he was summoned to the officers' tent. The colonel wanted to see him.

He stood to attention at Colonel Putnam's desk. The colonel had just finished lunch and seemed to be in a good mood. He smiled. 'At ease, son,' he said and he picked up a paper from his desk. 'I have a few notes here about you, young man. It seems you had a commission lined up with the British but you preferred to come to us. That correct?'

'Yes, sir.'

'Why was that? It's not easy to get a commission with the British Army. Plenty of advantages to be gained and excellent prospects for a young man like you.'

'I'm not British, sir. I'm an American.'

Colonel Putnam nodded and smiled in approval. 'So what do you think of this war we're fighting?'

'I think we can't lose, sir.'

'And why is that?'

'Well, if we Americans were fighting to hold on to England or France and the English or French didn't want us there we'd have one hell of a job on our hands, a losing battle, as you might say. It's the same thing in reverse. We're not going to let some nobody three thousand miles away tell us what to do. Not for much longer anyway.'

'And you're ready to fight to prove that?'

'Certainly am, sir.'

'Well, how do you feel about taking up a commission in our army, Blanchard? I reckon you'd make a good officer.'

'Thank you, sir.'

'You would accept?'

'I would, sir, yes.'

'Then I have to say this, Blanchard. It seems the British are attempting to infiltrate our forces with bogus volunteers, spies on the inside. A young man like you could well be a candidate for this kind of assignment. I understand two such individuals have been uncovered so far. They were taken out and shot. No quarter given.'

'No less than they deserve, sir.'

'Quite.' The colonel relaxed a little. 'You will be known as Lieutenant Blanchard. There is no elaborate training scheme involved. Your captain will discuss your duties with you. All right? Good. Then

I will make the necessary arrangements.'

'Thank you, sir. And, sir, what about my brother? He turned down a commission, too.'

The colonel smiled. 'I know, and I'm due to see him next, make him the same offer. Could mean you splitting up, of course. Separate commands. Almost certainly will mean that.'

'Yes, sir!' Tom saluted smartly, as he had been taught to only that morning, and turned on his heel. Then he hesitated, half-turned back, a question unasked.

The colonel raised his eyebrows. 'Something else?'

'Well ye-es, sir. A bit of advice, if you don't mind.'

'You need some or you want to give me some?'

'I need some, sir. Some help.'

The colonel sat back in his chair. 'So what can I do for you?'

Tom told him about Jimmy, what a fine soldier Jimmy was and how this true American had been turned away at the whore tents.

The colonel was sympathetic, but he didn't think there was much he could do. 'One of those things, son.'

'I was wondering,' Tom said. 'If you could ask Auntie Moll, the whore lady, if she could provide a girl for Jimmy, a Negro girl.'

The colonel laughed aloud. 'You want me to be a pimp, a procurer of women!'

Tom looked suitably abashed. 'I'm sorry, sir. I didn't mean. . . .'

'Go on,' the colonel said, still laughing. 'Get outa here!'

'Yes, sir.' Tom backed away. 'Sorry, sir.'

'No, wait,' the colonel said. 'You really are this fellow's friend, Blanchard. Now why is that?'

'I don't know, sir. It's just that . . . he's a man. A good man.'

'He's a black man.'

'I don't see why he should be a *slave*.'

'That's just the way it is, son.'

'The way I see it, sir, this King of England wants *us* to be *his* slaves and we're not having it. Why should any man be a slave?'

'Our job is to win this war,' the colonel told him soberly, 'not change the world.'

A few days later one of the men came and sat on the grass across from Tom and Hank. 'So what 'ave you been up to, Tom Blanchard?' he asked. 'You been gettin' rough with one o' them whore women?'

'How do you mean?' Tom asked.

The man stood up and slapped Tom on the back. 'Auntie Moll wants to see ya.'

'He's ruin' one o' the girls!' someone shouted.

'Bin goin' like a stallion,' said another and with the ensuing hilarity came a flood of obscene and bizarre accusations. Tom hurried off in search of Auntie Moll.

She was smoking a pipe, still wearing her multi-coloured shawl and was clearly not stopping. 'You, Banchard?' she guessed as if she was in a hurry.

'*Blanchard*. Tom Blanchard.'

'Colonel says you wanna Negra gal.'

'Well, not for me personally,' Tom said. 'But yes.'

She eyed him curiously, her bloodshot gaze heavy with the cynicism of the years. Then, through the smoke from her pipe, a faint light dawned in the bleary eyes and she almost smiled. 'Ah know you,' she claimed. 'You is the one who got that Negra boy as a friend. It's for him, huh?'

'Yes, ma'am,' Tom acknowledged.

'Well, you tell him she ain't just for him. She's a good looker for a Negra an' there's plenty fellers'll pay good money for some black meat. He'll just have t' take his place with the rest.'

'When do you expect the young lady?' Tom asked politely.

'Huh?'

'When will the girl be here?'

'Friday. Friday nigh'.'

'What time Friday?'

Auntie Moll ran out of patience. 'Ah don' know what time, boy! Hell, if your Negra friend wants t' be first in line he'll just have to be first here.'

Later that day Tom and Hank told Jimmy they had a special treat lined up for him. 'It's for your birthday,' Hank said.

'What birthday?' Jimmy asked. 'Ah don't have a birthday.'

'Everybody has a birthday,' Tom told him.

'Well, ah don't. Leastways, if ah do, ah don't know when it is.'

'It's Friday,' Hank declared. 'Friday night. Make a note of the date. From now on your official birthday is Friday. Or you'll think it is when you see what we've got for you. That right, Tom?'

Jimmy looked at Tom.

'You're coming with us to the tents,' Tom said. 'Friday night.'

'Oh no.' Jimmy was adamant. 'I ain't goin' nowhere near them whore tents. Not Friday. Not ever.'

Sarah was determined. She was going to leave the convent at the first opportunity and she was going to go to Boston. Imelda's letter had contained a note from her aunt, Imelda's mother, to the effect that she was more than welcome to stay with them for as long as she wished. Sarah wanted to go to Boston to discover what had happened to Tom Blanchard.

For several weeks there was no way of getting to Boston from the convent. The roads were too dangerous. Marauding rebels and drunken soldiers roamed the highways. And an assortment of vagrants and petty criminals were taking advantage of the situation. Most didn't clearly understand why but they knew there was a great deal of unrest and they would probably not be called to account for minor crimes and misdemeanours.

The mother superior forbade Sarah to leave by the regular coach, which had been held up twice in the past month, the occupants robbed and subjected to various indignities. It was simply not safe for a young girl or for any lady travelling alone, the mother superior insisted, and in view of what had happened to her family Sarah could only agree.

Then one day a platoon of British soldiers was installed in the village close to the convent. They were awaiting a General Howe who was *en route* from Philadelphia. The general was to travel on to Boston by the local coach and the platoon were to provide an escort. When Sarah succeeded in obtaining a seat on the coach the mother superior could raise no further objection.

On the appointed morning the coach stopped at the convent and Sarah took her seat, waving goodbye to the nuns who had come to see her off and sinking demurely into a corner. The general and his aide-de-camp sat facing Sarah and the other two travellers, an elderly lady who announced haughtily that she was going home to England and 'civilization', and a diminutive clergyman who seemed unsure of his role. All three of the general's non-military fellow travellers had been carefully vetted, Sarah included.

Politely, after exchanging pleasantries with the other two, the general said good morning and asked Sarah why she was going to Boston. She was going to Boston, she told him, to stay with her aunt and uncle, a Mr and Mrs Harvie. Ah! he said. He knew Mr Harvie well. A fine gentleman, a loyal subject of his Majesty the King, he gushed and the elderly lady nodded in approval. Sarah's response was subdued. She liked her aunt and was extremely fond of Imelda, but she had never felt the same about Uncle Max.

The aide-de-camp watched her obliquely, but said little. He was a handsome man, a major as far as Sarah could judge from the insignia and markings on the sleeves and at the collar of his rather splendid uniform. His glossy black hair, swept back, and his heavy black eyebrows accentuated his deep dark eyes and a smile seemed to hover permanently over his strong features.

All through the slow journey Sarah felt his eyes on her face and neckline – so much so that she twice adjusted the chiffon at her throat. He was certainly good-looking, she conceded. But there was a hint of danger about him, something not quite trustworthy.

From the mostly one-sided conversation between the two military men it soon became apparent that General Howe was to take command of the British Army in Boston. The general, from an aristocratic English background and therefore oblivious to the presence of servants and lesser mortals, evidently believed that military matters in any case were beyond the comprehension of an elderly lady, a timid clergymen and an innocent girl and could be freely discussed. Sarah listened carefully to every word.

The general was clearly concerned at the way things were in Boston. The new commander of the rebels, George Washington, was successfully instilling order and discipline in the flood of volunteers. The rebel soldiers were now better fed and better equipped and many were housed in hastily constructed barracks, built by men who were used to erecting their own homes. The majority of the British, by contrast, were still living in serried rows of tents that were bearable in summer but barely adequate for anything more than the mildest of winters.

In Boston the days were bright with the last rays of summer, but in the ranks of the British there were dark rumblings of discontent. The most senior officers were living well enough, having taken up residence in the homes of well-to-do citizens who had left for safer climes. But the troops who roamed the otherwise empty streets were a less happy breed. Many were troubled by flux and many died for want of fresh food. Fish and salt pork of dubious quality made up their main diet and when a ship arrived with fresh provisions these were too highly priced for the common soldier. Scurvy and dysentery were rife and as the blockade around the city tightened and summer gave way to a wintry fall shortages became even more acute. Stealing food was considered an extremely serious offence. Those caught were severely punished, often with the lash of a cat-o'-nine tails.

Advance intelligence had informed the general that the robbery and violence against the people who had remained in the city had reached unacceptable proportions. He intended to change all that with public floggings, even public executions. He would appoint, he told his dark-eyed aide, an executioner who would accompany the provost marshal on his rounds and carry out executions, hang a man on the spot, without benefit of a trial if such a course was warranted. He didn't say, Sarah noted, who would decide if such a course was warranted.

At a comfort stop a few miles from Boston the general's aide introduced himself to Sarah as they stepped from the carriage. His name, he said, was Major Danvers. He was aware, he added, that she could not have failed to overhear the general's remarks and he hastened to assure her that though the city was in turmoil many of the grander houses and estates were off-limits to the rank and file. Her uncle's home, he assured her, was intact and the family were in no danger.

The truth was that many of the grander homes and estates had been commandeered and high-ranking officers had moved in. They were enjoying their stay in a way that, denied to their men, could only foster resentment. General Howe's predecessor had lived in comfort in the house of an eminent businessman, John Hancock. He had entertained his fellow officers and their wives with lavish dinners and musical evenings and he had slept with the Hancock's housekeeper. Fine wines and the best food available had appeared on the general's table and on evenings when official meetings were called and wives were not invited a good supply of the local whores were readily available for later. But things would be different now. General Howe was said to be a family man devoted to the wife he had left in England. Womanizing and merry-making were not the general's style though this was not the case with his handsome aide.

Major Danvers had taken more than a passing interest in the quiet girl in the opposite seat and his interest was further stimulated by her genuinely unaffected lack of response. He was charming and he was an attractive man, but at that first meeting he had no way of knowing he had little or no hope of success with Sarah. For almost every waking moment Sarah's thoughts were with Tom Blanchard, where he was and in what danger he might be.

'I am indeed delighted to have made your acquaintance, Miss Dowling,' the major told her, flashing his white teeth and she felt the light brush of his moustache as he stooped to kiss her hand. 'I sincerely hope that we will meet again.'

Ben Withers had intended to make only a brief stop at Melanie's house but Mrs Stokes insisted he stayed for a meal and hurried off into the kitchen. The moment Ben and Melanie were alone they fell into each other's arms with eager kisses until they slid to the floor and Melanie was forced to call a halt.

'Not here,' she whispered urgently.

'Melanie,' Ben said. 'My God, I've missed you!'

'Tell me,' she said. 'Tell me what happened.'

He told her of his meeting with John Foster and how when John was killed he believed he would have to look elsewhere for the information he needed. But, along with the orders for his transfer, John had left him a message. The man Ben was searching for was with the British Legion in New Jersey and, with John's help, Ben had been posted there.

'If anything should happen to you . . .' Melanie began.

'I'll be fine,' he assured her. 'All I want to do is come face to face with this Sergeant Duckett. Then I'll be on my way. I'll join the rebels, catch up with Tom and Hank.'

'How long will it last, Ben? When will it be over?'

'Four, five years maybe. It'll take time. But the British can't win. If they had any sense they'd know that. This is our land and we're going to kick them out once and for all.'

Melanie smiled. 'Sounds funny from a man who wears a red coat.'

'I only wear it when I have to and I don't want you ever to see me in it. I got permission to wear mufti for this trip. Travelling as far as New Jersey, alone in a red coat would be madness. I wouldn't last two minutes out there.'

'It's a dangerous game you're playing. What if. . . ?'

He covered her mouth with kisses. 'War is a dangerous game,' he murmured. 'But this is a war we're going to win. We have to.'

There was a light knock at the door. 'Food's on the table,' Mrs Stokes called, but she didn't open the door. 'Come along now.'

'I want you to do something for me,' Melanie whispered. 'For us.'

'What?' He smiled down into her blue eyes. 'Anything.'

'Later,' she said. 'I'll tell you later.'

They took their seats at the kitchen table and Mrs Stokes lifted the lid from the hot soup dish. 'Help yourself now,' she ordered. 'And see that this boy eats plenty, Melanie. He tells me he has a long way to go tonight.'

'Tonight?' Melanie's bright eyes registered alarm.

Ben nodded. 'I must leave tonight. Otherwise I'll have trouble getting out. Sentries at every crossing and I have no authority to be here. I should be well on my way to New Jersey.'

The talk at the table was subdued now and when, finally, Mrs Stokes brought in a pitcher of elderberry wine Ben thanked her for the lovely meal and for allowing them to be alone together.

'And now,' Melanie told her mother with a smile, 'we'd like to be alone again. Just for a little while.'

Mrs Stokes was almost as fond of Ben as Melanie was. She adored the way he so obviously loved her daughter and she him. Without being obtrusive their devotion was almost palpable. It was something she had never seen before and didn't expect to see again. Even in her own long and relatively happy marriage she had not known the kind of bond that bound these two.

'I want to take Ben up to my room,' Melanie said, her eyes begging her mother not to object.

Mrs Stokes merely nodded and Melanie kissed her cheek and led Ben by the hand up the stairway to her bedroom. It was already dark outside and the moon was clouded over. The sound of marching feet came by, crunching down the lane. An hour. Or not much more. That was all they had. And Ben would be gone.

TWELVE

AUNTIE Moll looked up at Tom Blanchard warily. 'Ah know you paid your money but. . . .'

'But what?' Tom was in no mood for excuses.

'This Negra gal – she ain't what ah expected.'

'In what way is she not what you expected? If she's black and she's a girl. . . .'

'Ah ast for a Negra *woman*. A Negra whore from Cambridge. This little gal don't look like no whore to me.'

'You mean she's too young?'

'Ah wouldn't say she was too young exactly. Ah'd say she was about seventeen. Some o' ma girls started out twelve, fourteen.'

'So?'

'You can have your money back. . . .'

'No,' Tom said, through his teeth. 'We promised him.'

'It's just that, to me, she looks like trouble.' Still she hesitated. Then: 'Well, all right. Your man can have his turn, ten minutes and no more. Then she's gotta go. Ah'm sending her back.'

'You said the men would like. . . .' Tom's voice trailed.

'A bit o' black tail? Yes, sah! Ah knows what ah said. But there's something ah don't like about this set-up.'

'Where did you get her?'

'Ah ast ma contact's in Cambridge an' this is what ah get,' she said, on the defensive now. 'Some Negra from a farm Lexington way brung her in. But ah reckon she belongs to someone, some white boss maybe, and ah don't want no one come lookin' for her.'

'All right,' Tom said. 'So I bring our boy over now and then you can send her back. Get it over with. That what you want?'

She nodded gratefully. 'Soon as you can.'

Tom turned away but then he turned back. 'You reckon this girl is new to all this? You think she hasn't done this sort of thing before?'

Auntie Moll gave a worried shrug. 'Ah dunno. Ah s'pose she must have. Most Negra girls her age been in somebody's bed. Most often the massah boss – and that's what scares me. She's a good looker for a Negra.'

Back at the tent Jimmy had Hank in an arm lock. 'Tryin' to make me go to that whore tent,' he complained when Tom put his head round the flap. 'Well, ah ain't going.'

'Listen, Jimmy,' Tom said, stepping inside. 'Let him go, for God's sake.' Jimmy released Hank who fell back on his bed, nursing his arm. 'Listen to me. You have to come with us to Auntie Moll's. Please. For us. For me. For Hank.'

Jimmy laughed aloud. 'For you and for Hank? Why? What's in it for you?'

'We want to help you with this, that's all,' Tom said in earnest. 'And we went to a lot of trouble to get you a girl, a black girl. And so did Auntie Moll. And she's not one of those regular whores. She's something special.'

'Have you seen her?' Hank asked, sitting up.

'No,' Tom admitted, 'but according to Auntie Moll she really is something special.'

'According t' Auntie Moll,' Jimmy scoffed.

'And she's young, too'

'How young?' Hank asked.

'About seventeen. No more than that.'

'She so special, how come she's a whore?' Jimmy demanded.

'Well,' Tom said. 'I don't know that she is. I don't believe she does this sort of thing on a regular basis.'

'Come on, Jimmy,' Hank urged. 'You can take a look at her.'

'And you'll have to be quick,' Tom added. 'If you don't show up Auntie Moll is going to sell her off to the highest bidder.'

A mixture of curiosity and concern for a girl who was being exploited by a grasping whore woman spurred Jimmy to stand up and announce. 'Well, all right. Ah'll take a look. But if ah don't like what ah see ah'll just say so.'

'Number one,' Auntie Moll said, looking Jimmy up and down. 'And you come right out when ah tell ya. Ten minutes, no more.'

Jimmy glanced back at Tom and Hank and their eyes registered encouragement. He went into the tent and slowly, apprehensive now, he held aside the flap on number one.

She was a small, slender girl with smooth brown skin and black hair cropped close to her head in tightly-coiled curls. She was thin, Jimmy noticed, but not undernourished, her legs drawn up beneath her, her shoulders hunched, her hands clasped tight as if in prayer. Sitting sidelong on a grey blanket that saw service several times a night, she looked as though she had withdrawn within herself and closed a door on the rest of the world.

When Jimmy appeared at the open flap she looked up at once like a startled doe, her black eyes wide and alert. For a moment he thought she might take off and crash through the fabric of the sun-scorched tent. But when she saw him some degree of calm returned. He was young. He was not some huge, overweight, ugly giant of a man whose rough aim would be to force himself upon her and tear her apart. And he was black.

Jimmy ventured inside allowing the flap to fall into place behind him and sank to his knees before her. The girl stood up dutifully and Jimmy gazed at her bare legs as slowly but entirely without rancour she raised her coarse shift above her head and allowed it to fall by her side. A square of cloth, tied in a bow on one hip, was all that remained to cover her. With eyes averted, her hands went to the bow.

She knew this was something she had to do. Her master's head boy had made her come and for this she would be well rewarded. If she refused she would be rewarded with a severe beating. And, he had threatened, her pretty little face would be permanently scarred. She would be disfigured for the rest of her life and this was something she feared more than a beating. She had been beaten before and she had survived. But her face was different. It was one of the few things she had that didn't displease her. One more thing, the head boy had told her – the head boy who was old enough to be her grandfather – the master must never find out.

Jimmy sat back on his heels and his hand reached out to hers, staying her from releasing the bow. The feel of her hand, small, delicate, was disturbing. But what Tom and Hank had evidently assumed was not so. To touch a woman was not entirely new to him. Three times when he was fourteen years old a maid at the home of his former master had helped him unravel some of the mysteries and he had been a willing and eager pupil. Yet now he felt no heedless lust for the fragile girl at his disposal. Nor did he pity her. What he felt was an overwhelming rush of tenderness.

He looked down at the hand in his and she watched him warily, awaiting his next move. Carefully he opened her hand and pressed the palm to his lips, then he closed her hand as if wanted her to hold his kiss and keep it safe. Holding her fist tightly closed she placed her free hand on her hip and gazed at him in wonderment. A little embarrassed Jimmy picked up her discarded shift and told her to put it on.

The girl turned away, hiding her naked breasts as if some subtle change had taken place between her and Jimmy and she wanted to regain her modesty. Jimmy watched as she raised her arms and wriggled back into the meagre shift and when she turned to face him she looked for a moment as though she might burst into tears. It occurred to him that his action in handing her the shift might have appeared to her like a rejection.

'Ah think you're lovely,' he said quietly, anxious to dispel any misunderstanding. 'You're the loveliest girl ah've ever seen.'

She looked at him uncertainly.

'What's your name?' he asked.

She hesitated. She was not sure she should give her name.

'Tell me,' he urged her gently, her hands in his as they knelt face to face on the thin blanket. 'Ma name's Jimmy. Jimmy Sunshine.'

For the first time he saw the hint of a smile in her dark eyes.

'It's true,' he insisted. 'Sun was shining at the time and ah chose it maself.'

Her smile broke out and Jimmy was captivated. Then he laughed and she laughed and they rocked back on their heels.

'You is even lovelier when you laugh,' he said.

Embarrassed again, she looked down at the blanket but she didn't take her hands from his.

'Tell me,' he said. 'Please. Ah have to know. What's yours?'

'Ma name is Chrissie,' she said softly and Jimmy fell in love again, this time with her voice.

'Chris'mas, really. Ah was born at Chris'mas.'

'Chrissie,' he breathed. 'Chrissie. Ma Chrissie!'

She smiled in surprise and then they both laughed and he guessed she had not laughed spontaneously like this in a long time. He stood up and pulled her to her feet and his arms went round her thin frame.

He held her close and carefully as if she was something fragile and very precious, something that must be handled with great care.

Unused to such tenderness Chrissie yielded totally, her body against his, her arms resting on his broad shoulders, her head against his chest. Locked in his tight embrace she felt safe and protected. She didn't want him to let her go. But then his hold slackened. She looked up at him, her head held back, her eyes wide and uncertain. Jimmy smiled down at her and kissed her gently but firmly on the lips.

Chrissie didn't know how to respond. Was this just a prelude to what she'd been brought here for? Was he really just like all the rest? Again he held her close but she couldn't relax now and when he spoke her whole body tensed.

'Chrissie,' he said softly, his deep soulful eyes looking down into hers. 'Ah think ah love you.'

Chrissie pulled away from him. 'You don't know me.'

'Ah've always known you,' he told her. 'An' you've always known me. It's just that we never met until now.'

She gave him a look that said plainly, 'You're mad.'

'All right,' he said. 'So ah'm crazy. But let me say this. You come here today . . .'

'Ah was brung here,' she corrected him, defiant now.

'You was brung here today and you didn't know what to expect. Well, neither did ah. You was ma birthday girl.'

'Your what?'

'Ma friends paid for you,' he said. 'It's ma birthday. You was to be a sorta treat. Ma birthday girl. And ah didn't know you'd be so lovely. You coulda been some fat ol' whore woman.'

Chrissie laughed.

'Instead of that you're this angel from Heaven.'

'Ah'm a housemaid for white folk in Lexington,' she told him. 'That's what ah am.'

'Not to me, you're not. And what's more ah'm gonna take you away from them and all that maid stuff.'

Her laugh was a little nervous now. 'Ah don't think so.'

'Oh yeah!' he told her. 'Ah'm gonna take you away. We're gonna go some place where no one will ever find us. But first of all we're gonna get married.'

Her eyes opened wide. 'You are crazy, Jimmy Sunshine.'

'Ah ain't never been so sane in all mah life.' He laughed. 'Ah'm gonna marry you, girl, whether you like it or not.'

'What's going on in there?' It was Auntie Moll. 'Time's up. Come on out 'ere. Right now!'

Jimmy drew Chrissie to him and held her tight. He kissed her again gently on the lips, then eagerly and she responded. But he didn't want to spoil what he'd established. This was love not lust and there was no time anyway. Their time was up.

'Come on! Come out 'ere.' Auntie Moll was getting agitated. 'That girl's cart is 'ere.'

'Half edge over Lexington way,' Chrissie told him in reply to his request for an address. 'Just by the drift.'

Jimmy had been there once with old Mabbutt's head man. He had seen the rapids where the river fell and the foam broke white on the rocks.

'Ah'll come for you, Chrissie,' he said. 'Ah promise.'

'When?' She had begun to take him seriously. She had never known anyone like this Jimmy Sunshine and if he was true to his word she was with him all the way.

'Soon,' he assured her. 'Ah promise, Chrissie. Some day soon we'll he together an' we'll stay together for always. Ah loves you an' ah think you feel the same way 'bout me.'

Chrissie didn't deny it.

'Somethin' wonderful happened today,' he murmured, holding her tight. 'Today is the day Jimmy Sunshine an' Miss Chrissie fell in love.'

Despite the swarms of rebel forces gathered on the outskirts of the city, life for the higher ranking officers of the British Army in Boston that summer was far from unpleasant. Though their men were suffering from an increasing scarcity of food and drink, the officers who were entertained nightly in the homes of well-to-do Loyalists were more than well catered for. One such home was that of Max Harvie. With an eye to a title for himself and access to the court of King George, he believed that the marriage of his attractive if fickle daughter, Imelda, to some high-ranking British army officer would greatly enhance his prospects of achieving his ambitions. As a result the guest lists at his frequent house parties were carefully composed.

When Sarah Dowling appeared at her aunt's house she found that a party had been arranged for that evening. It was already mid-afternoon and she was tired from the long rumbling coach ride from Philadelphia.

'But you must come to the party,' Imelda told her. 'The British will be here in force. Think of all those dashing young officers in their best blues just dying to meet young ladies like us.'

'I have no wish to meet young British officers, Imelda, dashing or otherwise,' Sarah said evenly. 'My concern is for Tom and Hank Blanchard. Is there any news of their whereabouts?'

'I'm afraid we don't mention the Blanchards any more,' Imelda said quietly.

'But Hank was your beau, was he not?'

'Only when we were very young and then not really.' Imelda dismissed Hank with a wave of her hand. 'I was betrothed to Lieutenant John Foster who was killed at Bunker Hill. He was fighting rebels like Tom and Henry Blanchard and from what I heard his head was taken clean off by a cannon ball.'

'Imelda!'

'It's true,' Imelda said and, as if she had realized she should be shocked not excited by the gory details, she added primly and in the tone her mother used, 'This really is a terrible business. Such a dreadful waste of young men's lives.'

Sarah had been sceptical of her cousin's play-acting since they were children. She looked at her askance. 'So what's this about you being betrothed? I don't believe a word of it.'

'He *did* ask me to marry him,' Imelda insisted, 'but I hadn't given him my answer. I scarcely had time to consider my answer before he was gone, taken from us.' She lowered her voice dramatically. 'I'm glad, in a way, that I wasn't ready to give him my answer. If I had refused him it would have seemed so . . . so callous. I mean, with him going off to war.'

'You always said you would marry Hank Blanchard,' Sarah reminded her as Imelda allowed her voice to fade in a bout of spurious compassion.

'Well, I did say that, yes,' she admitted, suddenly brisk. 'But not any more. I told you, Sarah, Henry Blanchard and his brother are traitors. Daddy says those boys are the enemies of our King. They have joined the rebels and I'm afraid they will come to a sorry end.' Once again belatedly aware of the effect of what she was saying she put her hands to her mouth. 'Sarah, I am so sorry. I know how you feel about Tom. But then you can't go on feeling that way. You can't love a man who is a traitor.'

'Perhaps Tom has decided his country doesn't need a king and perhaps he is right.'

'Sarah, you mustn't let Daddy hear you say that.'

'I'm sorry,' Sarah said. She was a guest in this house. It would be wrong, she recognized, to be discourteous to her host.

Already Imelda's butterfly mind had alighted elsewhere. 'You must rest now and be ready to come down to the party. When you see the young men Daddy has invited you'll forget all about the Blanchards and the war and all that.'

Sarah really was tired now and, when she fell asleep on the comfortable bed in the room her aunt had set aside for her, she didn't wake until she heard the chimes of eight from the clock in the hallway downstairs. From the large annexe below the strains of a minuet drifted up the curved stairway and under her closed door. Sarah realized where she was and that the party would be in progress. She didn't want to go to a party and would have gladly gone back to sleep but the door opened and her aunt appeared. Smiling, she brought a tray to Sarah's bedside. 'I hope I didn't wake you, dear,' she said. 'I thought you might like a little light refreshment.'

'I'm so sorry,' Sarah said, sitting up. 'I'd no idea it was so late.'

'Hush now. There's absolutely no need to apologise. You were very tired.'

Sarah glanced at the tray. She had assured her aunt earlier that she was not hungry and would not be down for dinner but she realized she had not eaten all day.

'It's so kind of you to have me,' she said.

'What nonsense! Your mother would expect no less. And Imelda is thrilled to have you. We all are. Now have something to eat and, if you feel you would like to come down, the party is far from over.'

The guest list that evening was even more distinguished than usual, but none was quite so young as Imelda had predicted. Not one of the officers was below the rank of colonel. Perhaps, thought Sarah when she saw them later, her cousin had come to recognize the undoubted advantage of marriage to an older man. In England, through marriage, a girl could become a titled lady overnight, a marquess, a duchess even. And Sarah was right. This possibility had not escaped Imelda who had of late taken to surveying herself in the cheval mirror in her mother's bedroom and silently mouthing the words, 'M'Lords, ladies and gentlemen, may I present Her Highness Imelda, the Duchess of Wherever.'

Most of the officers present were heavily powdered, self-important and over indulgent at the food and drinks tables. Even Imelda didn't fancy any of them. But one of the few who appeared in any way youthful, a man with a black moustache, dark laughing eyes and the aura of a courtly playboy had caught the attention of most of the ladies in the room. Apparently he eschewed the elaborate hairpieces of his fellow officers, preferring to wear his own sleek black hair unpowdered and tied at the back by a ribbon. A colonel with many campaign ribbons, he was probably, Imelda decided, nearer forty than thirty.

Mr Harvie clearly felt the dashing colonel was a highly acceptable suitor for his marriageable daughter and introduced them at once in his, to Imelda, over effusive and slightly embarrassing way. The colonel was utterly charming. He danced with Imelda, escorting her to and from various groups of guests in a most solicitous fashion, and Mr Harvie beamed happily, thrilled that the two had, as he told his wife, 'hit it off'.

Imelda was charmed yet a little fearful of the colonel's attentions. She looked up at him as they danced, at his dark brown eyes, his black moustache and his, surprising for a serving soldier of whatever rank, strong white teeth. No matter how she tried to whiten her own teeth they remained a stubborn ivory. Perhaps, she thought, when she knew him better, she could ask him what he used.

The colonel had arrived late and had not had time to sign any of the dance cards and some of the other young ladies were becoming restive now as Imelda held on to him until eventually, for the sake of decorum, she was obliged to give him up and let him dance with someone else. From then on she set about finding out all she could about him. He was, she learned, well-known to and highly thought of by hostesses in London and he had many lady friends. Among his army colleagues he was known – and mostly without rancour for he was undeniably good-looking – as 'Handsome Jack'. And he had only that day arrived in Boston to take up a new post that carried with it a promotion from major to lieutenant colonel.

It was late, almost midnight, when Sarah Dowling, suitably refreshed, decided that she really ought to attend the last half-hour or so of her uncle's party. Somewhat nervously, she appeared now at the head of the sweeping stairway. At once she caught sight of Imelda and the handsome partner she had somehow managed to reclaim. The two stopped dancing or, rather, the colonel did and Imelda was brought to a halt beside him. Together they looked up at Sarah.

'You must meet my cousin,' Imelda said, sensing even then that her partner, Handsome Jack, had lost interest in her.

Sarah came down, slowly, gracefully, to the foot of the stairs, smiling politely in recognition. She had not expected to see him again and certainly not so soon.

Ben left Melanie as the church clock chimed midnight. His shoulders hunched, he hurried through the moonlit streets, aware of the shadows, the doorways where soldiers and street women performed their loveless and grotesque routines. By the ale house a man lay in a drunken sleep in the sloping gutter, forming an island in the stream of foul, brownish water that flowed from a line of broken latrines. Against the grimy wall another man sat back, legs splayed, and stared with glazed eyes at a reeling world as a barefoot urchin filched what was left in his ragged pockets.

At the street corner a group of soldiers, clearly the worse for drink, were noisily engaged in some dispute. One of the soldiers shouted something in Ben's direction but he crossed the road and turned down a side alley. He was not looking for trouble. All he wanted now was to be on his way.

His new route took him past the Harvies' house where even at this late hour the doors, though heavily guarded against intruders, were open and yellow lights glowed in all the windows. Ben paused for a moment as the sedate sound of a string quartet filtered out and lent the night an aura of gentility.

If he had taken Max Harvie's offer of a commission, Ben reflected, he might well have been a guest in that affluent household. Melanie would be turning heads in a stunning ball gown and he would be sporting the dress uniform of a British officer. But he had made his choice. He was not an officer and he was not British. He was an American and he was proud of it and the purchase these people had on the land of his birth would very soon be wrenched from them forever.

The saddle was shiny and new but his Blanchard bay seemed happy with it. The road ahead was lit by the moon and the stars and he planned to ride most of the night. But by the bridge where the Charles River held precious memories he slowed to a halt. The little Irishman was waiting on an army grey. 'Paddy!' he said, eyes wide. 'What in the name of God are you doing here?'

Paddy leaned forward, his puny frame crooked in the saddle. 'Sure an' I'm waitin' for you, am I not? I knew you were off to see your lady love, but I also knew you would have to be leavin' tonight and you would have to pass this way. An' I'm here, so I am.'

'But why?' Ben asked.

Paddy grinned, his face creased and he looked more than ever like a mischievous leprechaun. 'I'm comin' wit' you is why.'

THIRTEEN

WHEN Jimmy got back from the whore tent Tom and Hank were waiting and they saw at once he was worried. He was troubled by the thought of what might happen to Chrissie. It was crazy, he told himself. An hour ago he didn't even know the girl. He had never met her. Yet here she was, suddenly central to his whole existence. Chrissie was what he cared about now and he knew that from this day forward it would always be that way.

'So how was it?' Tom asked eagerly.

'It was . . . It was just wonderful.' Jimmy's face and eyes lit up in a broad, beaming smile.

'You enjoyed it, eh Jimmy?' Hank said in a way that implied he was experienced in these matters.

'Ah sure did,' Jimmy told him. 'But not the way you mean.'

'Oh?' Hank felt he had somehow been reprimanded.

'Her name's Chrissie,' Jimmy said reverently, 'an' ah love her.'

'You *love* her?' Tom said. 'You don't know her.'

'Ah know her,' Jimmy said with total conviction. 'Ah've always known her.'

Tom looked puzzled. 'How do you know her? You met her before or something?'

'You can't love her,' Hank said disparagingly. 'Even if you know her. The girl's a whore. She sells her body to horny bastards like us.'

Jimmy looked ready to square up to Hank. 'Don't you say that. Chrissie is *not* a whore. She was forced into this. She ain't never done this kinda thing before.'

Hank grinned. 'That what she told you?'

'It's the truth!' Jimmy was angry now. 'She's just a kid. She lives on a farm out Lexington way an' she got forced into this. You told the

117

whore woman to find some gal for me an' she did. She sure did. But Chrissie is no whore. Chrissie is just the most beautiful gal in the world.' He smiled dreamily and it might have been funny if he had not been so serious. He shook his head as if he couldn't believe his luck. 'An' she's just a kid.'

'Makes no difference how old she is,' Tom said. 'If she's that good-looking some old farm manager or more likely the owner of the place will have had her by now.'

'Ah'll kill any man touches 'er,' Jimmy said violently and there was a look in his eyes Tom and Hank had not seen there before. 'Ah swear it,' he said. 'Ah'll kill any man harms 'er.'

The boys were bemused, didn't know what to say. 'Where is she now, Jimmy?' Tom asked gently. 'Gone back to the farm?'

'Yeah,' Jimmy said. 'The man brung 'er here gotta have 'er back in just a coupla hours. An' that man oughta know better. He's a Negra himself an' ah know him now. Got a good look at him.' He scowled. 'One o' these days he's gonna answer to me.'

'You can't go getting yourself into trouble,' Hank said. 'Not over a girl you'll probably never see again. We'll be moving out soon.'

'This ain't just any girl,' Jimmy said. 'Chrissie is ma girl from now on an' ah'm gonna marry 'er.'

It was clearly no use arguing with him. 'We have a war to win before you marry anyone,' Tom said.

It'll wear off, Tom told Hank later. Jimmy would soon forget her, he said. But Jimmy didn't forget her. He didn't ever forget her.

That night when Auntie Moll was closing the flaps on the whore tents Tom called to see her.

'Closed, soldier,' she said with a little smile. 'You'll just 'ave to jiggle yourself around 'til Friday night.'

Tom had never met a woman as coarse as Auntie Moll. He'd led a fairly sheltered life in Boston as had most of his friends and her vulgarity still embarrassed him.

'I'm all right, thank you,' he said, his face reddening. 'I want to ask you something, that's all.'

'Oh yeah? What you looking for, huh? Somethin' different? Three in a bed? Naughty peep show? Auntie Moll can set up most things.'

'I want to ask you about the Negro girl you brought in,' he said. 'Chrissie.'

'Chrissie, huh? That her name? Well now, it sure is a shame. Ah guess there's lotsa young fellas like you an' sum not so young would sure like a little roll around with a good-looking kid like Chrissie. But she ain't for sale. Not any more.'

'Why is that?'

'Ah'm sorry,' Auntie Moll said. 'You ast me to find a nice Negra gal for your friend an' that's what ah did.'

'I know,' Tom said. 'And I'm grateful.'

'Well, all right. But ah can't get her again. Ah can maybe get another Negra – ah don't know.'

'It's not that,' Tom said. 'I don't want a Negro girl. I just want to know about *this* girl – Chrissie.'

'Ah don't know any more than you,' she said defensively. 'Ah didn't even know the gal's name.'

'I want to know where she came from, who brought her here.'

Auntie Moll looked worried now. 'Ah don't think so,' she said, shaking her head. 'Ah don't want no trouble.'

'She's not a whore, is she?'

'Ah don't call ma girls whores, young man. But no, you is quite right. She is not of the profession. Ah got her through a contact in Lex. The Negra boy who runs the farm there brung her an' he had to have her back by tonight 'case the bossman want her.'

Tom frowned.

'Aw come on, you know how it is,' Auntie Moll said. 'You ain't that innocent.' She looked at him closely. 'Are you?'

'You mean the owner of the farm?'

'Yeah, yeah,' she said, impatient with him now. 'If the owner want her in his bed she in his bed. They all do it. They work the boys to death an' they bed the young women. A good-lookin' kid like this Chrissie ain't goin' escape.'

Something was still bothering Tom and Auntie Moll took pity on him. 'What's the problem, son? Didn't your boy like her?'

'He liked her all right,' Tom said. 'I just feel I may have started something here I'm going to regret.'

'Ah don't want no trouble.'

'There won't be any trouble. Not for you anyway.'

'Then what?'

'Our man thinks he's fallen in love with her and he wants to marry her.'

Auntie Moll laughed uproariously. 'Won't be the first fella to fall for one o' ma girls,' she declared proudly. 'But hey listen! Can't worry about that. He'll forgit her soon as you boys move out. They always do.' Lowering her voice, she added, 'An' ah hears you boys is movin' out any day now. Sunday maybe, next day at the latest.'

'I hear that, too,' Tom agreed.

'Then don't you worry none,' she told him. 'Coupla weeks he won't even remember that girl's name.'

The arrival of the newly promoted Colonel Danvers at the gathering of the Harvies and their friends had caused a stir among the guests. Those who knew him well dismissed the sobriquet Handsome Jack with a smile and agreed he was a jolly good fellow, not in the least vain, a first-rate soldier and a fine and loyal ally. Those who didn't know him well were often less welcoming but he had little difficulty in winning over those he wanted to win over.

His procedure at parties such as this rarely varied. He would go out of his way to acknowledge all the male guests and gain their goodwill with a series of warm smiles and firm handshakes. His technique was to give each one his close attention and the respect they evidently craved. Having accomplished this and with the eyes of most of the younger women present drawn to his disarming smile he would then seek out several of the older ladies who would quickly succumb to his undoubted charm. Any potential hostility dispelled, he was free to train his dark smiling eyes on whatever took his fancy.

Mr Harvie knew Danvers and was well aware of his potential. A colonel already, he would be well received on his return to England. He had fought with distinction at Bunker Hill and was highly regarded by Generals Howe and Burgoyne. At thirty-two he was unmarried and, though twelve years older, he would make an excellent choice of husband for Imelda. There was also every chance that Danvers would one day be knighted or afforded an even higher honour. The King himself was said to be fond of him and he had achieved this happy state of affairs without, apparently, incurring the displeasure of the King's courtiers. Max Harvie was ambitious and had long coveted a knighthood for himself. With a rising star like Jack Danvers as his son-in-law and his own not inconsiderable work on behalf of the Crown his ambition, he believed, was achievable.

But Imelda Harvie was far too frivolous and empty-headed for Jack Danvers and when Sarah appeared on the stairway he almost propelled Imelda towards her.

120

'You must meet my cousin,' Imelda said, somewhat piqued at his undisguised interest in Sarah.

'Miss Dowling,' he said softly, and he raised Sarah's fingers to his lips. 'How lovely to see you again so soon.'

'Major Danvers,' Sarah responded.

'*Colonel* Danvers now,' Imelda corrected though this seemed of little consequence. 'So you two know each other?'

'We shared a coach,' Danvers said with a smile.

'With three other people,' Sarah added.

Imelda felt she was in the way. 'In that case, please excuse me,' she said. 'I imagine you two have much to discuss.'

Sarah raised her eyebrows, surprised at her cousin's abrupt departure, and in the entrance to the main reception room Max Harvie frowned a little as he watched his daughter hurry away.

'I don't think we have much to discuss, *Colonel*,' Sarah said quietly. 'Imelda seems to have the wrong impression.'

'On the contrary,' Danvers said, 'I think you and I might have a great deal to discuss.'

Again Sarah raised her eyebrows.

'For instance,' he said, with what he obviously thought was his most captivating smile, 'where did you find such beautiful green eyes? I mean, they're not the sort of eyes one could easily forget.'

His words were so blatantly flirtatious that it was difficult not to laugh. Sarah did her best to keep a straight face but found this impossible to sustain when he went on and on with his outrageous flattery. 'Really, Colonel Danvers,' she said. 'I don't. . . .'

'Do you know,' he interrupted, suddenly serious as he steered her gently into the small ballroom, 'that when I was a boy I had a dream in which this very old soothsayer came to my bedside. He told me that all my life I would want to be a soldier of the King in the belief it would bring me lasting joy and true contentment. But this, I would find, was only a means to an end. Being a soldier would mean I could travel the world in search of what I really needed for this true and lasting contentment. I would not know what this thing was until I found the words and the words would be contained in a small box. In time, of course, I forgot about the box. I became a soldier, travelled the world, but I have never found that true and lasting contentment. And, until I arrived here in Boston, I had never found the box.'

Despite herself, Sarah was intrigued. Half-smiling in disbelief, she

GERARD MAC

said, 'You found the box?'

'I found the box.' His handsome face was still now as he paused before going on, making her wait for the conclusion of his story. 'After we left the coach General Howe and I were shown to our respective quarters. I now have a small but adequate room at the barracks on North Street.' He regarded her quietly, testing her patience. 'On my desk with a short note was a small box.'

Sarah was openly curious now and to others, watching in the small ballroom, she and Danvers appeared to be immersed in some deeply engrossing conversation.

Max Harvie beckoned his daughter to his side and urged her to intervene, break them up. I can't do that, Imelda said. They're friends. They already know each other.

'Beside the box,' Danvers told Sarah, 'was this note that said an old man who looked like a beggar but claimed to be a wizard had left the box which must only be opened by Colonel Jack Danvers.'

Sarah's sceptical smile had gone. She wanted to know what was in the box and Danvers knew he had her undivided attention.

'Slowly,' he said, 'I opened the box and inside – what did I find?'

'What?' Sarah demanded.

'Another little note. And this one said, quite simply, you will never find true joy and contentment until you meet and marry a girl with green eyes.'

Sarah burst out laughing and several heads turned towards her. At once she regained her composure and a measure of decorum. 'I must admit,' she said softly, 'you had me believing your story, Colonel Danvers.'

'Ah, but it's true,' he said laughing. 'And now I have met her, the girl with the greenest eyes in the whole world.'

'If I did not know you are a responsible officer of the British Army, I would believe you are quite mad.'

'Ah, but are we not all quite mad, my dear Miss Dowling? I must confess, I certainly am. If I were not I would by now have abandoned this excessive formality and I would be addressing you as "Sarah" not Miss Dowling.'

Sarah averted her eyes and made no comment.

'If we are to be friends,' he went on, 'and I sincerely hope we are, then I request your permission to address you as Sarah.'

He had left her little option. 'If you wish,' she said with a shrug.

He was looking at her curiously and she wanted to be free of his attention but she didn't know how to extricate herself without causing offence. 'I really didn't intend to come down this evening,' she said feebly. 'I was very tired after such a long journey.'

'Quite so,' he said. 'I felt the same, but then when I realized if I came I might see you again I couldn't resist.'

Sarah looked embarrassed, obviously wanting to escape but too young and inexperienced to realize her indifference would only strengthen his resolve. Danvers seemed so much older than she and even here, in her aunt's house, she was a little afraid of him. She cast around for a means of escape and was relieved to see her Uncle Max and Imelda approaching.

'What do you mean, you're coming with me?' Ben asked.

'I've left the 29th,' Paddy told him. 'I'm moving on.'

Something about the little Irishman's creased features and his almost toothless grin made Ben smile. 'You're a deserter?' he said evenly. 'You're running away?'

'If you like.'

'Then I suppose I should take you back.'

'But you won't.'

'I won't?'

'No,' Paddy said confidently. 'An' I'll tell you for why. One, you're my friend an' you wouldn't do that to me. And two, if you go back to camp now they'll wan't to know where you've been an' why you are not in New Jersey where you should be.'

'The army's going to miss you,' Ben said.

Paddy made a noise in his throat. 'They won't care if I'm there or not. They never really wanted me anyhow. Didn't fit in, did I? When they tell that drill sergeant I've shipped out he'll think it's his birthday.'

'Well, all right,' Ben said. 'But if they catch up with you they'll shoot you on the spot. And I don't want them coming after us.'

'They'll not come after me,' Paddy said with a laugh. 'They'll be glad they got rid of me. And anyway, once we get away from the Neck and we're out in the open country they wouldn't dare follow. Too scared, I bet.'

'There'll be other units along the way.'

'Ach, that's not a problem. Nobody would believe I'd been a soldier anyway. I never looked right in that uniform. That red coat they gave me was too long. It was trailin' the ground. I felt like I was the Pope in his flowin' robes, so I did.'

Ben looked at Paddy's horse. It was an emaciated little nag, a horse that at some time had been badly treated. 'I don't like people who are cruel to animals, Paddy.'

'I know he needs some care and attention,' the Irishman said, 'and I intend to see that he gets it.'

'Well, I'd say you are going to have to carry him.'

'Sure an' he's not as bad as all that. I'll treat him good. I'll give him plenty o' rest an' walk with him when I can. He'll be all right, so he will.'

'Well, you know I can't go slow. I've got to join my unit. I mean, we'd never get to New Jersey.'

'I'm not going to New Jersey,' Paddy said. 'I'm going to New York and I'm not in any hurry. I'll get there in my own good time. I just thought I'd like to go a little o' the way wit' you.'

Ben nodded. 'But why New York?'

'I t'ink that's where the future is. For me, anyway. This war won't last. An' when the British have gone New York will be the place t' be.'

'You sound pretty confident the British are going.'

'The British have no chance, Ben. An' they know it.'

They were walking side by side, their horses in tow, along the moonlit ribbon of road. Ben liked the Irishman. Paddy was a man who had nothing or so it seemed. No home. No family. No Melanie waiting for him. He had told Ben he had no interest in women, adding with a laugh it was probably because no woman had ever shown any interest in him, not even his mother. His mother had abandoned him on a back street more or less as soon as he could walk. Yet he had told Ben all this without bitterness. This life is just a game of cards, he'd said, and we can only play the hand we're dealt. In other words he had accepted things the way they were and with good humour and Ben admired him for that.

They parted where the coach route diverged, Ben to join the British Legion, Paddy to what he called 'pastures new'.

'And what will you do in New York?' Ben asked as they gave each other a parting embrace.

'Whatever I can at first. But one day I will own my own tavern, so I will,' Paddy told him. 'An' if you ever find yourself in town, Benny boy, just be sure to look out for Hogan's Tavern.'

FOURTEEN

UNDER Colonel Putnam's direction the rebel volunteers near Roxbury were gradually becoming more organized. They were formed now into four companies. As newly appointed lieutenants, Tom and Hank Blanchard were given Company B and Company D respectively. Jimmy Sunshine had been allocated to Company B and would therefore retain at least some contact with Tom. But the three of them no longer shared a tent. Tom and Hank had moved into what served as officers' quarters.

The tall thin drummer, also allocated to Company B, had succeeded in claiming Tom's old space in the tent next to Jimmy but Jimmy was not sure this was a good idea. The drummer was 'all right' but Jimmy didn't want to be part of what might become some kind of subtle segregation, unintentional or otherwise.

None of this appeared to have occurred to the drummer or, if it had, it didn't bother him. 'Hey, Jimmy,' he said one evening. 'Ah got somethin' for you to see.'

'Oh yeah?' Jimmy said tolerantly.

The drummer sat down beside him and pulled out a tabloid bulletin sheet.

'What is it?' Jimmy asked.

'It's one o' them newspapers.'

'You can read it?' Jimmy was impressed.

'Hell no,' the drummer said with a laugh. 'Ah can't read it. But ah know what it says.'

'Yeah? What does it say?'

The drummer folded the paper and put it inside his shirt. 'You know the fella thinks he knows everythin? Talks like some kinda professor?'

Jimmy nodded. 'What about him?'

'Well, the professor reckons you an' me are in the wrong army.'

'What're you talking about?'

The drummer lowered his voice. 'He sez the English in Virginia are giving slaves and servants there freedom. He sez we should be fightin' for them.'

'Gimme the newspaper,' Jimmy said. 'I'll get Tom to read it.'

All it said in the news bulletin, Tom told him, was that some Lord Dunmore was recruiting black men for the British Army. According to the paper any slaves or servants who joined would become free of their indentures and would be well taken care of by the British after the war. Tom said maybe it was just a newspaper story, a piece of propaganda, but he would find out what he could. True to his word, he raised the question at the next officers' meeting with the colonel.

Colonel Putnam confirmed that the story was substantially true. The Loyalist Governor of Virginia felt he was not getting sufficient support from the British in Boston and had decided to launch an initiative of his own. At first it seemed like a clever move on the Governor's part. Many Negroes were disaffected and easy prey to such inducements. In the South blacks widely outnumbered whites and the threat of insurrection was enough to make many leading rebels return home to secure the stability of their plantations, thus weakening the rebel forces.

It was in April 1775 that Lord Dunmore made known his plans. In May his relations with organizations representing Loyalist plantation owners soured and by early June, though assured he was not in any danger, he left his official residence in Williamsburg and set up his base aboard the man-o'-war *Fowey*. News now travelled quickly that Dunmore was sailing up and down the coast and river, plundering farms and plantations and taking aboard 'freed' slaves. By November Loyalist slave owners were incensed and deeply opposed to his policies. They began to spread rumours and damning forecasts of his intentions. Slaves were warned that Lord Dunmore only wanted able-bodied men who were willing to fight and die for him. There was no place for women and children or the elderly. Also, it was said, if the British were defeated, recruited slaves would simply be sold off in the West Indies.

Fortunately, Colonel Putnam told his officers, this Lord Dunmore had little knowledge of military strategy. A successful surprise attack on a company of rebels at a place called Kemp's Landing on the Elizabeth River had further inflated his already swollen ego. But his sense of superiority did not last long. Early in December at Great Bridge, a few miles from Norfolk, he suffered a humiliating defeat with many casualties and the loss of several of his officers.

Many slaves had rushed to embrace this promise of freedom but now, with the threat of execution facing those runaways who were recaptured, it was proving a difficult choice to make. Slave owners had decided to offer an amnesty. Return within ten days and all will be forgiven. Many were returning, the colonel said. And there were rumours that among Lord Dunmore's army, living aboard a variety of vessels and with no land base, many had fallen foul of smallpox. It's difficult to know the truth right now, Colonel Putnam said. But the high and mighty lord sure made a big mistake when he upset those loyalist landowners.

Tom Blanchard told Jimmy all this without embellishment. It was up to Jimmy, he said, to do what he thought was in his own best interests. There were new recruits to the rebel camp every day, many came and many left. If Jimmy stayed, then fine. If he left then he and Hank would understand and wish him well.

It was true, Tom added, that if he left and was granted his freedom by the British there would be no question of him losing it again after the war. If he returned to Boston, that is. There was already a groundswell of opinion in Boston that slavery was wrong. According to the Quakers, Tom said, to keep a person in bondage was against the will of God. It was different in the South, of course. And if these promises came only from this Lord Dunmore, a man who was not exactly popular with his own people, who was to say they would be honoured when the war was over?

On the other hand, Tom said, if he left he wouldn't be on his own. The drummer seemed a good man to have with him. Maybe they would be all right, get what they wanted. Whatever Jimmy decided, he and Hank would always regard him as a special friend and they would always be glad to see him if he returned to Boston. They hoped he would stay but, of course, it was his decision. One that only he could make.

Jimmy was confused. He didn't know what to do. He knew he was not yet free of Mabbut and no matter what Tom said he would have to disappear when the war was over or he might be made to return to that old slave driver. There was no way he was going back to the kind of back-breaking work old Mabbut put him through and the kind of non-existence he suffered as a farm slave. He would rather die in battle than go back to that. And there was Chrissie now. He needed to be free for her sake. If he didn't gain his own freedom he could never call and claim hers. Not only did he need to be free, he somehow had to set Chrissie free, too.

He was wide awake when the drummer stirred in the next bed but he lay still, kept his eyes almost closed. The drummer drew himself up and paused for a moment, looking down. Jimmy didn't move. But the drummer knew he was awake and, down on one knee, he whispered close to Jimmy's ear, 'Not comin' den?'

Jimmy opened his eyes, shook his head and whispered, 'Good luck, drummer.'

The drummer nodded and straightened up.

'An' take care,' Jimmy added and the drummer was gone, out into the night and to a road that would lead him to who knows where.

For a brief instant Jimmy was tempted to race after him, tell him to wait. But he didn't. He closed his eyes and lay back. If he hadn't met Chrissie he would have gone. He was sure of that. There was nothing for him here.

The drummer had set up a lot of questions, questions he couldn't answer. The Blanchards for one. Why should they care what he did? Did they care? Maybe Tom more than Hank. Hank had just gone along with what Tom said and did. It was Tom who offered him the ride in the cart, Tom who offered him the drink from his canteen, Tom who treated him like he was a real person. But why? Why should someone like Tom care about him?

That morning the company sergeant wanted to know why he was three men down. One was in the sick bay, he was told, and another was on an errand for the colonel. But nobody had seen the drummer. Anybody know where he is? What tent is he in? He's gone, sarge, someone said, and his bedroll's gone with him. Gone to join the slave lovers, someone else suggested and one or two sniggered.

'Maybe he just wanna be free,' Jimmy murmured.

By the middle of February, 1776, the rebels were under the

command of General Washington. The general, appalled at the unwashed state of most of the rank and file and the evident lack of discipline he found when he first took over, systematically imposed his will and gradually created what was virtually a new force. Those who could not or would not take the restrictions and the rigorous drill routines he imposed soon deserted and Washington and his generals knew they were better off without them. Now he had the makings of an army he could view with pride and, after months of stock-piling supplies and ammunition, he was ready for the fierce battles that lay ahead.

One morning early in March Colonel Putnam assembled the four companies under his command and told them they were to be addressed by the adjutant general. Major General Gates, who had played a significant role in reorganizing the rebel army under Washington, at thirty-seven, was five years older than his chief. But he looked much more. He had grey hair and he wore spectacles and when he walked he seemed to stoop forward. He looked more like an academic than a soldier but he was a shrewd administrator and he knew how to talk to the men.

'When our chief, General Washington, first took over,' he told them, 'he did not like what he saw. Many of the men camped hereabouts were a disgrace to our cause. They were not fit to be called soldiers. And frankly, the general was glad to see the back of them. And so should you be. Those who deserted in the face of a little tough training would surely desert when face to face with the enemy. Those of you who are still here, I am pleased to say, have proved yourselves to be real soldiers, true patriots and good men. Our equipment may not yet he entirely to our liking but it is much improved. Likewise our arms.' He told them of the many cannons and mortars captured by rebel soldiers, with the help of an unruly group known as The Green Mountain Boys, at a place called Ticonderoga. 'Our uniforms are still makeshift,' he went on. 'But at least we can recognize each other now – if only by our coonskin caps.'

There was laughter in the ranks and the general continued, 'As you know the British are in Boston. But they are worried men. We are going to run them off our land and they know it! We are going to run them into the sea and they can swim back to England for all we care!'

The rows of men raised a cheer.

'So we have no worries about General Bloodyback Howe and his men in red coats. He can't hold out in Boston forever. Our boys are ready and waiting, all set up on Dorchester Heights. Any day now he's going to have to fight and take a beating or sail away. Now – how does this affect you boys here? Well, by order of General Washington himself, I am to tell you that, as one of the finest battalions in our new United Colonial Army, you can be put to better use elsewhere.'

Whether what General Gates then said was true or not, he added with a smile and with the desired effect, 'What General Washington actually said was, it will not take his best men to crack a soft old nut like General Howe.'

There was more laughter. But Tom and Hank Blanchard at the head of their respective companies exchanged glances and back in the ranks Jimmy Sunshine murmured, 'Come on, General, tell us the rest.'

The general turned to Colonel Putnam. 'Colonel?'

Colonel Putnam went into his tent and returned with a furled flag. 'This, gentlemen,' he announced, 'I am proud to tell you is our new standard. The flag of the United Colonial Army.'

He released the ties, unfurled the flag and as he held it aloft it opened out and fluttered in the mid-morning breeze. And at that a resounding cheer went up. Then the assembled rebels stood to attention and saluted.

Colonel Putnam smiled broadly as a sergeant major stepped forward to take the flag from him. 'And so,' the colonel said, addressing his men, 'at first light in the morning we move out.' He glanced at General Gates. 'For obvious reasons I am not at liberty to tell you exactly where we are going but we are to move south. I can, however, tell you that where we are going there will be plenty of action.'

The probability that the town might soon be abandoned by the British was the all consuming topic of conversation in most Boston households that March morning and nowhere more so than at the Harvies. All that was delaying an evacuation was a shortage of ships. The weather was cold still, the conditions were wintry and General Howe's 12,000 men were miserable and thoroughly dispirited. There was little for them to do but wait. Food in the town was in short supply and many of the soldiers were guilty of thieving. Houses were burgled, stores were broken into, smallholdings were robbed of poultry and though those caught were publicly flogged the transgressions continued. Law-breaking had become a major problem and so blatant that an executioner was appointed to accompany the provost marshal who had been given the authority to hang miscreants on the spot without the benefit of a trial.

At first General Howe had planned to attack the rebel forces surrounding the beleaguered town but those people in the know, people like Max Harvie, knew he had abandoned this plan and was simply waiting for enough ships to arrive to transport his men and their equipment to safety. By early March the rebels had consolidated their positions and General Howe had again considered engaging them in battle but the poor weather had worsened. The heavy rain had become a torrent and with good sense the general had again abandoned any plan to attack.

On the morning of 16 March Max Harvie and his wife, their daughter Imelda and their niece Sarah Dowling, with a sense of foreboding, were sitting quietly at the breakfast table.

'General Howe has informed me, my dear,' Max Harvie told his wife in a subdued tone, 'there will be places for us on one of the British ships.'

'We are to leave?' Imelda asked.

'I'm afraid so,' her father replied. 'Temporarily, of course. But, yes, we must leave. When the British go this rabble will come down from the hills. And they will be thrown out just as soon as reinforcements arrive. In the meantime we must take General Howe's advice and move to a safer place.'

'But why must we?' Sarah asked reasonably. 'This is our country. Surely we have nothing to fear.'

'We are loyal to the Crown, Sarah,' Max Harvie told her in a voice that was almost a reproof. 'These roughnecks are not. They want to pull down everything we stand for, everything we have worked so hard to build.'

'But where would they take us?' his wife asked.

Mrs Harvie had feared this would be the outcome. She would be forced to leave her home, the house she loved. Her husband, she knew, was too embroiled in the business of recruiting loyalists and disseminating propaganda on behalf of the British to attract anything but abuse and worse from the supporters of the rebels. And this was the dilemma. Mrs Harvie didn't want to go but she knew she couldn't stay. Worst of all she felt, in her heart, that her husband was wrong.

131

The people were right. Why *should* they be taxed and ruled from a foreign country with a pompous king 3,000 miles away? She had never said this to Max and now it was too late. She wished she had taken a greater interest at the outset. She might well have persuaded him then that he was wrong. He was not a bad man. There was a great deal of good in him and he could be kind and generous. It was just that he was too easily impressed by the trappings of titles and high office, and he valued prestige and position a little too highly.

'Where will we go?' she asked.

It was then she realized he didn't know, he had no idea where they would go. It could be England. But who did they know in England? They would have no home there and very little money.

Max Harvie was red-faced and flustered. He threw down his napkin. 'They will take us to a place of safety,' he insisted.

Someone had arrived at the front door and Alfred, the Harvies' manservant, appeared from the hall. 'Visitor, sah.'

Harvie went into the large hall and Sarah recognized the deeply resonant voice of Colonel Danvers.

'How nice to see you, Colonel,' Harvie responded. 'Do come in. Alfred, show Colonel Danvers into the living room.'

But Colonel Danvers waved Alfred away and followed Harvie into the breakfast-room. Resplendent in the red coat of the King's Own 4th Foot Regiment, his regimentals faced in gosling green and laced silver, his rounded hat, which he doffed with a flourish, decorated with a cockade and feathers, the colonel bowed low. 'Mrs Harvie. Imelda. Sarah. Please forgive this intrusion.'

All eyes were on the handsome colonel but he turned with some urgency to Max Harvie. 'There is room on a ship tonight, sailing at midnight. Two cabins for you and your family.'

'You are very kind, Colonel,' Harvie responded warmly.

'It is essential that you leave then.'

Harvie nodded and Danvers turned back to the table. 'I'm sorry there is so little time, ladies, but it cannot be helped. I suggest you bring with you only what is absolutely essential. There will be little room and the cabins are very small. Most passengers will have only the open deck.'

'Must it be tonight, Colonel?' Mrs Harvie asked.

'I'm afraid so, ma'am. The city will be evacuated tomorrow at first light. Many, I fear, will be left behind. We will leave from the harbour but there will be no shots fired and this rabble from the hills will he free to move in. They have cannon and other heavy artillery out there on the heights but they have promised not to bombard the town. There will be little damage done provided the evacuation is carried out swiftly and efficiently.'

'You're just going to abandon the city?' Imelda asked scathingly. 'Just let them walk in?'

The colonel smiled. 'It is all part of our strategic plan. We will be back. Have no fear.' He stepped forward took Mrs Harvie's hand and held it to his lips. 'I must leave you now, ma'am, ladies. There is much to be done.'

'We are extremely grateful for your kind assistance, Colonel,' Mrs Harvie told him.

'Of course, of course,' Max fussed. 'Forever in your debt.'

Colonel Danvers paused at the door. 'There is one other thing, Max, if I may.' He bowed again to the ladies and indicated that he wished to speak to Harvie in private. In the hallway he added quietly, 'There is a condition to all this.'

Max frowned. 'A condition?'

'Let me put it this way, Max, as clearly and as bluntly as I can, in order that there is no misundertanding. There are two cabins available for you and Mrs Harvie and for your daughter Imelda on condition you are accompanied by your niece Miss Dowling.'

'Sarah? Well, of course, Sarah will come.'

'Let there be no mistake over this. The ship sails at midnight. I suggest that you and your family arrive at the dock no later than ten thirty. My aide will be there to receive you and to guide you aboard. He will recognize you, Max. He tells me he knows you by sight. However, and I must stress this again, if your niece is not with you neither my lieutenant nor the ship's captain will permit you to board.'

'But why?' Harvie asked. 'I am quite certain Sarah will come.' He laughed nervously. 'But why is it so essential? She is just a girl, an ordinary girl. She is not important.'

Danvers was deadly serious. 'She is of great importance,' he said, 'to me. See that she is there.'

Ben Withers made steady progress, careful not to over tire his mount, resting early each evening and setting off each morning at first light. Once, as he rode steadily through a barren valley, a line of braves appeared on a hilltop. They watched his progress all the way and Ben knew that if he urged his horse to a gallop they would come down from the hill and take up the chase. They were like wolves. If you ran and showed fear they would enjoy the chase. The danger was that they would take his horse. The bay was a beautiful animal, a possession they would prize.

Ben took a gamble. He slowed to a halt, dismounted and began to examine the horse's front left shoe. After a moment he set off slowly on foot, leading the horse and limping slightly to put the idea into their heads that the horse had gone lame. He had his musket and he knew he could make a fight of it if he had to. He didn't want to kill any Indians but he didn't want to be scalped either. The incident passed and as he reached a gently flowing tributary of the Hudson he allowed his horse to drink before setting off again.

Later that afternoon as he followed the river, something by a copse caught his eye. It looked like a small mound of clothing until he drew near and saw it was a body. The man had been dead for several days, the body crawling with bluebottles. Even from several feet the stench of the putrefying flesh in the heat of the day was stomach churning.

Ben forced himself to look closer and guessed the man had been one of the express messengers the army employed. His despatch bag lay nearby. Ben touched it with his foot but he didn't want to look inside. It occurred to him that he ought to bury the body but he was not carrying a spade and he realized it was dangerous to tarry. The man had been scalped, the line of flesh where the scalp had been taken a bloated green.

The act of scalping had appalled him since as a small boy he had witnessed a simulation of the process. The method the Indians used apparently, as demonstrated by a bloodthirsty youth, was to place a foot on the victim's neck, twist one hand in a clump of hair to tauten the skin and with the razor sharp scalping knife in the other hand swiftly remove the scalp.

Ben drew back, mounted the bay and rode off at speed. He felt guilty leaving the body to the flies and the howling wolves he heard at night but he consoled himself that he didn't have the means to bury the poor man or the time. He convinced himself that his journey was already taking far longer than it should and he must be on his way.

His thoughts throughout his long ride had been concerned mainly with how best to confront Sergeant Duckett. Now the body of the dead messenger had given him an idea, a plan of action, a plan he would pursue immediately he reported to his new commanding officer.

FIFTEEN

'I'M not going,' Sarah said flatly.

Max Harvie was in no mood for girlish tantrums. 'Don't be ridiculous, young lady,' he said with a sweep of his hand. 'You have to go. We all have to go.'

Sarah's Aunt Mary was less dismissive. 'You can't stay, dear. There's no telling what these people might do.'

'Aren't you forgetting what they did to your mother and your family?' Imelda asked. 'For goodness sake! Aren't you afraid of what they might do here?'

'What about Vanessa and Alfred. They have to stay.'

The Negro housekeeper Vanessa, who was not much younger than Aunt Mary, was clearing the table. Sarah appealed to her with wide green eyes.

Vanessa merely smiled. 'Negras is of no account, Miss Sarah.'

'Vanessa will stay, of course,' Aunt Mary said. 'This is her home. These people will not harm her and they may not harm the house if Vanessa and Alfred are still living here. But you have to come, Sarah. We couldn't possibly allow you to stay.'

Sarah shook her head. 'Then I'll go back to Philadelphia.'

'Colonel Danvers wants you to come with us,' Max told her.

Sarah shrugged. 'I don't owe Colonel Danvers anything.'

Max Harvie was exasperated. He turned away and glared, his face red and angry, at his wife. Then he left the room. Aunt Mary left her seat and followed him out into the hall.

'Max! Max, what is it?'

'That girl has got to come with us and she is coming whether she likes it or not.'

'If she really doesn't want to come,' Aunt Mary said, 'perhaps we could arrange for her safe return to the convent.'

'She *has* to come,' Max insisted.

'We can't force her to, if she really doesn't want to,' his wife pointed out reasonably. 'And you said yourself the rebels have promised not to damage property and . . . and houses . . . and things and if Sarah is here whilst we're away and Vanessa and Alfred are here then when this awful business is over we will have our home to come back to.'

Max was silent, furious that he'd been placed in this invidious position by this man Danvers.

'Max?' Aunt Mary watched him anxiously.

He took her by the shoulders and looked deep into her eyes. 'Colonel Danvers insists that Sarah comes with us.'

'Colonel Danvers? He can't do that. If she doesn't come she doesn't come.'

'If Sarah doesn't come we don't go.'

'But why?'

'The offer of two cabins on one of His Majesty's ships is conditional on Sarah coming with us.'

'And why is that?'

'I would have thought it was obvious, woman. The man *wants* her. He wants her for himself.'

'Max! That is outrageous. I thought Colonel Danvers was a man of honour, an officer of the King. You must speak to General Howe.'

'General Howe would not be interested in the fate of one girl. And before you say any more, stop for a moment and think. *Think*, Mary. Would it be such a bad thing? What I mean is, if Danvers wants Sarah for himself I will insist he marries her. Then, eventually, he would take her home to England with him and that could work out well for us.'

'For us?'

'Well, Sarah is our niece, is she not? And Colonel Danvers is, I hear, expected to receive at the very least a knighthood on his return. Sarah would be Lady Danvers.' Max paused wistfully. 'I had hoped he would take to Imelda in that way but there we are. He chose Sarah. Such is the way of these things.'

'Sarah is a very pretty girl.'

'I wouldn't say *pretty* exactly. Not as pretty as Imelda.'

'She is a strikingly attractive girl, Max. I am quite sure that many men would be drawn to her and those beautiful eyes.'

'Mm, yes. I suppose so.' Max was reluctant to praise Sarah. 'The point is, how do we persuade her to come with us?'

'Imelda could try.'

Sarah and Imelda had remained at the breakfast table.

'I don't want to upset Uncle Max,' Sarah was saying, 'but I really would rather stay here and I don't see why it matters what I do.'

Imelda laughed. 'It's not Daddy who wants you to go. It's Colonel Danvers, you ninny. It's obvious the colonel is smitten. And any girl would consider herself fortunate to be courted by a man like Colonel Danvers. Not only is he rich and of very high rank in British society, he's handsome, too! What more could a girl ask for?'

'Love?' Sarah suggested. 'I don't love the man.'

'You could learn to. I'm sure I could.'

'Imelda,' Sarah said with a smile, 'you are not only my cousin, you are my friend and I love you. But you must understand, to become involved with a man I must be *in* love with him. Colonel Danvers, I know, is an extremely attractive man but I already have a man.'

'You have?'

'You know I have.'

'You are not still thinking of Tom Blanchard? He's a traitor. He went off and joined the rebel army. The people who murdered your own family, Sarah. You can't still want *him*!'

'Tom Blanchard had nothing to do with what happened at the farm. And we don't know for sure that any of the rebels did. We only have the word of a frightened little boy.'

'Are you saying it was the British?'

'I'm saying it could have been either side. I went to visit my family's grave in Roxbury and the pastor said that sometimes, in floods and fires and war and pestilence, a certain type of person takes advantage of the situation. There is always good and bad, he said, on both sides.'

'That may be so,' Imelda allowed, 'but you just listen to me. You can forget Tom Blanchard and open your eyes. Colonel Danvers is a far better prospect.'

The sky above Boston was a dark grey that morning and by noon the rains came. It was a Saturday and the streets around the docks were busy with families from in and around town seeking to buy in whatever provisions they could. There was a sense of urgency as if a period of severe austerity was on the way and whatever food was available was in great demand. Street traders and tinkers lined the pavements with makeshift stalls and at regular intervals platoons of soldiers in short red jackets, red waistcoats and black leather caps, men of the 38th Foot Regiment, marched down to the seafront, scattering all before them.

Word had gone round that the British commander, General Howe, had finally abandoned any hope he might have had of engaging the rebel army. He had decided to wait no longer for further vessels that could aid an evacuation and to leave with what he had. By evening the rain was falling in windswept sheets across the harbour front as hordes of frightened Loyalists converged on the dock, clasping whatever belongings they could carry.

Watching the chaos in the street from a high window Max Harvie was gripped by panic. He knew he was probably one of the most unpopular men in Boston and that he would undoubtedly be a target for the rabble. He stormed downstairs in search of Sarah. It was monstrous that this girl should put them all in danger and after all the hospitality she had received in his house.

A coachman was at the door. 'Beggin' yer pardon, sir. Colonel Danvers of His Majesty's Army has instructed me to transport you and your family to the east dock at once.'

'Yes, yes,' Max replied. 'Imelda! Find your mother . . . and Sarah.'

Mrs Harvie and Imelda were ready, bags in each hand.

'As few possessions as you can, if you please, ma'am, miss,' the coachman said apologetically. 'There's little enough room and the master won't allow anyone aboard with extras.'

Frightened but in control, Mrs Harvie nodded, aware of the anxiety in her husband's eyes.

The coachman said, 'Mr Harvie, sir. I take it this is Mrs Harvie and this is Miss Sarah?'

He held a hand out to indicate Imelda and for a moment it crossed Max's mind that they might board the ship without seeing Danvers until they were well under way. Perhaps he could allow the coachman to believe Imelda was Sarah.

But Mrs Harvie said, 'No, this is my daughter Imelda. I'm afraid my niece Sarah will not be coming.'

'Ah!' The coachman looked genuinely perplexed. 'In that case, ma'am, my instructions are. . . .' He looked from Mrs Harvie to Max. 'I'm very sorry, sir, but. . . .'

Then they all turned as Sarah came down the stairs carrying her travelling bag. 'My name is Sarah Dowling,' she said quietly. 'Pray take us to the ship.'

'So what was it like at Long Bridge?'

Ben Withers' question hung in the air and the others waited as if he had lit the fuse to a wagonload of explosives and there was nowhere to run.

The Scot, a sergeant who had been steadily drinking himself over the edge, blew up. 'What was it like?' He banged the top of the long mess table with his fist. 'What was it like? I'll tell ye what it was like!'

He was well known, apparently, for his sudden outbursts. When he was sober he rarely spoke but when he was drunk it all came out. He had been through the worst of the disastrous campaign in Virginia and nothing in his previous military career, mainly as a foot soldier in the war against Spain, had prepared him for what he witnessed there. Though his superiors had not recognized it he was suffering, as were many of his contemporaries, from a severe attack of battle fatigue.

The other senior NCOs around the table in the mess tent began to drift away until only Ben remained. He felt obliged to stay and listen. It was he, after all, who had asked the question.

'Generals!' The Scot looked at him with pale watery eyes beneath bushy ginger-grey eyebrows, his coarse hair now more grey than red. 'Generals! Bloody useless parasites! They do nothin' but send good men to their deaths.' The eyes had Ben fixed in a glare and there was no escape. 'Generals who listen to half-wits! The Governor of Virginia is a bloody half-witted buffoon! And the generals listened to him. Can ye believe that? They listened to *him*!'

Ben could only nod, eager to escape from the manic Scot but at the same time curious to know what happened.

'Twenty miles south of Norfolk,' the Scot intoned as if reciting some epic poem. 'Twenty miles south an' a causeway. A narrow track over a filthy swamp an' the other side, waitin' for us, jus' waitin' to blow us apart, thousands of these militiamen, rebels, call 'em what ye will. An' all of 'em crack shots. They earn their livin' huntin' an' shootin' an' I tell ye they could hit a mallard from a hundred yards. Aye, an' a man's a bigger target.'

He checked to make sure Ben was listening.

'Ridiculous, it was. An' most of all, unnecessary.'

'What happened?' Ben asked quietly.

'What happened? I'll tell ye what happened. Our boys were made to walk up this causeway in single file, one at a time in full view of these bloody crackshots. The enemy was nice and cosy behind this stockade, just' waitin' to pick us off. An' pick us off they did. The captain, fine young feller, shot down after just a few steps. Three lieutenants all hit. No chance. They might just as well have thrown down their arms and said, "Will ye shoot me now, please?"'

'The other side couldn't believe their eyes. Men marching up the causeway to be killed, one by one. They were brave men, staring death in the face. Or stupid men. Who can say? But I'll say this for the Americans. They were men of honour. When they saw what was happening they held their fire and they allowed us to bring in our dead. We were told these people were barbarians, the lowest of the low. Yet they behaved with great dignity and respect for our dead and wounded. What we were told was all lies, I tell ye. All lies.

'An' what was it for? We had no chance yet our bloody generals didn't seem to notice. They'll send us all to the same senseless fate. You watch. An' for what? This war is not worth fightin', laddie. It's already lost. We might as well stow our kit and sail away.'

The Scot's tirade had become treasonable. Defeatism was a cardinal sin in the army. And Ben was no longer nodding his head in approval. He couldn't afford to be allied to this kind of talk. He wanted to carry out his own private mission then go on his way. But there was no escape just yet.

'Then there was Sullivan's Island. Another disaster! We were supposed to attack but our brilliant leader had lost the track and landed us up to our arse in a swamp. And these so-called rebels, these *amateur* soldiers were there again, jus' waitin' for us. Shot to pieces we were an' so were our ships. The two biggest were damned near blown out o' the water. They'd brought down these reinforcements to Cape Fear. The *Bristol* and the *Experiment*.'

He was calming down considerably now and, having found a listener, was intent on telling his story. Ben could see he had been affected deeply and so he listened with manifest concern, not wanting to appear in any way discourteous.

'The *Bristol* lost her main mast and her captain was mortally wounded. The *Experiment* fared little better and her captain lost an arm. All of our frigates were damaged and had to run for cover and one was set on fire and abandoned. More than two hundred of our lads were killed in that crazy misguided engagement and the Americans lost no more than ten or a dozen dead. We were defeated, demoralized, humiliated. But they won't tell ye that, laddie. They won't tell ye anythin'. Oh no, we'll keep all that quiet. Well, I'll tell ye. Bloody disaster all the way. That's what it was.'

A sergeant-major appeared behind the Scot, gently easing the whisky glass from his hand. 'Come on, Jock. Bedtime. We want you fit an' well for the morning.'

The Scot laughed in a crazed way as he was hauled from his seat at the dining table and hustled away by two of his fellow NCOs. 'They want me fit an' well in the morn, so's they can send me to meet the Reaper!' he cried in Ben's direction. 'Did ye no hear that, laddie? They want me fit an' well so's I can be killed.'

The sergeant-major stayed behind and nodded at Ben. 'Too much of the bottle,' he said. 'He'll be all right tomorrow.'

Ben had arrived at the fort just after midday. He'd reported to the adjutant's office, been allocated quarters and told to report back at nine next morning. Listening to the Scot had focused his mind. 'He's seen a few campaigns,' he ventured.

The sergeant-major nodded again. 'And he'll be seeing some more any day now.'

'I only arrived today,' Ben said. 'Ben Withers. From Boston.'

He explained that he was new to the army and, though he'd been based at Boston, he hadn't seen any real action.

'Well,' the sergeant-major said. 'Can't tell you much but I can tell you this. You won't have time to get settled in here. As the colonel says, the enemy awaits.'

'I was wondering,' Ben said. 'Is there a Sergeant Duckett here?'

'Duckett?' The sergeant-major frowned. 'He a friend of yours?'

'I sort of knew him once in Boston.'

'Friends like him you won't need enemies.'

Lying in his bunk, Ben told himself that time was running out. He didn't want to find himself facing his own people in battle. He must deal with Duckett now and make his escape.

The long march south had taken its toll and the day after their arrival Colonel Putnam gave his band of rebel troops a day off. Spirits had been lifted in New York by the publication of a draft of the Declaration of Independence and though many were keen to get on with the job and go back home the city was new to them and they were curious and eager to sample its delights.

It was early in July, a hot summer's day, when Tom Blanchard, his brother Hank and Jimmy Sunshine went down to a tavern at a place called Bowling Green. The three were clearly rebel soldiers but neither Tom nor Hank was wearing a badge of office. It was the first time since being promoted that they had been able to join Jimmy without the trappings of rank.

The city was in ferment, the streets alive with the excitement of the day. It was as if there was something in the air, as if something wonderful was about to happen. Inevitably, this had brought out the drunks, the thieves, the pickpockets, the whores, and children who begged and danced in the gutter for the price of a bite to eat.

At the tavern the ale flowed fast. 'Must get myself a woman,' Hank declared after only two jugs of the landlord's 'special' brew.

Tom and Jimmy laughed. 'You talk as if you reg'lar gets yourself a woman,' Jimmy said, 'when you only ever had just the one.'

'And we don't know how that one worked out,' Tom added.

A large blowsy woman well past her best flopped herself down on Hank's knee and announced coyly, 'I'm a woman.'

'Coulda fooled me,' Jimmy said.

'You watch yer tongue, Nigger boy,' the woman hissed.

Jimmy reached for the sheathed knife he had placed on the table beside his glass. 'An' you watch your ass or I might just slice it off.'

Tom laughed to ease the tension. 'Then where would you be, eh ma'am? Out of business, I guess.'

The woman looked around for support. Niggers ought to know their place in New York and she was not going to have no Nigger talk to her that way. But at that moment a diversion arrived in the shape of two young rebel soldiers who began handing out copies of a printed sheet. Tom took one and began to read in the daytime dark of the tavern.

'What is it?' Hank asked. 'Price list for whores?'

'Declaration of Independence,' Tom read.

A quiet man at the next table nodded soberly and said, 'Read that and read it good, boys. It's just what we need.'

'It's to tell them British we is independent an' we is gonna stay that way,' another man announced.

The document had been published a few days earlier, fourth of July,

143

by order of the Second Continental Congress in Philadelphia. It was written largely by one of their leading members, a planter from Virginia named Jefferson.

Hank had a copy now and he and Tom read their respective copies in silence. 'What's it say?' Jimmy demanded in frustration.

'It's great!' Tom was enthusiastic. 'Great stuff!'

'Read it!' Jimmy urged and a small group gathered around their table in support. There were many in the tavern who couldn't read and they were all eager to know what the document contained.

The noise died down as Tom began to read and someone called out, 'Speak up, son!'

Encouraged Tom stood on a chair and by the second paragraph even the two barmen had stopped serving to listen. '*We hold these truths to be self-evident,*' he read, '*that all men are created equal; that they are endowed by their Creator with certain inalienable rights; that among these are life, liberty, and the pursuit of happiness . . .*'

The cheering broke out before Tom had finished reading and continued outside and along the unmade roads and walkways of the crowded city. As if by common assent a large crowd had gathered and become a mob bent on destruction, drawn as if by magnet to the nearby statue of George III. The low railings surrounding the large statue proved no obstacle as the mob surged forward to knock off the head. The head was heavy requiring three men to carry it back to the tavern where it was put on display. To cheers and singing the headless body was then carried off to be melted down and made into bullets.

Back in the tavern there was great hilarity. A shapeless hag of a woman was on a small stage, lifting her skirts and sticking out her naked rear for all to see as she sang a bawdy song called, 'An' it's *that* to Georgie Porgie!' The large whore had returned to Hank's knee, behaving now as if Jimmy didn't exist and a younger, slimmer girl who might have been pretty if she washed occasionally and combed her hair was clinging to Tom. She was evidently impressed that he could read and stir the crowd with the power of his words. She was gazing at him as if the words were actually his and she had fallen in love with his eloquence.

'This is quite something,' Tom said to the sober man at the next table. The words of the Declaration had affected Tom deeply and his voice felt constrained. 'Quite extraordinary.'

The man nodded in quiet agreement and Jimmy said, 'Read that bit again, Tom, That bit about the truths . . .'

Tom looked down at the printed sheet. '*We hold these truths to be self-evident . . .*'

'Yeah!' Jimmy cried. 'That's it!'

'*. . . that all men are created equal.*'

Jimmy's eyes shone as Tom read on. Maybe this war was worth fighting for, after all. Maybe a thing like this was worth dying for, he thought. And for the first time in his life Jimmy felt he was a part of the whole. All men are created equal. The governors were actually saying so. At least now, he and people like him would be allowed to live their lives with dignity. He was for that. He would fight to the death for that.

'Death to the British!' he cried out, loud and clear, and his cry was taken up. 'Death to the British!' The chant went round the tavern and nobody seemed to notice he was a Negro. They had listened to him. 'Death to the British!' he cried. 'Death to the bloodybacks!'

The quiet man at the next table caught Jimmy's eye and held up the printed sheet. 'Fine words,' he said soberly. 'But the man who wrote this owns slaves himself and I bet he has no intention of setting 'em free.'

Later, on the way back to camp, several of the boys lay drunk on the moonlit flatboard wagon, Hank among them. Jimmy, wide-awake and with a clear head, stared gloomily at the road that rolled away beneath them. Tom had also drunk rather more than he was used to but not so much that he didn't sense Jimmy's mood.

'What's got old Jimmy then?' he asked hazily.

'Ah, it's nothin'.'

'Come on,' Tom said. 'I know you.'

'Do you?' Jimmy asked, almost aggressively. 'Know me?'

'Sure I do. You're my old pal Jimmy Sunshine. And I know when something's bothering you.'

Jimmy was quiet for a moment then he said. 'Ah'm sorry, Tom. It's . . .'

Jimmy's words hung in the air.

'It's what?' Tom demanded. 'Come on, out with it.'

'It's just ah was talking to the man at the next table . . .'

Tom had noticed that beneath all the raucous behaviour, the singing and chanting in the tavern Jimmy appeared to be having an earnest conversation with the quiet man. The man had a red face and a rather large nose, Tom remembered, but his eyes were intense and somehow darkly compelling.

'He was British,' Jimmy said, his eyes wide, 'but he was with us. He told me the Quakers is right an' that slavery is all wrong.'

'Well, that's right,' Tom said.

'Yeah, an' he gave me this paper an' ah has to tell him ah can't read. That's the shame of it. Ah wanna learn to read, Tom. Ah know it ain't supposed to be allowed for Negras. But now, well, maybe this independence sez we can.'

Tom took the paper and in the moonlight, his head still fuzzy and his eyes unfocused he had difficulty at first in reading it. 'It's a pamplet,' he said at last. 'It's called *Common Sense* by some fellow called Thomas Paine.'

'Yeah,' Jimmy said, excited. 'The man sez he was called Tom.'

'I'll read it in the morning,' Tom said. 'Tell you what it says.'

'Yeah,' Jimmy said with a nod, 'but what ah really want is for me to read it for mahself.'

'Well,' Tom said magnanimously, aware even then that he might regret it in the morning, 'perhaps I could teach you.'

Jimmy gripped his arm. 'You could? You'd do that for me?'

'Yeah, sure I will,' Tom said and he lay back on the cart and closed his eyes. 'Tomorrow. We start tomorrow.'

All that summer General Washington had been preparing for the defence of the city. The news from the South was good. The British under General Clinton had failed to take Charleston in South Carolina and Clinton's now ragged and worn-out army had sailed north. General Howe had been run out of Boston, humiliated there by a strong rebel force, and the new British aim was to capture New York.

These two armies now joined forces at Staten Island to await the arrival of General Howe's brother Admiral Viscount Howe. The admiral had been appointed naval commander-in-chief in North America and his job it was, with the use of force if necessary, to restore the peace to the colonies. But General Washington was not prepared to meet him and Congress flatly refused to withdraw their Declaration of Independence.

Howe now had 30,000 troops at his disposal, many of them Germans, Hanoverian mercenaries. These troops, far more than Washington could muster, were in better shape and much better disciplined than the previous force he commanded. With ten ships and twenty frigates in support, Howe was now ready to divide and rule, to take command of New York and the Hudson River and in so doing cut off the rebels in the north from their allies in the south.

SIXTEEN

A FTER enduring a cold and miserable two week voyage to Nova Scotia, the Harvies and Sarah Dowling spent late March and most of April 1776, in Halifax. The ground was frozen, the snow lay thick and food was scarce and expensive. Housed in a less than comfortable boarding-house, sharing a freezing attic with Imelda, Sarah now questioned the wisdom of her decision. She had been adamant she would stay in Boston but when her aunt explained that unless she went with them none of them could go she had relented. Everything had been done with such haste it was only later that she asked why it was so essential she should go. Colonel Danvers, Aunt Mary told her, had insisted.

Max Harvie was still frantically pursuing his master plan and it was just before they left Boston that he perpetrated one of his most despicable acts. That night before they sailed he prevailed upon his wife to offer the coachman some light refreshment.

'Some pie perhaps,' he suggested. 'A glass of wine?'

'It's kind of you, sir,' the coachman said apologetically, 'but there's little time.'

'Half an hour,' he said, leading the coachman to the kitchen. 'No longer. I promise. There is something I must do.'

Mrs Harvie and Vanessa made up a plate of cold meat and some salad and the coachman sat at the kitchen table, resigned but grateful and ready to devour whatever he was offered.

In the hallway Harvie told his wife he was going out. He would be half an hour at the most. There was something he had to do before he left Boston. Used to accepting his instructions without question Mrs Harvie merely nodded and returned to the kitchen.

As his horse trotted down North Street Harvie saw the crowds in the side roads leading to the docks. Everyone knew the British were leaving and already those who had collaborated, openly declared their loyalty to the Crown, were stricken with anxiety. Should they stay and face the now open hositility of neighbours and the wrath of the incoming rebels or should they leave their homes, flee to the harbour and beg for a place on one of the ships that were soon to depart? The word was that the redcoats had formed a cordon round the docks area and no one was to be allowed to board until the next day, Sunday.

There had been heavy rain and the crowds had turned the unmade roads into mud. Max Harvie, high in the saddle, rode alongside the slow-moving lines, careful not to catch anyone's eye. He wanted to get to the small print shop, one of several businesses he owned, and back to his home without hindrance. But on a corner, standing disconsolately with several bemused workmen, was a man he had once employed as an overseer on one of his many building projects.

The man was an untrustworthy fellow, a troublemaker, and Harvie had found reason to sack him. Harvie turned his horse away but the man had seen him and from the sudden change in his expression it was clear he saw the situation as an opportunity to right the wrong he felt he had suffered. Harvie spurred his horse and galloped away up a narrow track that led back to the main throroughfare but here he was met by further scowls of recognition. There was much animosity towards him and men of his kind, rich men who, for their own ends, had pandered to the British, and the less fortunate people of Boston were ready and eager to let them know it.

Harvie arrived at his office to find the door broken open and the window shattered. His desk and other items of furniture had been ransacked. Two doors away was the print shop and there was a light at a window in the darkening afternoon. He hurried along the boardwalk, looked in at the window and saw his longtime employee Ezra at work, his grizzled head down over a printer's chase and a small stack of printing blocks.

'Ah, Mr Harvie. . . .' Ezra began, his face without expression.

'I'm leaving tonight, Ezra,' Harvie told him hurriedly and in his usual imperious manner. 'I'm leaving with General Howe. But I'll be back before long, have no fear.'

'Mrs Harvie and the girls going, too?' Ezra asked.

'Yes, yes, of course,' Harvie said but he didn't ask what Ezra's plans were. Ezra had a wife and three daughters but it didn't occur to Harvie to ask about them. 'We are leaving within the hour,' he went on, 'but just as soon as the British reinforcements arrive this rebel trash will be dealt with and dealt with severely. I'll be back soon and everything will return to normal.'

The previous day Ezra had received a visit from a representative of the rebel army. He had told Ezra the print shop would not be damaged. The rebels proposed to use it and to employ him. When Ezra told Harvie this Harvie had looked as if he might explode with rage but he had contained himself. If they wanted to use the print shop to print their piffling little pamphlets, he decided, then so be it. At least there would be no damage and everything would be in working order when he returned.

The man had left a list for Ezra to print, a list of rebel soldiers killed in action. He had printed a similar list of the British lost at Bunker Hill. The rebels wanted him to do the same for them.

'Do as they say, Ezra,' was Harvie's reaction. Then: 'I take it you intend to stay – if only to safeguard your future here.'

'I have nowhere else to go,' Ezra said mildly, 'and I must think of my wife and my girls.'

'With that horde descending on the town,' Max Harvie said, as insensitive as ever, 'I should lock up your daughters. You heard what happened to my niece's family.'

Ezra made no comment. The rumour was that the British were responsible for that particular act of brutality not the rebels.

'Take your pay from the money coming in and take the rest to Mr Dawkins at the bank each Thursday, there's a good fellow. And there'll be a nice little bonus for you on my return.'

What money? thought Ezra. He couldn't see the rebels paying for any work he did for them. But again he didn't comment. It was pointless with a man like Harvie.

'Now where's the list of dead they wanted?'

Ezra pointed to a small pile of printed posters. 'All done,' he said.

The previous day Harvie had written at the top of the list: *Print in alphabetical order.* He had also added two names. He looked at the finished product now, nodded in satisfaction and rolled up the top two sheets to take with him. This was what he wanted. A printed list of rebel dead that included the two names: Thomas Blanchard and Henry Blanchard.

It was 22 August, 1776. Throughout the previous night the wind had howled across Staten Island. Then, at first light, an armada of small boats carried British soldiers and German mercenaries across the dark choppy waters to Long Island. The forces under General Howe consisted of almost thirty thousand troops, seven thousand of them well drilled, disciplined mercenaries. Less than successful against what their leader had called 'amateurs', the British and German troops were eager now for battle. Bayonets fixed they sat closely packed into the small boats like tightly coiled springs ready for release.

The first batch landed unopposed. Reconnaisance groups from the rebel army drew back, torching any building that might offer shelter or cover to the incoming invaders. Then, as the British force advanced, nearing the village of Flatbush, they came under heavy fire and suffered nearly forty casualties. On the eve of the 26th, after a brief respite, they moved forward again. Attacking the rebel defences on their left they then turned in on the rear. At the same time a force of nine British battalions attacked the rebels' right. In the centre a force consisting chiefly of Germans commanded by a General von Heister attacked the main body of rebel resisitance.

The British plan of campaign was a success. The rebel soldiers were outmanoeuvred but the British lost about 400 men and twenty-one officers were killed or wounded. Rebel casualties came to more than 3,000 and there was great panic and distress as many tried to escape through swampland which proved as treacherous and unforgiving as the enemy pursuing them.

Tom and Hank Blanchard were at the head of their respective companies in the centre of the rebel defence, waiting in the wind and rain to face the full brunt of the British attack. It was their first experience of battle at close quarters and they had little idea of what they might expect. Jimmy was in Tom's company, close at first to his leader, but the rebel force quickly became fragmented and in the resultant chaos they lost contact.

The noise was deafening and the sight of relentless, running foot soldiers with murder in mind was terrifying. Tom could see a line of redcoats in their white breeches and white belts, muskets at the ready with bayonets fixed. There was enemy fire all around and though

151

many British soldiers fell dead or wounded there were simply too many of them to repulse, as they screamed madly and ran into battle, seemingly heedless of the danger they faced.

But for Tom there was no time to think, no time to contemplate death. The enemy was in close and the redcoated invaders were bayoneting at random, even running through those who turned and raised their hands in surrender. A batch of about twenty men of Tom's company broke ranks and fled and he was powerless to stop them as a group of rebels ahead also ran for cover. At this Tom gave up any hope of holding his men together for there was panic all around and his one concern now was to find his brother. He ran from side to side, searching for Hank and found him standing, still as a statue, as if transfixed as the retreating horde raced by. Tom grabbed him, turned him round and ran with him and the rest of the hurriedly retreating rebels.

A man racing between Tom and Hank, elbows raised, suddenly fell, hit in the back of the neck at close range by a shot from a musket. His scream of pain galvanized Tom and Hank and they ran as they had never run before. Whichever way they turned they could glimpse the red and white of the British or the blue of the Germans as horses, driven wild by the noise in a stampede of confusion, ran amok among the terrifed soldiers of both sides. The only escape seemed to lie ahead and into what looked like a small lake fringed by green-barked trees and marshy land.

Already many of the rebels were attempting to swim to freedom but as they were driven forward many realized the lake was no more than a treacherous swamp and turned with their hands in the air to surrender. Again several of the British soldiers ignored the obvious acts of submission and, perhaps propelled by their own fear and exultation, simply ran them through. The blood of the wounded oozed into dark red spreading stains and many fell dead as the bayonets were withdrawn and plunged again and again into by now defenceless men until a young British officer, his sword raised above his head, rode in to halt the massacre, ordering his men to stop the killing and to take prisoners.

Slowly the panic subsided and the noise, but for a random shot here and there, died to an eerie calm across the battlefield. The screams now came from the swamp where men were mired and crying for help. Tom watched open-mouthed as a rebel soldier tried to drag himself clear of the mud that gripped his knees and was dragging him down and down, to his waist, to his chest, to his shoulders. There was no escape and slowly, with a look of horror and disbelief, he sank beneath the thick grey surface.

Others in the swamp were suffering or about to suffer the same fate and Tom ran to a British officer on horseback who had a coil of rope hooked to his saddle. 'Do something, man. Throw them your rope. Let your horse drag them out.'

Surprised by Tom's spontaneous outburst the young officer, fresh from his military academy, looked down his nose at Tom and told him with a superior air, 'My dear fellow, if you wish to save them by all means do. You have my permission to embark on your mission of mercy and enter the swamp.'

Tom turned away in disgust and felt the tap of a sword on his shoulder. The young British officer leaned forward on his mount. 'May I remind you, sir, I am an officer of His Majesty the King and you are my prisoner. To turn your back on me is both ill-mannered and impertinent.'

'Lieutenant Blanchard of General Washington's Continental Army,' Tom said. 'I would remind you, sir, I am entitled to the same respect you rightly expect from me.'

The officer gave a short derisory laugh. 'We don't recognize any *continental* army or any self-styled *General* Washington.'

'You will,' Tom promised.

'Sit down, damn you.'

It was raining now, not heavily but in relentless sheets of wind that swept down from the hillside. The captured rebels had been ordered to sit close together and remain seated in the mud and they did, cold, exhausted and dejected. At the swamp the last of the drowning men had sunk beneath the surface and all was still again. Tom glared up at the young officer. 'You could have saved some of those men with that rope.'

The officer reined his horse in tightly. 'This rope is for hanging rabble and you'll be the first in line if you don't do as I say.' He leaned down and looked Tom in the eye. 'Now hold your tongue, *Lieutenant*, and sit down.'

Foot soldiers with muskets were stepping among the prisoners to relieve them of their weapons and anything worth taking. One man was ordered at gunpoint to remove his boots and the soldier who

153

threatened him tried them on, decided they were a good fit and promptly discarded his own which the robbed man hastened to retrieve. Any boot was better than none in that comfortless terrain.

In the nearby woods the British and German troops were warily stalking snipers and rounding up those in hiding. The defeat of the rebels was total and for now, at least, the British were the victors. But the British had not yet worked out what they were going to do with so many captured.

Crouching a little the lean muscular figure of a rebel soldier in grey breeches and a coarse grey shirt picked a way through the groups of sitting prisoners. Tom and Hank raised their hands in the air delighted to see that Jimmy Sunshine was alive and well.

'Sit down!' a watching guard bellowed.

But Jimmy carried on, making his way towards his friends. The British officer on horseback turned and urged his mount through the seated prisoners who quickly made way to avoid the horse's hoofs as Jimmy dived for a place beside the brothers.

On horseback the officer towered above them, his long sword aimed at Jimmy. 'You,' he said. 'What do you think you're doing?'

'Beg pardon, sah?' Jimmy responded.

'You were ordered to sit, not scamper about like a demented rabbit,' the Englishman warned him.

'Oh yes, sah,' Jimmy said, full of apology. 'Ah'm just a stupid Negra boy, sah. Ah just don't know no better.'

Some of the rebel soldiers nearby smirked and the young officer sensed that Jimmy might be making fun of him. But he was not sure how to react. 'Then sit down, you stupid fellow,' he ordered. 'Sit down and stay down or I'll run you through.'

Ben Withers had his meeting with his company commander the morning after his arrival at the legion's camp, partly because the sergeant-major had suggested that Ben might have been affected by the drunken Scot's treachery.

'You must disregard what that madman has been saying, especially about the Carolinas,' the company commander told him. 'His view is jaundiced. I understand he is upset, disappointed at his lack of progress. He has been passed over for promotion on a number of occasions. He is not a man one should allow oneself to be unduly influenced by, if you take my meaning.'

'No, sir,' Ben said. 'Of course not.'

Most of the British Army officers Ben had encountered, with the exception of homegrown Bostonians like John Foster, were irritatingly supercilious and this company commander was no less so. He also had a disconcertingly odd glint in his eye.

'What do you think of him?'

'I really don't know the man, sir.'

'No, quite so. Well, I can tell you. The man is a traitor. He's a treacherous drunkard who has no right to wear the insignia of a non-commissioned officer in His Majesty's Army.'

The glint in his eye, the hint of madness was there again. His judgement seemed more than a little harsh, thought Ben. By all accounts the man had fought hard and well in the Carolinas and no doubt he had seen many disturbing things. He'd probably had enough. But Ben knew the best course was to say nothing. This was not his problem. Yet in spite of this, he heard himself say, 'Perhaps he is just sort of . . . I don't know.'

'What?'

Ben rose to the challenge. 'Perhaps he is just suffering from battle fatigue, sir. I understand he saw a lot of action in Virginia.'

'He is a soldier, Sergeant. It is his job to see action, as you put it.' The company commander was clearly in no mood to consider any extenuating circumstances. 'He sets a bad example to the men with his constant whining and his defeatist talk. He will be tried by a field court martial and sentenced to death by firing squad – the only just fate for traitors. You must put this Fraser out of your mind; forget you ever met him.'

Fraser. So that was his name, thought Ben. The poor man had been found guilty and sentenced to death before his trial and this crazy colonel was setting him up for a firing squad. It was the colonel who was mad. Not Fraser. But the voice of reason told him not to get involved. This was not his army and the Scot was not his problem. The game he was playing was dangerous enough.

'I'm grateful that you agreed to see me, sir, so soon after my arrival,' he said, ready now to play his hand. 'Please allow me to introduce myself. I am not Sergeant Withers from the 29th at Boston Neck. I am Lieutenant Withers from Special Services here on behalf of Lord Cornwallis.'

The colonel sat up straight behind his desk. Ben, seated opposite now, leaned forward confidentially. 'I had hoped you would have received some notification of my credentials but on my way here I came across the badly mutilated body of the express messenger.'

'Badly mutilated?'

'He had been scalped, sir, and the contents of his bag scattered to the winds. The papers he was carrying would not have been of much use to the enemy, I'm pleased to say, and certainly of no use whatsoever to an Indian. They were encoded.'

The colonel was nodding.

'B3, sir,' Ben said. 'You are familiar with B3, of course, colonel?'

It was a codename Ben had invented on the spot but the colonel coughed and nodded with a grunt, anxious not to lose face.

'My instructions are to make my way behind enemy lines in New York.' Ben paused and looked around. 'Strictly for your ears only, colonel, my mission is to assassinate a certain rebel leader. I cannot say more, I'm afraid. Even to you. It is considered safer for us all at this stage that the identity of my target is not revealed.'

The colonel nodded, his eyes wide, the glint of madness bright.

'I am to leave early in the morning,' Ben said. 'My orders are to expedite this mission as soon as possible, certainly by the end of the month. I'm afraid I'm already behind schedule.'

'If we can help in any way,' the colonel said.

Ben could scarcely believe his luck. The man was totally duped. 'Thank you, sir. There is one thing.'

The colonel spread his hands to indicate his willingness to help. 'Whatever you need.'

'I am to borrow one of your senior NCOs, a Sergeant Duckett.'

'Duckett?' The colonel frowned. 'I think I know the one.'

Ben anticipated the colonel's question. 'Why him? Because I understand he is familiar with the patterns of procedure we must follow. He was once with the 29th, was he not?'

'I don't know,' the colonel said. 'He may well have been. But he may not be the man you need for this. He's not entirely reliable. Perhaps I should bring in the adjutant, find someone else.'

'No,' Ben said firmly. 'We don't want to set off any speculation, colonel. Confidentiality is everything in matters of this kind. My instructions are to collect a sergeant by the name of Duckett and I must follow these orders religiously. With your permission I will leave with Sergeant Duckett in the morning and I will report to his lordship that you provided me with the utmost co-operation.'

SEVENTEEN

ALL was calm now on the damp fields where hundreds of rebel soldiers sat quietly, cold and hungry and barely speaking as they waited for something to happen. The smoke of the battle had drifted away and been replaced by a light mist. Tom Blanchard crouched on his haunches, sucked on the rounded stem of a blade of grass and looked out across the treacherous stretch of water. A flock of wild geese had gathered on the far bank and it occurred to Tom that if someone started shooting at them they would take flight. Some would be shot but most would escape. That's what would happen to us, he thought. If we all suddenly took off some of us would be shot in the back. But most of us would escape.

The surface of the water, lightened by pale sunlight, apart from a ripple here and there, was undisturbed, a silken coverlet for the countless bodies sucked down into the underlying swamp. This was the way the world was, he told himself. Tranquillity on the surface. Carnage below.

Sentries were posted in twos at vantage points and the men of an infantry platoon were rapidly erecting tents in a field on some higher ground. To the right of the swamp and rising steeply were the wooded slopes of the hillside. Tom's thoughts were already on escape. He had no intention of suffering a long dreary march to some prison compound or wilting away here in the open, prone to the same weary inertia that seemed to have gripped most of the others. He had heard how the British treated prisoners of war. If they were not exactly maltreated they were neither fed nor watered with any frequency, coming as they did well down the list of priorities, somewhere below the battalion's horses.

Jimmy Sunshine was of the same opinion. Escape was preferable to incarceration and the sooner they escaped the better. 'Once they get us lined up in them columns they can count us an' keep us in some kinda order,' he said. 'If we're gonna go we gotta go soon.'

'And where are we going to go?' Hank asked tolerantly.

'Any place is better than this,' Jimmy said.

'Jimmy's right,' Tom said. 'Tonight. We go tonight.'

The next hour or so they spent edging their way towards the side nearest the woods. Ignoring the grumbles from those who had to move to let them through all three made it to the outer edge of the huge band of seated or sprawling rebels without once standing up.

'Where the hell you think you're goin?' one demanded, irritated at having been disturbed. Out of this lot, Hank told him. Want to come with us? The rebel soldier looked at him as if he was mad, then he moved over and allowed him to pass. 'Best of luck,' the man said. 'I reckon you're gonna need it.'

At the first opportunity Tom grabbed his brother by the arm and whispered urgently, 'We don't want a mass outbreak, Hank, and we don't carry passengers. Just the three of us OK?'

'What do you say we take a little break?' Jimmy said. 'Rest awhile. Then when it gets dark we can make a run for it.'

They were almost where they wanted to be but their movements had not gone unnoticed. A British officer on horseback rode up, brandishing his sword at Tom. 'You! You over there. Yes, you. Sit still, damn you. Don't let me see you move again.'

Dutifully Tom sat still and he stayed still until the bewigged and powdered officer turned his mount and trotted on down the line.

Many of the soldiers on both sides were tired and worn-out and long before dark they were asleep, some snoring loudly, others wrestling with their dreams, weary and dispirited after the alarms and the near death battle of the day and the long cold uneasy wait that followed.

The sun glowed, a bright red yolk just above a range of hills, and those still awake watched as it sank with quiet majesty as if bringing down a curtain on the day's events. There were few stars but those there were glistened hard and bright as the moon cast a pale light over the outstretched men.

'Funny things, aren't they?' Hank murmured.

'What?' Tom responded.

'Stars. What do you reckon they are?'

'Stars?' Jimmy said in a loud whisper. 'A preacher man once told me they was cracks in the floor of Heaven.'

Tom and Hank smiled. 'Cracks in the floor of Heaven,' Tom said. 'I like that.'

'Shut up and get some sleep,' someone nearby said.

'I do believe that sentry over there is sleeping,' Hank whispered, hunched forward on his knees in the damp grass. 'Let's go, huh?'

The three of them moved out to just a few grunts and grumbles from those they disturbed but one man sat up. 'I'm comin' with you.'

Tom shrugged. They couldn't stop the man. If he wanted to come that was up to him. So now there were four of them, moving out, ready to run, then Tom gave the order. 'Go! Let's go!'

The four figures detached themselves from the mass and ran, dark shadows running for the even darker shadows of the woods. The sentry, who had been dozing fitfully, saw them, picked up his musket and ran out and down to where they were headed.

They reached the wood a few yards ahead of him but soon found they were bunched together in a clearing. The sentry hesitated. He was reluctant to create a disturbance. If he fired a shot it would be like waking the dead. 'All right!' he barked. 'Stop right there!'

He trained his musket on the four. 'Don't move until I tell you.' He came closer. 'I want you to walk back, one at a time. All right? And there'll be no more said. I want you to go back and lie down.'

Tom shook his head almost imperceptibly at Hank and Jimmy. The other man waited, motionless. 'Ready?' Tom said. 'Go!'

All four turned and ran, zig-zagging through the trees, and the sentry hesitated, his musket poised, finger on the trigger. But he didn't shoot. He was a placid man and he didn't want any trouble. If he fired a shot the whole hillside would erupt. There would be questions and recriminations and nobody would get any sleep, including him, and his tour of duty was almost over. If he fired a shot and they still got away he'd be in trouble. So did it matter? Four of these ruffians would not be missed. He was sure of that. There were nearly 2,000 of them back there. And anyway, they would only run into swampland, probably drown. He just hoped nobody else had seen them go.

Tom and the others ran and kept on running until they realized there was no one in pursuit. Pleased with their escape yet wary of what lay ahead they carried on at a gentle jog before slowing to a walking pace in the bright moonlight.

'We need horses,' Tom said.

'Yeah,' Hank said. 'I could eat one right now.'

Round a bend in the road the low outline of a farmhouse came into view. The four approached it quietly, unsure of their reception. The front door was open. Tom knocked but there was no one about. They went inside, looked in every room. The owners, they decided, must have fled when that morning's battle commenced. By the light of the moon through a window they found bread and milk and a platter of cheese which they shared equally and devoured in seconds.

Out back there was a stable with a small corral and just one horse. The horse looked well cared for and automatically, as if out of habit, Jimmy filled the trough with water from a pump. A well-worn saddle hung behind the stable door.

Inside the farmhouse looked as though it had been abandoned in a hurry and the four were grateful now for the shelter. They had decided they would rest here until morning and Hank had already stretched himself full length on the main bed.

For the first time Tom had an opportunity to scrutinize their uninvited companion. He was not a young man. About forty, Tom guessed. He looked tired, his eyes watery and his beard in need of a trim, which was understandable. But he also had the sagging shoulders of defeat and dejection in his demeanour.

He saw Tom was looking at him and he decided it was time to speak. 'This war is over for me, boys,' he said. 'I'm going home.'

'And where's home?' Hank asked, sitting up.

'Way up north,' he said. 'I've just had enough.'

'But this was one battle,' Tom told him. 'All right, so we lost. But we had the beating of them in the south. We kicked them out of Boston. And they haven't got New York City yet. Why, this is only the beginning.'

The man shook his head. 'Not for me it ain't.'

'You can't give up now,' Tom said. 'None of us can.'

'Washington's army is no match for the British,' the older man said. 'They got warships in the East River. They got control of the Hudson. They got reinforcements – more of them Goddamned Germans – on the way. Washington don't stand a chance.'

'Ah guess it's a good thing we don't all think like you,' Jimmy said, addressing the man for the first time.

The man looked at him sharply, a new faintly hostile look in his tired eyes. He was not sure who this Negra boy was, what was his standing or why he was with them. One thing was certain. He was not used to being spoken to in this way by a Negra.

Tom, sensing trouble, said with a smile, 'We've got to win now. Right is on our side. You seen the Declaration?'

'I seen those fancy notices before,' the man said. 'All these high flyin' ideas are fine. But who wins the war is what matters in the end. Not some piece of paper.'

'Well then, sir,' Tom said, 'we wish you well.' Hank and Jimmy nodded and Tom went on, 'We offer you our very best wishes for the future to you and yours, but if that is the way you're thinking we don't want you with us. At daybreak we say goodbye. You go your way, we go ours and no hard feelings. If you change your mind we're heading for the river and you're welcome to join us. As far as we know General Washington still holds Brooklyn Heights and that's where we're heading. We're going to join up again and we're going to win this war, come what may.'

The man merely nodded and started to make a bed on the floor. It was still cold in the farmhouse but much better out of the wind and the rain and they slept soundly. At least three of them did until they were awakened by the whinny of a horse and the pounding of hoofs. All three rushed to the window in time to see the quiet man riding off into the night on the only available mount.

In Halifax there was little news. General Howe and his men had sailed for Long Island. At the garrison only a token force remained. There was no one of any real authority Max Harvie could ask about the progress of the war.

Sarah was taking a lead from her Aunt Mary and doing her best to stay optimistic, but Imelda was difficult and it was not entirely her fault. She was not as sturdy as Sarah and she had little resistance to the cold. Her face was pinched, her nose was red and runny and she was thoroughly miserable.

'I heard they don't have spring in Nova Scotia,' she whined, as she sat huddled by the fire, 'and I wouldn't be surprised if they don't have summer either.'

She was constantly asking Sarah to stoke up the fire, but Sarah told her every time, 'We have to conserve the logs. Uncle Max says they are getting scarce now like everything else.'

161

Sarah was sorry for her cousin but she was glad when Imelda fell asleep and she could sit quietly by the fire and look for pictures in the flames. She had done this since she was a little girl and her mother's maid, Pansy, had told her if you look in the flames on a cold day you will see pictures.

So much had happened since then. When she was a little girl her life was good. She was happy and she had everything she needed. Her pony and then her horse. Her mother, her father. The tears welled up and she knew she mustn't think about her family and what had happened to them. She thought instead of Joseph and Pansy. Joseph was a lovely man. He'd known her since she was a baby. And Pansy. Pansy was her friend.

There were tears, too, when she thought of Pansy, that lovely black face and those bright shining eyes. Pansy had a little boy whose name was Joshua but everyone called him Buzz. Sarah wondered what had happened to him. She'd heard he'd gone to work at the Mabbuts' place but she didn't really know them. She just hoped they were treating him kindly. For some time now she'd had a notion, a plan she hoped she could carry out one day. She would get a place of her own and she would find the little boy Buzz and bring him to live with her, take good care of him as Pansy would have wanted. And if she was married, married to someone like Tom Blanchard, she could have children of her own and they could all live together and be happy.

She thought of Tom and that evening at the Harvies' when they walked around the garden. She looked in the fire and saw that big room and heard the music, the lilt of the two-step and Imelda taking over, changing dance cards, and John Foster towering over her and Tom trying to butt in, so stupid and clumsy and red-faced, but she was drawn to him. She just knew then that he was the one and she felt a glow now, just remembering. It was love at first sight. Mad, crazy, but that's what it was.

Imelda stirred and Sarah poked at the fire to turn a log. Their world was in turmoil and terrible things were happening but she knew she must not complain. So many people were much worse off. She had Aunt Mary and Aunt Mary really cared about other people. Not like Uncle Max. All Uncle Max really cared about was himself and his social standing.

The night they left Boston Aunt Mary told him he should say something to Vanessa and Alfred, some words of comfort and assurance. He had said a few hurried words. *They mustn't worry. He would soon be back.* That sort of thing. But the servants knew they had little to fear from the rebels. And they were not stupid. They also knew that allowing them to remain in the house might save the place from going up in flames.

The coach ride to the ship had taken longer and was much more tortuous than it might have been had Uncle Max not delayed their departure. Huddled back in their seats they found the journey to the dockside terrifying. The unmade, ill-lit streets of Boston could be a daunting prospect in ordinary times but now they were choked by the less fortunate, all heading in the same direction. Whole families, children, parents, grandparents, gripping what possessions they could carry, struggled fearfully towards the dock where a space aboard a ship might or might not accommodate them. Groups of men, many the worse for drink, were gathered at street corners, ready to peel away to rob or molest the most vulnerable. Once, as a young woman was lifted bodily by two reeling men and carried into an alleyway, kicking and screaming and clearly fighting a losing battle, Imelda cried out in fear. Cowering back in their dark interior Sarah and Imelda saw hostile eyes turn towards them and felt the angry rocking of the coach. Only the coachman's whip, the threat of his co-driver's musket and the flailing hoofs of the rearing horses kept the anxious malcontents at bay.

The dockside was no less congested. Long queues had formed desperately hoping to board a vessel out of the driving rain and out of the dangerous cauldron their city had become. The coach trundled at last into a restricted area and the coachman and his assistant helped Max Harvie and his family down the two steps as a seaman came forward to carry their baggage. A dour-faced first mate barred their way until the coachman invoked the name of Colonel Danvers. Heads down now against the wind and the rain they were led up the slatted gangway and, as they stepped aboard thankfully, Sarah looked back at the chaos.

The days were long now with no news and all Sarah could do was wait. The fire had burned low. Time for another log.

'I'm cold,' Imelda said, waking up and pulling her shawl tight about her shoulders. 'Look at the fire. You don't care, do you?'

Sarah built the fire up. 'You're the one who doesn't care. What about our friends? Where are they? What's happened to them?'

'Who do you mean?' Imelda asked, a silk handkerchief at her nose as she blinked at Sarah with watery eyes.

'Melanie. Ben.'

'Melanie will be at home in Boston, praying for Ben's return, and Ben will be doing his duty, fighting to put things right and get us all back to normal.'

'And your intended?' Sarah asked with a mischievous smile. 'Henry Blanchard.'

'He is not my intended. Not any more. Henry Blanchard is a traitor. I don't even want to think about him.' Imelda looked at Sarah sharply. 'And neither do you. What you really want to know is what happened to his brother. Well, he's a traitor, too. You must forget him, Sarah. Put him out of your mind. You mustn't care about *him*.'

Sarah merely smiled. She did care about Tom Blanchard and every day and every night she thought about him, about where he was and what he was doing, and how when the war was over they would be together again. But Max Harvie and his friend Jack Danvers had other ideas for Miss Sarah Dowling and the course of her life was soon to take another direction.

'This is Lieutenant Withers,' the colonel said.

The young adjutant looked at Ben and his sergeant's stripes.

Ben smiled. 'Lieutenant Withers, Special Services. I'm here incognito, masquerading as a sergeant.'

'I see,' the adjutant said.

'We can't tell you much, in fact, we can't tell you anything,' the colonel said airily, 'about Lieutenant Withers' mission save to say he is to take with him one of our sergeants.'

'A Sergeant Duckett,' Ben said.

The adjutant raised his eyebrows. 'Duckett?'

'Does this pose a problem for you?' Ben asked.

'Well, it's not for me to say. . . .'

'No, please,' Ben said. 'If there's something I should know . . .'

The adjutant looked at the colonel.

'Go on, man,' the colonel said. 'Say what you have to say. I've already told Lieutenant Withers that this Duckett is a menace and has been all the time he's been with us. In fact, we'll be glad to be rid of him.'

'What has he done?' Ben asked.

'There was some trouble locally,' the adjutant said. 'Duckett was in a tavern in a village Crosswicks way and he was causing trouble with the locals. It seems he got into an argument playing cards with some of the local men and they threw him out. But, foolishly, he went back with his musket and, we're not sure what happened, but he shot and killed a little boy. He had to be rescued and now he's under investigation. It was very bad for the regiment.'

'Then perhaps it will be a good thing if I take him away for a couple of weeks.'

'Perhaps,' the adjutant agreed and he added, 'I'd say he's lucky to be alive. If he sets foot around there again the whole village will slaughter him. They want him to hang for murder.'

EIGHTEEN

THE war now was at a critical stage. Washington's army of rebels had suffered a serious and demoralizing defeat. Out-manoeuvred and overrun, those who could had retreated and regrouped on Brooklyn Heights where Washington gave the order for all the men under his command to be evacuated across the river to Manhattan Island.

The three escaped prisoners of war were saddened by what they saw. They were tired, worn out from walking night after night, unsure of the route they had taken, aware that at any time they might run into a contingent of British or German soldiers. But they were not so utterly dejected as the columns of weary men they joined at the waterfront where countless small boats were gathered to carry them to temporary safety.

Sodden feet slowed to a shuffle. Heads dropped against the wind and the incessant rain. Weapons were clogged with mud, powder was rendered wet and useless and an aura of defeat hung over the whole operation. In fours they stepped forward through the puddles and the pounding rainwater and climbed aboard the rocking and sliding boats that bumped alongside the jetty. Each boat was filled to capacity and sometimes a boatman would refuse to sail until the load had been lightened and one or two of the men stepped back ashore.

Dawn was coming up and the scale of the retreat would soon be revealed to the British. But that day good fortune was on the side of the rebels. At daybreak a heavy mist appeared and cloaked their movements. Before the British look-out men and their advance guard could report back, all of the rebel soldiers and what equipment they had saved had been transported across the East River.

Tom Blanchard sat in the prow of a fishing boat and reflected on the way things had turned out. The battle, if that's what it was, had been a wild, disorganized disaster in which no one on the rebel side had given orders or co-ordinated a defence or attack. No one had taken command. In fact, both sides had hit out in a wild panic like two pugilists, both lacking in skill, flailing away at each other until inevitably the bigger and the stronger of the two found the sheer brute force to overcome his opponent. Or that was the way it seemed to Tom. The British claimed later their superior tactics and skill at outflanking the enemy won the day and this was true. The rebels had lost over 3,000 men. A further 2,000 had been taken prisoner and many of those who died had drowned in the treacherous swamp that cut off their retreat.

It was now that the British made a disastrous tactical error. If they had followed the rebels across the East River, as many of their officers wanted to do, and continued their advance the war might well have been over and won. But the British, perhaps with the heavy loss of life incurred at Bunker Hill in mind, did not follow. Commendably, General Howe harboured the hope that the war might be won without further bloodshed. As he told his detractors, he did not wish to kill 'good' Americans. He merely wanted to rid the country of the 'bad' few, bring these pointless battles to an amicable end and restore the previous status quo. His estimate of the strength of feeling in the country turned out to be woefully wrong.

For the rebels the war did seem lost. Royal Navy ships patrolled both the East River and the Hudson and, despite their miraculous escape, the rebels were at this point totally defeated. Convinced the war was lost, many of Washington's men simply went home. Others, with looting and robbery in mind, stayed in New York.

For the next two weeks there was an uneasy lull with nothing much happening on either side. Then, in mid-September, with the Royal Navy bombarding the rebel camps, the British crossed the East River and landed in Manhattan at a place called Kipp's Bay. The constant barrage from the ships was a success and the comparitively small British advance force quickly established a strong position where they could await reinforcements. In the course of this encounter the rebel army again proved unreliable and made a hurried retreat in a disorderly run for cover.

Once more many of the rebel soldiers, about 800 men, surrendered and were taken prisoner. But Washington succeeded in regrouping his

167

disorganized force and took up a position on Harlem Heights. The British, unopposed, entered New York to a tumultuous welcome as Loyalists flooded the streets, marking the homes and properties of known rebels with a large letter R and waving replicas of the British flag. But no sooner had the British occupied the city than a fire broke out in a timber yard.

No alarms could be sounded. The usual method of ringing church bells was not possible because nearly all the bells had been melted down to provide ammunition. The flames quickly spread, unchecked, through the narrow streets and alleyways and before the fire could be brought under control more than 400 buildings were destroyed.

The British, naturally, suspected this was the work of rebels left behind in the retreat for this specific purpose. Whether the fire was started by rebel soldiers or their sympathizers was difficult, if not impossible, to determine. But several men were caught in possession of matches and fireballs. One man was apprehended as he lit a firebomb and was promptly thrown into the flames. Others were shot or hanged on the spot. But the fires delayed the British advance and again Washington was afforded precious time to reorganize his dwindling army.

This time Washington was so disgusted and so disappointed with the behaviour of the men under his command he lost his legendary patience. 'Good God Almighty!' he exclaimed, at the depleted ranks of hangdog men. 'Have I such troops as these?'

It was mid-October before the British began a new offensive. On opposite sides of the Hudson, Washington had set up two garrisons, one at Fort Lee, the other at Fort Washington. In addition, a series of entrenchments along the Bronx River as far as the small settlement of White Plains was created. The plan was to defend steadfastly every step of the way.

The battle, begun on 28 October, proved to be the fiercest yet. This time Washington's men stood their ground, repulsing the first onslaught which came from a detachment of German mercenaries. The British advanced in solid columns. Cannon, howitzers and mortars rent the air in a deafening crescendo of exploding shellfire peppered with the crack of muskets, and the surrounding hillsides smoked as though on fire.

Men lay dead or wounded, their bodies broken, many with arms and legs shattered or blown off. One man had caught the full force of a cannonball in his gut, another ball had taken out a man's hip bone. And slowly, relentlessly, the British advanced, only coming to a halt at noon the next day.

By 31 October the British were ready to make a final onslaught, but heavy rain delayed them yet again. The British advance had cut off the rebel strongholds at Fort Washington and Fort Lee. On 15 November a drummer and a soldier carrying a white flag were despatched with an invitation to the commander of Fort Washington to surrender in order to avoid further loss of life. If the commander refused, the message added, when the fort was taken, as it undoubtedly would be, no one would be spared. The colonel in command of the fort replied that he and his men were fighting 'for the most glorious cause mankind ever fought in' and they would 'fight to the last'.

Without further delay the British attacked on four fronts strongly supported by a continual bombardment from a navy warship in the Hudson. At last, surrounded by heavy artillery and troops with fixed bayonets, the rebel colonel sent out a flag of surrender. Over 2,500 prisoners were taken and a large store of ammunition and guns were commandeered.

The British now had the whole of Manhattan Island and they lost little time in knocking out the other rebel stronghold at Fort Lee. So savage and swift was the attack on Fort Lee that the rebel company entrenched there had little time to escape. But escape most of them did, leaving pots still boiling on camp-fires, tables laid for the officers' dinner and weapons and equipment they could ill afford to lose. Only twelve men, all of them drunk and incapable, remained as the British overran the fort.

Washington and what remained of his rebel army were pursued as far as Princeton. By the time he crossed the Delaware River at Trenton many of these men had deserted. It seemed clear now that the British, with their superior forces, their command of New York and the news that they had captured Rhode Island unopposed, were set to end the war victorious. All but a few on both sides believed the rebel uprising had at last been put down.

Tom with Hank and Jimmy had been with Washington's main force since the retreat from Brooklyn Heights and never once had they harboured a thought of leaving. But all three had been changed irrevocably by what they witnessed in the closely fought battles along the way. The taste of fear, the stench of death, the sight of indescribable mutilation had led to a numbing of the senses. Exhausted, inured now to the horrors of the battlefield, they snatched at bouts of sleep at every opportunity.

Of the three Jimmy had survived the best. He appeared to have gained in stature and authority. His colonel had noticed his resilience and selfless dedication under fire and there was little doubt if he had not been a Negro promotion would have rapidly come his way.

Jimmy it was who rallied the men in his platoon with good-natured jibes. Jimmy it was who laughed and sang in the face of weariness and depression. And when someone called him 'a crazy Nigger' it was in a friendly way, there was good-natured inclusive laughter and Jimmy was not offended. But Jimmy was no clown. Jimmy it was who urged the men forward in battle, and Jimmy it was who soothed their nerves and cajoled and restored their pride and enthusiasm. And the men it was who protected him from any hint of prejudice.

'We is independent, boys,' he cried. 'We have our Dec'aration an', by the good God Almighty, we're goin' to fight to keep it. No bloodyback is gonna take that from us. No, sah.'

Max Harvie was not happy. In Halifax he had no power, no position, no influence and very little money. All his important contacts had gone south with Howe and though the general feeling was that the war would soon be over he had no news of how it was progressing. Then, one afternoon in the dingy boarding-house where he and Mrs Harvie and the girls were living, he had a visitor.

Jack Danvers had been recalled from New York where he had been based since the British marched in. Max Harvie was delighted to see him and still more delighted with the news he brought. General Howe had routed the 'rabble' army, as Danvers liked to call it, on every front and everyone knew this man Washington and his motley mob of renegades were demoralized and defeated. Summer would flush them out and there would be an end to all this nonsense once and for all.

'Does this mean we can return to Boston?' Harvie asked.

'Yes, of course,' Danvers said. 'But not just yet. As soon as hostilities cease and that can't be long now. But don't look so disappointed, Max. I have news, good news, for you. You will need to stay a little longer here, in Halifax, but not in this miserable hole.' He looked around, wrinkling his nose at the dark shabby room. 'I have secured for you and Mrs Harvie, and for your daughter and niece, rooms at the Grand Hotel.'

'The Grand Hotel!' Harvie was impressed The Grand was the best hotel in Halifax. In fact, it was the only hotel of any distinction. But, as far as Harvie knew, it had been taken over completely as officers' quarters and, on the ground floor, the army's administration offices. 'But I thought General Howe had commandeered the Grand.'

'He has,' Danvers confirmed. 'But that doesn't mean we can't find respectable accommodation for a close friend and ally. I told the general I was not happy with the quarters you were having to endure and I suggested rooms at the hotel should be made available to you. I'm sure you will be much happier there.'

'You are too kind, Colonel, and I hope you will convey my heartfelt thanks to General Howe. But with no income coming in from my various businesses at present, funds are – how shall I say? – in short supply. I doubt that I could afford the Grand.'

Danvers waved his hand airily. 'Ah, nonsense, my dear Max. The accommodation is free, gratis, compliments of His Majesty.'

Harvie preened himself, genuinely flattered. 'I . . . I don't know what to say.'

'Then just say yes and move in as soon as it is convenient.'

Harvie was overcome. 'This is excellent news. Mrs Harvie will be delighted. Colonel Danvers, I am forever in your debt.'

'No, no,' Danvers said, 'not at all. Although there *is* something.'

'Anything,' Harvie offered.

'I have been recalled to England to take up a new appointment. I will be leaving at the end of the month. The appointment is as an equerry at His Majesty's court.'

'Really?' Harvie was deeply impressed. 'You are to work for His Majesty? But that's splendid news!'

Danvers' dark eyes were smiling. 'Strictly between ourselves, Max. I should not be telling you this, not before it has actually been announced, but I am to receive a knighthood.'

'Oh, my dear fellow, my heartiest congratulations. Colonel Sir Jack Danvers! Splendid! Splendid!'

'However,' Danvers told him, 'as I said, there *is* something, a little, as yet, unresolved problem. The position I am to take up requires that I am married, Max. I have to find a wife, a young lady who will, indeed, become a titled lady when we are married.'

171

'Lady Danvers,' Max said, his eyes shining.

'Precisely,' Danvers said.

Max Harvie's scheming mind was racing ahead. 'And is there someone?' he asked quietly.

'I have a young lady in mind,' Danvers said, with a smile.

'Colonel?'

'Come on, Max. You must know who I mean. Your niece, Sarah, of course. I need your help to become better acquainted with the young lady. I am sure she would make an excellent lady at court and I really am quite taken with her.'

Max nodded. 'Leave it to me, colonel.'

'I think it's time you called me Jack,' Danvers said.

Harvie couldn't wait to tell his wife the good news. He found Aunt Mary two doors away with the girls. 'Be ready to move, ladies,' he told them exuberantly. 'We are to leave here at last.'

'We're going home?' Sarah asked.

'Yes, oh yes. But not yet. The war is almost over. The rebels are defeated and soon we can go back. But for now we are to move to far more salubrious surroundings. We are going to live at the Grand. The Grand Hotel!'

'Oh lovely,' Imelda said. 'All those handsome British officers . . .'

Aunt Mary was quiet, wanting to discuss this with her husband alone, find out what was really going on.

'So the war will soon be over?' Sarah asked.

'The rebel army has been defeated on every front.' Her uncle repeated what Colonel Danvers had told him. 'They are totally demoralized. Have no fear, as soon as the weather improves they will be flushed out and dealt with once and for all.'

'What will happen to them?' Sarah asked.

Harvie dismissed this with a wave of his hand. 'I don't know. I expect they will get what they deserve. Now be ready to leave here in the morning. Mother and I will go to the Grand today, secure our new accommodation.'

Back in their own room Aunt Mary questioned her husband closely. She always suspected Max and his often devious way of doing things. Nothing was ever quite so straightforward as he made out. He told her of Colonel Danvers' visit, referring to him now with a new familiarity as 'Jack'.

'General Howe,' he said, 'is just waiting for the summer and then he will bring an end to the war and all the nonsense that's gone with it. The people don't want this rebellion, Mary. They never wanted it. Why, Jack told me that when they marched into New York the city streets were filled with cheering crowds, waving the British flag. It's all over, Mary, bar the shouting.'

'What a terrible waste of young lives,' Aunt Mary said. 'So sad. All those fine young men.' She looked at her husband squarely. 'On *both* sides, Max. All those fine American boys, dead or mutilated.'

'Ah yes,' Max felt that this was his cue, the right moment. He went to his small hide despatch case. 'I think now might be the time to show Imelda this.'

'What is it?'

He drew out the rolled poster Ezra had printed for him in Boston. 'The rebel army took over my printing plant.'

'What about Ezra?'

'Oh, Ezra will be all right. They need him to work the press. They want to print bulletins apparently and lists of their own people killed or missing similar to the notices we printed of British casualties. It's all propaganda, I suppose, to show their supporters the sacrifices they're making.'

'Max, these are mere boys. Many of them we knew. They have been to our home. You can't just dismiss them.'

Harvie unrolled the poster. 'I didn't want to have to show this to Imelda,' he said. 'There was a time when she was quite fond of young Henry Blanchard.'

He held up the poster for her to read and her hand went to her mouth. 'Oh no. That poor boy. Henry Blanchard, dead. And Tom. Tom Blanchard, too. Their poor mother . . .'

'I think it would be better if you told Imelda, Mary,' Harvie said. 'She might be quite upset. Although she may not be as affected as she once might have been.'

Harvie decided to keep the rest of his news to himself. Let the girls absorb and recover from the news of the Blanchard brothers' untimely deaths. Imelda, he knew, would be only superficially affected. Mild histrionics, perhaps. but no more than that. Sarah was the one. She had to understand she must forget this Tom Blanchard. Her future lay elsewhere. But he would wait a day or two, he decided. Let her get over this, then he could bring up the pressing subject of Jack Danvers and his search for a suitable wife.

The war was going badly for the rebels and the news of the fall of New York came as a shock to Ben Withers. Ben's own personal goal was in touching distance and if he accomplished what he had set out to do he could throw off this offensive red coat he found it necessary to wear and join his friends and his comrades in the rebel army where he belonged.

With any luck, he told himself, by tomorrow evening he could be crossing the country in search of General Washington's army. But even this was not what he really wanted. All he really wanted was to return home to Melanie. That was all. That and an end to all hostilities. With so many men dead or maimed for life on both sides there were too many losers. But nobody ever wins this kind of war, he decided. If there has to be a war it should be a war of words – no more than that.

Yet he couldn't reconcile this with his own private war against this man Duckett. He had to make the man acknowledge what he had done then kill him. It was irrational, perhaps, but with Ben the need to do this had become an obsession. The memory of what happened that day in the woods near home when he was a boy would haunt him for the rest of his life unless he did something to expunge it. Even then, he knew, the pain of it would never really go away. He tried not to think about it but often, when all was quiet and he was alone, the sounds, that whimper, the full horror of that day would return.

Ben wanted to get the deed done and done quickly but now there was to be a further delay. The adjutant had joined him at breakfast in the officers' mess. 'You were hoping to leave today but I'm afraid it can't be done, old chap. I understand the CO is back this afternoon and he wants to see you.'

'The CO? But the colonel . . .'

'Is not the CO.' The adjutant smiled. 'Colonel Miller is a sort of supernumerary. Nominally in charge when the CO is away.'

'I see,' Ben said, trying to hide his frustration.

'The real CO is Lieutenant Colonel Tarleton.' The adjutant said this as though the name held some special significance.

'Tarleton?' Ben said.

'You must have heard of Colonel Tarleton,' the adjutant said. 'Everybody else has.'

Ben smiled. He liked the rather worldly-wise adjutant. Without actually saying so he seemed to view the whole business of army life and its hierarchies as some mildly amusing pantomime.

'Colonel Tarleton has quite a reputation.'

'For what?' Ben asked.

'For everything. He has distinguished himself in battle and in many ways. Why, as a young officer it was he who captured one of the rebel army's top men, a General Lee. Caught him with his pants down, so to speak.'

Ben raised his eyebrows.

'This General Lee was relaxing in a tavern, a bawdy house by all accounts. Quite a blow for the rebels and quite a coup for Colonel Tarleton. But his exploits are well known on and off the field. It is said that he has killed more men and bedded more women than any other officer past or present.'

'Said by whom?' Ben asked.

The adjutant's eyes twinkled but he made no comment.

'So what would the good colonel want with me?'

'I suspect he wants to hear your story from you yourself. And he'll need some convincing to release one of his sergeants.'

Ben could only wait. He had been keyed up and ready to go. Now he had more time on his hands. But one thing he intended to do before he left was say goodbye to Fraser. He left the mess and strolled over to the tent where the Scot, Sergeant Fraser, was held under armed guard. The guard who had been sitting cross-legged on the grass, dozing in the weak mid-morning sun, jumped to his feet.

'Lieutenant Withers,' Ben said, though he was not wearing a uniform or offering any badge of authority. 'Permission of the CO,' he added and went through the flap.

Inside, Fraser was at a small field table, sitting astride a stool. He looked up as Ben entered. 'And what do you want?' he asked in his usual no nonsense manner.

'I expect to move out today,' Ben said. 'I came to say goodbye.'

'Is that so?' Fraser said. 'I'm moving out today, too. So goodbye.'

There was a voice outside and a young officer ducked in at the flap. He glanced sheepishly at Ben and handed Fraser a gun box. Then he stepped back, saluted smartly and left with what looked like indecent haste.

'Ach, the poor laddie's embarrassed,' Fraser said.

Ben's eyes asked what the gun box was for.

'Like I said,' Fraser told him. 'I'm moving out, too. I called for a pistol. And the regiment was quick to oblige.'

It was a custom of the regiment. An officer accused of cowardice or treason or some similarly reprehensible act could opt for suicide rather than face a court martial. In that way there would be no trial and no conviction and there would be no record of the disgrace at home. He would simply be listed as a casualty of war. His fellow officers would remain silent and any benefits that might be due to his dependants would be paid as if he had died in battle.

'You can't do that,' Ben said when Fraser explained. 'You must stand trial. You could be found innocent.'

Fraser laughed aloud. 'But I'm not innocent. Colonel Tarleton is a tart, General Howe is a fornicating fool and the King of England is a pot-bellied lunatic.'

Ben smiled. 'How do you know these things?'

Fraser looked at him curiously. 'I'm beginning to wonder about you, laddie. Where have ye been? Ye only have to look at this Tarleton and everybody knows Howe has been knocking off Mrs Loring for years and the King, well . . .' He was lost for words.

'I wouldn't have put you down as a gossip, Fraser.'

'All right. So ye want some real treason. Well, the British have no right to be here and the sooner they admit it and get out the better. There! I've said it all again and I'll go on saying it.'

Ben smiled at the man's bravado. He appeared to have a death wish. And though he agreed with every word of Fraser's treason and would have liked to have said so openly he was not yet ready to die. He had too much unfinished business. 'Listen,' he said, 'why give up? Why don't you try to escape?' He lowered his voice. 'Perhaps I could help.'

'Steady now!' Fraser warned. 'You're an officer of the Crown, Lieutenant Withers. Ye canna allow yourself to get mixed up with someone like me. Go on your way, laddie. Live your life.'

'But you could start again. America is a big country. You could lose yourself here.'

'I could be an Indian chief. I could wear a kilt and a sporran and I could lead the tribe into battle with my bagpipes.'

'I'm serious.' Ben said.

'Ach, I've already lost myself. And I wouldn't want to start again. All I know is soldiering, son. It's all I've ever done. And anyway, I've just had enough.'

176

'I wish I could help.'

'You go on your way, son, and take good care o' yourself. An' when all this is over you get out. Go home, find yourself a nice lassie to keep ye warm in bed o' nights. Have lots o' wee bairns an' name one of 'em after me. Angus. Angus Fraser. Tell the wee laddie about this mad Scotsman ye once knew.' He opened the gun box. The polished pistol in the velvet gun-shaped well shone in the light from the tent lamp. 'I'll say goodbye now,' he said. 'An' I wish ye luck in all that lies ahead.'

It was ridiculous, Ben told himself. He had only known Fraser since the day before yet he couldn't trust himself to speak. He embraced the Scot, stepped back and nodded once as a tear pricked his eye. Then he turned and left the tent.

Moments later, as he strode across the grass, he heard the shot.

NINETEEN

THAT winter General Washington was almost in despair at the state of his rebel army. Many men had deserted and still more were ready to leave just as soon as the term of their enlistment was up. But the Blanchard boys and Jimmy, as eager to fight and win this war as ever, were still there and they were present the day the general called his men together at his headquarters on the Delaware.

It was a cold, chill December day and the mood of the men was sombre. Most were poorly clad and many had holes in their shoes or, in some cases, no shoes at all. Thievery and corruption was rife in the ranks and the reputation of the rebel army had sunk amongst the populace to its lowest ebb. They were poorly drilled, a ragged lot with many marching out of step, their sullen, defeated faces reflecting their mood. They'd had enough of war and though drums beat to rally support there was little response.

'My brave fellows,' General Washington began, addressing the men from his horse, 'you have done all I asked you to do, and more than could be reasonably expected. But your country is at stake, your wives, your homes, and all you hold dear. You have worn yourselves out with fatigues and hardships, but we know not how to spare you. If you will consent to stay for one month longer, you will render that service to the cause of liberty, and to your country, which you probably never can do under any other circumstances.'

The drums beat again and this time many of the men who had been moved by the general's words and the kindly, affectionate way he had addressed them were ready to respond.

Tom looked at Hank and then at Jimmy. Maybe the war was not lost. Not yet anyway. 'I'm staying,' he said.

A soldier nearby said, 'So'm I.'

Another said, 'I ain't no quitter.'

Several men stepped forward, others followed and soon most of those who were fit enough and some who weren't had elected to stay. The general with his kind and considerate words had created a new mood. But his army was still in a sorry state and the ragged appearance of the men, their 'uniforms' worn and limp, their faces pale and drawn, was hardly an incentive for new recruits. Yet new recruits were sorely needed.

General Washington, who by now had less than 3,000 men, exhorted Congress to raise an army of volunteers and to persuade young gentlemen of good character to enlist as officers. Congress agreed but the raising of such an army would inevitably take time and for the general time was running out.

Tom and Hank were called before their colonel later that day. They'd lost the companies under their command because they'd been unable to maintain control in the wholesale panic of the battle on Long Island and they admitted as much to the colonel.

'You will do better next time,' was all he said.

'But we failed, sir,' Hank insisted.

'You didn't fail, son,' the colonel told him. 'You escaped. You rejoined your regiment. You showed resilience, resourcefulness and, in that way, you gained experience. We are regrouping and you, gentlemen, will lead new companies, four platoons of volunteers each. I want you to knock them into shape, make something of them.'

'Yes, sir,' Tom said and he saluted smartly. Hank followed suit. Then they looked at each other.

'Something else?' the colonel asked.

'We were wondering, sir,' Tom said, 'if you would consider our friend Private Sunshine. He's been with us every step of the way.'

'And he proved himself a far better soldier than either of us,' Hank said. 'He'd make a fine offficer.'

The colonel, a fair-minded man, listened politely. He'd heard excellent reports of the Negro private, he said at last, of his valour under fire, his good spirits under the most difficult of conditions and of the high esteem in which he was held by his fellow men. 'I hear what you say of him,' he told the brothers, 'but I can't make any promises.' He stood up from behind his desk and shook them both by the hand. 'You will receive your orders later today.'

General Washington was deeply concerned now that the British would target Philadelphia. A diversion was needed and a victory, however small, to boost the flagging morale of his troops. About 500 men under the command of Major General Gates and a number of new volunteers had joined the rebel army to make up a force of about 6,000 men.

It was on Christmas night that Washington chose to attack Trenton where an arrogant and dismissive German colonel was in command of a regiment of mercenaries. The Germans were inclined to make much of Christmas with lots of dancing and carousing and Washington guessed correctly they would not, next day, be in a fit condition to fight.

Despite the sleet and heavy rain that night Washington's men ferried through the icy waters of the Delaware and marched towards their target. The colonel believed he could easily put these 'amateurs' down and refused to prepare his defences. If they came, he said, he would despatch them with bayonets.

Early next morning, despite a biting wind, Washington's men were in place and ready to attack Trenton. The German colonel, who had been drinking heavily the night before, rushed from his bed to summon his men and was killed in the street fighting that had already broken out. By that evening Washington had gained a notable victory. Over a thousand mercenaries had been captured along with, to the delight of the rebels, large quantities of rum.

The British in Princeton were stunned by this setback and an army, 7,000 strong, promptly set off to finish the rebels once and for all. It was a ten mile march along difficult muddy roads and they decided to delay their attack until morning. The river was frozen preventing the passage of boats but the ice was not thick enough to take the weight of men on the march. The rebels, it seemed, were cornered.

Then, in the middle of the night, Washington's army crept away by a devious route, leaving the fires of their camp burning brightly. In confident mood they were ready to take on the token force of about a thousand men the British had left behind at Princeton. At sunrise on 3 January, an American general, Hugh Mercer, was fatally wounded and his men retreated before the bayonets of the British who were refusing to take prisoners.

Tom Blanchard and his four platoons had held fast. Now he and his men were inspired by the sight of their commander-in-chief, General

Washington, oblivious to his own safety, racing to the front line on his white horse and putting a stop to the retreat. A short-lived and bloody battle ensued but the rebels won the day with the British losing more than 300 men and most of their weapons.

The success at Princeton brought fresh hope and optimism to the rebel army and, most importantly, renewed support for the revolution from the people who felt they had suffered the presence and the pillaging of foreign troops for far too long. The alleged robbing of innocent families, the theft of food and belongings, the stories of cattle stolen and even of wives and daughters abducted and raped, were often exaggerated and enlarged upon but this was what people chose to believe and volunteers began to come forward in increasing numbers.

Throughout the spring and summer of 1777 the rebel army grew in size and strength. Uniforms, though, were in short supply and many companies were distinguished only by the sprigs of green they wore in their hats. Most of these men were poorly drilled raw recruits but by September, General Washington had a force of 16,000 troops at his disposal, gathered at Brandywine Creek near Philadelphia.

Despite the shortage of men with first-hand experience of battle there was no sign of any promotion for Jimmy. But he was not aware of the brothers' efforts on his behalf and it had not even occurred to him that he might be considered. Throughout those months he was assiduously learning to read, prevailing on Tom or Hank, whoever was available, to help.

The quiet man in the tavern in New York had told Jimmy if he wanted to learn to read he must first learn to speak. No more 'dese', 'dem' and 'dose'. This had greatly amused Tom and Hank who listened for any slip-ups in his speech. For every lapse he was teased remorselessly. But he was learning and he was enjoying learning, poring over every printed piece, lips moving silently, until he had a grasp of the content.

Most nights now Jimmy would lie awake thinking of Chrissie. He was looking forward to the day when he could read her a story or, better still, read their children a story. Somehow he was going to get enough money to go to Lexington and buy her freedom. Either that or, if he didn't have the money, he would steal her. But it wouldn't really be stealing. She didn't belong to some slave owner. People don't *belong* to people. Nobody *belongs* to anybody.

Except children. Until they're older they belong to their parents. And people like Chrissie and me, he told himself, people like us belong to each other.

He asked Hank one day what he thought about when lying in bed at night. Jimmy was serious but, as usual, Hank turned the whole thing into a joke. 'I think about that big fat whore used to come to the tents Friday nights.'

Tom said he often thought about what would happen when the war was over, how the country would be run and who would run it. He didn't add that most of the time he thought of Sarah, where she was and how she was. Had she got over what happened to her family? Although no, he realized. No one could ever get over something like that. Maybe in time it would get a little easier but however it was, wherever she was, he wanted to be with her. He wanted to find her and spend the rest of his life with her.

'Imelda!' Max Harvie summoned his daughter. 'Would you come into the parlour, please? And bring Sarah.'

There was something in her father's tone. Imelda looked at her mother who pressed a lace handkerchief to her lips and looked as if she was about to cry.

'What? What is it?'

The two girls were in their hotel room when Imelda's father called them, surroundings far better than their earlier dingy accommodation, but there was still little for them to do in the military garrison Halifax had become and the weather was bad. Harsh winds had blown away the white fronds that hung like Christmas decorations from the branches of the trees, the heavy rain turning the snowdrifts into black slush, but slowly the town was being relieved of its winter clothes.

Once, when Imelda and Sarah had been permitted to go to the general store by the dockyard they had seen great slabs of blue-veined ice in the harbour where ships and many smaller craft had not moved for weeks and were wreathed in mantles of sagging snow. Now, with the coming thaw and if the war was going well, perhaps they could go home.

'Come, sit down,' Imelda's father said, with a frown. 'We've received some news. Not *good* news, I'm afraid. But your mother and I thought we should inform you at once.'

The two girls exchanged glances. They had followed him into the rooms he shared with Imelda's mother and were seated, primly now, on the edge of the plush sofa.

'Daddy, please!' Imelda said. 'What is it? What's happened?'

'Imelda,' Harvie began, then he looked at his wife for support but, with a little wave of her hand, Aunt Mary indicated she would prefer to leave it to him.

Harvie hesitated and in the silence that followed a brightly burning log shifted in the grate. 'Ezra has sent some papers and documents from the office,' he said. 'And some proofs of work he'd done before we left. It's a matter of habit with Ezra. He likes me to see and approve proofs though, under the present circumstances, what I could possibly do if I wanted to change anything I don't know.'

'Daddy, please! What is it?'

'Er . . . yes,' Harvie said apologetically. 'I'm just saying at least we still have Ezra and the print business.'

'Is the war over, Uncle Max?' Sarah asked suddenly.

Harvie shook his head. 'No, dear,' he said slowly. 'I did say it was not good news. I'm afraid the war is not over, not yet, and inevitably there are . . . casualties.'

Sarah looked up at him quickly, catching on much faster than her cousin. Casualties? Who could he mean? Was it the colonel? Handsome Jack, the dashing colonel who went to embarrassing lengths to pursue her. She hoped not. She didn't want all the attention he gave her but she didn't wish him any harm.

'As I said, I have received a proof from Ezra. It's a copy of a poster Ezra received for printing just before we left. You will remember the army printed a list of dead officers after each engagement. That was how we came to hear so swiftly of poor John Foster's untimely end.'

'Is it Edward?' Imelda asked. The last they'd heard of her brother he was serving with General Clinton in the Carolinas.

'No, thank God!' Harvie said fervently. 'It isn't Edward. As far as we know, your brother is safe. . . .'

'Then what?' Imelda's patience had run out. 'Who?'

'Max!' Mrs Harvie intervened.

'Well,' Harvie told them, 'in the same way as the army posts lists of officers killed in action, these so-called rebels have made Ezra print a list of their people, rebels killed in action.'

'Henry Blanchard is dead,' Aunt Mary said.

Harvie faced Imelda. 'I know how at one time you were close to Henry Blanchard, my dear.'

'Hank?' Imelda's eyes registered alarm. 'Oh no. Not Hank. He's just a boy.'

'They are all just boys,' her mother said, stifling a sob.

'He joined the enemy, Imelda,' her father said sternly. 'He chose to fight against his own kind, people he has known all his life, loyal supporters of His Majesty the King, and I'm afraid he has paid the ultimate price.'

'Hank?' Imelda said, her hands covering her face.

'Henry Blanchard's name is on this list of rebels killed,' her father confirmed, 'along with that of his brother.'

'Tom?' Sarah was shocked. She had pictured in her mind the fair-haired younger brother of the man who was always in her thoughts. Now she felt a sudden chill as if the brightly burning flames of the fire in the grate had gone out. 'Tom Blanchard is dead? Is that what you are saying, Uncle Max?'

Max Harvie nodded. 'I'm afraid so, Sarah.'

Imelda was ringing her hands theatrically. 'It isn't fair.'

Her father produced the list and there were the names, third and fourth down in alphabetical order. Anderson, John, Andrews, Robert, *Blanchard, Henry, Blanchard Thomas.*

Sarah wanted to be alone. She wanted to get away from the unctuous Uncle Max and his bad tidings and from the genuine distress of her aunt who could only make matters worse with her words of comfort. 'I'm sorry,' she said, avoiding eye contact with any of them. 'You must excuse me.'

'Sarah,' Aunt Mary said.

Aunt Mary looked around for Imelda but Imelda was lying on the sofa, her face buried in a cushion, her words muffled. 'Why them? They were not real soldiers. They were boys. Just boys.'

Sarah didn't want to be unkind to Imelda but she didn't want to be coupled with her in grief. As when news of John Foster's death arrived, her tears seemed too much like crocodile tears.

'Excuse me,' Sarah said and she left the room.

'So Lieutenant Withers, how many women have *you* had?'

Ben was new to the mess table and apparently fair game for the young commander. The other officers sniggered dutifully.

'Had, sir?'

'Had, Lieutenant.'

Ben answererd truthfully. 'Not many, sir.' In fact there had only been Melanie. She was all he had and all he wanted.

'You are an American, I understand. A Bostonian.' The voice was high-pitched and precise with a faintly sardonic note. 'Loyal to His Majesty. Very commendable. But we are all friends here. Gentlemen of the world. You need not be shy.'

Ben's dislike of the young chief had been instant and it was increasing. 'I am far from shy, sir,' he said in a measured tone that carried its own implied warning. 'I assure you.'

'A-ah!' Tarleton felt his bait had been swallowed. 'Our guest is made of stern stuff, I perceive.' More sycophantic sniggers. 'Tell us about the trips you American boys make to the Indian camps. For a few pence, I'm told, one can have a very good time.'

All eyes were on Ben. The other officers were waiting to be entertained. Clearly he was not going to escape without some kind of response. But perhaps it was nothing personal. Perhaps all new boys were put through this procedure, he told himself. After all most of these powdered pansies were the product of aristocratic English schools where putting a new boy through some sort of initiation ceremony was traditional.

'You have been misinformed,' Ben said, dropping the 'sir'.

'Really?' Lolling back in his seat, Tarleton held up his glass of rum. 'Then perhaps you will correct this misinformation.'

Ben sat up straight. 'When you say "Go to the Indian camps" this creates an erroneous and, indeed, dangerous impression. If I or any of these gentlemen were to go to an Indian camp with the express intention of offering payment for the company of a squaw we would, without a doubt, return minus our scalps . . . and probably minus our balls.'

The assembled officers were silent, unsure of their chief's reaction, and after a moment, Tarleton said quietly, 'Go on.'

'It is true that there are wandering groups here and there of unfortunates, anything from half-breeds born outside of their tribe to a brave who has offended some tradition, or code of behaviour, and has taken to the grog after being thrown out. Some of these people, though by no means all, will sell you a woman for the night or for an hour or for as long as you wish. But they are not representative of the

Indian. The Indian is a proud and honourable man. He is well able to take good care of himself and his people and we cross him at our peril. His women are not for sale.'

'Thank you, Lieutenant,' Tarleton said, with a smirk towards his assembled officers. 'Thank you for the lecture and for improving our deficient education.'

'But Indians steal white women, do they not?' demanded a portly captain with a bluish pitted nose.

'Not in order to lie with her,' Ben said.

'And for what other reason would one take a woman,' Tarleton asked in his most insulting tone, 'if not to lie with her?'

'In my experience,' Ben told him, 'in our collective experience, in America, the Indian will only take a white-man's possessions in retaliation. A brave of an honourable tribe, and most of them are honourable, will not steal a woman or cattle or anything else from the white man unless he has been wronged in some way, or is at war. If he is at war, or has been wronged, he will take both men and women, but for their scalps. He does not want a white woman for anything else. He has his own women. And he will protect them with his life.'

'Then tell us why these honourable Indians murdered our express messenger,' Tarleton invited sceptically, 'the messenger bringing the authentication for your mission.'

'Because the Indian considers he is at war with the British.'

With a smile and a sweep of his hand Tarleton turned to the rest of the table. 'So next time you gentlemen feel like dragging some squaw into the bushes keep your hat on and hold on to your balls!'

The sycophants laughed uproariously and Tarleton had clearly tired of the Indians. 'You still have not told us how many women you have had,' he said, but he didn't pursue the subject. He had become engaged in a discussion with the officer on his right.

Ben regarded him from down the table. His name was Banastre Tarleton. He was a man whose reputation, wherever he went with the British Army and beyond, travelled ahead of him. At first sight Ben hadn't liked the look of him and still didn't. From what he had heard Tarleton, who was only a year or so older than himself, had been in action in most of the engagements in which General Clinton had commanded the British. He was now in command of a mixed force of cavalry and light infantry. By all accounts he was totally ruthless and prepared to annihilate anyone who stood in his way. He was quick-tempered, arrogant and, in the eyes of many, including his own, extremely good-looking. Not handsome in a masculine way, his beauty was more feminine with full, pouting lips and long, luxuriant eyelashes.

Newspapers and pamphlets sympathetic to the rebels attributed many unsavoury activities and exploits to the 'devilish Tarleton' as they labelled him. But Tarleton revelled in his reputation, boasting openly that he had 'butchered more men and lain with more women than anyone else in the army.' He had certainly killed many opponents in battle, as those under his command would testify. And if the word 'lain' was to include the women and girls he had raped, his second boast was probably also true.

Ben Withers, in his clean-cut, outdoor way, was both bigger and better-looking than the powdered and pampered Tarleton and he had little regard for the man. Yet the following day he found there were several things to admire about the young commander. Tarleton was without doubt a fine horseman. He was also a strong disciplinarian, an ideal chief, a man who men would follow to the death.

But Ben's grudging admiration was soon dispelled when he witnessed the way Tarleton chose to break in an unruly horse. Wearing huge spurs and wielding a heavy whip with a piece of iron knotted in its tail he lashed the unfortunate beast until the blood poured from its flanks and foam frothed through its teeth.

Ben wanted to intervene, to drag the little poseur from the horse and beat him senseless, but he turned away, his blood in a turmoil, and fought to remain calm. He could not bear to see an animal, any animal, mistreated. But he dared not become involved. He would be embroiled in some sort of disciplinary procedure, a complication at this stage he could not afford. He had come this far, he told himself, for one purpose and for one purpose only.

Ben turned away, hating himself for not rushing to the horse's aid. It was then that he saw the thick-set, dark-eyed sergeant with the long scar over his left eye. The man was leaning on the gate to the small corral, grinning approval at his commanding officer who had so brutally subdued the horse. Could this be him? The infamous Duckett? He was a sergeant, about the right age, and he hadn't changed much in eight years. Ben was sure it was him.

Their eyes met briefly across the corral but there was no flicker of recognition from the sergeant and there was no reason why there should be. Duckett had probably long forgotten what he did that day all those years ago. But Ben Withers hadn't.

TWENTY

THE summer of 1777 in New York was hot and oppressive and with so many people living in close proximity disease was rife. The smell from the docks at low water and the stench from the narrow polluted streets had become unbearable. Food was in short supply and expensive, there was much thieving and petty crime and the British, their morale at a very low ebb, were no longer welcome.

The aim now was Philadelphia. Towards the end of July, leaving a much reduced force of infantry and cavalry to hold New York, about 14,000 troops embarked on an ill-judged and uncomfortable voyage and were landed in late August at a small town called Head of Elk in Maryland.

In low spirits the British troops marched towards Brandywine Creek where the army of General Washington was entrenched. At dawn on 11 September the British attack began. All day the battle raged back and forth but gradually the superior strategy and outflanking movements of the professional soldiers forced the rebels to withdraw. By nightfall the Americans had lost over 1,000 men killed or wounded and almost 400 more were taken prisoner. The British losses, dead or wounded, were nearer 500.

The next day the British moved forward again and Washington crossed the River Schuylkill leaving a detachment of men known as 'the Pennsylvania line' to delay the advance. To eliminate this delaying force the British sent three infantry battalions to attack the Pennsylvanians by night. Guided by the camp fires the British took the rebels completely by surprise close to an inn known as the Paoli Tavern. The rebels ran in all directions but the British bayoneted every man they caught up with and the next morning hundreds lay dead, all killed by the bayonet.

The massacre was total and the way was clear for the British to advance to the Schuylkill where they crossed the river at Flatland Ford. On 25 September their bands blaring in triumph and with a show of heavy artillery the British marched into Philadelphia.

The British objective now was to open up the Delaware River. From bank to bank many obstacles had been sunk into the river-bed to prevent safe passage and until these were removed supplies had to come by land, a much longer and more hazardous operation. Opening up the river had become a priority and a large detachment of troops was detailed to carry out the process.

General Washington now saw an opportunity to attack the reduced numbers at the temporarily vulnerable British headquarters based at Germantown. In the early hours of 4 October the attack began but conditions were far from ideal. A thick fog greatly reduced visibilty as a furious and confused battle ensued, neither side certain in the smoke and fog who was the enemy. The fighting, which went on for almost three hours, was finally concentrated around a large stone house in the centre of the village.

The British charged and at first the rebels gave way but again and again they returned and in greater numbers until, for the first time, the British were forced to sound their bugles to retreat. As General Howe rode up and saw what was happening he poured scorn on his men and ordered them to form up and fight back, claiming they were only facing a scouting party. But when a large column of rebels came into view and cannon fired on his position he realized this was no scouting party and rode off at high speed.

Losses on both sides were heavy yet neither Washington nor Howe felt anything had been gained. Washington had failed in his attempt to retake Philadelphia and Howe, having succeeded in reopening the Delaware had suffered many casualties. Though he had captured the country's capital and most elegant city and though the men of the Continental Congress, who were ready and waiting to form the first independent government, had fled to York, a hundred miles away, he felt no elation. The man who had been hailed as victor after he entered New York, fêted at home where there was the erroneous feeling that the war was all but won, now felt he had achieved little in the past year. Numerically, the rebel army was stronger than it had ever been and the British were still unable to force them into one decisive confrontation. Deciding to spend the coming winter in Philadelphia, General Howe despaired of ever bringing a successful end to hostilities and he was on the verge of resigning his post and returning home. His message to London was that without massive reinforcements he would not be able to finish the job.

General Washington was equally dissatisfied with the progress of the war. He had regrouped his army at Whitemarsh, about fifteen miles from Philadelphia. He now moved a few miles west to Valley Forge. The difficulty here was in maintaining morale throughout the coming winter. Again there were desertions with some men simply going home. For those who remained there were few comforts and the situation was not helped by the lurid stories of the British enjoying what someone called 'the fruits of Philadelphia'. Several prominent citizens, unwilling to stay and submit to Loyalist rule, reported that 'the British officers are revelling in balls and music and sumptuous dinners as their vile men plunder and pillage and go about deflowering virgins and carousing in drunken orgies.' To the two generals, Washington and Howe, with so many men dead, the battle for Philadelphia seemed like a battle both sides lost.

Tom Blanchard knew his brother was safe and well. They saw each other most evenings in the officers' mess. But apart from an occasional raised hand across a crowded parade he had seen little of Jimmy. Now, having lost a sergeant at Germantown he again approached the colonel on Jimmy's behalf. This time, not wanting to say no to Tom who had proved himself a brave and reliable leader in battle, the colonel agreed. A week later, Jimmy joined Tom's company.

'They sure mus' be scrapin' dat ol' barrel,' he said with a laugh, holding up his three stripes.

'I reckon you're right, James,' Tom said in disgust, emphasizing the correct pronunciation. 'They must be scraping that old barrel. Haven't you learned anything?'

'Sorry. Ah . . . I forget.'

The colonel, still unsure of how the men would react to a black sergeant, had expressed his reservations. Tom told Jimmy to get his stripes sewn on and next day he marched his four platoons to an outfield away from the main camp and allowed them to sit on the grass and relax.

'We're lucky,' he told them. 'We have a new sergeant and I can tell you he's a man you can trust. I know he won't let me down because he's the best there is. This company is under my orders and Sergeant

Sunshine is my man. You do as he says.' He waited but nobody spoke. 'Good. We got that straight.'

A young farmhand, sitting cross-legged, said, 'Sure is one hell of a name. Sergeant *Sunshine*.'

The men laughed but in a receptive way. They seemed too tired and resigned to their fate to show much interest.

'Well, I'll tell you,' Tom said. 'When he was a boy, Sergeant Sunshine was a slave to one of these Loyalist pigs, but Sergeant Sunshine is nobody's slave. Soon as he could he got himself free and he took another name. Now what's wrong with Sunshine?'

There were a few smiles but not much response. Tom and his fellow officers had been told to guard against the boredom the long winter would bring, to try to keep the men's spirits high. Tom's men had been intensely loyal. They'd fought hard and well at Brandywine and at Germantown but now there were rumblings of discontent and a vague disenchantment with the war as if a debilitating malaise was taking hold.

'Look,' Tom said, 'I think it's time we had a little talk.'

Unknown to Tom the colonel and his aide had strolled to a few yards behind him. Jimmy saw them but the colonel smiled and shook his head so there was no way he could warn Tom. All the men knew the colonel was there and they sat up straight. Tom was pleased. He thought they were keen to listen to what he had to say. But then they did listen and so did the colonel.

'I know conditions are not ideal here. We're short of supplies, but we're not going to starve and even if we have to chop down the entire woods we are not going to freeze to death either. We hear these tales from Philadelphia about what a great time their fellows are having. Well, if it's true, we're going to make them pay. We can't lose this war, boys, because it's *our* war. A war we have to win. And we can't lose because – you know why? If we have to give in to them, let them run our country, it'll all happen again. Our children will start another revolution and another and another until we do win. As long as it takes, we will win. And you know why? Because right is on our side.'

Tom was warming to his subject and his men were listening intently. 'The bloodybacks have stolen our country and we want it back. It's not about robbery and rape and God knows what else. We know all that goes on, but both sides have been guilty. No. It's about living under the thumb of foreigners. A mad king three thousand miles away. Why should we build up our country and send him the proceeds? They say we must pay their duties. *Stamp* duties. They say the money is to pay for their army to stay and protect us. Protect us from what? The French? The Indians? We can protect ourselves. You know that. We don't need 'em. We don't want 'em. And, by God, we're not going to have 'em.'

There were stirrings of assent. Men nodded and repeated the slogan. 'We don't need 'em. We don't want 'em. And, by God, we are not going to have 'em.'

'But we're not going to leave it to our children to clear these people out,' Tom went on. 'We're going to do that ourselves. We'll see this winter through and we'll be ready. We're going to run the bloodybacks and their powder-puff bosses into the ocean and they can swim home.'

'Yeah!' a cheer went up and gradually the men came to their feet to clap their hands and chant. 'Death to the bloodybacks,' was the cry. 'Kill the buggers!'

The colonel and his aide clapped their hands to join in the applause. Tom spun round, surprised. 'Sir! I'm sorry,' he said. 'I didn't know you were there.'

'That's all right, Lieutenant,' the colonel said, and with a bow to acknowledge the assembled company, he strolled away, his aide in attendance.

'Future Congressman there,' he was heard to say.

For several days Sarah stayed in her room, unable to face the outside world. Even when Colonel Danvers arrived to pay his respects she refused to appear and her Uncle Max was furious. Of course the death of the Blanchard boy was sad but it could not mean so much to her, he complained. She barely knew him.

Aunt Mary offered the colonel a glass of rum and hoped he would return at a later date. Her daughter and her niece had received some very bad news from Boston, she told him. Two of their young friends, mere boys, had been killed in the war.

'Really?' Danvers looked concerned. 'Please, Mrs Harvie, you must give the girls my most sincere condolences. Do you know what regiment? In what campaign they were engaged?'

As always, Aunt Mary was scrupulously honest. 'I'm afraid the boys were not in the army, Colonel. At least, not in the British Army. They joined the rebels.'

Danvers frowned. 'Friends of Sarah, you say?'

'Well actually, they were schoolfriends of Imelda. Sarah only came to know them later.'

Max Harvie came bustling into the room, angry with Sarah for refusing to come down. He caught the end of the conversation and said at once, 'Two brothers. Imelda had a mild flirtation with the younger boy some time ago. He seemed a nice enough boy, from a respectable family. We didn't know he would turn out the way he did. A traitor. Disloyal to the throne.'

Danvers, darkly handsome, resplendent in his uniform, turned to Aunt Mary. 'Then why, may I ask, should this affect Sarah? Why will she not come down?'

'Sarah knew the other brother, Colonel, but only briefly. She probably sees this as a mark of respect – for a former friend.'

Not entirely convinced, Colonel Danvers bowed to Aunt Mary and nodded at Harvie. 'Perhaps I will see Sarah the next time I call. Thank you, Mrs Harvie, for the drink.'

From her third-floor window Sarah watched the colonel leave, tall in the saddle of his well-groomed horse, his broad shoulders showing off his splendid uniform. There was a light knock at the door and Imelda came in. Sarah turned and sat down on the bed.

'You are going to have to see him sooner or later, Sarah.'

'Why? Why should I?'

'Well, he's been good to us. He got us these rooms after that awful hovel. You hated it there. We all did.'

'I don't want to see anyone ever again.'

'You were waiting, saving yourself for Tom,' Imelda said gently.

'That night,' Sarah said. 'The ball at your house in Boston. It was the first time I spoke to Tom. I'd seen him earlier, out in the street. You remember? The riot? I knew then. I knew then he was the one. The one for me.'

'What's happened to us, Sarah?'

'That was the night you were with John Foster. Tom and Hank were there and you were flirting with everyone.' Sarah smiled. 'Everyone except Hank.'

'Oh, that didn't mean anything.' Able to cry at will, Imelda sobbed. 'Hank knew me. That was what I loved about him. He knew I would always come back to him.'

'What about John Foster?'

'Well, yes. John asked me to marry him. And I liked him, I liked him a lot. But I never had any intention of saying yes. It was just flattering, I suppose. Now Hank, Hank would never ask. I always knew that when the time came I would have to do the asking.'

'And you didn't mind?'

Imelda shook her head. 'I always knew that Hank would say yes.' She was smiling at the image of Hank in her mind, the open face, the clear blue eyes, the tousled hair, the innocent boy. That's what he was. *Innocent*. Then she remembered he was dead. 'Oh, Sarah,' she cried. 'Why did they have to join the rebels? Why did they have to join anything?'

'You know why,' Sarah said dully. 'They had to join *some*thing. And your father was pressing them to join the British.'

'They could have taken up commissions. It was all arranged.'

'They could have joined the British,' Sarah said, 'and had their heads blown off like John Foster.'

'What will we do now, Sarah? What will become of us?'

'I don't know,' Sarah said. 'We'll probably go back to Boston when the war is over.'

'I don't think I'll marry anyone now. Not now Hank has gone.'

'Nor will I,' Sarah said decisively, as images of Tom brought tears to her eyes. Tom standing awkwardly at the edge of the dance floor. Tom rowing along the Charles after church on a sleepy Sunday. Tom sitting on the porch in the moonlight at Melanie's house that time when they were all together.

'The sensible thing,' Imelda said, 'would be for you to marry Colonel Danvers. He has so much to offer.'

'He isn't Tom.'

'You have to be realistic, Sarah. Tom was a once in a lifetime thing. But he's gone now. You have to think about the future.'

'You sound like Uncle Max.'

'Daddy is right. Colonel Danvers is probably the best catch in the whole army. And besides . . . you have to admit, he's just about the most handsome man either one of us has ever seen. Some girls would kill to marry him.'

'Imelda,' Sarah said, 'I'm not interested.'

'Well, you should be. You are just being silly. Daddy says that Colonel Danvers is very well connected in England. He's rich. He's a landowner. He has two big houses. And, strictly between ourselves, he is to receive a knighthood. You could be Lady Danvers. Lady Sarah Danvers. Wouldn't you just love that?'

'No,' Sarah said truthfully. 'I don't want to be Lady Danvers or Lady anything. All I ever wanted to be was Mrs Tom Blanchard.'

'I know,' Imelda said, suddenly contrite. She realized it was callous of her to be talking like this so soon. Yet she couldn't help adding, 'But I can think of a lot of worse fates than having to share a bed with Handsome Jack Danvers.'

Any day now a messenger would arrive with the news that neither headquarters nor Special Services had ever heard of this man Withers and had no idea what his game was. Ben could not afford to delay any longer.

It was a cold night, the dark-blue sky moonlit and studded with stars. Winter was coming in and it occurred to Ben that heavy snowfalls could render the roads impassable. Not yet sure of his plans he decided to seek out Duckett.

He wandered vaguely towards the marquee that served as the sergeants' mess and as he passed the stables he saw that a single lantern was burning in one of the stalls. Ben looked in to where a small man with two stripes was kneeling in the straw beside the horse Tarleton had almost flogged to death.

'How is she?' Ben asked, kneeling beside him.

'Not going to make it,' the little corporal said, not sure who Ben was or if he should call him sir.

'Lieutenant Withers,' Ben said. 'I saw what happened today and I thought it was pretty disgraceful.'

The corporal looked at him, wanting to comment, but wary of criticising his CO. 'It's . . . er . . . very sad, sir.'

'It's more than that,' Ben said, unable to control his renewed anger. 'It's bloody dreadful and unnecessary.'

The corporal was holding a basin of water. He put it to the horse's mouth but the horse was unable to raise its head. The corporal poured the water gently from the side into the horse's mouth and the horse shook its head and writhed momentarily. Tenderly the corporal stroked the quivering body where it lay and caressed its mane. 'Can't take it in, sir. She's too far gone.'

The horse was dying before their eyes, its flank grey, flies hovering already over its exposed wounds.

'I'd like to horsewhip the bastard,' Ben said.

The corporal remained silent, not daring to even nod, though he agreed wholeheartedly with the sentiment.

'What have you got?' Ben asked urgently. 'You must have something we can give her.'

The corporal shook his head. 'I asked the doc but he said no. Medical supplies are for men not animals.'

'Sometimes, Corporal,' Ben said, 'I prefer animals to men.'

'Yes, sir,' the corporal said.

'We'll have to put her down. Can't allow her to suffer like this.'

The horse's plight had obviously affected the little corporal as much as it had Ben. He wiped a tear from his eye. 'Can't, sir.'

'Why? A bullet is the only charitable way.'

'I know, sir. But they won't give me one. The armourer says his orders are no firearms to be set off in case the enemy is in the vicinity. We don't want to reveal our position. And it's true, sir. We have been told that.'

'There's no enemy round here,' Ben scoffed. 'Have you asked Tarleton?' Then he toned down his anger. 'The colonel would understand, I'm sure.'

'I asked Sergeant Duckett to ask the colonel but he said no. The armourer is right, he said. Bullets is for the rebels.'

Ben was furious. He paced the straw-strewn floor of the stable then came back to the stall. 'We have to do something, Corporal. The poor thing is obviously in great pain.'

The corporal stroked the horse's neck and ran a finger gently above her eyes to soothe her.

'Perhaps we should smother her,' Ben said. 'Put an end to it.'

'If you don't mind, sir,' the corporal said, tears running down his ruddy, weather-beaten cheeks. 'I'll jus' sit here with her. She won't last the night. She might go peaceful like.'

Ben nodded and left the stables, again his blood boiling at the insensitive barbarity. It was time to seek out Duckett, prepare him for a trip. At the sergeants' mess it was not the done thing for a commissioned officer to enter without an invitation. Ben had arrived as a sergeant and most people at the camp didn't know what to make of him. There was speculation about him in the ranks but he wore no insignia, just a rough shirt, a lambskin jerkin and riding breeches.

He stood just inside the marquee. Most of the activity was at the bar but several tables were occupied with men drinking and relaxing. The light was poor, a small lantern on each table, the bigger lanterns along the bar. An orderly from the cookhouse dispensed drinks. Ben stood to one side, mostly in shadow. His back to Ben, Duckett was holding forth at a table with five or six younger men in attendance. Ben sat at the next table, picked up a glass and poured some water from a pitcher in the centre.

Three of the sergeants with Duckett were fresh-faced and new. One looked no more than fifteen, half a lifetime younger than Duckett. 'What's it like, Sarge?' one asked. 'I mean, a real battle, hand to hand? All we've done so far is wait.'

'Yeah!' another said with alacrity. 'You've been in lotsa scraps, Sarge. What's it really like? Face to face.'

'Yeah!' several voices endorsed the question.

Duckett needed little encouragement. He glanced back at Ben. He'd seen Ben earlier in conversation with Colonel Tarleton and wondered who he was. Now he wondered why Ben was here.

'Yes, Sergeant,' Ben said, pulling his chair round. 'I'm new to all this, too. I've never been in a real battle. It'll be good to hear it from a man who knows what he's talking about. Tell us. What is it *really* like?'

Rum had already loosened Duckett's tongue and he was enjoying being the centre of attention. 'What's it *really* like?' he responded and he turned back to face his audience. 'Well, I'll tell yer. It's like runnin' through Hell. Or as near to Hell as any of you could ever imagine. Why, I've been in scraps where yer lose all sense of time or place. Yer get so close to yer man yer can tweak the bastard's nose. And then it's him or you. The bayonet or the bullet and yer got to get in first or yer dead. Whether it's hot or cold the sweat runs down yer back. Yer hands get so clammy yer can hardly hold yer musket straight. An' yer facin' 'em, their muskets aimed at yer, loaded, cocked and ready to blast. Yer stop breathin'. Yer scream but yer can't 'ear yerself 'cos all around the noise is smashin' yer eardrums. Yer run at 'em. The muskets flash an' smoke. The man beside yer goes down. But yer keep goin'. An' suddenly yer there. Face to face an' he's as scared as you. But it's you or 'im. Yer go for the guts or the throat. Stick it in, twist an' out. Yer mouth is dry. But it's you or 'im. Then it's you or the next man an' the next an' the next, until maybe it's you. Or maybe it's over and yer still alive – or maybe yer dead.'

The men sat still, absorbed, living the melodrama.

'An' that's why weapons training is so important,' Duckett said quietly. 'Know yer musket, know yer bayonet. An' above all know yerself.' He held an imaginary bayonet, demonstrated. 'An' always, always remember, when yer stick yer pig it's in, *twist* an' out. Not in an' out. It's in, twist an' out. Otherwise yer could lose yer blade. Then where would yer be?' He took another gulp at his rum and added, 'An' just remember, you lads belong to Colonel Tarleton's Legion. We have the reputation for bein' the finest scrappers in the British Army and we aim to keep it that way. We fight dirty an' we kill clean – all right? An' we don't take prisoners. Colonel Tarleton's men don't take prisoners – they kill 'em.'

Saluting smartly a very young orderly approached Ben Withers. 'Colonel Tarleton wishes to see you, sir.'

'Colonel Tarleton wishes to see me,' Ben said for Duckett's ears. 'Of course. I'll come right away.' He stood up, bent forward close to Duckett and said, 'I enjoyed that, Sergeant. Very graphic.'

At Tarleton's tent a guard announced, 'Lieutenant Withers, sah.'

'Come in, come in.' Tarleton was wearing a frilly white blouse with frilly cuffs. His powdered wig made him look even more like a girl. 'Come in and sit down, Lieutenant.'

Ben pulled up a wicker chair. 'You've had some news, Colonel?'

'Not yet,' Tarleton said.

'Time is important,' Ben said. 'Much more of this delay and my mission may well be aborted.'

'Your mission.' Tarleton faced him, elbows on his desk, his chin resting on his intertwined fingers, his eyes fixed questioningly.

Ben returned the look almost to the point of insubordination, then said, 'My mission is to carry out a covert operation. I am not at liberty to tell you more.'

Tarleton was clearly irritated, though not because he was eager to know what this so-called covert operation entailed. It was the fact that he was not in the know. He was being excluded and he had not been able to either bully or charm the information out of this man.

'You ride in here, to my camp, wearing three stripes. But you inform my . . . er . . . deputy, you are not a sergeant. You are, in fact, a lieutenant. Lieutenant Withers of Special Services. You are on a secret mission, a mission to assassinate a leading rebel leader.'

Ben looked round uncomfortably. 'Colonel . . .'

Tarleton held up his hand. 'You have no papers. No advance intelligence. Nothing. Because, you say, the express messenger delivering this coded information was intercepted and butchered by your noble Indians. I am to allow you to leave and take with you my best sergeant. The sergeant reviled by all except me. A man reviled because he is ten times more ruthless than anyone bar myself. Sit in my chair, Lieutenant, if indeed that is what you are, and tell me you would swallow this cock and bull story.'

Ben shrugged. 'I have nothing to say, sir. Except, perhaps, that Lord Cornwallis will be less than pleased.'

Tarleton bristled, as if this was a slight to his authority. 'I am to attend a conference tomorrow of some very senior officers in Trenton. I may well be able to shed a little light on this matter.' Regaining his poise, he smiled cordially at Ben. 'I will be back in the late afternoon. Tomorrow evening I would like you to have dinner with me. Just the two of us.'

Ben stood up and bowed. 'You're very kind, sir.'

Apart from the mystery surrounding him there had been from the beginning something about this man that sparked Tarleton's innate competitiveness. Clearly he was an enigma, unfazed and unimpressed by Tarleton's assumed superiority, his presence or his reputation. Obviously he would be attractive to the ladies and, grudgingly, Tarleton admitted to himself the man did have a kind of quiet charisma.

'Lieutenant,' he said as Ben turned to leave, 'you never did tell me how many women you've had.'

Ben smiled. 'Some matters are private, sir.'

'There you go again with your secrets,' Tarleton said, then a light dawned in his eye and he, too, smiled. 'Perhaps, Lieutenant, you are of another persuasion.'

If this was what he wanted to think, so what? Ben didn't care. 'As I said, some matters are private, sir.'

Tarleton nodded as if satisfied with this. Ben saluted and, as he left, it occurred to him that all the boasting of how many women he'd had might be Tarleton's way of forestalling any speculation or suspicion that he might be of another persuasion. In dress and manner the colonel certainly looked that way.

Ben strolled back to his temporary quarters, to his army issue bedroll and his small pack and the picture of Melanie. Now was his chance. Tomorrow with Tarleton out of the way he could leave and take Duckett with him. He put his pack away and went out again. If Duckett had carried on drinking he'd be in a pretty befuddled state. With some advance warning tonight he may well remember a little in the morning.

He was in luck. The marquee was almost empty but Duckett was still there, swaying on his seat, eyes half-closed. Ben sat down beside him and gave another man at the table a look and a little jerk of his head that said his presence was not required. The man stood up, swayed slightly and left.

'I know you,' Duckett said thickly.

'And I know you,' Ben said. 'My friend Colonel Tarleton tells me you are the best man he's got.'

Duckett swayed back a little, his chest out. 'Bloody right.'

Ben leaned forward, braving Duckett's foul-smelling breath. 'That's why he wants you to join me on a special assignment.'

Duckett's expression tried to register. 'A what?'

'He has a special job he wants me to do. That's why I'm here. And I need a man to help me. Colonel Tarleton tells me you are the perfect man for the job, the only man he can trust. The colonel says he would trust you with his life.'

Duckett was nodding, taking in what he wanted to hear.

'But I don't know,' Ben said. 'Maybe I should ask him for someone else. We have to leave tomorrow and, well, you've had rather a lot to drink.'

'No, no,' Duckett argued. 'I always 'ave a lot to drink. I'll be fine tomorrer. Colonel wants me, colonel shall 'ave me.'

At eight o'clock the following morning Ben watched as Tarleton, in his green jacket and high cocked hat, accompanied by a captain and two bodyguards, rode out of the camp gates in a cloud of dust.

Duckett was in the sergeants' mess. Still without insignia of any kind, Ben had no hesitation in stepping inside. He found Duckett at once and stooped to whisper in his ear. 'Colonel's office after breakfast, Sergeant,' he said, then, 'Oh, and have a good breakfast.'

Ben smiled and left, murmuring to himself, 'The condemned man is entitled to a hearty breakfast.'

Half an hour later Ben was at Colonel Miller's desk. If there was to be a problem with the sentries or anyone else he wanted to have the uneasy colonel's support. 'The CO will have told you Sergeant

Duckett and I are leaving today, sir.'

Colonel Miller looked at him wildly. 'Oh ... er ... yes. Yes, of course.'

'As you know, permission came through last night.' Ben knew he was treading on very thin ice. He could easily fall through if the much more perceptive adjutant appeared. 'It's a difficult assignment and I would deem it a favour, sir, if you would offer the sergeant a word of encouragement.'

'Yes, yes, of course.'

'Lord Cornwallis will be made fully aware of the help you have given me in allowing me to stay here. I am most grateful, colonel.'

Right on cue, an orderly announced Duckett's arrival.

'Ah, yes,' Colonel Miller said, still basking in Ben's praise, his wild eye beaming madly at Duckett. 'You are to be congratulated, Sergeant, on being chosen for this very special assignment. I'm sure we have the right man for the job. Thank you and good luck.'

Ben shook hands with Colonel Miller then Duckett saluted and together they left.

'Crazy bastard,' Duckett was heard to mutter but Ben chose to ignore this as he watched the body of the horse that had died during the night being dragged on three bound planks across the parade ground to where a pile of wood formed a pyre.

The little corporal was standing by the stable door. He went inside and reappeared leading Ben's bay and the horse Duckett had chosen. 'They're a bit jumpy this mornin', sir,' the corporal said. 'I covered her in straw but they all knew she was there an' it makes 'em nervous. They always know, sir.'

Ben nodded and stroked the bay's neck.

'Silly ol' bugger,' Duckett said as they led the two horses away. 'Thinks they're 'is bloody children.'

'They are his children,' Ben said. Then he stopped and faced Duckett. 'You remember what I told you last night, Sergeant?'

'Most of it.'

'Well, let's see. My orders are that one Sergeant Duckett is to accompany me on this very special mission. If the mission is completed successfully there will be a substantial reward.' Ben didn't say what the reward would be but he noticed a quickening of interest in Duckett's eyes.

Duckett, in a grey jerkin over a blue workshirt, wore brown riding breeches and he was booted and spurred.

'No uniform,' Ben said appreciatively. 'I see you remembered that bit. Perhaps you were not as drunk as I thought.'

'I can hold my drink,' Duckett boasted.

'As I said,' Ben went on, 'no uniform. We will not want to be identified as British soldiers. And no weapons. What we'll do won't take long. Half a day at most. And you know everything you need to know for now, Sergeant. So come on, let's go.'

TWENTY-ONE

SHE was not very tall and she had shiny black hair swept back in a tight bun, pale clear skin and the longest, darkest eyelashes Hank had ever seen. She was wearing a dark-green ankle length skirt, a long sleeved, high-buttoned white blouse and a square of green cloth folded into a triangular neckerchief and secured by a leather toggle. Yet despite her demure dress she looked supple and slender in an athletic way, tomboyish almost, and with the cuffs of her sleeves turned back she looked briskly efficient. On her left arm, Hank noticed, a pale-blue armband signified she was a nursing auxilliary.

The scene was harrowing, a huge tent filled with long lines of broken bodies, the air fetid with death and decomposition, the living among them twisting, writhing in varying degrees of agony. Limbs gouged by cannon, eyes still or swivelling wildly, so much blood that on many it was hard to find and stem the source. A minister in black moved along the lines, closed eyes and folded lifeless arms on stilled chests for the corpse removal corps to identify the dead. Desperately short of morphine, quinine or any kind of palliative, febrifuge or sedative, just one doctor tended the sick and dying. And yet this lovely girl, seemingly oblivious to the putrid mix of stale bodies, congealed blood, excrement and vomit, with a cooling cloth to mop foreheads, attempted to calm the deranged and comfort the desperate.

The sounds and stench of this nightmare would haunt Hank for the rest of his life yet even here, in the full horror of that day, in a glance, a quickening of interest passed between him and the girl. Carrying a tray of implements she passed close by where Hank was standing and briefly, for only an instant, their eyes met. His undisguised admiration brought an embarrassed smile to the corners of her mouth. But it was not a dismissive smile and in the sidelong glance she gave him before modestly averting her eyes it seemed obvious to Hank that his interest was reciprocated and that an exchange of pleasantries, anything to further what appeared to be an instant mutual attraction, would not be rebuffed.

He hovered in the entrance to the hastily constructed hospital tent. He could see the girl clearly but she was engrossed in her work, too much in demand to give him any of her time. For now he would have to settle for that brief timeless encounter.

The doctor, who had been aware for some time that a polite-looking if rather clumsy young man was getting in the way of his helpers, asked quietly, 'Is there something you want, young man? A limb that requires amputation, perhaps?'

'No, no, Doctor,' Hank said stupidly. 'I'm fine, thank you.'

The doctor was washing blood from his hands. 'Then might I suggest that the passage of those engaged in urgent business in these rather cramped conditions would be less impeded if you were to remove your large and inconvenient presence?'

'Oh, yeah. Sure.' Hank was embarrassed but despite the mild rebuke the doctor didn't seem unapproachable. 'Sorry, sir. But I was wondering . . .' He pointed a finger in the direction of the girl. 'Do you know the name of that beautiful nurse?'

The doctor looked along a row of bodies as if there was more than one nurse to choose from. 'I ought to,' he said, with the hint of a smile. 'She's my daughter.' Then he looked at Hank with a puzzled frown. 'What are you doing here, son?'

'I'm the officer in charge of these men,' Hank said and he spread his hand to indicate the orderlies. 'We're here to help.'

'Then help,' the doctor said and he thrust a tray of surgical instruments in his hands.

All that day Hank followed the doctor from patient to patient, cleaning wounds, extracting shards of metal from shattered skin, gently pouring water over cracked lips, whatever was necessary, much of the time on his knees. By the time the light began to fade the bodies of the dead had been removed, the moaning and the anguished cries had been calmed and some degree of quiet and peace had been established. It was time for Hank to gather his men and find them food. The doctor thanked them all for their help and, left alone with Hank, he said, 'I've told your colonel I can only give him today.'

'You won't be back tomorrow?'

'Afraid not, son. I'm a country doctor. I have my own patients.'

'I thought this was a pretty remote place. I thought that was why we came here.'

'Not as remote as you might think. Quite a few homesteads and small communities and they all need their doctor.'

Hank nodded. 'We should be grateful you're on our side.'

'I'm not on anybody's side,' the doctor said.

'You're not a rebel and you're not a Loyalist. Then what?'

'I'm a Quaker and a pacifist. I don't believe in war, any war.'

Hank was too weary to enter into a discussion. 'Thank you, sir,' he said politely. 'Thank you for your help.'

They shook hands then as they parted the doctor looked back. 'Oh, and by the way, the young lady's name is Kathleen.'

Already the supply of food was strictly rationed and nobody was happy with what they got. Watery beef soup and doughy wheat cakes. 'Enjoy it now, boys,' the quartermaster said. 'Ain't gonna get no better.'

It was almost midnight when Hank returned to the small tent he was to share with Tom and two fellow officers. Every bone in his body it seemed was aching and all he wanted to do was lie down. The short last leg of the seven day journey from Whitemarsh had begun at first light, then the brief respite and the warming rum, then the long day's stint in the hospital tent.

The two lieutenants were asleep, one snoring loudly. Tom was sitting cross-legged, his head in his hands. He looked up as Hank raised the flap, came in and sank in a heap beside him on the damp grass. 'How did you get on?'

'We cleared out the dead but there'll be more in the morning. What have you been up to?'

'Ach,' Tom said wearily. 'Building cabins. My boys were split into eights and the same with 'C' company. We're here for the winter and we're going to need something more than tents.'

'Why did they choose this Godforsaken place?'

'Safer than Whitemarsh, I suppose. The hills behind us, easier to defend.'

'But there's nothing here,' Hank said with a yawn.

'We don't know that yet. Got to get settled, then we'll see.' Tom glanced at his brother and saw that he was asleep already, his shoulder pack for a pillow.

The army had marched from Whitemarsh only thirteen miles away, yet it had taken seven days. The rain and the wind, the sleet and then snow had slowed them down and beat them back but they had marched on, many with boots worn thin, some with no boots at all, their freezing feet wrapped in ragged strips of cloth. The footprints in the snow were specked and stained with blood from lacerated feet. Many fell and were helped up or in desperate cases left to perish. Young faces made old, hardened by the driving wind, stared, eyes wet or dimmed by snow, at the monotonous road ahead. Many had the shakes and debilitating bouts of uncontrollable shivering, hands too frozen to lift the caps on the shared canteens.

At first those who fell or were unable to continue were carried solic-itously to the roadside but as the long march progressed and the wearying days and nights passed the ragged columns of men stepped over their fallen comrades and carried on, too weak to help. Hungry and sick, they had been pushed to the limit.

The first day a tin whistle had played 'Yankee Doodle'. With their shoulders erect, they had stepped out almost jauntily. But the music had died away and they had trudged on in silence, their footsteps muffled in the snow.

Several times Tom had found the snow inviting, as if to fall and lie there might be a good way out. He'd been totally exhausted before, after a day in the field from sunrise to dusk at harvest time, but never was it anything like this. His bones felt hollow as if drained of marrow and his spirits began to sink. They seemed to be walking from nowhere to nowhere. But the sight of Jimmy, Sergeant Jimmy, grinning along the lines and trying to raise morale, kept him going.

When they did arrive at the chosen place there seemed to be nothing there. They would have to build the camp before they could bed down and it was going to be a long hard winter.

'It's our job to hold things together,' Hank said. 'I guess that's what an officer has to do.'

'I've lost three men already,' Tom said.

'Dead? Couldn't make it?'

Tom shook his head. 'They told me they'd had enough. They were going home and they just walked away.'

'Weren't you supposed to shoot them?'

'I couldn't do it. Could you?'

Hank shook his head. 'I guess not.'

'Listen,' Tom said, 'if the British come now they can finish us off. Right now we couldn't fight a herd of sheep.'

The main reception room at the Grand Hotel in Halifax had become a meeting place for high-ranking army officers like Jack Danvers, for exiled business men from Boston and for leading local supporters of the British cause. There was also a smaller room with a bright log fire and a door opening to a quiet square of garden where, well wrapped against the biting cold, Sarah and Imelda, and occasionally Aunt Mary, would take a breath of fresh air. It was deep mid-winter, bleak and cold, and the maple trees were bare. The narrow paths and the garden seats were covered in snow but Sarah felt she knew every corner and often she would venture out alone in search of the solitude so elusive in her room.

It was one such time that something happened, something that was to change the course of her life. She was standing before an oak tree with which she had conducted several silent and one-sided conversations. She wondered, she told the tree, what lay ahead and what might have happened if Tom Blanchard had lived. Would he have come in search of her? If he had lived and the rebels had lost the war would he have been detained for months, perhaps years, in some prison camp? Would the day have ever dawned when they could meet freely and declare their feelings for each other?

Standing there, alone, that winter in Halifax, Sarah felt a sharp pang of regret for what might have been and now could never be. It was over and she knew in her heart there would never, could never be another. Tom had been so obviously right for her and she for him. If she was to go on with her life it could only be in a mechanical way. She would be expected to marry. Other women, many other women, had done this. They had married and they had borne children. But they had lived out their lives with a man they could never know with that lifelong closeness, that total commitment that sometimes two people are lucky enough to share.

Tom! She closed her eyes as she stood before the oak tree. She wanted to shout his name at the grey, dismal sky, to recall him from Heaven. Surely the heartbreak in her voice would cause any compassionate God to relent and send him back. She opened her mouth, her face turned upwards as she prepared to play out in silence her little fantasy. But something, a presence, made her stop and turn to face the intruder. It was Jack Danvers.

'Colonel!'

'My dear Sarah,' he said. 'I'm so sorry. I had no wish to startle you. Your Aunt Mary said you were out here.'

The cold weather and her unexpected visitor had reddened her cheeks and her silent soliloquy had brought tears to her eyes.

'What is it?' Danvers asked. 'Are you all right?'

'It's nothing,' she said and she forced a small smile. 'I suppose I've been standing out here too long.'

'Please,' he said, showing great concern. 'Allow me to escort you indoors. There's a lovely fire burning inside.'

Sarah refused his arm. 'Thank you, but there is really no need. I'm quite all right. Just a little cold, that's all.'

She led the way back to the smaller of the two public rooms where the fire was burning brightly. She wanted people around her. She didn't want to be left alone with the colonel, attentive and handsome though he was. She felt there would be safety in numbers and with others present she would not be obliged to converse with him. But there was no one about and the hotel seemed strangely quiet.

'Where is everyone?' she asked, her unease evident in her voice.

'Mrs Harvie was here,' Danvers said brightly. 'I expect she'll be back shortly. Perhaps you would like to sit by the fire, restore a little of your natural warmth.'

Sarah glanced at him quickly, detecting a hint of irony. 'I'm so sorry, Colonel. I'm afraid I'm being most ungracious.'

'No, no. Not you, Sarah. You couldn't be. Please sit down.'

The colonel's eyes never left hers and she felt uncomfortable, concerned that they were alone and she had no idea where either her aunt or Imelda might be. Uncle Max had found a temporary office for himself by the harbour and would not be home for another hour or more.

'Tell me, Colonel,' she said, removing her bonnet and shaking out her hair as she searched for a topic of conversation that was both pertinent and impersonal. 'How is the war *really* going?'

'Who is winning and who is losing?' he said with a smile. 'Well, of course, the tide has turned in our favour as we always knew it would. We are winning on all fronts and we have this so-called General Washington at our mercy. When we capture him, and it's only a matter of time before we do, then in my view the war will be over. Without

209

him the war will simply peter out. The opposition will disappear overnight.'

'What would happen to the general were you to capture him?'

Colonel Danvers was happy to talk and to get Sarah to talk. He felt she was frightened of him, frightened of being alone with him and this was something he had not experienced before. Most of the young women he knew and had known were eager to be left alone with him.

'We'll treat him well,' he told her, 'like the fine and honourable gentleman he is. We'll probably wine and dine him, welcome him to our top table.'

Sarah raised her eyebrows.

'Then we'll take him out,' he said, 'and shoot him.'

Danvers laughed as if this was a huge joke but Sarah couldn't bring herself to join in. 'Tell me, Sarah. You say were *you* to capture him, not were *we* to capture him. Are you not one of us then? Do you not support His Majesty in such matters?'

'I hate wars, Colonel,' she said boldly. 'From what I have heard and seen wars seem equally bad for both winners and losers.'

'Sometimes,' Danvers said seriously, 'a war is necessary. Not desirable, perhaps, but necessary. Sometimes one must fight for what is right.'

'It robs people of their homes, families of their fathers, wives of their husbands, lovers of the one they love.'

'You have in mind the young man you knew in Boston.' It was not a question. It was a statement and, for Danvers, a statement that had to be made and faced.

Uncle Max or her aunt must have told him about Tom. 'I was in love with a young man named Tom Blanchard. I still am, in fact, but he was killed in this awful war.'

'He was on the wrong side,' Danvers said.

'What does it matter which side he was on? He could have been on your side. He might still have been killed. People on both sides are killed every day. It could have been you yourself.'

Danvers looked down into her earnest green eyes. 'And you wouldn't want that?'

'No, of course not.'

'But you would rather it was me than this . . . this rebel.'

'I don't want anyone to die.'

Danvers turned away. 'Life can be very strange, Sarah. Some people live long empty lives, others die young. There appears to be no sense, no pattern, to our existence.' He turned back to look at her again, took her by the shoulders. 'What matters now is that you are here and I am here. We are alive and I'm glad. Because I came here today to make a proposal.'

'A proposal?'

'A proposal of marriage. I want to ask you for your hand, Sarah. Your uncle has given his approval and this permits me to make this approach.'

So this was why the room was empty; this was why she had been left alone with the handsome colonel. Sarah hoped they were not all waiting outside, ready to burst forth in celebration the moment she said yes. If they were they were going to be very disappointed.

'You don't have to make a decision now,' Danvers assured her, disconcerted by her lack of response. He had never asked a woman to marry him before and he had always assumed any such invitation would be accepted at once. 'But I assure you, if you answer yes you will never have cause to regret it. I want to marry you, Sarah, to take care of you for the rest of your life.'

He smiled down at her, a kind and courteous smile, and she saw how genuinely handsome he was. 'You need time,' he was saying, 'but not too much time. I have been recalled. My tour of duty here is at an end. I must return to London where I understand a knighthood and a further promotion await me.'

'I'm pleased for you,' Sarah said with a genuine smile.

'This means,' he went on, 'whoever I take as my wife will be presented at court to His Majesty the King and become Lady Danvers. Life in London can be very pleasant for the highly placed and socially acceptable and, as my wife, you would most certainly be in that enviable position.'

'Thank you, Colonel,' Sarah said decisively. 'You do me a great honour, but my answer must be no.'

Danvers nodded soberly and said, 'Might I ask why?'

'Because I am not in love with you,' she said honestly.

He laughed and again he took her by the shoulders. 'Is that all? I am certain, given time, I can make you love me.'

Sarah shook her head. 'I don't think so, Colonel,' she said, a little coolly now.

'But I do,' he said, not in the least deterred. 'And to make a start I would be happy if you would call me Jack. Colonel is a little formal between two people who are to be married.'

The morning was cold but bright with a latent threat from the dark clouds on the nearby hills. The land was almost bare, the grass sparse, poor grazing country. Not Indian country, not farming country, not anything much. Ben Withers needed a smaller space and a tree where he could sling a rope. He rode steadily with Duckett close behind.

Duckett was bemused. He had not been told anything, except that he had been chosen for this assignment. But he had no idea what this assignment was and he knew very little about the man ahead, Lieutenant Withers. All he knew was that he was from Special Services and he was close to Tarleton, the top man. Now Duckett was interested, curious to know where they were going and why. Yet, like the trained soldier he was, he followed orders. He rode steadily behind the lieutenant, raising no objections, not asking questions, not even speaking until they came to a weather-beaten signpost on the otherwise poorly marked highway.

Riding slightly ahead Ben put out an arm to indicate the road he wanted to take. Duckett drew his horse to a halt at once and the horse reared slightly. 'Can't go that way, sir,' he called, as he brought the horse expertly under control.

'We have to go that way,' Ben said, turning back, 'that way and beyond. It's the quickest route.'

'Look, Lieutenant,' Duckett said. 'I got in a bit o' trouble down there, in the village. I swear, if they see me they'll come after me. It could mess up your plans.'

Ben laughed. 'You scared of a few village people?'

'You don't understand,' Duckett said.

'The colonel told me all about it,' Ben said. 'You shot some kid and you were wearing your red coat. But look at you now. Who's going to recognize you? And we'll be through there in no time. In fact, we won't even go through the village. We'll skirt around it.'

'I don't know,' Duckett said. 'They're a pretty wild bunch down there. They'd tear me apart.'

'Listen, Sergeant,' Ben said firmly. 'That's the way we're going and that's an order.'

Ben rode on and reluctantly Duckett followed. There was a cart track to the right of the village where Ben turned off, away from the huddle of small buildings in what was really no more than a tiny hamlet with a dozen houses, a store and a tavern. He didn't want to be seen just yet any more than Duckett did.

The cart track led up a slight incline into a more wooded area and just over a low hillock edged with trees, bare now since the late fall in a carpet of brown crinkled leaves. This was it. Quiet, secluded, just what Ben was looking for. It wasn't exactly like that day eight years ago but that was in early summer.

It was all boiling up inside him again and maybe, he thought, this was the only way he would ever get rid of it. Now was the time to confront the tormentor and this would be the place. Ben pulled up and slid from the bay.

Duckett pulled up behind him but didn't dismount. 'We can't stop here,' he said.

'Get down,' Ben said quietly.

He took a coiled rope from his saddle, looked at the trees and chose the one with the sturdiest branches. He tied one end of the rope to a low branch on the next tree and slung the other end over a higher branch on the taller tree. Then he jerked the rope forward until it caught and held in a fork to stop it slipping back and left the rest of the line dangling. Back at his saddle-bag, he pulled out a pistol and a cartridge case and, without comment, proceeded to load the pistol.

Duckett leaned forward in his saddle. 'You said no weapons.'

'That's right,' Ben said, pointing the loaded pistol at him. 'I also said get down.'

Duckett's dark eyes narrowed and he stepped down. 'Are you going to tell me what this is all about?'

'Yes,' Ben said. He put his hand deep in the saddle-bag and drew out his own red coat. 'But first you put this on.'

Duckett's mouth fell open. 'Are you crazy?'

'Absolutely,' Ben said. He threw the coat at him. 'Put it on.'

Duckett caught and held the coat. 'I can't do that. Not here.'

'Put the coat on,' Ben said menacingly. 'Or else . . .' He raised the pistol, aimed at a point between Duckett's eyes.

Duckett struggled into the coat.

'Button it up,' Ben ordered. Duckett did as he was told. 'Now turn around and put your hands behind your back.'

Duckett turned around, his back to Ben, his hands behind his back. Ben put the pistol on the ground, took a lanyard from his pocket and

213

tied it tight to secure Duckett's hands. He picked up the pistol and prodded Duckett in the back. 'Over there,' he ordered and he pushed him towards the tree.

At the tree Ben tied a noose in the loosely hanging rope, placed the rope over Duckett's head and tightened the noose.

'Hey!' Duckett was scared now. 'What the hell is this?'

Ben stepped back and nodded, pleased with his handiwork. 'Now Sergeant Duckett,' he said calmly, 'I'm going to tell you a little story.'

Duckett was tense, holding himself erect to stop himself from shaking. His head was in a noose, his hands were tied behind his back, he was wearing a red coat just a short walk from a village full of people who wanted to tear him apart and this crazy bastard was pointing a pistol at his head.

Ben tied the bay's reins loosely to a tree then he whacked Duckett's horse lightly on the rump and sent it scampering down the cart track.

'Hey, no!' Duckett cried. 'We've got to get away from here.'

'It's story time,' Ben said. 'Now shut up and listen. Cast your mind back, if you've got one. Cast your mind back eight years. It's a hot sunny day. Not like today. I mean, today looks like winter's coming in.'

'For Chris'sake!' Duckett said in exasperation.

'Lovely summer's day,' Ben said. 'Clear blue sky. A boy out in the woods, Roxbury way. He's running through the wood, not a care in the world, chasing his little dog. Great little dog. Terrier called Billy. And he comes across these two soldiers. Two British soldiers. They're lying there in this clearing with a cask of brandy or rum or, I don't know, some kind of hooch and there's a couple of horses tied up nearby.

'One of these soldiers jumps up and he catches Billy. Scoops him up in his arms. And as the boy comes through the trees the other fellow grabs him. Then the fellow with the dog says, "We're gonna have a bit of fun here", and he gets a rope from his saddle. You know, just like mine. And he slips the rope in a noose round the little dog's neck. Then he sets the little dog down and it runs away until he hauls it back by the rope around its neck. And he keeps doing this. He keeps giving the dog a bit of length then hauling it back by the neck. I bet it hurts like hell that, don't you? Only the soldier thinks it's funny. And so does his pal.

'Then when he gets tired of this he slips the rope over the branch of a tree and he hauls the little dog up by its neck. The little dog's kicking and struggling and swinging about in mid-air as it tries to get free. And the boy's crying and shouting for him to stop and let it down but the other soldier's got the boy in an iron grip.'

'What're you talkin' about?' Duckett asked.

'You mean, you don't remember?' Ben looked surprised. 'It was only eight years ago. The boy remembers. The boy remembers every detail. He remembers, for instance, that the fellow who held him back so he couldn't help the dog was a man called Johnson.'

'Johnson,' Duckett said, a light dawning in his eyes. 'Yeah, Johnson. I heard he got killed at Bunker.'

'Yes,' Ben said. 'Lucky for him that he did.' He looked at Duckett steadily and there was something in his expression, a bleakness that further alarmed the captive sergeant.

'This boy,' Ben went on, 'he remembers something else, too. He remembers that you were the man with the rope.'

'Who are you?' Duckett asked, trying to contain his fear.

'You don't know? Why, you're dumber than I thought, Duckett. And I didn't think that was possible.'

'It's you, isn't it? You were that kid.'

'I was that kid,' Ben confirmed.

Duckett tried to laugh. 'All this is for a dog?'

'It wasn't a dog, Duckett. Billy wasn't just any dog. He was *my* dog. And you do remember now, don't you? You let him run away and you hauled him back with the rope round his neck. Maybe I should do that with you.' Ben paused. 'Yes, maybe I should.' Then he said, 'Billy was yelping at first and I was crying and fighting this Johnson. But then Billy was sort of whimpering, begging, in his way, for mercy. But you didn't let him go, did you? You slung the rope over a branch and hauled him up by the neck and left him to swing there, kicking and struggling for his life. Then you climbed on your horse and Johnson let me go and climbed on his. And I was jumping up as high as I could to reach Billy but he was too high. I tried to climb the tree but there was no way up and all the time Billy was struggling and squealing and trying to breathe. You and Johnson thought it was funny. Then, worst of all, I ran to you and begged you to let him down. I said you can't go, you can't leave him like this. So what did you do? You shot him. You shot him and you just laughed and rode off and left us, me heartbroken and Billy hanging there dead.

'I stayed with him until dark when my dad and my uncle came looking for me. They asked me who did this terrible thing and I said I didn't know your names but I would find out. Dad said if you do you must tell us and we'll get them. But when I did find out, when you were in trouble and you got your thumbs branded for manslaughter when it should have been murder, I was a little older and I decided I would get you myself. And now I've got you.'

'This is insane,' Duckett said.

'I know,' Ben said. 'But Billy was my little dog and I loved him. And you, you are a sad, evil murderer and you're going to die. Now. Today. You are going to hang by your neck until you are dead. And if you don't die, I'll shoot you.'

Duckett's horse had run a little way down the track and stopped by some foliage. Everyone knew everyone else in the village and most people knew and could recognize other people's livestock. A boy of about fourteen had been trapping rabbits and when he saw the horse he looked around for the rider. He didn't recognize the horse and he didn't recognize the saddle. He walked on up the cart track and, as he neared the top of the slightly rising track, he caught a glimpse of a red coat. He dropped down behind a bush. Since a drunken argument led to a redcoated sergeant randomly shooting and killing a local boy named Joey Carter the attitude of the villagers to the British had been extremely hostile and they were wary now of what they openly called 'bloodybacks'. After a moment the boy peered round the bush and witnessed a very strange sight.

A man was aiming a pistol at a bloodyback whose head was in the noose of a rope slung from a tree. The boy looked closer at the bloodyback. It was him! The boy was certain. It was the one who killed Joey Carter. Great! Somebody got him. But it wasn't Mr Carter or any of Joey's family. Mr Carter wasn't there. There wasn't anyone there except this man whom he'd never seen before. He backed off down the slope. He had to tell someone, everyone, about this and he raced to the village, still clutching his rabbit traps.

Sergeant Duckett was shaking now. There was no doubt in his mind that this madman meant what he said. He was going to die and there was no way out. 'I'm sorry,' he said, fear constricting his voice. 'I'm sorry about what happened.'

'So am I,' Ben said.

'It was jus' the drink. We'd been drinkin' all mornin'.'

'Too late. You have to die.'

'No, please. You can't do this.'

'Watch me,' Ben said. He took the rope from the lower branch, wrapped it around his hand then slowly started to haul Duckett upwards. Duckett's eyes bulged but Ben pulled on the rope until his toes were barely touching the ground.

'I can't breathe.'

'Good,' Ben said. He walked across to where the ground sloped and sat down facing Duckett. He had this man exactly where he wanted him. He'd had this moment in mind for eight years Yet he felt no elation. He didn't want to enjoy it. That would make him as bad as Duckett. He must either cut him loose or kill him. But he couldn't cut him loose. That wouldn't bring an end to the matter. He had to kill him. Duckett was looking across at him, pleading with bulging eyes, as he dangled on tiptoe. Ben aimed the pistol and Duckett opened his mouth, horrified.

'No! Please!' he cried. 'You can't!'

Duckett was right. He couldn't do it. He couldn't kill in cold blood, even though that was exactly what Duckett had done to Billy. He just couldn't do it. But he couldn't let him go, either. Duckett would go straight back to Tarleton and Tarleton would send half the British Army after him. Perhaps he should put the pistol back in the saddlebag, out of reach, and tell Duckett it's to be an even fight. Man to man. No weapons. But a fight to the death. That would be the honourable thing to do.

Ben stood up to tell Duckett what he proposed but he paused. There was a strange murmuring sound. A noise, like the noise of a crowd, and it was getting louder. He looked back and from the track a group of about twenty or thirty people, men, women and children, came bearing sticks and stones. They were chanting something, then when they saw Duckett they were all talking at once, shouting abuse at the man in the redcoat. Then they ran forward, ignoring Ben, or perhaps not even aware of him, as they hurled stones and beat Duckett about the head and body with their sticks to cries of 'Bloodyback murderer!'

Ben watched, transfixed, as two of the men took the rope from the lower branch and hauled Duckett upwards. There were shouts of approval as Duckett was hauled high, his feet kicking out as he swung madly at the end of the rope. He tried to scream for help, but if he made a sound it wasn't heard in the cries of the jubilant mob. Ben felt sick and he had to turn away when a young woman stepped forward with what looked like a halberd and plunged it deep into Duckett's midriff. The writhing stopped, his head fell forward and Duckett hung there, his body speared, dead at last.

The boy who had alerted the village was looking curiously at Ben. It was time to go. Ben didn't want to speak to anyone. He didn't want to answer any questions. His mission here was over. He just wanted to ride away now, far away, find the rebel army and join in the much bigger fight that was still raging.

He went to where he had left the bay, took the reins and led the horse past the still chanting villagers. He swung up into the saddle, nodded at the boy then rode down the track towards the open country. The boy watched until he was just a small figure out on the plain and wondered who he was.

TWENTY-TWO

A T Valley Forge the rebel army was all but defeated. It was General Washington's darkest hour. Many of his men, officers included, had deserted and of the remnants many, only there because they had nowhere else to go, were demoralized. Physically the men were exhausted, still not recovered from the thirteen mile march from Whitemarsh. Many were sick, many afflicted by a maddeningly itchy skin infection and many were covered in unsightly scabs.

Food was in very short supply. There was no meat and very little bread. The army was surviving on what were known as 'firecakes', lumps of flour baked on hot stones. Housed in tents and hurriedly erected log cabins, there were few, if any, comforts to see them through the winter weeks ahead. Parades were irregular and when they were held the men who turned out looked like fugitives from a charnel-house. Some even appeared wrapped in worn blankets in place of uniforms. Sickness and scurvy plagued the camp and every day officers resigned their commissions and many more in the ranks deserted.

The mood in the camp was not improved by the tales from Philadelphia. Brought by hooch sellers at the camp gates and sometimes whores who were under the misapprehension that the men had money, stories of the high life being enjoyed by even the lowest ranks of the british Army were not appreciated. British officers, it was said, were enjoying sumptuous dinners, fatted calves, the best that Philadelphia had to offer in elegant balls, the theatre, limitless wine and compliant courtesans. The rank and file, it was also said, were having the time of their lives, every night spent in taverns, cavorting merrily with the local harlots.

Discipline in the camp was virtually non-existent. Many of the officers, who were frequently drunk and often entertained whores in their tents, had lost the respect of the men and on one occasion this lack of respect turned into resentment and open hostility. Some of the men had their families with them and one soldier, released early from guard duty, returned to find his captain in bed with his wife. The soldier fired a pistol at the officer and wounded but didn't kill him. The soldier was tried and hanged that same evening.

This, and other inequitable situations, was leading to anarchy and something had to be done. Conditions in the camp had rapidly deteriorated. Carcasses of dead horses were allowed to lie around for weeks and putrefying offal and other waste lay dangerously close to the flour stores. Hunger, filth, cold and the unremitting wind and rain all added to the discomfort, a climate in which even the brothers Blanchard found reason to become estranged.

Hank had been unable to get the girl, Kathleen, out of his mind. She had been friendly in a distant way and he realized he could not have cut a very attractive figure. He felt dirty, unwashed, his beard was long and at the straggly stage, his hair felt coarse and unkempt and in need of cutting. He didn't smell too good, either. Why would she have looked twice at him? She was simply being polite, he supposed. Well, one day he would show her that he could clean up well. But would he ever see her again?

They had gone now, the doctor back to his country practice, his daughter to whatever she did with her life. Nursing, perhaps. He knew next to nothing about her. All he knew was that there was something there that made him catch his breath. And her name was Kathleen.

It was with considerable surprise then that, from the parade ground, he saw the doctor. He told his sergeant to take over and hurried across to greet him. With no legitimate reason to delay him, he cried, 'Doctor!'

The doctor, who was with another man, stopped in his tracks and smiled as Hank came running over.

'Doctor,' Hank said breathlessly, 'you remember me, I hope? Henry Blanchard.'

'Lieutenant Blanchard, of course.'

Hank stood there, lost for words.

The doctor turned to the man beside him. 'This young man was a great help when the army first arrived. Lieutenant, Mr Dodd.'

Mr Dodd smiled and nodded at Hank.

'I thought you said you wouldn't be coming back, sir,' Hank said.

'Mr Dodd is a surgeon,' the doctor told him. 'You have a young man here who must have an amputation. Gangrene, I'm afraid. Mr Dodd has generously agreed to perform the operation.'

'That's very kind,' Hank said to Mr Dodd. 'I hope all goes well.'

The two men turned to go on their way and Hank blurted out, 'Is Kathleen with you?'

The doctor smiled. 'I'm afraid not, son. She was just helping out that day. She's back at her own work.'

Hank looked at him like a helpless puppy. 'Her own work?'

'She's a teacher at the junior school in Fourways.'

The junior school in Fourways. For days after this Hank pondered how he could get to see her. Fourways, he found, was one of the few villages in the valley, a small settlement near a major crossroads, about an hour's ride away. He couldn't wait to go there and see her, but first he needed to clean himself up. He sought out Jimmy, the man who knew everyone.

'Hey, Jimmy!'

'Yes, sir. Lieutenant Blanchard, sir,' Jimmy said, caressing every word. 'Sergeant Sunshine at your service.'

Hank looked down at the heavy volume Jimmy was carrying. 'Still reading I see.'

'Every chance I can get,' Jimmy said. 'Minister let me borrow this. Have you ever read the Good Book? The Bible?'

'We always had one at home, but I can't say I ever read it.'

'Some strange words in here, Hank. Did you ever begat anyone?'

'Not as far as I know,' Hank said, 'but – hey! – never mind that. Where can I get a mirror?'

Jimmy looked horrified. 'A mirror? Mirrors are banned. You know that. We ain't . . . we are not allowed to look at ourselves. We might scare ourselves to death.'

'I'm serious. A mirror. Where can I get one?'

'Well,' Jimmy said. 'There's a young fellow in D company. Used to be a barber.'

'A barber? Has he got his stuff, his equipment?'

'I think so. I'll ask him if you like.'

'Great!' Hank said. 'And you know, Jim, you sound good. I mean it. You sound almost intelligent.'

Jimmy arranged for Hank to get his hair cut and his straggly beard straightened up the same evening. The young barber did have a mirror and initially Hank was shocked by what he saw.

'Cut the beard down,' he said. 'Close as you can.'

He washed his threadbare shirt and dried it, shivering, before a blazing fire. He scraped caked mud from his jerkin and slept with his pants carefully lined up under the blanket he slept on.

'What's going on?' Tom asked. 'You going to a wedding?'

'I hope so,' Hank said, and he told his brother about the girl.

'You can't go,' Tom said. 'It's too dangerous. In any case, you can't just go off to see some girl. You're an officer, for God's sake. Too many officers wandering off. Think of the men. How do you think they feel?'

'She's not *some* girl.'

'Your place is here.'

'I'm sick of here,' Hank said. 'We're beaten anyway. Anyone can see that.'

'You're no better than the rest,' Tom told him

For a moment it looked as if they might square up to each other, but Hank turned on his heel and went to the stables. The corporal normally in charge was not there. Hank found one of the few healthy-looking horses and without a word to anyone he rode out of the camp. He was going to find the girl called Kathleen and nobody was going to stop him.

But Tom was right. The indiscipline of the officers had led to the present state of chaos and apathy. It seemed that most of the men were just waiting for the end. Conditions at the camp, the mood of the men, filled General Washington with dismay. He knew only too well it would be a simple matter for Howe's men to dispose of the rebel army once and for all at Valley Forge and it was a surprise to many that they didn't.

Some said the British general was far too busy to give the necessary order. He was sampling the fruits of Philadelphia, entertaining his notorious mistress, Lizzie Loring, attending 'official' functions that were simply an excuse to eat, drink and be merry. All this as Washington worried about the lack of food, that his men were inadequately clothed and had not been paid for weeks and the ever present danger that disease might spread through his depleted force.

In the rebel officers' mess the consensus was that the move to Valley Forge was a massive error of judgement. The general had been swayed in his choice of site by men who knew nothing of military matters and even less of the bleakness of the place.

All ranks, officers and men, held General Washington in high regard. They appreciated his sympathetic concern for their well-being and his always kindly attitude towards them. But there was also a strong feeling that he was too weak to win this war and far too courteous to his advisers who, according to their critics, were both ignorant and ill-informed.

Why General Howe didn't annihilate them there and then was inexplicable, but he didn't and the rebel army survived the worst of the winter. The British general's excuse was that armies traditionally did not do battle in winter and this was true. But the intelligence he was receiving must have told him that an attack on Valley Forge at that time would not have entailed a battle, merely a rout.

'Is it true?' Imelda burst into the bedroom. 'Colonel Danvers has asked you to marry him?'

Sarah shrugged, unable to raise any enthusiasm.

'Oh, Sarah! What did you say?' Imelda was brimming with excitement. She took Sarah's hands in hers and they sat side by side on the bed. 'Surely you didn't say no.'

'I can't marry Colonel Danvers, Imelda. You know that. I still love Tom.'

Imelda's face clouded. 'Tom Blanchard is dead,' she said gently. 'You have to accept it, Sarah. You can't mourn Tom forever. He wouldn't want that. Your life must go on. You're young and alive and – Colonel Danvers! Why, he's the most eligible man in the whole of the British Army – and the most handsome!'

'You knew about this,' Sarah said accusingly, though she was not angry. She could never be really angry with Imelda. 'You knew the colonel wanted to get me alone. You, Uncle Max, even Aunt Mary. Where were you all, for goodness' sake?'

'Well, I suppose it wasn't entirely proper,' Imelda conceded. 'It was Daddy. He wanted us all out of the way so the colonel could speak to you in private.'

'You were wasting your time, all of you. I told him no and that's an end to it.'

Imelda shook her head. 'I don't think so. Colonel Jack is not a man to take no for an answer. I suspect the ladies always say yes to Colonel

Jack.' She grinned wickedly. 'If you know what I mean.'

'Imelda Harvie!' Sarah pretended to be shocked.

Imelda laughed. 'Colonel Jack will be back and he'll sweet talk you into his arms. You'll see. He's a man of experience. When he gets to work on you, you'll just crumble.' She skipped out of the way as Sarah tried to hit her with a cushion. 'All I can say is, I wish it was me. He can sweet talk me into his bed any day.'

Sarah heard no more of Colonel Danvers for several days. Her Uncle Max, obviously aware of her refusal, was more than a little cool and impatient towards her. But Aunt Mary was the same as always. Kind, gentle, comforting. She was a lovely lady, thought Sarah. But how on earth, she wondered, did she come to marry Uncle Max? She was everything he was not and Sarah hoped Imelda realized just how lucky she was to have such a mother.

Sarah wished her own mother was here. She needed her now. But, of course, if her mother was still alive Sarah would still be at the farm. War or no war, Sarah's family would never have left the farm. They had nothing to fear from the local people. They had many friends and twice a year in May and September her father threw open the gates and there was feasting and dancing that went on half the night. Sarah thought of those warm nights when as a child she was allowed to stay up with Cousin Imelda until they fell asleep on the veranda and were carried upstairs by Dad or Joseph and Miss Pansy would put them to bed. Aunt Mary and Imelda always came but Uncle Max was never there. Uncle Max always had business to attend to.

Her mother's eldest sister, Aunt Alice, never came either. She was all right in her way but, as children, Sarah and Imelda had always been a little frightened of her. She was even now rather strict and forbidding as Sarah discovered when she went to stay with her after what happened at the farm. Aunt Alice was family it was true, but Sarah became much more relaxed when she went to stay at the convent with the nuns.

How different things would have been if her family had not been murdered. Many times Sarah had gone over the details of what happened that day or, at least, what she had been told had happened and she still couldn't believe any local people would do such a thing. Once, when she had mentioned these doubts, her Uncle Max had flown into a rage. What are you suggesting, girl? That this was the work of His Majesty's loyal soldiers? She was not suggesting anything, she had told him meekly. But her doubts had remained.

Tears always threatened to engulf her when she thought of her lovely parents and Joseph and Miss Pansy and little Buzz and she knew she mustn't dwell on the past. She must force herself to think of something else. Right now, with Colonel Danvers pursuing her, she needed to think carefully about her future.

Her options were limited. If she returned to Boston she would not be in any danger. She was of no consequence to either side, rebels or redcoats. But she had no family there now, unless the Harvies returned with her and that seemed unlikely. Uncle Max had his heart set on a life in London. He would go and he would take Aunt Mary and Imelda with him. All Sarah would have was Aunt Alice. Her Aunt Alice would take her in, of course, but she probably wouldn't really want to and, in truth, Sarah told herself, she wouldn't want to live with Aunt Alice.

There was only Tom's family but she had met his parents only once and now with Tom gone there was no connection. Why did these things happen? Why did fate have to be so cruel? Why did there have to be a war? If Tom was alive she would marry him now, today. But he wasn't and she had to face it. Tom was dead. He was never coming back.

In Boston she knew Melanie Stokes. And there was the little boy Buzz. If she could she would find Buzz and take care of him, for Miss Pansy's sake. She could find a small house and take him in and perhaps work as a teacher to earn a little money. After all she would not be penniless. Her father's land and the farm were hers now though Uncle Max thought she should wait until the war was won and things returned to normal before selling up. There would be lots of takers then and she would get a good price. But Sarah didn't want to think about that. The farm held so many memories. She had lived there all her life.

The weather was less severe now and people were venturing out more. A number of social events were arranged and one Saturday the Harvies and Sarah were invited to an evening at home in a large house rented by a prominent Loyalist family, Bostonians in exile.

The house was brightly lit, the light from the tall windows turning the surrounding snow a warm yellow, and the strains of a string quartet could be heard faintly as the Harvies' carriage crunched up the driveway. Uncle Max and Aunt Mary exchanged glances. It was all so reminiscent of home.

'Oh, Daddy,' Imelda said. 'We used to do this.'

'And we will again, my love,' Max promised.

It was a little after eight when the Harvies' entourage arrived and they immediately caused a stir. The level of conversation dropped and many eyes, some hard and hostile, but mostly with at least the pretence of friendly appraisal, turned towards Sarah.

'Aunt Mary,' Sarah whispered in alarm, 'what is it? What is everybody looking at?'

'They're looking at you, dear,' Aunt Mary told her gently. 'I expect they've heard of the colonel's proposal.'

Imelda was revelling in the attention as if it was partly directed at her. 'Isn't it lovely? Everyone wants to know us. Our darling Sarah is to marry an English knight and become a lady.'

'But it isn't true.' Sarah was alarmed. 'I told him no.'

'Of course it's true. You want to be a lady, don't you?'

'Imelda!' Aunt Mary scolded. 'Now stop it. This minute. And another thing, Sarah does not have to marry to become a lady. She is already a lady – unlike some.'

But Aunt Mary's efforts to diffuse the situation went unheeded. Three simpering girls clustered fussily around Sarah to offer their congratulations on her engagement and before her denials could be heard the hostess, a Mrs Prence, a florid lady who was doing her best to be gracious, claimed Sarah as a 'special' guest.

'Oh, my dear,' Mrs Prence gushed, 'we are all so pleased for you. You must allow me to introduce you to the governor's lady. Soon you will be going off to London no doubt, but everyone here is simply dying to meet you.'

Sarah was overwhelmed. She knew neither how to respond nor how to escape. She looked back at Aunt Mary who obviously felt great sympathy for her but could do little to help. Uncle Max was smiling magnanimously now, holding his glass of wine high, as he held court with several self-important gentlemen like himself.

It was clearly of great import to Uncle Max that she didn't dispel the various misconceptions and she didn't want to upset either him or Aunt Mary. She felt she owed them both a great deal. Imelda, too, was enjoying her new found connections. Sarah decided, for the moment, not to spoil the party. It was simply a mistake. She had told Colonel Danvers in the clearest possible terms that her answer was no. She understood he was expected later. When he arrived then she would

THE WAY IT WAS

ask him to put the matter right.

Bowing and barely listening to the platitudes on all sides, Sarah was accepting too many glasses from the punch bowl. Once, when she encountered Imelda, she whispered, 'I'm getting quite merry.'

'Lovely!' Imelda was of little help. 'Let us both get merry. We can dance and sing and scandalize the lot of them.'

'I thought you'd have found a handsome cavalry officer by now.'

'Have you seen them?' Imelda said. 'They're all old men. They're so arthritic they can barely stand up never mind ride a horse!'

Sarah smiled and moved away, aware that Imelda was rather more merry than she was. She would wait now as she had planned. She would resolutely avoid the people who sought to press intoxicating drinks upon her and confront the dashing and presumptuous colonel the moment he appeared. Then she saw him. He was in the wide entrance hall, handing his fur-collared cloak to a manservant.

Uncle Max almost ran through the slowly-moving crowd to greet him and steer him into the small ballroom where most of the guests were gathered. Colonel Danvers kissed Aunt Mary's hand but his darting eyes were scanning the busy room until he saw Sarah. Without a word to Max Harvie, who for a moment was left talking to himself, Danvers strode across to face her with his darkly handsome smile.

Nervous earlier, Sarah now regretted having accepted the glasses of punch. She offered her hand. 'Colonel Danvers.'

'Jack,' he said. 'You promised.'

'I don't remember promising anything,' she told him, swaying a little. 'And I have something to say to you, *Jack*.'

He smiled down at her, realizing she must have had a glass of wine or something and this amused him. Far from making her seem older, more sophisticated, it made her seem even younger.

'For some reason,' she said, 'everyone here seems to think you and I are to be married.'

'Sounds like a nice idea,' he said, still smiling.

'But we're not,' she told him. 'You know we're not.'

The string quartet were playing a waltz.

'Allow me,' he said and he swept her out to the dance floor.

227

TWENTY-THREE

BEN Withers opened his eyes. The man who had kicked his leg was holding a pitchfork to his throat. From where he lay Ben could see farm boots, a rough woollen greatcoat, a man of about fifty in a woollen hat looking down at him.

'This is my land,' the man said.

Ben started to get up but the man held the pitchfork closer. 'I'm sorry, sir,' Ben said. 'I was taking a rest and my horse is tired.' He was aware that he was trespassing. He'd passed a sign on the high road that read Lowe's Farm. 'Would you be Mr Lowe?'

'Could be,' the man said.

'Well, as I said, sir, I'm sorry. I don't mean any harm. If you are Mr Lowe I wonder if I could buy some bread and some fodder for my horse.'

Mr Lowe relaxed a little. 'Where are you heading?'

Ben smiled apologetically. 'That's it, sir,' he said. 'I'm not sure.'

The farmer frowned. 'What do you mean you're not sure? Where'd'you come from and where're you goin?'

These were difficult questions. Ben had no idea where the man's sympathies lay. Was he for the rebels or was he for the redcoats? 'Well,' he said, 'I'd like to go home, up north. To Boston.'

'Boston, huh? Rebel army's got Boston.'

'So I heard,' Ben said.

'You look a fit enough young feller. Why aren't you in the army?'

The question had to be answered one way or another. 'Sir,' Ben said respectfully, 'I don't know if your loyalty is to the British or to the Congressional Army, so I'm going to have to tell you the truth. All I ask, sir, if you think I'm on the wrong side, you allow me to go on my way. Give me, say, a half-hour before you raise the alarm.'

Mr Lowe laughed and Ben sensed that he was not a hard man. In some ways he resembled what Ben remembered of his father. 'Maybe I should turn you in for trespassing.'

'If I've done any damage, I'll be happy to pay for it.'

'And how would you do that?'

'I could give you a half day's work. I'd work a full day but I need to get something to eat. And something for my horse.'

'You want me to pay you?'

'No, sir. I'd pay for the food and I'd work for nothing. I want to put things right between us. I'm an honest worker, Mr Lowe. I promise, if I can, I'll do whatever needs doing.'

'Great one for striking bargains, aren't you, son? So tell me, which army should you be in?'

There was no way out. 'Well, as you said, sir, the rebels are in Boston. But I hear we lost Philadelphia.'

The farmer's eyes crinkled even further. 'Come on up to the house. And bring your horse down to the stables.'

Ben walked ahead of Mr Lowe, leading the bay. There were two other horses in the stable. Ben led the bay to a trough and the horse lapped up water as the farmer found a nosebag and filled it with fodder. Ben lifted off the saddle, fixed the nosebag then put an arm around the horse's neck and hugged her.

'What's in the saddle-bag?' Mr Lowe asked.

'Change of clothes, hunting knife and a pistol,' Ben said.

The farmer nodded and led him into the house. 'Got a visitor,' he called and Mrs Lowe came from the kitchen. 'Young feller joining us for breakfast.'

Mrs Lowe smiled at Ben and offered him a seat at the big old table. 'And does this young feller have a name?'

'It's Ben, ma'am. Ben Withers.'

'Needs feedin' up,' Mr Lowe said. 'Got a day's work ahead.'

Mrs Lowe's breakfast of eggs and pancakes and slices of lean bacon and fresh bread with half a pint of hot tea seemed like the best breakfast Ben had ever had and he was ready to show his appreciation. All morning he chopped cords of beech and maple and stockpiled the hardwood in a reserve shed ready for seasoning. The farmer was already into this winter's wood and to help store a new supply Ben was just what he needed, someone to swing the axe and fill the reserve for next winter. He'd been troubled with his shoulder this year and the

229

kind of aches and pains he'd never had before.

At midday Mrs Lowe brought more tea and thick wedges of cheese sandwiches. Then Ben carried on working all afternoon.

'Listen, son,' Mr Lowe said, as the sky was darkening, 'you don't have to leave tonight. We can find you a bed and you can make an early start in the morning.'

'Well, thank you, sir,' Ben said, 'but I think I've put you and Mrs Lowe to enough trouble.'

'No, no,' Mr Lowe said. 'Mrs Lowe'll be pleased to have you. We got room. We got two boys and right now they're away with General Washington.' He winked an eye. 'But we don't tell folk that. And besides, you can tell me all about yourself and what the hell a boy from Boston is doing out here.'

'I will, sir,' Ben said, 'and I promise you, you won't believe it.'

Later, after he had cleaned up and ventured meekly into the Lowes' big living room, Mr Lowe handed him a warming glass of rum and they sat by the blazing fire with the enticing aroma of Mrs Lowe's cooking drifting in from the kitchen. Ben noticed the table had been laid for four.

It was all very homely and much more than Ben could have hoped for that morning but he wondered about the fourth place. Who was it for? Was Mr Lowe really a rebel supporter or had he somehow alerted the British? Maybe Colonel Tarleton will join us for dinner, Ben thought resignedly, with a phalanx of guards waiting to take me off to a place of execution.

The wheels of a cart crunched on the icy snow outside. Mr Lowe stood up. 'Ah,' he said to Ben, 'my friend the professor.'

Ben could hear voices in the kitchen, Mrs Lowe and a male voice, then a tall stooping rather elderly gentleman appeared.

'Come in, come in,' Mr Lowe said. 'Let's take off that cloak.'

The tall man nodded at Ben as he was relieved of his cloak and went to rub his hands before the fire. 'God, it's cold out there!' he said. 'And how are you, Charlie?'

'Fine, fine, we're all fine. We've done a hard day's work today. We've not been poring over old books in a warm study. Ben, this is my friend the professor, as fine a reprobate as you could wish to meet. Joe, this is Ben, a young tramp I picked up this morning.'

'Don't be offended, son,' the professor said. 'You'll get no fancy introductions from Charlie here. Nor will I.'

'I'm pleased to meet you, sir,' Ben said as Mrs Lowe called them to the table and showed them where she wanted them to sit.

'Eat now, talk later,' Mrs Lowe said, as she came in bearing bowls of soup, and they did as instructed.

'Ada,' the professor said, as he dispensed the brandy he'd brought with him and Mrs Lowe poured the coffee. 'I won't say that once again you have surpassed yourself because that, I think, adds quite unnecessary pressure. But you have, my dear, you have.'

'He means he enjoyed it,' Mr Lowe said to no one in particular.

'That I did,' the professor said. 'That I did.'

'Be quiet, both of you,' Mrs Lowe ordered and this amused Ben. She appeared to treat both her husband and the professor as if they were children. 'We want to hear from Ben.'

'Yes,' Mr Lowe said. 'I believe our young friend Ben is going to entertain us with the story of how he comes to be here tonight. A story, he tells me, we'll find hard to believe.'

All three – Mr Lowe, Mrs Lowe and the professor – coffee and cognac to hand, looked at Ben expectantly. Ben decided to begin at the beginning and tell them the story of the little boy and the terrier, Billy, in the woods near Roxbury eight years ago.

They listened fascinated to the point where the villagers killed Duckett and Ben wandered here in the snow that began to fall two days ago and had fallen steadily ever since. He wanted to join up with General Washington's army, he told them, but he didn't know this part of the world and he was not sure he was heading in the right direction.

The professor was the first to speak. 'Well now,' he said, 'that story is so unbelievable it must be true.'

'Why don't you just go home, Ben?' Mrs Lowe said. 'Things are not going well for General Washington's army. The war will soon be over. Nobody believes Washington can win now.'

'Please don't say that, Mrs Lowe,' Ben said. 'We have to win.'

'It's true Washington's in trouble,' the professor said. 'His army's penned in a place called Valley Forge but they're not beaten yet.'

'If the British come out of Philadelphia,' Mr Lowe said, 'they can end it right now. Don't know why their man Howe doesn't do it.'

'I don't think Howe wants to fight,' the professor said. 'I'm sure he'd like to end it peacefully. I believe what he has wanted all along is for the Congressional Army to call it off, disband, say it was all a mistake. He'd like to say all is forgiven and just go back to England.

That way a lot of lives could be saved.'

'But is it really that bad?' Ben asked.

'Well, it is in General Washington's camp but General Gates has done a lot better in the north. The British sent this general over to sort things out. Gentleman Johnny Burgoyne. Bit of a character, by all accounts. But, to be fair, he didn't get the kind of support he was promised. He made a few pretty serious mistakes, too.'

'Employing those Indians was a big mistake,' Mr Lowe said.

'Yes,' the professor told Ben. 'When the reinforcements he'd been promised didn't materialize he put a lot of Indians on his payroll and told them they had to behave like soldiers. They didn't know what he was talking about. They got completely out of control, went around terrorizing folk and scalping those they captured. British lost a lot of support over that. Wherever he went, he'd been told, there'd he Loyalists waiting to join him. But it didn't happen. Then at Saratoga he found he was trapped, there was no way out and he was forced to surrender.'

'So Gates is a hero,' Ben said.

'Gates gained a lot of respect all round. Seems he behaved like a true gentleman. Treated his prisoners well and he was civil and courteous to Burgoyne.'

'So,' Mr Lowe said. 'Washington lost Philadelphia and Gates won at Saratoga. Lots of calls for Gates to replace Washington.'

'That would be a mistake,' Mrs Lowe said. 'Everyone loves George Washington. Ordinary people, I mean. And anyway, you can't change your leader in the middle of a war.'

'Well, I don't know about that, Ada,' the professor said. 'The British are not happy with Howe and it seems he wants to go home anyway. I reckon they'll make a change in the spring.'

They talked well into the night but it was not until after Mrs Lowe had gone to bed that the professor told Ben, 'It would be a mistake to go to Valley Forge, son. Didn't want to say this in front of Mrs Lowe with her boys being there, but I understand conditions are pretty bad. Short of everything, food, clothing, decent shelter. You'd be better off joining Gates's army.'

Ben nodded. 'If I can find them.'

'What do you think, Joe?' Mr Lowe asked.

'Well,' the professor said, 'we can arrange for him to go up north by river. Best way. Most direct way. Saves riding around for days on end. Safer, too. Less chance of riding into trouble.' He turned to Ben. 'We have a boatman who'll know exactly where to take you, an old Indian guy. He's out every day and he looks like he's just trawling for fish so nobody bothers him. But he works for us.'

'For us?' Ben queried.

'Yes, son. We have a network of folk working to secure our country's future. Most of us are too damned old to fight but we're not too old to spread propaganda and false information and help undermine the British at every opportunity.'

Ben nodded appreciatively. 'So I go by river.'

'Soon as it can be arranged,' the professor confirmed.

'One problem, Ben,' Mr Lowe said. 'Can't take your horse.'

Ben looked pained. He'd grown fond of the bay. 'Would you have her, Mr Lowe? Take good care of her?'

Mr Lowe nodded. 'Sure I will. And when we've won this crazy war you can come back and claim her. You can bring that lovely girl you got up in Boston.'

Ben smiled. He had shown Mrs Lowe the portrait of Melanie. 'I will. I promise.' He looked at the professor. 'We are going to win, aren't we, sir?'

'Sure we are,' the professor told him confidently. 'And you know why? Because nobody loves the British. The rest of Europe hate them for their supercilious ways. We are going to keep at them and nobody but nobody is going to come to their aid.'

He held up his glass of brandy and the flames of the fire danced in the golden liquid. 'When I say nobody likes the British,' he said carefully, 'what I really mean is nobody likes the *English*. Most British soldiers are uneducated oafs and the English officer class treats them like human excrement. Most of them have no idea where they are or why they're here. Nobody tells them anything. They're professional soldiers. Their job is to stand up and die. Whereas our men know exactly why they're here and they have everything to live for.

'General Howe's campaign is seen by many as a dithering mess of missed opportunities. In fact, it may well be that Howe is the only civilized man among them. But have no fear. Most English officers are a product of one or two snot-nosed schools. Like their so-called aristocracy, they suffer from delusions of superiority. And that's what'll bring 'em down.'

TWENTY-FOUR

H ANK rode fast, so anxious to see the girl Kathleen that he arrived at Fourways before lunch time. The junior school was the first thing he saw. As he rode down the hillside towards the village he saw a long low building with what was clearly a school playground. And there she was.

Through a large window he could see a dozen rapt faces of seven or eight year olds and Kathleen sitting on a child's desk apparently reading aloud. He tied his horse at the two-bar fence and leaned on a post. The playground had been cleared of the deep snow but a fresh fall had left a new thin layer. Already there was a long, icy, child-made slide. Behind him snow-decked pines covered the hillside like a thousand Christmas trees. Maybe next Christmas, he told himself, the war will be over and things will be different.

Kathleen had her back to him but he knew that tight black bun and he could see her profile as she turned her head. A small boy looked through the window, saw Hank and Hank made a face that made the little boy laugh. Kathleen glanced up and said something to him. She carried on reading aloud, but those nearest the boy were looking out of the window at Hank who was entertaining them with funny faces.

She turned and looked out at him in surprise. Hank raised a hand and waved. Kathleen frowned at him, said something to the children and left the classroom. Moments later she was in the playground. Hank vaulted the low fence.

'Can I help you?' she asked.

Hank looked at her as if struck dumb.

'Are you looking for someone?'

'You,' he blurted out. 'I'm looking for you.'

She looked at him curiously, her head on one side, and he was not

234

sure whether she remembered him or she was paying him back for the intrusion.

'Your father said your name is Kathleen and you work at the school in Fourways.'

She nodded. 'Then he's correct. My name is Kathleen, I do work at the school and this is Fourways.'

'Yes,' Hank said.

She looked at him blankly. 'So?'

'We met at the camp when you were helping him out. I was in charge of the helpers. Not you, I mean the soldiers.' He was making a mess of this and he knew it.

Kathleen relented. 'I know who you are but you look different.'

'I've had a wash,' he said, feeling stupid as soon as he said it.

'Oh good,' she said, 'and not before time if I remember rightly. So what can I do for you?'

'Well, the thing is,' he said, 'I had to come and see you because, well, I mean, we don't know each other.'

She was nodding as if attempting to understand. 'Is that a good idea? Going to see someone you don't know?'

'No, no,' he said. 'I've come to see you because of the war.'

'Because of the war?'

'Well, yes. I mean, there's so little time. I don't know how long we'll be at Valley Forge. I don't know what's going to happen to us. We need to come to an arrangement.'

She stood before him, in the playground, her arms folded, as all the children in her waiting class watched from the window.

'We have to come to an arrangement,' Hank repeated. 'Look, Kathleen, if I can call you Kathleen, this is the craziest thing I have ever done in my life. But there's so little time. There's a war on and we don't know what's going to happen. Everything has to he speeded up. Real fast, if you know what I mean. If things were different I'd be asking you to walk out with me. I'd be asking your father for permission to visit you.'

'I thought he'd already given that,' she said.

'Well no, not exactly,' he admitted. With a sweep of his hand he indicated the school building. 'If this place was a grand hall and there was music I could ask you to dance. I would ask you for your card and I'd fill in every space. I wouldn't want you to dance with anyone else but me.'

She smiled and he was encouraged.

'I'd take you for boat rides on the river and I'd take you home for tea then, after a suitable time, I'd ask you to marry me.'

Kathleen looked at him wide-eyed, incredulous.

'But there isn't time for all that in a war,' he told her.

'You're mad,' she said.

'I know,' he agreed. 'But there are times when one has to be a little mad. The thing is, I've no time to wait. So I'll tell you now. I want to marry you.'

'You want to marry me,' she said, trying but failing to conceal her amusement. 'So hadn't you better tell me your name?'

'Hank,' he said. 'Henry Blanchard. My brother and my friends all call me Hank. We're from Boston.'

'From Boston,' she said, as if implying that explained everything.

Then she laughed and the curve of her lips, the high colour in her cheeks, her dark eyes, her dark shiny hair made him want to take her in his arms.

'Lieutenant Blanchard,' she said, 'you are going to have to leave now. I have a class of seven year olds waiting.'

'You won't forget me, will you?'

'How could I?'

'Promise. Promise you will never ever forget me.'

She backed away. 'I promise I will never ever forget you.'

'And I can come and see you? After the war?'

His mention of the war that seemed far from over and in which so much could happen saddened Kathleen. 'I hope so,' she said.

'I'll write to you,' he called. 'Care of the school. Fourways.'

She nodded from the doorway and he turned and bowed with an extravagant flourish at the watching children and they all laughed and waved. Then she watched as he rode away.

Back at the camp Hank sought Jimmy. He had only been away a few hours, half a day at the most. But he wanted to know what if anything, had happened in his absence.

'The general has issued new orders,' Jimmy told him. 'Place has to be cleaned up. Men got to stay in camp, stop stealing fences and stuff for fuel. Officers got to stay put, too. Set an example. No more riding off to see pretty schoolma'ams.'

'Right,' Hank said. 'So nothing's happened.'

'We have a new sergeant,' Jimmy said.

'Oh yes?'

'A Sergeant Ray. He used to be called Sergeant Sunshine but that sounded kind of silly. So he's changed it. He's still a Sunshine, only now he's a ray of sunshine. What do you think?'

Hank laughed. 'Jimmy Ray? Fine, if that's what you want.'

'Well, as you weren't here,' he said, 'I asked Tom and he said it would be OK. He'd inform the colonel. My promotion has not been prom— what is it?'

'Promulgated,' Hank said.

'My promotion has not been promulgated. So when company orders go up, if the colonel says it's OK, I'll be Sergeant Ray.'

'Congratulations,' Hank said, with a smile.

'Oh, and by the way,' Jimmy went on, 'I hear we have a new Inspector General. Mr Conway – that his name? – Mr Conway has been sacked. We now have a German gentleman, a baron no less. I think they say his name is Baron von Steuben.'

'And what's he going to do?' Hank asked sceptically.

'Knock us into shape by all accounts,' Jimmy said.

Colonel Danvers had danced with Sarah all evening, as if this was his right. She had been unable to do anything about it and he had not made any announcement regarding the engagement. The problem now was that the governor, prompted by his wife, had invited the pair to a grand ball at his official residence, an invitation that was difficult to refuse. Aware that several glasses of punch was rather more than she could safely cope with, Sarah had remained silent. She was still acquiescent when the colonel informed Max and Aunt Mary of the invitation. Imelda wanted to know why she was not invited and the colonel gave her his most charming smile and said he would 'see what he could do'.

It was not until the following morning that Sarah felt able to assert herself. But by then a young subaltern had been detailed to partner Imelda and Sarah found she was part of a foursome.

'Sarah, please,' Colonel Danvers implored her when he called that afternoon, 'please think about what I have to offer. Your future would be secure. We would be presented at court. I have a country house in Buckinghamshire and a pied-à-terre in the city. My mother has a large house in Northumberland, a lovely part of the country where we would be most welcome. Come with me to England and in due course we will be married in the village church. We would then take the Grand Tour. Paris, Venice, Rome.'

It was all very seductive. 'But are you not concerned that I don't love you?' she asked.

'If the young man you set your heart on were alive I would help you find your own home in Boston and I would wish you luck in waiting for him.'

'But why? Why should you care?'

'Because I love you,' he said. 'I want you to be happy. But I don't want you to return to Boston and an uncertain future. You are free to marry and I have asked you to marry me. You say you don't love me. I would consider it a privilege if you would allow me to spend the rest of my life in earning your love.'

Sarah didn't know what to say. He seemed so genuine.

The colonel laughed. 'Please don't look so alarmed. We have time to think this through. In the meantime, let us enjoy Nova Scotia. The weather is improving and the governor's ball must surely be the most prestigious event in this God-forsaken place.'

In spite of herself, Sarah was wavering. After all, there was nothing for her in Boston.

'You can't refuse to accompany me to the ball, young lady,' the colonel said. 'Your cousin Imelda is expecting you.'

Sarah laughed, knowing this was true and there was no escape. She would go to the ball. But first, she told herself, she would consult the only person she felt she could really trust, the only person she had left to consult.

The governor's ball proved a splendid affair held in the State House, the governor's residence. Once again most of the ladies present were of an older generation, the wives of high-ranking British officers, government officials and local dignitaries. Sarah and Imelda shone like jewels on a tray of marbles, Sarah in a demure yet elegant dress put together in five days and nights by the celebrated dressmaker whose help Aunt Mary had enlisted.

Gilded mirrors and grand portraits adorned the walls. Scores of candles in shining chandeliers and elaborate candlesticks lit the privileged scene and the gentle music of flutes and violins filtered through the low-pitched buzz of the chattering guests.

Sarah, accepting a tall glass from a silver tray, remembered at once the previous occasion and at the earliest opportunity poured the drink into a flower filled vase. Imelda looked down her nose at the effete young officer delegated to escort her and chose to dance with a fur trader from Toronto who, in spite of his wandering hands, succeeded in making her laugh.

As a newly engaged young lady Sarah was not required to carry a dance card. As if by right, Colonel Danvers claimed all her dances, stayed by her side and took her by the hand to accompany him wherever his presence was required. All that evening the resplendent colonel romanced her persuasively and when carriages were drawn she was delivered, along with Imelda, safely back to her temporary home at the Grand Hotel.

It had been yet another charm assault by the dashing colonel and the next morning Sarah was still reeling from the impact. She had been dazed by all the attention. She had enjoyed it, slowly feeling herself drawn into and engulfed by the aura of glamour that surrounded him.

'You had a lovely time,' Aunt Mary said at breakfast. 'I can tell. Imelda is still in bed. Too much wine, I expect. That girl doesn't know when to stop and she thinks I don't know. But I have my spies.'

'She's lovely,' Sarah said loyally, 'and so funny. I do hope she finds some handsome young officer. Nearly all the men last night were far too old for her. And married, most of them.'

'She said you spent the whole evening with Colonel Danvers.'

Sarah smiled. 'I had little option. He was always there. But he's . . . very nice.'

'You like him?'

'It's difficult not to, Aunt Mary. But you know, he's quite a lot older than me.'

'Eight or nine years? That's nothing, dear.'

'It's twelve actually. He's thirty-two. Tom was only a year older than me.'

'I know,' Aunt Mary said quietly. 'But these things happen, Sarah. Your life is only just beginnng. I'm sure you would have been happy with Tom. I remember him well. Always very polite and pleasant, a gentleman. As was his brother Henry. A credit to Mrs Blanchard. She must have been very proud of them and I'm sure she must be devastated at losing them. I mean, to lose one of them is bad enough but to lose them both. . . .

'You know, I really thought that Henry Blanchard would marry Imelda and so did Imelda. And I think he would have if he had lived.

She really was very fond of him. It would have been nice to have you married to Tom and Imelda married to Henry and everything the way it used to he before this dreadful war.

'But now, now we have to move forward. No use looking back. What's happened has happened and I see a bright future, indeed a glittering future for you with Colonel Danvers. I really do.'

'Even though I don't love him?'

'Time changes everything, Sarah. You may come to love him one day. You don't exactly dislike him and that's a good start.'

'But that isn't fair to him. I'm sure he could find someone who would truly love him.'

'He doesn't want that. He wants you.'

'But why?' Sarah was genuinely perplexed. 'Why me?'

'I think the plain truth is that he's a man born and brought up as a member of the English upper classes where he has always been given or taken whatever he wanted. If something is denied him he wants it all the more.'

'And if I agreed to marry him,' Sarah said, 'he would soon grow tired of me and start wanting someone else. Our marriage would become a pretence.'

'Quite possible,' Aunt Mary agreed. 'But if that did happen it wouldn't be so bad. It happens, I believe, in the majority of such marriages. The husband takes a mistress but his respectability is maintained. His home and his wife and family are sacrosanct.'

'I'd be miserable.'

'Many ladies are miserable. But they find their own outlets and, as they get older, they become thankful. It's far better to be miserable in comfort, Sarah, than to be miserable and poor.'

'You sound as though you approve.'

'It's the way of the world, dear.'

'Is that what happened with you and Uncle Max?' Sarah asked innocently.

Aunt Mary smiled. 'No, he doesn't have a mistress. Although he does actually. His business career is his mistress. That's what he lavishes most of his attention on.'

'And you don't mind? I mean, do you love him?'

'Not in the way you mean. I'm fond of him, but that's all I've ever been really. He's taken good care of me and Imelda and Edward and we've always been comparatively well-off. Uncle Max has always been very ambitious, you see. I thought all that might have cooled a little by now. But it hasn't. He wants to make his mark in England. That's why he's so eager for you to marry Colonel Danvers. If it was Imelda, he would insist.'

Sarah laughed. 'I don't think he'd have to. Imelda thinks the colonel is wonderful.'

'Well, in some ways, he is.'

Sarah nodded. 'But what about you? Are you happy?'

'Reasonably so,' Aunt Mary said wistfully. 'If you don't expect too much out of life you won't be disappointed.'

'Oh, but that's so sad.'

'Don't listen to me, dear. I'm happy with Uncle Max.'

'Where is Uncle Max this morning?'

'Down at his little office. Things to do, he says. He wants to go to England as soon as possible. But first he must return home. He has matters to attend to in Boston. The sale of the house for one thing and he has his various business interests. And, of course, there's your claim to the farm. I think he wants to cut his ties in America and centre his activities in England.'

'But what about the rebels? Is it safe to go back?'

'People seem to think so. They say the war is all but over.'

Ben had expected to leave within two or three days, as soon as word came from the professor. But the snow fell steadily for the next two weeks and the Indian boatman was unable or unwilling to brave the ice floes in the freezing river. Ben felt he must repay his hosts' hospitality and he did this at every opportunity, helping Mr Lowe to repair a part of the barn damaged by heavy gales in November, feeding the horses and pigs, doing the early morning milking and collecting the eggs daily from the coops.

'It's very good of you to allow me to stay like this,' he said one evening at dinner.

'You can stay forever, son,' Mr Lowe said with a laugh. 'You do the work an' I'll put my feet up.'

'We love having you here, Ben,' Mrs Lowe said. 'And you can stay as long as you have to. So we'll say no more about it.'

The thaw didn't arrive until early February when the professor was able to pay a visit. Even then it was several weeks before he could bring news of the Indian. He did have other news though, news of

General Washington's army. According to the professor things were looking up at Valley Forge. He didn't know much, he said, but there was a good deal of optimism once again.

The professor didn't know why or what had changed the situation but volunteers were pouring into Valley Forge and the general's army was every day gaining in strength. He brought news, too, of a Franco/American alliance. The French, he explained, had lost a great deal in their seven years war with Britain and they were ready to hit back by assisting the rebel army whatever way they could. Money and arms had been flowing secretly across the ocean for some time, he said, and arms from France had played a major part in General Gates' victory at Saratoga.

The British are running scared, he said, of another war with France right now. But if it happened, Mr Lowe said, that sure would be good news for us. Exactly, the professor agreed. The British would need to withdraw half their troops to set them against the French.

Ben was barely listening to the armchair analysts. He felt he had been kicking his heels long enough and he was anxious now to join up with the rebels, clear his name with his friends. Every day that passed he thought of Melanie and every night. Now Tom and Hank Blanchard were on his mind, too. Where were they? Who were they with? Were they at Valley Forge? Most of all, what did they think of him? If they thought of him at all, he told himself, they would class him as a traitor. That was something he had to put right and maybe he could. The bleak weather was easing now. The professor seemed to think the Indian would be out on the river by the end of next week.

Ben was spending his evenings with the Lowes, listening to Charlie's erratic banjar playing and it emerged that Mrs Lowe loved poetry. All she had was a Bible and a couple of battered books her boys had brought home from school and forgotten to take back. She quizzed Ben, prompting him to remember the poems, if any, he'd learned at school. He wanted to please her but the only poem he could remember was one the boys at school had loved, mainly because it made the girls blush.

'I don't know, Mrs Lowe,' he said. 'I don't know if it's right to say it. Girls at school always said it was embarrassing.'

'I won't be embarrassed,' she laughed. 'I'm too old for that.'

'You'll not escape, Ben,' Charlie said. 'Oh no. You gotta pome. She gotta have it.'

'It's by someone called Andrew Marvell,' Ben said. *'But at my back I always hear Time's wingèd chariot hurrying near.* It's about this boy telling his girlfriend not to be so coy. It'll be too late, he says, when we're dead.'

'Well, go on,' Mrs Lowe said.

'It's sort of saying that when you're dead . . . *Then worms shall try that long preserved virginity.'*

'Don't rhyme,' Charlie said.

'Shut up,' Mrs Lowe said. 'Go on, Ben.'

'And your quaint honour turn to dust and into ashes all my lust. The grave's a fine and private place, but none I think do there embrace.'

'Why, that's lovely,' she said.

'Sounds dirty to me,' Charlie said.

Later that night Ben began to write a letter. It was possible, he realized, maybe even probable, that he would be killed in some battle somewhere and he needed to write to Melanie now, tell her yet again how he felt about her, how he had always felt about her. And how, no matter what happened, no matter where he was, his last thought would be of her. His dying wish would be for her to go on and live her life to the full.

He agonized over his words for several nights before finally giving the letter to Mrs Lowe. She would need to keep it until the war was over, he told her. If she sent it now by messenger it could fall into the wrong hands and she and Mr Lowe would be exposed. They would be arrested for harbouring rebels. If he did survive the war he would write back at once and they could arrange to meet. He would bring Melanie to see them or, if they preferred, he would arrange for them to come to Boston. Mrs Lowe said she would take good care of the letter and she promised, when the war was over, she would make sure Melanie received it.

Three days later, after a bear hug from Charlie and a tearful embrace from Mrs Lowe, Ben lay hidden beneath a tarpaulin in the prow of a boat steered by a silent Indian in an Indian shawl and a black hat with a rounded brim.

TWENTY-FIVE

A rebel soldier at the entrance to the mess tent spoke to the catering officer. 'Tom Blanchard,' the officer called out. 'Colonel wants to see you.'

'What have you been up to?' Hank asked.

'Something's going on,' another lieutenant said. 'Lot of comings and goings at the chief's tent today.'

Tom had no idea why the colonel would want to see him. He shrugged helplessly at Hank and followed the messenger.

'Come in, Blanchard,' the colonel said, 'and sit down.'

Tom sat down, facing the colonel across a desk. It was like being summoned before the headmaster at school. Tom wondered what he had done wrong.

'I'll get straight to the point,' the colonel said. 'What would you say to a promotion? Captain on full pay.'

Tom smiled.

'I know,' the colonel said. 'I know you haven't been paid since we got here. None of us has. But you have your IOUs and they will be honoured in full – some day. But forget the money. What do you say?'

Tom frowned. 'I'm flattered, sir. Of course, I am.'

'But?' The colonel was surprised at his reticence.

'Well,' Tom said, 'with respect, sir, I think I can do more good where I am, close to the men.'

'Go on,' the colonel said.

'I think maybe we have too many officers. Too many captains, too many colonels. I don't mean you, sir. You do a very difficult job and you do it very well.'

'Oh, thank you,' the colonel said ironically. 'But we're supposed to be talking about you.'

244

'Yes. I'm sorry, sir,' Tom said. 'But you know what I mean.'

'Tell me,' the colonel said.

'May I speak freely?'

The colonel nodded. 'Say your piece, Lieutenant.'

'Well, it seems to me that everyone with any sort of non-job is a captain or a colonel or – dare I say it? – even higher. Most of them don't seem to have any real duties yet they strut about the camp, demanding respect. It's very demoralizing for the men. They see what's going on and they look on these officers with contempt. Not all officers, of course. But too many of them are missing half the time. They bring whores into the camp. They buy that ghastly hooch those old hags sell at the camp gate. And they actually drink it. They're drunk out of their minds and then they're ill. Most of the men, well, the men in my company anyway, wouldn't touch the stuff. They have no respect for these 'officers', none at all.

'Men like General Washington and the French officer, the Marquis de Lafayette, are held in high regard. Of course they are. And you yourself, the men have great affection for you. And that's because you treat them like human beings and with some respect. But there are too many officers who treat them like dung and command neither affection nor respect.' Tom calmed down, feeling he had said far too much. He stood up as if to leave. 'I'm sorry, sir. I myself have been disrespectful to my fellow officers and I regret that. But I feel it needed to be said. May I go?'

'No, you may not,' the colonel said. 'Sit down.'

'I'm sorry for the outburst, sir,' Tom said, genuinely repentant.

'Well, I'm not,' the colonel said. 'It was like a breath of fresh air. What you say is right and today we have made a good start at sorting things out. Three colonels and seven captains have been sacked, booted out, cashiered, call it what you will, without pay or IOU.'

'Can you do that, sir?'

'We've done it, Tom. And they've been told to take us to court if they want compensation. Can't see anyone doing that. They'll not want their *good* names dragging in the mud. Anyway, several officers have gone and I need a captain to work with Baron von Steuben. He's a military genius, or so I'm told. And he's here to make an army out of the poor disheartened men we've got. It's a tough job, but he says he can do it and he wants an assistant. His title is Adjutant General. He's replaced Mr Conway and he wants a man who is close to the men, a man who can maintain morale and motivate them. They've had a long hard winter but that's coming to an end. We have supplies coming in now and things are going to get better all round. I want you to take up this challenge. What do you say? Can you do it?'

'Yes, sir,' Tom said. 'I'd be delighted.'

'Good. Report to Baron von Steuben in the morning. Six o'clock at his tent.'

'Six?'

'That's what he says.'

'Right,' Tom said. 'I'll be there.' He hesitated.

'Something else?' the colonel asked.

'My brother's a good officer, sir. Will there be other promotions?'

The colonel looked at him. 'You Blanchards,' he said. 'Well, there will be, yes. But your brother has a few questions to answer. He was missing from camp yesterday. Seems nobody knew where he was.'

'He's a good man, sir,' Tom said. 'That was just once.'

'Go on, get outa here,' the colonel said. 'I'll tell the baron to expect you.'

The baron had joined the army of General Washington on the last day of February, 1778. That first morning when Tom arrived at 6 a.m. to report for duty the baron was already fully dressed. He was standing outside his tent, taking in deep gulps of the fine morning air. The sky was light, no dark clouds threatened and for once there was a feeling of well-being abroad, a feeling that was soon to convert the general aura of defeat into one of pride and confidence. Tom didn't know it at the time but he was about to work with one of the most extraordinary men he would ever meet and when he reflected years later on the presence of the baron that first morning he knew it was the effervescent baron who sparked the change in outlook that gradually transformed the rebel army at Valley Forge.

The man was alive with a breezy *bonhomie*. His brisk marches up and down, his clicking of heels, his swift about turns and his ebullient *joie de vivre* led Tom to believe he was something of a joke. But Tom was soon to discover the baron might well be a joker but he was certainly no joke.

In a fractured and limited English he succeeded in conveying his philosophy to the ragged battalions he confronted every day for the next three months. You men, he somehow told them, like to sleep. You like your bed. Well, that's good. And if you are fit and healthy and absolutely exhausted at the end of the day you will enjoy that bed even more. And when you awake, like me, you will have a renewed appetite for life. Look at me! I love every moment of every day and, I promise, you will too.

Two hours of marching up and down in squads of eight every morning. An hour's rest and two more hours of arms drill. At midday another break during which time the NCOs were given special training. More parades after lunch and courses in tactics for the officers as well as instruction in how to get to know and gain the confidence and respect of the men under them.

This isn't work, the whole assembly were told. This is fun and one day it might save your lives. Enjoying life is a state of mind. You are good men. Tough men. A good friend to the man next to you, to all the men in our great army. Enjoy it! You belong. You are one of us. You would give your lives for each other and with that knowledge you can face anyone. You can beat any army. You can win any war. Let us make sure we win this one.

With this kind of rhetoric in his limited English, peppered as it was with obscenities and his frequent descents into farce and intentionally comic strutting about, he won the hearts and minds of the men and gradually a new atmosphere of resolve began to take hold. They did care about the next man. They did want to win as the baron forged them into a formidable fighting force.

There were more smiles. There was more laughter. There were many jokes about the crazy baron. But there was never anything malicious in the jokes and his comic antics served only to endear him further. Baron von Steuben, the Prussian military man, had told the Continental Congress he could do it and he had done it.

Food and clothing, especially good footwear, were now arriving at the camp. New volunteers were coming in and many who had left in disillusion were returning. The coming of spring added a new dimension and what emerged, as if from a doomed chrysalis, was a fighting fit band of brothers, eager to take on the British.

Before the British in Philadelphia fully realized just how much this metamorphosis had transformed their opponents it was too late for any walkover. Now they had a fight on their hands.

Communications were poor and nobody in Halifax, Nova Scotia, was aware of the resurgence of the rebel army or of the continuing hold the rebels had on Boston. Apart from mopping-up operations Washington's army was defeated and totally humiliated. The rebel uprising had been quelled once and for all and General Howe felt able to leave Philadelphia for a well-earned rest. It was safe now for the Loyalist exiles to return home and many were eager to do so, anxious to reclaim their homes and take up their lives where they had been so rudely disrupted. This then was the erroneous impression those who had fled from Boston were labouring under, Max Harvie included.

Max had a number of business matters to attend to before he could leave for England. There was the disposal of his share in various enterprises he had undertaken over the years. A laundry, a chandlery, the print shop and several more. There was the house and the sale of the Dowling family farm. So many loose ends required his attention, it would take at least three months, he estimated, before he could leave.

Imelda was not happy with this. She wanted to go with Sarah. But arrangements had been made for Sarah to travel in the care of a dowager, Lady Welles, who would deliver her to the family home of Colonel Danvers' sister on the Thames at Kingston to await her wedding day.

Sarah was more than happy for Imelda to accompany her but Aunt Mary felt this would be an unwarranted intrusion into the clearly well-laid plans and Max said definitely no. Imelda must go home with them. There would be plenty of time for her to see Sarah when they arrived in midsummer.

Those last weeks in Halifax consisted of parties and dances and musical evenings and Imelda desperately trying to find an acceptable suitor who would whisk her away to his family seat in what she perceived as the promised land. Sarah's head was in a whirl. She had little time to consider what was happening. But she was enjoying every day and she was happy to see Jack when he arrived to escort her, no longer protesting when he was referred to as 'her colonel'.

She had said no frequently to his proposals of marriage and she had never once said yes. Yet he had never accepted no as her answer and marriage and a new life in England seemed inescapable. It was an option that was becoming increasingly attractive. She felt nothing now, she told her aunt, for Boston. That was where the people Jack called 'the rabble' had murdered her family and Pansy and everything she loved. Then fate had taken Tom Blanchard in the wrong direction and he was dead. There was nothing for her there, she said. And if

Imelda and Uncle Max and you are going to England then she would too. And marry Jack, Aunt Mary said. Sarah smiled and shrugged. It seemed inevitable. It was all she had and her previous life was receding, back into the past and, for now, out of her mind.

In early May, 1778, after a tearful farewell on the quayside, Sarah said goodbye to the Harvies and left Halifax with Lady Welles knowing that Jack would follow on the next ship. Three days later Max, Aunt Mary and Imelda sailed for Boston.

Without a word the Indian dropped Ben at a narrow creek and as he pushed the boat off he pointed to a path through the trees. The path was no more than a foot wide and not very well-trodden. Ben looked back and raised a hand but the boat had turned and was already on its way.

He set off with the sun high above the tall trees and for at least half a mile he saw and heard nothing but the twitter of birds and the occasional loud buzz of a bee. He had no idea where he was or where he was going but he followed the narrow path until a voice behind him brought him to a halt.

'Stop right there,' the voice ordered.

He looked back and saw two scruffy-looking men levelling rifles at him, a tall one and a short one. At least, they were not redcoats, he thought, though they could be scouts for the British.

'Where do you think you're going?' the tall one asked.

What the hell? thought Ben. He would just have to trust his luck. 'I'm looking for the Congressional Army,' he said.

'The what?'

'I'm trying to find the rebel army.'

'And why would you want to do that?'

'Because I want to join them.'

'Keep walking,' the tall one said.

After another fifty yards or so they came to a road and across the road the entrance to what was obviously an army camp. But there was no sign of redcoats and there were no recognizable uniforms. The tall one pointed to the camp entrance. 'In there, turn left.'

Ben crossed the road and, as with the Indian, he turned to raise a hand in thanks but the two men had already gone, presumably back into the woods.

Ben turned left and found he was in a queue, a motley crowd of new recruits. Volunteers were flooding in and a lot of it was down to stories about the behaviour of the British. Previously communication had been slow, but now graphic reports were coming in, especially from New York. Thieving, it was said, was rife. Foraging parties in the surrounding countryside would take anything edible or drinkable and the badly disciplined military would raid homes, smashing down doors and breaking windows.

No woman was safe. Many were abducted and if a civilian male attempted to intervene he was soon outnumbered and severely beaten. On one occasion sixteen young women were chased from a Presbyterian church. Pursued by rampant soldiers they were seized and carried off into a nearby wood. None escaped. One man was forced to witness the rape of his wife. A girl of thirteen was taken from her bed, carried to a barn and ravished by at least five men. These and still more lurid tales were widely reported now, mainly in the rebel press, but no one doubted their veracity and the name and the reputation of the British Army could never have been held in lower esteem.

All of this provided great ammunition for rebel propaganda and, for the first time, the rebel leaders were able to choose the men they required. Leaders like the old campaigner, Dan Morgan, were able to use the unacceptable conduct and savagery of the British to incense local communities and drum up a new anti-Loyalist fervour.

On one occasion the wily Morgan is said to have told Congress: 'The British soldier is an animal and his aristocratic officers are no better. In fact, gentlemen, his officers are even more depraved than he is. When they are not out attempting to ravish our women they are busy buggering each other.'

When Ben's turn came he stepped forward smartly, gave his name and said he was from Boston. The recruiting officer was seated at a desk. He asked first if Ben could read to which Ben replied, 'Of course, sir.'

The officer looked up at him. 'There's no "of course" about it around here, son,' he said and he asked Ben about his schooling before indicating a half-dozen young men who were standing to one side and instructing him to join them.

As the long line of recruits filed through the recruitment tent the small group grew until, when they numbered fifteen, they were led away to a second interview. With so many new recruits coming in, they were told, it was necessary now to find suitable candidates for officer training. Twelve officers were required immediately and Ben was one of those selected. The chosen twelve shared a large tent and were told to be on parade by eight next morning. It had been a long day and Ben was happy to roll out his bedroll and fall asleep.

In the days that followed there were intensive courses in arms drill, weapon training, field manoeuvres and tactics, behaviour in battle – the list of topics seemed endless. Then one morning they were called to account, one by one. Ben was asked if he had brought with him a recommendation or reference of any kind. He said he hadn't because he was prepared to serve in any capacity. He had not assumed he would be offered a commission. Was there someone who could be consulted as to his suitabilty and his patriotism? He thought of Tom and Hank.

'Friends from home,' he said. 'Two brothers. They volunteered some time ago. I'm sure they will be commissioned officers by now. They would certainly vouch for me.'

'What makes you so sure they will hold commissions?' he was asked.

'Well,' he said, 'if you are considering me, sir, you would certainly have considered them.'

'Their names?'

'Blanchard. Tom and Henry Blanchard. I don't know where they are, sir, but they were with General Washington. If they are still alive, I would guess they're at Valley Forge.'

TWENTY-SIX

Hank Blanchard put his head round the tent flap. 'You wanted to see me, sir?'

'Come in, you big loon,' Tom said. 'Great news!'

Hank came inside. 'What? What's happened?'

'Ben,' Tom said. 'Ben Withers is alive. He's with General Gates.'

'That's great! How do you know?'

'I got this message. Benjamin Withers is on a course for potential officers, it says here. He's given our names as referees. CO wants to know if we know him and, if so, what do we know about him.'

Hank grinned. 'We know him all right. He joined the British.'

Tom looked around. 'Shut up, you idiot. Someone might hear you. We know he joined the British for a reason. Melanie said one day we would understand why and that's good enough for me. He must have done what he wanted to do and now he's doing his duty.'

'Right,' Hank said. 'So what do we tell the colonel?'

'You don't need to tell him anything. If you're asked just say yes, he's a good man. Leave the rest to me.'

'But what about. . . ?'

'That's an order, Lieutenant Blanchard,' Tom said with mock severity.

'Yeah, OK,' Hank said. 'Good to know he's alive and kicking.'

'Now,' Tom said, 'you don't know this if anyone asks. But we're moving out soon. Keep it to yourself but by the end of next week we'll be on the move.'

'About time, too,' Hank said. 'Listen, I've got news for you. Some fellows came in from Boston last night. Haven't had chance to talk to them yet.'

'Where are they?'

'Probably being scared stiff by the baron,' Hank said with a grin.

At noon Tom saw a group of men waiting by the cookhouse. Most of them were wearing a kind of dark-blue jerkin over their own non-military clothing but it came as close as any he'd seen to making a rebel uniform.

'You the fellows from Boston?' Tom asked.

'Yessir,' said one.

'Who's your chief?'

'Lieutenant Coley, sir.'

There'd been a family named Coley out Prospect way. They were not well known around town, kept themselves to themselves mostly. But Tom had come across them once or twice. Two or three brothers, he remembered, boys who might well be serving with the rebel army. Certainly their old man would not be keen to pay taxes to the British.

Coley was dressed in a dark-blue jacket and white breeches. Tom recognized him at once. There was a Brad, a Brett and a Beau, but he couldn't be sure which one this was.

'Lieutenant Coley,' Tom said.

Coley stared at him for a moment as if he'd seen a ghost.

Tom smiled. 'Tom Blanchard from Boston.'

'Blanchard,' Coley said. 'Tom Blanchard. I remember.'

'Your brothers in the army, too?' Tom asked.

'Brad's up north with St Clair and Beau's runnin' the farm.'

Tom nodded. 'Then you must be Brett.'

The lieutenant held out a hand. 'Brett Coley.'

'I remember your father's place. Over Prospect Hill way. Cattle and wheat and Indian corn, if my memory serves me right.'

'In a small way,' Coley said. 'It's me and my brothers now. Pops don't do much no more.'

Tom grinned. 'Real old rebel though, eh?'

'Oh, sure. Got no time for those fancy British. He says they're more like women in their frills an' powdery wigs.'

'I reckon he's right, too,' Tom said with a laugh, 'and damned bitchy women at that. But tell me, how was it in Boston?'

'Well,' Coley said thoughtfully, 'it was getting better, I suppose. Not too bad before we left. Things had been tightened up a lot.'

'How do you mean?'

'Well, when the British pulled out all hell let loose. You know how it is down there by the docks. Pretty rough best of times. But when they left – hell! Lootin' an' robbin'. Some people seemed to think everythin' was there for the takin'. An', man, did they take! Then we came in from the hills an' we started to sort things out.'

'Some pretty wild fellows in Boston, I guess,' Tom said.

'Sure are,' Coley agreed. 'An' that's it. It wasn't the British did the damage. They promised there'd be no trouble if we let them go peaceful an' they kept their word. It was when they left things got out o' hand.'

'What happened to people like Max Harvie? You know him. He had his sticky fingers into everything.'

'I know him all right. Grabbin' bastard,' Coley said. 'Hope he's not a friend of yours.'

'No, no,' Tom said truthfully. He had never liked Max Harvie, though he had always thought highly of Mrs Harvie and sometimes wondered how she came to be married to such a man. 'I knew him, that's all, and I knew his family. His daughter . . .'

Coley shook his head. 'Beats me how a man like him could have such a cute little doll of a daughter.'

'What happened to them?' Tom asked keenly. 'His family, I mean. Did they leave with the British? They wouldn't be too popular in town. At least, Max wouldn't be.'

'That's right. He left with the British on one of their boats. Had to, I guess. Went off up to Nova Scotia with Howe's men. An' I reckon he'd better stay there.'

'What happened to Mrs Harvie and Imelda? They go with him?'

'I expec' so. Why? You sweet on Imelda?'

'No, but I'm interested to know what happened to Imelda's cousin. Girl called Sarah. She was living with the Harvies.'

'Oh yeah! I remember her,' Coley said. 'Now she really was worth checkin' out. Fine-lookin' girl. An' there was somethin' about her.'

'She had these gorgeous green eyes,' Tom said.

'Is that right?' Coley grinned as if to say so it's her you're sweet on. 'You know what happened to her?'

'Well, if she was livin' with the Harvies like you say, an' I think she was, she'll be up in Halifax with the rest of them Loyalists. They all went. All the King's bootlickers who could pull the right strings, that is.' He smiled. 'Don't say she's one, of course. She's just a girl. Girls got to go with the hand that feeds 'em. But if she went with Harvie I don't reckon you'll see much of her back in Boston.'

'I don't know about that,' Tom said. 'Harvie will have to come back at some stage. He must have a lot of business interests to sort out.'

'Well, it's true a lot of folk are driftin' back. When we left word was goin' round that General Washington was finished. We didn't know what to think but now we're here we can see that isn't so. An' I'll tell you this, if Harvie shows his face in Boston again it'll be the last thing he ever does. They tar an' feather fellows like him.'

'He owns property up there,' Tom said. 'He's got a finger in pies all round town. He'll have to come back to sort it all out.'

'Only if we lose,' Coley said, 'an' that isn't gonna happen.'

Tom held out a hand. 'Good to talk to you.'

'Say,' Coley said, 'you had a brother – Hank.'

'That's right.'

'Is he dead?'

Tom smiled. 'No. He's down the line. C company.'

'Well,' Coley said, 'back home I got the impression both you and your brother were dead.'

'Well, if we are,' Tom said, 'nobody told us yet.'

'When I get back to Boston I'll put folk right.'

'You going back?'

'I brought this company down here and I'm going to bring back some more. Recruits are flooding in up there and soon as they're ready they're drafted. Trouble is, we're short of officers to move 'em around.'

'Well, look,' Tom said with a frown, 'if people really believe we're dead I need to get a message to my old man. Could you tell him you've seen me and that Hank's OK, too?'

'Sure I will,' Coley said.

'And could you find out what's going on at the Harvies?'

Ben recognized him at once. Racked by sciatica and rheumatism, his sardonic expression more lined now but, as always, defying the pain, he was still the charismatic figure Ben had first set eyes on at the Assembly Hall where he had conducted his illicit recruiting drive. The only difference Ben could see was that he was no longer a colonel. He was Major General Dan Morgan and that morning on the parade ground the twelve newly commissioned officers were lined up for his inspection.

Followed by a captain, he came along the line, pausing here and there to ask a question or make a comment. When he came to Ben he stopped and looked him up and down. Ben felt uncomfortable. The blue jacket he, like the others, had been issued with was all right but the white breeches were far too short and too tight, 'half-mast' as one wag observed.

'Somebody die?' Morgan asked.

'They're too short, sir,' Ben said idiotically.

The general smiled. 'What's your name?'

'Withers, sir,' Ben said, towering over him.

'Seen any action?'

'No, sir. I only just arrived.'

'And why is that?'

'I had things to do, sir,' Ben said and he realized at once it was the wrong answer.

'We all have things to do, son,' Morgan said and moved on.

At the end of the line of twelve he walked back, the captain in attendance, to the tent he used as an office and they went inside. The captain emerged moments later.

'Dolan, Hayes, Withers are to join General Morgan. Report to the orderly room. Rest dismissed for now.'

Dan Morgan had often been criticized and accused of over-familiarity with those of lesser rank. But nobody could deny his powers of leadership, his tactical skill and knowledge on the battlefield or his personal bravery which had been tested many times. He believed that his men, through their officers, should have full access to him. If they had something to say they must be allowed to say it. For his part, he vowed, as far as possible, he would always make himself available.

In the evening he liked to dine with his officers and not always his most senior officers. He wanted, he said, to keep them informed. The British, he told them, were now concentrating their efforts in the South with an attack on Charleston in South Carolina. After a discussion of the strategic implications General Morgan went on to mention the increasingly reported activities of a British officer by the name of Banastre Tarleton. Ben sat up and took notice.

Tarleton was in command of a cavalry and light infantry brigade known as the British Legion. He was acknowledged as the most successful and also the most notorious of British cavalry officers. There was no denying his skill in battle, the general said, yet he encouraged his legion to attack with a ferocity and a disregard for human life, slaughtering civilians or a surrendering enemy alike, that was inexcusable, even in a struggle so partisan as ours.

In South Carolina the British Commander-in-chief, Sir Henry Clinton, had sent Tarleton to make a surprise attack on a rebel base at Charleston. The attack was a complete success but it was marred by the unnecessary brutality meted out by Tarleton and his legion. Rebels, hands in the air, their weapons cast aside, were mercilessly cut down and Tarleton became known as 'the Butcher'. Most of his fellow officers were appalled.

Charleston, after ceaseless bombardment, finally surrendered to the British but, when news that the French were sending over substantial support for the rebels was received, Sir Henry Clinton deemed it necessary to return to New York and leave Lord Cornwallis to command the British forces in the South. Dan Morgan, with a smile, always laid emphasis on the words *Sir* and *Lord* as if he found them highly amusing.

Lord Cornwallis's strategy, rebel intelligence had discovered, was to leave a small army of occupation in Charleston and divide the rest into three columns. One was to march upon the oddly named village of Ninety-Six, another was to go for Augusta, the third to the town of Camden.

It was then that a regiment of Virginian rebels, led by a Colonel Buford, set out to rid Charleston of the British. Lord Cornwallis ordered Tarleton to intercept the rebels and with great enthusiasm, as usual, Tarleton's legion took off immediately. After a long hard ride they caught up with Buford's men on the border that divides North and South Carolina. In the late afternoon the Virginians, about 400 strong, turned to face the oncoming British.

The Virginian rebels formed a long line with strict orders to hold their fire. The cavalry came on and on and the rebels waited and waited but the order to fire came a fraction too late. The speed of the horses, their riders wielding sabres, could not be stopped and once again the death and destruction inflicted was so ferocious the rebels were ordered to surrender.

The ensign who raised the flag was immediately cut down and it was clear that Tarleton's men were not prepared to show mercy. Realizing this, many of the Virginians took up their arms again but the barbarous British Legion hacked them down and amid scenes of indiscriminate carnage not a man was spared. Bayonets were plunged into any body that showed signs of life and where several men had fallen in a heap the dead were cast aside to get at any living soul beneath.

The massacre provoked a prolonged brutal reign of civil disorder where Loyalists, encouraged by the rout of the Virginians, set out to settle old scores and terrorize known rebel supporters. 'The whole country,' Cornwallis reported, 'is in a state of rebellion.'

Houses were broken into and people were robbed as gangs of opportunist thieves roamed the countryside stealing anything of value from food and drink to horses and cattle. There was even talk of sea captains who packed more than 2,000 stolen slaves into their ships' holds for sale in the Caribbean. Most of this lawlessness was the work of so-called Loyalists who followed the British and enriched themselves with the plunder they took from the local inhabitants who were unable to defend themselves. And Dan Morgan was quick to see the propaganda value of such behaviour both in stirring up his men and in recruiting still more.

Cornwallis was finding his troops were now spread too thinly, a fact that was not lost on the rebel leaders. His 4,000 men were in garrisons as far apart as Savannah and Charleston and, with Augusta, Ninety-Six, Camden and several more outposts to sustain, he had not enough men to maintain a hold on South Carolina. His problems increased with the news that a widely experienced Indian fighter by the name of Thomas Sumter leading a growing force of rebels was rapidly approaching one of his garrisons. General Gates, it seemed, was also moving South with the main American force.

It was in the middle of the night that a British force of just over 2,000 men came across General Gates's army at a stretch of open land known as Parker's Old Field. There was an outburst of gunfire then all was quiet until morning. The rebel soldiers were ill-prepared for battle. They had been short of adequate food, a long difficult march had taken its toll and a debilitating sickness had spread through the ranks. But there was no alternative. They were forced to face the enemy and fight.

Cornwallis decided to attack at sunrise. Forming two brigades, one to the left and one to the right, with two battalions of Highlanders in the centre and the cavalry of Tarleton's British Legion drawn up behind them he was ready.

At sunrise a line of rebel militia advanced tentatively to engage the enemy. At once Cornwallis ordered his vanguard to attack. The militia turned and fled. Assuming this first line was a decoy the British regrouped and attacked the main body of Gates's army. For the next forty minutes the rebels fought bravely and well but then Tarleton's legion, having trotted away in a wide semi-circle, suddenly appeared and attacked them from the rear. Surprised and defenceless as the horses charged at them the startled rebels scattered, but the maniacal horsemen lashed out with their deadly sabres, cutting down all before them. Yet again the carnage was inexcusable. The rebels had run for their lives and, as if demented, the riders of the legion had followed, slashing at them with an unwarranted ferocity until before long the field was strewn with the bodies of the dead and the dying.

The rebel army, under General Gates, lost almost a thousand men and many more were taken prisoner. Provisions, weapons and heavy artillery including several cannon were lost. General Gates himself simply fled and didn't stop running until he had put many miles between himself and the scene of battle. His reputation as a general to be admired was now destroyed and even Dan Morgan, uncharacteristically allowing himself to criticize another general, at least in the presence of his junior officers, said he was surprised and disappointed at the general's apparent cowardice and abject focus on saving his own skin.

Thomas Sumter and his men who had been steadily advancing on Camden were now obliged to reconsider their position. But Cornwallis lost no time in sending Tarleton's men in search of their retreating column. In makeshift overnight accommodation Sumter's men were in the throes of preparing a meal when they were startled by the sudden appearance of the legion. Tarleton's men, with their customary bloodlust, delighted in slaughtering every rebel soldier, armed or unarmed, they could find. Sumter escaped but more than 150 of his men were killed.

By now Tarleton and his legion, well-known for their ferocity in battle and their reluctance to take prisoners, were widely feared though not by General Morgan. Dan Morgan told his assembled officers he would welcome an opportunity to confront Tarleton and his fellow butchers.

'Pretty boy,' he announced, 'has to be stopped.'

TWENTY-SEVEN

SIXTEEN days after leaving Halifax, Nova Scotia, the cargo ship bringing home Max Harvie, his wife and daughter docked in Boston. Vanessa, as instructed by Max Harvie's agent, had sent a carriage to meet the ship and bring them to the house. The big rooms, closed since their departure, had been reopened and aired, and they were happy to find their home intact. Happy, that is, until they heard from Vanessa how things were in their native city. The war appeared to be over in Boston. The British had gone but, according to Vanessa, law and order had gone with them. Gangs of men and youths, who seemed to think that freedom from the British meant freedom to do just whatever they had a mind to, roamed the streets unchecked. The streets, she warned them, were not always safe in broad daylight let alone at night time.

And what other news did she have? Aunt Mary asked. What else has been happening while we've been away? 'Well, ma'am,' Vanessa told her, 'the happiest news we heard was about the Blanchard boys. I always liked those two. Real gentlemen.'

Max Harvie was at the drinks table by the large fireplace. He was about to pour for himself a large glass of wine. At Vanessa's words he looked over his shoulder and Aunt Mary caught the expression of apprehension on his face. Vanessa went on to say, 'We heard Mister Tom an' Mister Hank was dead. But a young man named Coley came by to tell Mr Blanchard they're both fine.'

Aunt Mary was visibly shocked. 'Vanessa, are you sure about this? Tom and Henry Blanchard are not dead?'

Imelda almost dropped the cup and saucer she was holding. 'Oh, Vanessa! Can this be true?'

'True as ah'm standin' here. This young man, Mister Coley, came by

260

to say Mister Tom asked him to ask about Miss Sarah.'

Aunt Mary was looking at her husband.

'Where are they now?' Imelda was excited.

'Well,' Vanessa said slowly, 'ah supppose you know they was with them rebels an', far as ah know, that's where they are now.'

'What did you tell the young man?' Aunt Mary asked. 'About Sarah, I mean.'

'Ah said she was with you up in Canada or somewhere,' Vanessa said defensively. 'Ah mean that's all ah knew.'

'Miss Sarah has gone to England to be married,' Max Harvie said brusquely, entering the conversation for the first time but still avoiding his wife's eyes.

'Did you hear what Vanessa said?' Imelda asked her father. 'Tom and Hank are alive. Isn't that wonderful? I must get a message to Hank somehow. I thought he was dead! And, oh Mother, we must get a message to Sarah.'

Aunt Mary knew most of her husband's facial expressions and certainly enough about him to know the look on his face when Vanessa mentioned the Blanchard boys was one of guilt. She wanted to get him alone, question him about the alleged deaths of Tom and Henry Blanchard but he evaded her inquisition by suddenly announcing he had to go down to his office now, right away, before dinner.

'How did you know the Blanchard boys were reported dead, Vanessa?' Aunt Mary asked when Max had left.

'Well, ma'am,' Vanessa told her. 'Everybody knew. Ah heard it first from the gal works at the market but then ah saw it with mah own eyes. It was on the poster.'

'The poster?'

'You know how they put up the names of the British killed. They put them up for the rebels, too, an' ah saw it right there. Lootenant Tom Blanchard an' Lootenant Henry Blanchard.'

'You can't read, Vanessa.'

'That's true, ma'am. But there's always someone there can read out the names. It's sorta become the cus'om 'round town. That ol' man work for Mister Harvie. He prints 'em an' he puts 'em up in the window of the print shop.'

Of course, thought Aunt Mary. Max had the means at his disposal. But would he do such a thing? *Could* he? She had to concede that yes, he could. He had certainly looked guilty when Vanessa mentioned the

Blanchards. It would mean he was prepared to do almost anything to ensure Sarah married Colonel Danvers. She picked up a shawl and announced that she was going out. She would not, she said, be long.

'Oh, ma'am,' Vanessa said in alarm. 'Do be careful. Streets is not safe. They just ain't safe no more.'

Even in the short distance to the street leading down to the waterfront it was obvious to Aunt Mary the city had changed and not for the better. There was much damage and no sign of any effort being made to put things right. The oldest and best stocked of the stores was barely recognizable. It had been burnt-out and almost totally destroyed, and what remained of the shop front was disfigured by roughly scrawled abuse.

'Arse-licking Loyalist Bastard,' Aunt Mary read and, as she coloured with embarrassment, she remembered the inoffensive owner of the store. Admittedly he was a solid supporter of the Crown but this could be because he was the main supplier of comestibles to the British Army garrison.

There was an unfriendly, alien feeling in the air, Aunt Mary was convinced, as she hurried along the main highway. Without the safety of transport or a companion she felt unprotected, exposed. She knew she should not have come out alone and already she regretted her haste. She realized it was some time since she had taken to the street, travelling everywhere as she had in comparative comfort. For one thing, her clothes marked her out as a lady of means. She was different. She felt different. Aware of the curious glances she attracted, she felt like some colourful caged bird that had been allowed to fly free along the hedgerows with drab sparrows and town birds.

She hurried on, anxious not to attract the attention of a group of unruly-looking men gathered at the intersection and the unruly-looking women who accompanied them. Glancing back she saw that two of the women were walking in an exaggerated fashion as if to mimic her supposed airs and graces. It occurred to her now that the print shop her husband owned might no longer be there and a panic gripped her heart. But thankfully it was and the door was not locked. She hurried inside.

A man of about forty stood at the printer's stone where Ezra, Max's oldest employee, normally reigned. For several seconds the man carried on doing what he was doing then, unsmiling, he looked up and raised his eyebrows imperiously.

'Would you inform Ezra that I wish to speak with him, please?'
Aunt Mary asked, not sure whether the man had recognized her as the
owner's wife or not.

'Who wants him?' he asked rudely.

'Would you tell him, please, that Mrs Harvie is here?'

The man looked her up and down with an unpleasant, insolent look
in his eye, revelling in her discomfort. 'Would that be Mrs *Max*
Harvie?'

'It would,' Aunt Mary said, rising to the challenge. She was not
going to allow this ill-mannered lout to intimidate her.

'Can't do that,' he said and went back to whatever he had been
doing as if he expected her to accept this curt dismissal and leave.

'Can't do what?'

'Can't tell ol' Ezra you're here, cock.'

'I beg your pardon!' Aunt Mary's cheeks coloured red for the
second time that afternoon.

'I can't tell ol' Ezra you're here, cos ol' Ezra ain't. He don't work
here no more.'

'Why is that? Is he ill? Has he retired? I know he was getting on in
years but. . . .'

'Nothin' like that, missus. We invited him to leave.'

'You invited him? Didn't he want to leave?'

'Had no option, did he? He was a supporter of Max Harvie and the
British. Any friend of Max Harvie ain't welcome in this town.'

Aunt Mary knew her husband had never been the most popular of
employers. She had not always approved of his dictatorial rule and the
way he had treated people in the past. Yet many, like Ezra, had
remained loyal. 'Could Ezra afford to lose his job? Did he have some
sort of pension to fall back on?'

'Not off your ol' man, missus, an' that's for sure. Wouldn't give you
the shit off his shovel, ol' Max.'

'I think you are a vulgar, offensive person, an absolute disgrace.'

The man stopped what he was doing and narrowed his eyes at her
menacingly. 'You better watch your mouth, Mrs *Max* Harvie.'

Aunt Mary suddenly remembered why she had come. 'I take it this
business is now owned by so-called rebels.'

'Not "so-called", missus. That's what we are. Rebels.' He raised his
fist in the air. 'Death to the British. It's the rebels what run this town
now and from now on.'

'Then perhaps you can help me,' she said, surprising him. 'I came here today to ask Ezra why the names of two rebel officers – Tom and Henry Blanchard – were printed on a list of the dead when they were and, as far as I know, still are very much alive.'

'Ah!' The man grinned, showing broken and discoloured teeth. 'That's easy. We had an inquiry into all that, didn't we? It was your husband what did it. He tol' ol' Ezra to put those names on the list. Ol' Ezra said so. It was him, all right. Max Harvie. He wanted folk to think those men were dead.'

'Whatever for? Why would my husband do a thing like that?'

'Well, the word is,' the man said, warming to his story, 'he did it cos one of 'em was sweet on your daughter or your niece or somethin' like that an' he didn't want no rebel officer in his family. Your husband is a boot-licking royalist, missus.'

'He wouldn't do a thing like that,' Aunt Mary said, though she knew he would and probably had.

'Well,' the man said, 'there was only him an' ol' Ezra could have done it an' ol' Ezra had no reason to.'

'But that's awful,' was all she could say.

'Sure is, missus. An' if ol' Max ever turns up in this town we'll have him. We're on the look-out for fellows like him. Traitors to their own folk. We'll have him drawn an' quartered, tarred an' feathered, thrown in the drink. You better warn him to stay away cos we're here, waitin'. An' we'll have him.'

Max Harvie had gone first to the city office of his lawyer and business agent but he was puzzled to find the place was closed and looked as though it had been closed for some weeks. In the same building was the office of a man he knew well, a quantity surveyor. A bell tinkled above the door as he pushed it open. A desk clerk in shirtsleeves was at the counter, poring over a ledger. He looked up at Max, obviously surprised to see him. A known Loyalist like Max Harvie was the last person he expected to see.

'Is your employer in?' Max asked imperiously.

The clerk bristled. 'I'll see if Mr Simpson is available,' he said, but the door behind him opened and Warren Simpson appeared.

'This gentleman,' the clerk began, though he knew Max Harvie's name well enough.

Simpson looked at Max, as surprised to see him as his clerk had been. 'Why, Max,' he said. 'Come in. This is a surprise.'

Max removed his hat and Simpson raised his eyebrows at his clerk as Max passed through to the inner office. Both men were bemused by his unexpected appearance. Known Loyalists were dead men in this town but Max Harvie didn't seem to know it.

As soon as the door to Mr Simpson's office closed the desk clerk almost fell down the single flight of steps to the street in his haste to summon one of the street urchins in the muddied road outside. With a few words of whispered instruction he pressed a coin in the boy's palm and the grubby messenger sped away.

In Simpson's office Max was growing increasingly concerned. 'Are you telling me there is a complete breakdown of law and order here?'

'Not exactly,' Simpson began patiently. He was a tolerant, kindly man and, though for some years he had disliked Max Harvie, his business methods and his attitude to people he considered socially inferior to himself, he had no wish to see him meet the fate that undoubtedly awaited him if he stayed in town too long. This was not solely out of concern for Max. Warren Simpson had known Max's wife, Mary, for many years, since early schooldays in fact, and he had always had a special regard for her. At one time he was actually considering proposing marriage to her when Max, an infinitely less attractive but far more ambitious suitor, stepped in and spirited her away. But a young man never forgets his first love and Miss Mary Lowell – as she was in those long gone days – had never been far from his mind.

'There are some people about – undesirables, Max, roaming gangs – who are actually searching for those prominent citizens like you who took the British side.'

'I came back here,' Max said, 'to sell my business and property interests. I do not intend to stay any longer than I have to.'

'You don't seem to understand,' Simpson told him calmly. 'You may not have anything to sell. Not here anyway.' He lowered his voice. 'Things have changed, Max, and in many ways for the worse.'

'What was mine before is still mine. No one can change that.'

'That may be so. But it will take a long time for things to settle down and then more time for you to lodge and win your claims.'

'Wadham has been my agent here for twenty years. He will have taken care of all that. Where is he anyway? Has he moved office?'

'I'm afraid Jack Wadham can't help you any more.'

'Oh? And why is that?'

'Jack Wadham is dead, Max. He was a known Loyalist, a supporter of the British, and some of the very people he employed, people he trusted, turned on him. A couple of weeks ago a mob came for him.'

'*Came* for him?'

'They took him from his office and they tarred and feathered him. Then they hanged him from a spar down by the docks.'

Max paled. He felt rooted to his seat. Warren Simpson had never been a close friend. He was more a business acquaintance. But Simpson, he knew, was a decent and honourable man, a man who would never concoct such a story out of mischief or for his own ends. This was trouble, big trouble, a possibility he, perhaps, ought to have foreseen.

'You are in danger here, Max,' Simpson said gently. 'If they'd do something like that to a man like Jack Wadham, what might they do to a man like you? You are a much bigger fish.'

'I always took care of my employees, paid them on time, kept them in work.'

'You supported the British. You recruited some of our best young men, secured commissions for them in the British Army. The British have lost the war in the North and it's only a matter of time before they lose the war in the South. Boston belongs to America now and Americans. To put it bluntly, Max, you backed the wrong side.'

'What should I do?'

'Is Mary with you?'

Max nodded. 'And Imelda.'

'Well, if I were you, I would leave town, go now before anyone knows you're here. Go back to Canada or wherever you've been and then, in a year or two, when things have settled down, you will probably be able to stake a claim to what is rightfully yours. Wait until the war is finally over then the voice of reason will prevail. I am certain we will not be enemies of the British for long. They will want to trade with us and we will want to trade with them. The unruly mobs will be put down and we Americans will want to do the right thing. When that day dawns legitimate claims will be heard I'm sure, yours among them.'

'I was planning to leave for England, take my family, everything, and settle there. I have friends in high places. . . .'

'Then do that and be patient.'

'I must leave at once,' Max said, convinced now of the urgency.

'Board whatever ship is available,' Simpson advised. 'One that's leaving in the next day or so. Go anywhere, but go. You can make your way to Canada or England from wherever you land. You simply must get away from here.' He rang a handbell on his desk. 'I will order a coach to take you home and to wait there to take you to the dockside.' The desk clerk appeared at the door, 'John, summon a coach, please. Mr Harvie is leaving.'

'Yes, sir,' John said and he hurried down the flight of stairs.

A small group of men had assembled at the corner of the block and others were making their way to join them. The desk clerk, worried now at his own part in alerting the mob, ran across the muddy unmade road and told the man at the carriage company that Mr Simpson required a coach at once.

A few minutes later when Simpson and Max Harvie appeared at the street door a hastily harnessed coach trundled from the yard across the road and turned to draw up alongside them.

'I'll go first to the dock office to reserve some accommodation.'

'Just go, Max,' Warren Simpson said, aware of the mob, 'and give my love to Mary.'

Max climbed inside and the coach moved off but as it gathered speed it was pursued by a growing crowd of angry men, women and jeering youths. It was brought to a halt less than 200 yards from the sea front.

The crowd swirled around the horse and carriage like a flood tide and the driver protested, concerned for the safety of the bodywork. He was dragged from his seat, his whip wrenched from his grasp, and he was hauled back over bobbing heads, to where he could do no harm. Then they began to rock the coach until it looked as though it might turn over.

Inside Max Harvie cowered back, frightened and outraged, barely able to believe that this could be happening to him, Max Harvie. But there was no escape. The jeering faces were on both sides of the coach and there were so many his view became a blur of snarls and shaking fists.

Some of the men forced their way into a wharfside yard where equipment was stored for running repairs to the many ships and small boats. They searched and found what they were looking for and they reappeared rolling out a barrel of tar. Pillows were quickly commandeered from the quayside hostelry and a space was cleared in the midst of the crowd.

'Get him out!' someone called and, as the door of the coach was wrenched open, the lid was prised from the barrel.

Max drew back but the door on the other side of the coach was also flung open and to chants of 'Out! Out! Out!' he was dragged forcibly from his haven.

When his panic-stricken white face appeared, a cheer went up and he was hoisted high horizontally. Grubby hands gripped his arms and his legs and, spread-eagled, he was carried above the heads of the crowd and set down in the clearing. Terrified, he scanned the crowd for a friendly face but all he saw were the hate-filled eyes and bared teeth of his captors. 'Where's the sheriff,' he cried. 'I demand to see the sheriff!'

'Yer demandin' days are over, Harvie,' a voice told him.

He swung round to face the speaker. 'I'll remember you, my man,' he threatened, 'see if I don't. And you'll pay for this.'

'You'll not remember anythin' when we're through with yer,' a second voice cried as the crowd closed in.

They tore at his clothing, ripping the coat from his back then lifting him bodily to drag off first his boots, then his breeches, everything, until he stood naked and shivering before them.

He tried to cover himself with his hands as they laughed and pointed at his pink, wobbly flesh. A toothless harridan cackled and made some obscene remark about his exposed anatomy. In response, her cronies and others joined in with obscenities and ribaldry of their own.

'Give me my coat!' he demanded. But one of the men, a burly thug who pushed him away with little effort, was going through the pockets in search of anything of value. Someone had already claimed his watch and chain and his diamond pin.

He darted for what he thought was a gap in the crowd but he was pushed back across the encircling ring of onlookers. Those on the other side simply pushed him back again and this became a game as he was pushed from side to side, reduced to tears of frustration and humiliation. Then he saw the barrel of tar and when he realized their intention he attempted to fight his way out with a new determined surge of strength. But most of the men were bigger, stronger and younger. The blows rained down on his head, on his chest and below the waist until he sank to his knees in defeat.

It was then that they lifted the barrel and slowly they poured the

268

contents over him. The shiny liquid fell smoothly like black syrup, covering him from head to toe. He tried to protest but he gagged as the slow swirl of tar entered his mouth. It closed his eyes, blocked his nose and filled his ears and he felt as if he had fallen into a smooth black swamp from which there was no escape. On his knees, his hands clawing at his face, he was a pitiful wretch of a man but there was no pity and there was no mercy.

The pillows were torn open and the cackling women took great delight in shaking the white and light-brown feathers out over his head. One pillow was sufficient but they had another and they were eager to use it. People who barely knew Max Harvie and certainly had not been misused by him had joined in and were delighting in the shamefully sadistic ritual.

Under the tar and the curly clinging feathers Max stirred. He could scarcely breathe and he was barely able to raise his bruised body. 'Please!' he begged. 'Please!'

'Into the drink!' someone cried and they prodded him with sticks to make him stand. 'Up! Up! Get up!'

Even now, in his distressed state, a new panic flared in Max. 'No, please! Please, no! I can't swim.'

But if anyone heard above the din of the crowd they took no heed. There was no stopping the heaving mob as they poked and prodded until he was teetering on the edge of the dock.

He stood there, bent over, and rushed to one side. The mob drew back to evade his tarred body. Then, with the glint of madness in his wild eyes, he staggered towards the other side and they drew back. He was a man fighting for his life and he knew it. All modesty and dignity gone, he didn't care any more. He was going to fight them all the way.

The water here was about twelve feet deep, a stagnant basin, murky with sewage and waste with drifts of scum floating grey and brown on its uninviting surface.

'In! In! In!' they chanted.

Then the sole of someone's boot was placed squarely in Max Harvie's midriff and he was sent backwards over the edge and into the water. A great cheer went up though some in the crowd, their blood lust for now assuaged, were having misgivings. What if he drowns? 'Throw him a line,' someone shouted.

But the majority held sway and when, after his initial desperate flailing about, Harvie failed to surface and the rings he had made gave way once more to an unruffled stagnation there were no volunteers to go in and fish him out.

TWENTY-EIGHT

Now from the South came news of a new, worrying defeat for the British. A Lieutenant Colonel Ferguson, a highly thought of Scot, had left the village of Ninety-Six with a force of just over 1,000 men, all of them American Loyalists. He was bound for Charlotte and along the way he planned to mobilize recruits for the Loyalist cause from the many small settlements by the Saluda River and in the foothills of the Blue Ridge mountains. It was a forlorn hope, for none was forthcoming. Instead he found an unruly army of backwoodsmen, many of them fine marksmen and all of them bent on his destruction.

Ferguson's men were hounded and harassed at every turn until they were forced to stand and face the enemy. They took up what they thought would be an unassailable position on the crest of a steep hill on what was known as King's Mountain. On one side was a sheer drop. No attack could come from there and Ferguson was confident he could defend his other two sides with ease.

Far better organized than Ferguson imagined, the backwoodsmen began their climb in four groups, the tall pine trees and the thickly wooded slopes allowing them to advance virtually unseen. In their dun-coloured buckskins and long dark coats they were able to climb close to the summit. Darting from tree to tree the backwoodsmen swarmed upwards at both the front and the side, firing sporadically then dodging back out of sight. Unable to foresee where the next attack was coming from man after man of Ferguson's army fell and a bewildered panic began to take hold.

The backwoodsmen were coming in so close now they could only he repulsed by bayonet. But still they came, swarming up and over the mountainside like ants covering a molehill. Brandishing a sword, Ferguson rode on horseback amongst his men, exhorting them to stand their ground. But the cause was lost. Wounded in the chest and in both arms, he charged madly at the enemy until a sustained barrage of shot brought him down. He fell dead from the saddle and his horse stumbled over the edge.

White flags were raised but many of the backwoodsmen were unaware of the surrender and continued their attack. Others, seeking revenge for the excesses of Tarleton's legion, showed no mercy. And yet again white flags were ignored and the dead and the dying lay scattered across the hilltop.

As the noise subsided and the smoke of battle drifted upwards and away the backwoodsman set about gathering and burying the fallen but this was not done well. Bodies were thrown into piles and covered with logs and rocks and loose undergrowth but this was not enough to save them from the hogs that came to devour the flesh, the vultures that hovered then landed on raised claws to pick at the bones and the roving wolves that came by night.

'This business on King's Mountain,' Tom Blanchard's colonel told him, 'is yet another tragedy. Once the battle is won it's over. Yet the killing goes on. So much unnecessary butchery.'

'The British are responsible for that, sir,' Tom said. 'allowing their man Tarleton and his legion to behave the way they do. Our people are simply seeking revenge.'

The colonel looked saddened. 'I know that's the excuse, Tom, but there's good and bad on both sides.' Then he brightened. 'The one good thing that comes out of all this is the sure knowledge that the British can't possibly win this war. They have no chance. Not with every backwoodsman in the country refusing to accept their presence. These village people are not going to be ruled by the British. Or by anyone else for that matter.'

Tom and Hank were constantly on the look out now for Ben Withers. They were under the command of General Greene who had taken over from General Gates. Greene had divided his army into two factions, one led by Dan Morgan. Ben knew, when confirmation came through that Captain Tom Blanchard and Lieutenant Henry Blanchard had expressed a willingness to be his referees, that they were still alive and he couldn't wait to catch up with them. He felt he owed them an explanation.

Dan Morgan was ready and spoiling for a fight with Banastre Tarleton. Aware of Dan Morgan and Morgan's reputation as a battlefield technician, Tarleton was more than ready to take him on. And so, one bitterly cold winter's morning, with 1,000 men at his disposal, including his legion and troops drawn from the British infantry, Tarleton faced Dan Morgan's army.

It was 17 January, 1781. At a stretch of land known as Hannah's Cowpens, on Dan Morgan's instructions, Ben and three other newly commissioned officers lined up the militia, those trained civilians who supplemented the regular Congressional Army. Carefully placed with their backs to the river, Morgan reasoned, there was no way they could back off.

Most of the militia were skilled marksmen. Their orders were to hold fire when Tarleton's men made their first attack, stand firm as the enemy approached, open fire only when the order was given. They must fire at least two volleys at the oncoming troops, they were told. Then they could disperse.

On a long sweep of gently rising ground Morgan's regulars formed the second line of defence. Hidden from view behind a steeper rise, Morgan's cavalry and mounted infantry lay in wait. He was ready now. The battle could commence.

The British had marched through a long night and throughout the ranks they were cold and tired but, as always, Tarleton was impatient to start and he began his attack at once. Confident he could drive the rebel militia into the river he lined up his men with fifty heavily armed cavalry on either side and gave out the order to advance.

Morgan galloped along his line, enthusing his men and ordering them not to fire until they could see the whites of the bloodybacks' eyes. As the British infantry came on, the militiamen stood firm. They waited, holding their nerve, until the enemy was less than fifty yards away and the order was given. The militiamen opened fire with a devastating first volley, their aim concentrated mainly, as instructed, on the officers and senior NCOs. A second volley was equally success-ful then, as expected, they began to disperse.

True to form, Tarleton sent out his Light Dragoons with orders to annihilate the fleeing rebels but the dragoons were startled to find themselves confronted by a cavalry charge that outnumbered them two to one. The sight gave heart to the rebel militia and with Morgan and his officers riding among them calling, 'Form up! Form up!' they reformed. In a staunch line they stood their ground, ready to fire a fresh volley.

Ben Withers galloped like Morgan along the lines, screaming at his men to turn and fight. He felt exhilarated. He had never been in such a battle before. He'd never been in any battle before. This was his first and it was a big one and it seemed to take him over as he cursed and shouted like a demon in the din. Get in line, he cried at a young man who had half turned away. The young man looked terrified. He'd been about to run but at Ben's order he stopped, decided to stand firm. He turned back and a musket ball hit him in the throat and neck and his blood gushed out. Ben looked away, aware that this horrific moment would return to haunt him. Nearby a boy was screaming on the ground, his leg detached in the mud. This was the reality. Ben had entered the battle, fantasizing he might come face to face with Tarleton and surprise the man. But now it was only too clear this was not a game. He wanted an end to the madness, to the frenzy, to the maniacal killing.

It was not long in coming. With the British infantry in a ragged broken line, Tarleton saw that he was fighting a losing battle. He ordered his cavalry reserve to attack the enemy's right. Morgan saw at once what was happening and ordered the battalion to his right to withdraw. The rest of Morgan's men, mistakenly thinking this was the prelude to a general retreat, also began to withdraw.

Now as the rebels made a smooth orderly retreat, their lines in good shape, the British looked increasingly ragged. Noting this, the colonel in charge of the rebel cavalry, William Washington, a relative of the commander-in-Chief, sent a message down the line to Dan Morgan. 'Give them a volley and we will charge.'

Morgan halted the withdrawal and ordered his men to open fire. The British, less than a hundred feet away, were brought to a shocked standstill by this unexpected turnaround. Some fell dead, others fled and Tarleton's dragoons galloped away. That morning, the British lost more than 100 men, killed or wounded. Almost 800 were taken prisoner. There could be no doubt. The rebels had won a famous victory.

It was then, with the battle all but over, that Ben Withers was despatched with two platoons of infantry to silence a small group of Highlanders who were refusing to surrender and a half-dozen artillerymen who were still manning a three pounder. Not fully recognizing the danger, Ben and his men walked into a barrage of gun and cannon fire. Less than ten minutes later the big gun was silenced, the resistance quelled but not before several rebel soldiers lay dead or wounded, Ben Withers among them. In a blur of flashing muskets and a thudding of heavy lead balls, he had felt a sudden dampness in an eye socket, a leg giving way beneath him and then . . . nothing, only a blackness as the sound of battle died away.

Dan Morgan had left the militiamen to care for the wounded and bury the dead and directed his army east to the Catawba River. General Greene and his men were not far behind with Lord Cornwallis in pursuit. Before leaving, Hank Blanchard rode across the body-strewn field at Cowpens. One group of militia had been detailed to collect the bodies and bring them to where a collective grave was being dug. They were dragging the bodies as if they were sacks of refuse and throwing them on to a pile.

Hank pulled up. 'These men have died honourably,' he told the militia. 'Just be careful how you treat them.'

'They're British,' one said scowling and adding a belated 'sir.'

'They're still men, you cretin,' Hank said angrily. 'Do as I say.'

Two of the men lifted a body and placed it with exaggerated care on the pile. But as soon as Hank had gone they reverted to their callous dragging and throwing.

Hank was angry because no one seemed to know what had become of Lieutenant Withers. Tom had been in talks with his senior officers and unable to help and Jimmy didn't know Ben. The search had been down to Hank. But he had found nothing.

'We must check with the field hospitals,' he told Tom when he caught up, though he knew this would be far from easy.

'If he's alive,' Tom said confidently, 'we'll find him.'

Their colonel, Colonel Putnam, was not in the best of health. The cold winter days and nights were taking their toll now and increasingly the weight of responsibilty for the battalion was resting on Tom's shoulders. He had much to think about yet, like Hank, he was concerned for Melanie Stokes.

'If anything has happened to Ben,' Hank said, 'Melanie will never get over it.'

Tom nodded. 'That's why we must find him. Or at least, find out what happened to him.'

In the days and weeks that followed General Greene was pursued by Lord Cornwallis across several treacherous rivers in high flood until

Cornwallis, giving up the chase as fruitless, established a camp near Wilmington and the coastline in North Carolina. Here, Greene decided, was the place to confront him. The rebel army had swollen to more than 4,000 men. The British, worn out and hungry, had suffered many losses. They were down to a mere 2,000.

The confrontation came on 15 March, 1781, at the County Court House close to Guilford. Though heavily outnumbered the British fought bravely and well, driving off the rebel militia who turned and fled, meeting the courageous resistance of the American Maryland brigades with heavy cannon fire and finally winning the day when Greene and his officers trotted from the field, leaving much of their armoury behind. It was undoubtedly a victory for the British but it was a pyrrhic victory for almost a third of Lord Cornwallis's men had been killed or wounded.

The victors, cold and hungry, not having eaten since the previous day, sank to their knees in the rain and lay down on a battlefield still littered with the dead of both sides. The rebel wounded had been carried into the Court House, the British wounded carried away, in more than fifteen wagons, to various field hospitals.

A month later General Greene was ready to attack the British again. There was a feeling now that with the constant strain of battle and the loss of so many men in every engagement the British resolve was beginning to break. Greene sensed that he didn't have to win these battles and rout the British. He simply had to weaken them at every turn.

Further south, close to Camden, at a place called Hobkirk's Hill, the British were led by the young Lord Rawdon who had seen many campaigns from Bunker Hill onwards. Far too good a tactician for Greene, Rawdon engaged the rebels in battle and won the day. But again the British losses were so considerable it was clear to their leaders and to the opposition that this was a costly victory. They were winning the battles but, by attrition, they were losing the war.

Rawdon's force was so depleted he felt it necessary to retreat further south but this exposed a number of British outposts to attack. One after another they fell. First the detachment at Fort Granby surrendered. Fort Motte, Orangeburg, Fort Galpin and Georgetown followed. Only Ninety-Six, now a stronghold of 550 men, still held. Mostly American Loyalists and fearful of the fate that might await them if they were captured, these men were prepared to fight to the death.

General Greene attacked with a force of 2,000, Lord Rawdon appeared with three regiments to reinforce the British and the battle that followed proved a bloodbath for both. The initiative crossed from side to side, from advance to retreat and back again and many lay dead. When the British line was finally breached the rebel infantry swamped the camp and swarmed in unopposed. Yet instead of pressing home their advantage the rampaging rebel soldiers stayed to raid the stores of the food and drink the British had stockpiled against a long siege. Many of the rebels, soon rendered drunk and incapable, were shot in the indiscriminate crossfire and the battle dissolved in confusion with losses on both sides of more than 500.

Hank Blanchard's company was at the heart of the breach, many of his men guilty of wholesale pillage. But there was not much he or Sergeant Jimmy could do to keep them in line. All Jimmy's threats as he raced among them, waving a pistol, were to no avail. Most of them were too drunk to care, others laughed in his face and he was tempted to shoot them on the spot.

It was a fruitless battle which neither side won and, as Greene withdrew to the north and the British withdrew to a place called Charleston Neck, the war in the Carolinas came to an end. Apart from Cowpens, the rebels had won none of the battles. But the British had beaten armies that did not know when they had lost.

With Greene's army, Colonel Putnam was too ill to remain in command of his battalion. He had fallen prey to an unidentified illness and it was clear that he could not carry on. Arrangements, which he resisted at first, were made for him to be taken to his home near Flatbush on Long Island. Before he left the colonel called his men together to thank them for their support and dedication. He was certain, he told them, that the day of victory was about to dawn.

TWENTY-NINE

AUNT Mary was glad to leave the print shop and the presence of the unpleasant man who had taken Ezra's place. She was anxious to see Max, too, and demand an explanation. Not even Max at his most schemimg could justify what he had done.

The moment she stepped back into the street she was aware of the noise, the tumult down at the docks. A swarming mass of people had gathered and there was something going on. She suddenly felt vulnerable and she was frightened. Ladies dressed as she was in fine clothes were not normally unaccompanied on foot in this part of town. She must go home, she decided. She would deal with Max later.

The mob, for that is what it was, an unruly mob, was coming her way, up the sloping street. She looked around for some form of transport but there were no coaches in sight and she was not near a livery stable. Across the street three unkempt women were hurrying down towards the docks, alerted by the roar of the crowd. When they saw Aunt Mary they came to a halt and looked at each other, their attention caught by her fine scarlet cloak and the glint of jewellery at her wrist. Aunt Mary walked briskly up the hill, willing herself not to break into a run. The women hesitated, torn between their curiosity about her and the pull of what was going on down the street. Aunt Mary didn't look back.

Ahead of her at the roadside was a pony and trap and as she approached the driver came out of a nearby building. She ran towards him, her hand held high. 'Wait!' she cried. 'Please!'

The man looked back at her, puzzled.

'Are you going up to North Street?' she asked.

'Might be,' he said non-committally. He glanced towards the docks, seeing that if he was going anywhere it would have to be by way of North Street.

'Will you take me, please? I'll pay you.'

The driver hesitated, slow to respond. He didn't normally carry passengers, especially paying passengers. But, well, if he was going that way. . . .

'Please,' Aunt Mary begged. 'I have to get home.'

He nodded and she climbed up on to the jump seat beside him. He stirred the pony from its nosing in the gutter and they set off at a slow pace.

'Could you hurry, please?' she asked.

The man made a face and urged the pony into a trot. Looking back Aunt Mary saw that the mob was well up the slope now about fifty yards behind them. She didn't know that the man at the print shop had come to the door to investigate the noise, heard of the fate of Max Harvie and, annoyed that Aunt Mary's visit had caused him to miss the fun, had taken pleasure in informing those nearby that 'the fine lady in the pony and trap was Max Harvie's wife.'

The three women had started the chase and the word had spread fast. Max Harvie's wife was on the street and the mob responded. Many slid away, aware that they had witnessed if not taken part in the murder of a man. But there were elements in the crowd, a hard, bitter core of men and women intent on revenge for ills real or imagined.

The pony and trap had a good start but the crowd was gaining ground. Aunt Mary clung to the seemingly flimsy contraption, searching for sanctuary as they rattled up the unmade road. The army barracks was close by but she was unsure of her reception there – if it still was an army establishment. So much had changed. The old constabulary, she had noted on her way down the hill, was now a derelict building, its calming presence gone.

The noise of the mob came closer and suddenly, as the trap turned on to the more level ground of North Street, the driver brought the pony to a halt.

'Don't stop, please,' Aunt Mary begged. 'It isn't far now.'

'These people are chasing you, aren't they?' he asked, as if he had only just realized he was aiding and abetting her escape. 'It's you they're after.'

Aunt Mary found her purse. 'Please! I'll pay you.'

But he didn't want to be seen taking money from her. 'You better go,' he said. 'Go on. Get out.'

'It isn't far . . .'

'Get out!'

She made up her mind. She would have to run the rest of the way and she set off running. She was not a big woman nor was she athletic but she ran as she hadn't run since she was a girl at school.

She looked back and saw that the mob had turned into North Street. She had a good start on them but as she ran she realized her home might not provide the safe haven she sought. There was nothing to stop this rabble from forcing their way into the house. But she had nowhere else to go and with a growing sense of dread she ran to her front door.

At a window, aware of the commotion, Vanessa saw Aunt Mary coming and guessed what had happened. Eyes wide, she opened the door and Aunt Mary almost fell inside.

'Lock the door, Vanessa,' she gasped.

Vanessa locked the door though she knew if these people had a mind to they would soon break the door down.

Aunt Mary collapsed on a sofa in the large circular hallway but her respite was short-lived. There was a hammering at the door and faces began to appear at the windows, wild resentful faces she had only ever glimpsed from the safe interior of a carriage.

The front door splintered and Vanessa put her ample shoulder against it but the pressure was too much and she was forced back. Aunt Mary's immediate concern was for her daughter.

'Mother!' Imelda was on the stairway. 'What's happening?'

At that moment the front door collapsed inwards and the mob spilled into the house. Someone wielding a wooden bar caught Vanessa a glancing blow on the side of the head and she fell and was trampled underfoot in the rush to enter.

'Go!' Aunt Mary cried. 'Hide! Lock yourself in your room.' But as the mob surged into the hallway with eyes like children at a toy fair two of the men had spotted Imelda and were intent on more than mere theft.

The three women who had first noted Aunt Mary and her air of affluence had been joined by others and there were looters in every downstairs room, gleefully going through the drawers and cupboards, grabbing whatever took their fancy. At the long sideboard in the dining room a one-toothed hag had removed her skirt to make a container which she was busy filling with the Harvies' finest silverware.

A man who had no particular grudge against Max Harvie was searching for a means of setting the house alight. In the past he had revelled in the glow of the burning homes of taxmen and others who had collaborated with the British. The opportunity to start a blaze of his own was too much for him to resist.

Two men were sitting on the stairway, guzzling bottles of stolen wine. They barred Aunt Mary's way as she tried to pass. She had abandoned her concern for what was happening to her home. All she cared about now was her only daughter, but the self-appointed guardians of the stairway pushed her back and when she persisted in attempting to pass they kicked out at her.

'Wanna go upstairs, milady?' one taunted. 'Fancy a roll aroun' the bed, do we?'

'Come on then,' the other said. 'We can give yer a better time than that ol' goat Max Harvie.'

She ran at them, tried to force her way through but they merely laughed at her and one of them tore off her skirt. But then there was a new surge as men and women pushed their way up the stairs intent on finding fresh treasure and Aunt Mary was knocked aside.

Upstairs on the landing the firebug had found the implements he needed in the housemaid's cupboard. Candles and tapers. He lit a taper, ran into a bedroom and, temporarily touched by madness, set one of the long draped curtains on fire.

Elsewhere rooms were ransacked, drawers strewn across the floor, cupboards robbed of clothing and, with no sign of the raid abating, the crowd inside the house seemed to be growing in numbers and rapacity. Anonymous now, of little interest to those present and of even less authority, Aunt Mary felt she was being carried along by a powerful current, struggling to keep her head above water. And there was no sign of Imelda. With any luck, she prayed, Imelda had become lost in the crowd, able to escape attention.

For Imelda there had been no such luck. From the moment the mob swept through the front door she had been a target for some of the less drunk and incapable marauders. More than once from the safety of her father's carriage she had looked out with disdain on the less fortunate men of the town and some now remembered this air of superiority. Three men, three men specifically, though they were later joined by others, made her their prime target and she saw the intention in their faces as she turned and ran up the stairway to lock herself in her room.

They hammered at her bedroom door. The door shuddered and looked likely to give way. Imelda looked round for a weapon. She ran to the window, forced the casement upwards. The drop looked daunting but the door behind her splintered, fell inward. She climbed out over the sill and lowered herself to arm's length. It still seemed a very long way down. Perhaps the fall would kill her. Better to die, she decided as a large gnarled hand gripped hers. She pulled free and dropped, her skirts billowing out. The fall seemed endless but she landed on her feet and there were no bones broken. She had twisted an ankle and as she put her weight on it the pain shot through her leg.

Imelda staggered painfully towards the stable. If she could find her racer she would somehow haul herself up and, saddle or no saddle, she would cling on, ride for her life. It was her only hope of escape. The men in the bedroom turned back on themselves and ran in a swarm for the door, forcing their way against the tide and back down the stairs.

As the men left Aunt Mary ran into Imelda's room and saw that she was not there. Already two women were at Imelda's wardrobe, fighting over her clothing though they were of such odd shapes it was obvious nothing of Imelda's could possibly fit them. Ignoring the intruders Aunt Mary ran back out to the landing. 'Imelda!' she cried, running from room to room now. 'Imelda!'

There was a startling whoosh as flames burst from a bedroom, crackling and licking greedily at the woodwork. Panic gripped the people on the first floor and there was a crazed dash for the stairs. Then the landing was engulfed and there was suddenly no way out. Aunt Mary saw the mad arsonist, his coat on fire as he laughed insanely in the flames, and she backed away, gasping for breath in the smoke-filled air. A man on fire, screaming in agony, fell at her feet and she realized she was trapped. Once more she called out her daughter's name, her eyes stinging in the heat, her lungs filled with the choking fumes, then part of the floor gave way and she fell with the flames to the floor below.

Imelda dragged herself towards the stable as the men after her were delayed by the fire. Painfully, hopping on one leg to keep the weight from her damaged ankle she tried without success to swing a saddle up into place. The horse waited dutifully but she couldn't do it. Then Vanessa, blood coagulating on the side of her head, came to her aid.

Without a word, Vanessa swung the saddle up and fastened the straps. On her good foot Imelda mounted and stooped to grasp Vanessa's hand. 'Where's Mother?' she asked. 'What happened to her?'

'Go, chil',' Vanessa pleaded. 'Go now!'

Vanessa led the horse from her stall and out through the big doors as five men came from the side of the house. Imelda set off, prepared to run through them. They rushed forward. The horse reared and one of the men was kicked in the face by a flailing hoof. Imelda tugged at the reins, dug in her heels. But again the frightened horse reared up. One of the men gripped her skirts and dragged her to the ground. Vanessa ran forward as the men moved in but a vicious hand knocked her back.

The house was a burning mass and many of the people inside were certain to perish. Yet, at the rear of the house, the five men were still fighting over Imelda until finally all five carried her aloft down the path to a wood. They ran with her deep into the wood until they fell to the ground with Imelda underneath.

Stiff with fear, unable to move or speak, she closed her eyes as several pairs of horny hands tore at her clothing. She was aware of men struggling, cursing, arguing over who would go first then a great weight bore down on her. The overpowering stench of a noxious smell and foul breath covered her face and she wanted to vomit. Then there was pain, excruciating pain.

Her arms pinned down, she gritted her teeth, fists clenched, her body rigid as one after another, with oaths and obscenities, spread themselves across her. It must end soon, she told herself, as she lost count. One, two, three, four and there were more now, waiting their turn in an incongruously orderly queue. She sobbed once then mercifully she passed out.

A large crowd had gathered in the roadway at the front of the house, aware that there had been a breakdown in law and order and that there were still people trapped inside. Arriving late, Melanie Stokes stood open-mouthed, shocked by what she saw. It was a house she had visited many times.

She knew the Harvies were home but she hadn't yet spoken to Imelda, an omission she now regretted. She didn't want to think the unthinkable but Imelda might well be one of those trapped inside. Bodies, she could see, were being laid out on the front lawn and more were being recovered.

Hearing the plaintive whinny of a horse, Melanie evaded restraining hands and ran down the side of the house to the stable she knew well. The horses would be terrified and she was anxious to calm them, lead them to safety. She found Vanessa sitting on the muddy, churned up earth, her head against the stable door, her face swollen and bloodied on one side.

'Vanessa!' Melanie went down on one knee. 'What happened. Where's Mrs Harvie, Imelda?'

Vanessa looked cowed and defeated. 'Oh, Miss Mel'nie . . .' Melanie had never seen Vanessa, a lady normally composed and self-assured, look so distraught. 'Where are they?'

'The missus was in the house.' She sobbed. 'Miss 'melda . . .'

'What?' Melanie demanded. 'What happened?'

'Those men they took Miss 'melda inta the wood.'

Melanie stood up, looked back at the house. The kitchen and the outhouse were not yet touched by the flames. 'The gun cabinet,' she said. 'Is it locked?'

'You can't go in there, Miss Mel'nie. It too dangerous.'

'Where's the key?' she demanded. 'Tell me!'

'Ah don't know, Miss Mel'nie. But you can't go . . .'

Melanie ran to the house. A back door was open. Cautiously she went inside and the smell of smoke filled her nostrils. She opened a door, saw the flames blazing at a stairway and closed it quickly. The gun cabinet was in a room beyond the kitchen. It was glass fronted. She didn't search for a key. She simply picked up a broom and rammed the handle at the glass until the glass shattered. Then she chose a long nosed rifle she knew how to handle. In the drawer she found the ammunition she needed.

When she emerged she was holding the rifle and a handful of shot. She looked back at Vanessa, then set off down the narrow track to the wood.

The track narrowed still further but she had only gone ten yards when she heard the low rumble of several men. From behind a thicket she could see three or four unclean-looking wretches standing in line. Two men crouching down obscured her view of anything more. She fired the rifle in the air and there was confusion ahead. She reloaded quickly, fired again and the men scattered, all except the two crouching down.

Melanie reloaded and emerged, levelling the rifle. One of the two was a callow youth with a look of an idiot, the other a much older man. She had seen the older man before but she couldn't quite place him. Pointedly she aimed the rifle at the boy. 'Run!' she ordered. 'Or I'll kill you!'

He turned and ran, leaving the older man who drew himself up and Melanie saw Imelda lying there now, inert, her clothing torn, her eyes wild and unseeing.

'Come to join in the fun, missie?' the man said leeringly.

'You're the leader here,' she accused.

'You could say that,' he admitted, with an air of bravado.

'Get back!' she said, the fury mounting. 'Or I'll kill you.'

With a swagger he came forward. 'You ain't gonna kill . . .'

Melanie shot him in the leg and he fell, holding his knee and howling. She reloaded the rifle and aimed it between his eyes. 'What's your name?'

Holding his leg he looked up at her in agony.

'Your name or I'll kill you.'

'Briggs,' he said, rocking back and to and moaning.

Melanie remembered him now. He had done some work on the barn for Mr Harvie. 'Well, listen to me, *Briggs*,' she said, spitting out his name with contempt. 'I hold you responsible for this outrage. I'll report this to the sheriff's office and if they don't do anything Hank Blanchard will. Hank Blanchard is Miss Imelda's intended and, I promise you, if you are not in jail he'll kill you. Probably still kill you when you come out.'

'It weren't jus' me.'

'You were the leader. You admitted as much. Now go, or *I'll* kill you.'

He drew himself up and backed off painfully, then he turned and staggered away into the wood.

Imelda was badly bruised but, worst of all, she seemed to have lost her mind. Melanie knelt beside her, spoke to her gently and touched her arm but she shrank back in terror.

'It's all right,' Melanie said. 'It's me. Melanie.'

Imelda looked at her without expression, her eyes vacant.

'I'm going to take you home,' Melanie said.

Hearing the shots and fearful for Melanie's safety, Vanessa had ventured a few steps into the wood. Now, when Melanie called, she ran to help and between them they lifted Imelda. Her arms on their shoulders, they carried her to the stable.

Melanie brought a horse and hitched up the small wagon. 'I'll take her home with me,' she told Vanessa. 'I need to get her to bed then I'll call Dr Crouch.'

As the disturbance at Max Harvie's house raged on, the more responsible citizens gathered to condemn what had happened. It was the sheriff's duty to control these mobs, they complained, and whether Max Harvie had been a Loyalist or not he and his family were entitled to civilized treatment. A message had been despatched to the sheriff's office but by the time he arrived the damage had been done.

The sheriff came under considerable criticism from leading citizens and he was eventually obliged to resign. Men like Mr Blanchard Senior were not prepared to tolerate such blatant disregard for law and order. It was true that, among others, Max Harvie had collaborated with the British. But such people could be made to realize they were no longer welcome and informed in a civil manner that they must leave town. There was no excuse for the mass pillage and burning of property that would inevitably give Boston, which responsible men were attempting to rebuild, a bad name.

The *Gazette* and the *Evening Post* took this line and the publicity given to the attack on the defenceless Harvie household brought a halt to any further mob rule. But despite the attention the affair received in the press and at many public meetings, the murder of Max Harvie was never investigated and though what had happened was public knowledge no one was brought to justice. Nor was there an investigation into the burning down and wholesale desecration of his home.

Among the last of the bodies to be recovered was the body of Aunt Mary, burned and charred almost beyond recognition but identified by Vanessa. As for what happened to Imelda, four men including Briggs were arrested and all except Briggs were discharged for lack of evidence. Briggs, though denying rape, admitted to being present. He was sentenced to three years in prison or a public flogging. He chose flogging, which Melanie Stokes felt was far too lenient. Imelda was left to live in a twilight world of her own, cared for now by Melanie and Melanie's mother and facing a long, possibly endless road to recovery.

THIRTY

THEY had no news of Ben Withers, no conclusive news that is. A lieutenant who was with Dan Morgan that day at Cowpens told Hank
he had seen Ben leading a small squad to knock out a troublesome
cannon. They did the job but there was one hell of an explosion and
most of them had died. *Most* of them? Hank pressed him. Well, he said,
I reckon probably all of them. It was not certain, Hank told Tom, but
it was the only news they had. It was rotten luck, Tom said, so sad to
lose him so late in the war. Tom was convinced the war was coming to
an end and the British position was weakening by the day. He was
not wrong.

There was dissension now at the top for the British, political in-
fighting and personality clashes that could only damage their
campaign. Sir Henry Clinton, the Commander-in-Chief, felt his
authority was being constantly undermined by Lord Cornwallis, his
successor-in-waiting. and that he lacked the support from home to
which he was entitled. A growing body of opinion in England wanted
him replaced and this knowledge caused him to defer more and more
to Cornwallis.

The British Navy urgently required a coastal town where they could
establish a naval base. The French fleet was well on its way across the
Atlantic with reinforcements for the rebels. And in New York Clinton
believed he would need the bulk of the army to repulse any attempted
onslaught. Clinton's problems were mounting. There were disagreements over the choice of a suitable coastal town. The French
reinforcements would help to swell the opposition to almost twice the
size of the depleted British Army. And Cornwallis saw no reason why
he should abandon Virginia and send most of his men to New York.

Now after much prevarication, made easier by the frequently

contradictory orders he received from Clinton, Cornwallis chose Yorktown as his headquarters. He contended that Yorktown was better placed to provide a safe harbour for the navy. It would also be easier to defend than most other options. The town of Gloucester was just across the York River, about a mile to the north. East and west were swamplands. Any attack would have to come from the south. It was here that Cornwallis constructed a line of stockades and a further line of redoubts.

With the British awaiting the support of their navy the French Navy took control of Chesapeake Bay. Waiting and begging for reinforcements that never materialized, Cornwallis found he had backed himself into a corner. With their French reinforcments, the rebel army now comprised over 15,000 men and it was clear the British could not hold out indefinitely. Cornwallis warned his superiors, 'If you cannot relieve me soon, you must fear the worst.'

The Commnder-in-Chief of the Americans, General Washington, was in high spirits as he marched his army out of Williamsburg in the early morning of 28 September, 1781. Well turned out in their smart new uniforms supplied by the French, uniforms of blue and brown faced with red, the rebel army was confident and resolute.

As they approached Yorktown they found several of the British outposts had been abandoned. Here the rebels prepared their ground and on the afternoon of 9 October George Washington fired the first shot from a heavy gun at a range of 600 yards. This was the signal for an intense bombardment. Sixteen mortars and forty cannon battered the town hour after hour. With little more than 3,000 men fit for duty the British, under heavy fire, were facing an army 15,000 strong.

The rebels stormed the redoubts and stockades relentlessly and by 11 October they had advanced to within 300 yards of the heart of the British defence. Morale in the town was at a dangerous low. Food had become desperately scarce. Much of what was left was mainly putrid meat or worm-ridden biscuits. Bodies, many headless or with arms and legs shot away in the incessant barrage, lay unburied. Horses, so weak from malnutrition they were unable to stand, had to be put down. With no safe refuge in the town some people fled to the banks of the York River in search of shelter but even there many were killed by bursting shells. Not surprisingly soldiers were deserting or going absent without leave in great numbers.

It was obvious that Lord Cornwallis's only possible escape route was across the river to Gloucester. Struggling to provide the necessary covering fire, he sent out his first batch of men. They reached the other side of the river safely. But the second batch were not so lucky. A heavy storm blew up and that night the boats were scattered, tossed about and damaged. There was little hope of getting any more men across and the hoped for wholesale evacuation had to be abandoned.

Early next morning, 17 October, the rebel bombardment began again. Cannon and mortar sent shot after shot hurtling at the British defences. There was a perfunctory response then all was quiet. And then . . . the diminutive figure of a drummer boy in a dusty bearskin hat closely followed by a British officer waving a white handkerchief emerged from behind the British ramparts and walked slowly down the slope through the drifting gunsmoke in surrender.

A rebel officer went out to meet them. The drummer boy he sent back to the British lines. The officer was blindfolded and brought to the rebel headquarters. General Washington listened to what the officer had to say then refused Cornwallis's request that civilians loyal to the crown and rebel army deserters should not be punished. Nor would the surrendering British be allowed to march out to the beating of drums and with their flags flying.

As the discussions continued rebel soldiers cheered in triumph. At last the war was over and they had won. Across the muddied slopes Tom Blanchard raised a hand in salute at his brother Hank and Jimmy thrust a fist in the air. Then Tom was saddened at the thought of all those fine young bodies he'd seen lying twisted and mangled in death. Casualties had been high everywhere and on both sides. Even here, in this last one-sided battle, the rebels had lost eighty men, the French 200, the British 600. Yes, the war is over, he thought soberly. But at what cost?

The negotiations went on for the next two days as soldiers on both sides, weary of the years of battle, lay down in the welcome sunshine. Softening slightly, General Washington agreed that the British could emerge from behind their lines with music, provided they did not play their version of 'Yankee Doodle' or any of the other American tunes they loved to satirize.

So the scene was set. On the field of surrender was a circle of mounted French hussars in blue jackets. Wearing new red coats issued that day and bearskin caps, leather caps or tricorne hats depending on whether they were grenadiers, light infantry or battalion men, the

British were marched down to the field where they had to pass between two lines of troops. French infantry men in their white unforms were on one side, American soldiers in their darker, less ostentatious outfits were on the other.

The British soldiers entered the circle of French hussars, some of them throwing down their arms angrily as if to smash them on the ground until ordered to conduct themselves with dignity by their commander. Pointedly refusing to look at the victors, many of the British rank and file appeared close to tears.

The Americans, according to one British officer, behaved with great delicacy and the French were profuse with their expressions of sympathy. When he visited their lines immediately after the parade had been dismissed, he said, he was overwhelmed by the civility of his late enemies.

There was much sickness and debility in the British ranks and, whether genuine or not, Lord Cornwallis took the opportunity to claim illness himself and announced he was not well enough to attend the ceremony. A Brigadier-General O'Hara was delegated to represent him. At the surrender O'Hara offered his sword to the French leader, Comte de Rochambeau, but le comte would not accept it. 'We are subordinate to the Americans,' he said. 'General Washington will give you your orders.'

O'Hara turned away to offer his sword to General Washington but as Lord Cornwallis was not present Washington declined to accept and left the ritual to one of his senior officers who simply tapped the sword in acceptance.

The American and French officers then entertained the British officers to a lavish dinner with music and copious amounts of wine. Banastre Tarleton, with whom the Americans refused to eat, was not invited.

In the weeks that followed the ending of the war the armies on both sides were gradually scaled down. In England there were rumblings in Parliament about a continuation of hostilities but the British public were no longer in favour of such action and most ministers had come to accept, if not publicly, that it was not possible to win such a war. 'The people of America may be defeated, though not without difficulty,' one newspaper columnist commented, 'but the country itself is unconquerable.' And most of those who had faced the rugged mountains, the inhospitable plains and the impassable swamps agreed.

Hank Blanchard was preparing to return to Boston and take Jimmy with him. Tom would follow a week later. He had been invited to join General Washington's personal entourage on a visit to New York. Tom had seen much of his homeland, he told Hank and Jimmy, and now that independence was in sight he wanted to help in the formation of the country's future. Recommended by General Greene he had become a highly regarded aide of General Washington and a junior role in future government was a distinct possibility. 'One of us will have to go home,' Hank told his brother with a grin. 'Someone has to look after the store.' Jimmy just wanted to see Chrissie.

Hank and Jimmy left as planned and Tom promised he would follow within the week. But there was much to do in New York and when he finally did leave for home he was asked to go first to Flatbush to pay the regiment's respects to the family of his old chief, Colonel Putnam, who had recently died.

He had arrived in good time for the funeral and the colonel's wife was deeply moved that General Washington had sent a letter of condolence and a personal representative. Tom was well received by the family but a little surprised to be asked to pay his respects in the form of a eulogy at the funeral ceremony.

That night he agonized over what he was going to say and by morning he still had no clear picture in mind. But in the little church as he ascended the pulpit steps and looked out at the congregation he was suddenly calm. The church was full and it seemed that the whole town had turned out. The colonel was a well-known figure, popular and well respected, and his family name was spread wide across Long Island. Tom looked at Mrs Putnam. She was in the front row, dressed all in black. Mrs Putnam nodded and smiled her encouragement. The family tributes had been paid. Tom needed only to speak of the man as he knew him, a colonel of the Congressional Army.

'Here was a man,' he began. 'He was a baker not a soldier. He was only a soldier when his country needed him. The call came and he answered that call. He left his home and his family to defend his country and to keep it from those who would take it from us. And so the baker, for a little while, was a soldier.

'But he didn't change. He brought with him all the love and all the goodness that was in his heart and that was why those men who served under him loved him as they did.

'He became a soldier, fighting for his country. But he didn't hate the enemy. He didn't hate anybody. And he certainly didn't want to kill anybody. He just knew that what he was doing was right. He knew that what he was doing was right for his children, for his grandchildren and for his country.

'And with that sure knowledge he knew that no matter how long it took, maybe not with this war and maybe not the next, he knew that he and his fellow countrymen would win in the end.

'Here was a man, ladies and gentlemen, a truly *good* man.'

As he stepped down Tom was barely aware of what he had said, but whatever it was he could see from the smiles and the nods of approval that his words had been well received. Later at the Putnam home as he accepted a glass of wine he was approached by a man of the colonel's age with a rather distinguished air.

'Good speech, son. Well done,' the man said. Then: 'Blanchard? I know the name but not the face.'

Tom smiled politely.

'You were with Colonel Putnam?' the man asked.

'All the way, sir.'

'At Valley Forge?'

'Why yes,' Tom said, a little surprised.

'Colonel Putnam was a good friend of mine. I'm from a place called Fourways not far from Valley Forge. I'm a doctor. I came that first day to help with the wounded. Officer in charge of the sick bay was a Lieutenant Blanchard.'

'Ah,' Tom said. 'My brother Hank.'

The doctor smiled. 'He worked hard that day. But I think the presence of my daughter might have had something to do with it.'

Tom laughed. 'The schoolmistress. Kathleen.'

'Yes,' the doctor said. 'He was quite taken with her and, perhaps I shouldn't say this, but I think she was quite taken with him, too. He actually rode out to Fourways one day just to say hello.'

'Yes,' Tom said. 'The colonel wasn't too happy about that.'

'So how is he?' The doctor was serious for a moment. 'He's all right, I hope? I mean, he survived the war?'

'Oh yes,' Tom assured him. 'He's fine. He's gone home and I'm going tomorrow. Ma won't believe we're safe until she sees us.'

'Give him my regards, son,' the doctor said warmly. 'And I'll tell Kathleen he's safe and well.'

THIRTY-ONE

J IMMY stood shyly in the hallway as Mr and Mrs Blanchard hugged and kissed their son Hank. They had so much to talk about, so much news to exchange. But there was plenty of time for all that. Hank looked back at Jimmy. 'Ma,' he said. 'Dad, I want you to meet my friend here. Sergeant Jimmy Ray, the best company sergeant the rebel army ever had.'

Mr Blanchard went forward, hand extended. 'I'm very pleased to meet you, son.'

'Thank you, sir,' Jimmy said. 'I'm very pleased to meet you.' He turned to Mrs Blanchard. 'And you, ma'am.'

Mrs Blanchard, overjoyed at seeing her younger son and with the knowledge that her elder boy would be home soon, took Jimmy's arm. 'Come and sit down and let me see what I've got for you fine young fellows. You must be starving.'

'I want to hear all the news,' Hank said.

'Where to start,' Mr Blanchard said, bringing a jug of wine to the table. He laughed. 'It was like all our birthdays came on the same day when that young fellow came to tell us you were still alive. Don't know how it happened but you and Tom were on a list of dead rebel soldiers.'

'Word was Max Harvie did that,' Mrs Blanchard offered. 'He wanted Imelda and her cousin Sarah to think our boys were dead.'

Mr Blanchard shook his head. 'Max Harvie was a strange fellow and he did some pretty strange things but I don't believe even he would do a thing like that.'

Mrs Blanchard put plates of cold chicken before the boys. 'This is just for now,' she said. 'Tonight we'll have a celebration dinner.'

'This is lovely, Mrs Blanchard,' Jimmy said. 'Thank you.'

Mr Blanchard had noted that this was no ordinary Negro. 'Our news will keep,' he said cheerfully. 'Tell us about our friend here. Sergeant Ray.' He looked at Jimmy with a smile. 'And you can tell us how you came to be mixed up with this crazy son of mine.'

Jimmy looked at Hank. He didn't know what to say or where to begin. Mr Blanchard was actually treating him like a human being.

'Well, I'll tell you,' Hank said, coming to the rescue. 'Jimmy was working on the Mabbut place. That day when Tom and I went over to the woodcutter's in Roxbury we saw this fellow carrying a goddamned firebox – sorry, Ma – a big heavy firebox and we stopped to offer him a lift. I mean, we were only just past Boston Neck and he was going to Roxbury. Still had a long way to go.'

'Mr Blanchard,' Jimmy broke in, 'I was going to Roxbury on foot and your boys were kind enough to offer me a lift. I was a slave, Mr Blanchard, a slave to Mr Mabbut. Anyway later, when I was running away, I met them again. They were off to join the rebel army and they invited me to go with them and I did. I served alongside them throughout the war. We went through some hard times together and we became very good friends. Now the war is over I suppose I should go back to Mr Mabbut. But I was one of those people who actually believed the Declaration of Independence meant what it said.' He stood up. 'I'm still a slave, sir. If you would like me to leave, I will. Right now.'

'What are you talking about?' Hank said.

'Sit down, son,' Mr Blanchard said. 'Please.'

'You can't go yet,' Mrs Blanchard told him. 'Oh no. You have to taste my blueberry pie.'

Jimmy sat down.

'When Tom gets back,' Hank said, 'we're going to see old man Mabbut. With Jimmy's service record he's entitled to his release.'

'I have to go, Hank,' Jimmy said. 'I have to find some place to stay. Then I want to go to see Chrissie.'

Mr Blanchard was intrigued by Jimmy. He didn't behave like a subservient slave and his beautifully modulated voice, slow and so precise, was fascinating to the older man.

'You can stay here,' Mr Blanchard said. 'Can't he, Ma?'

'Of course he can,' Mrs Blanchard agreed. 'He can have Tom's room. Then when Tom gets home we can sort something else out.'

'You're very kind,' Jimmy said.

Mr Blanchard laughed. 'Have another drink,' he said, 'and you two can tell me about these hard times you been through.' He looked at Jimmy. 'And you can tell me how you got to talk like some professor.'

Jimmy explained that he had always wanted to read but at Mabbut's place it was forbidden for slaves to learn. Then Hank and Tom taught him between battles. Learning to read was the most wonderful thing that ever happened to him, he said. Now he read everything. Notices, bye-laws, announcements. And any book he could get his hands on.

'You see, Mr Blanchard,' he said, 'if you can read a word you can see how to say it properly. That's why I try to say everything right.'

'Well,' Mr Blanchard said. 'All I can say is, you make me sound like some kind of hillbilly.'

'I'd like to start a school, Mr Blanchard,' Jimmy said seriously. 'A school to teach black children how to read.'

Mr Blanchard nodded. 'It's a nice idea, son,' he said. 'But you know as well as I do there'd be a lot of opposition to something like that.'

'Come on,' Hank said, changing the subject. 'Jimmy has things to do first. Hey, Ma! Jimmy has a girlfriend. Lovely girl called Chrissie.'

'That's nice,' his mother said. 'You must. bring your young lady to see us, Jimmy. Where is she? In Boston?'

'She's at some place over in Lexington. Half Edge, I think they call it. She's a slave like me and I want to buy her out. But hey!' he said to divert attention from himself. 'How about Hank? He has a girl, too. A doctor's daughter from Valley Forge way.'

Hank shrugged. 'Well, I don't really know her.'

'Oh yes?' his mother said, doubting this. 'What's her name?'

'Kathleen. But I only met her a couple of times.'

'Too bad about Imelda,' his father said.

'Why? What happened?' Hank asked.

Mr Blanchard looked at Mrs Blanchard. 'We don't really know what happened,' he said. 'But the Harvie place got burned down. Terrible business. Mrs Harvie died in the fire.'

'Oh no!' Hank was shocked. He had always liked Mrs Harvie. 'I heard they were in Nova Scotia.'

'They were,' his father said. 'But for some reason they came home. They must have thought things were back the way they used to be but they weren't. And they won't ever be now.'

'So where's Imelda?'

'Don't know, son.' Mr Blanchard looked uncomfortably at his wife.

'Some pretty strange stories about that.'

'What? What stories?'

'Hank,' his mother said, 'Mrs Harvie died in the fire. Max Harvie is dead, too. And Imelda, I'm not sure, but I know she was with Melanie Stokes for a while. Where she is now, I don't know. But if you're interested best person to ask is Vanessa.'

The next morning Hank and Jimmy walked over to North Street and people who knew Hank stopped to shake his hand. He was a hero, he found, of the Revolutionary War. When they reached the Harvies' home Hank couldn't believe it. He opened the gate and Jimmy followed him inside. Hank shook his head. 'My God!'

Jimmy remained silent. He had little idea what this place was or what it had been but it was obvious that Hank was deeply affected by what he saw.

Hank walked on, down the side of what had been the centre of so many civic evenings, soirées and celebrations. It was the home of so many of the memories of his youth, so many images. The shadows of the dancers on the tall windows as he arrived here with Tom, the string quartet and Imelda manipulating the dance cards that evening when his brother first met her cousin, Sarah, Tom in a trance for weeks after.

With a smile he remembered the time Imelda tried to lure him into bed and how she pushed him unceremoniously out of the window when her mother came home unexpectedly. Poor Mrs Harvie. She was a lovely lady, a lovely person, and he couldn't bear to think of her perishing here in a fire.

Here was the kitchen, too, or what was left of it. The kitchen where, when they were small boys, Vanessa could always find an apple each for him and Tom. And this was the rose garden where Max Harvie had tried to recruit them into the British Army.

It had been a big house, a substantial house, one of the biggest in town. Now all that was left was a pile of rubble. Hank turned to Jimmy. 'Who would do a thing like this?'

Jimmy could only nod his head in sympathy, conscious there was something here that clearly meant a great deal to his friend.

There was someone in the stables. Hank strode across, pushed open the door. It was Alfred, the Harvies' elderly manservant.

'Missah Blanchard,' Alfred said, surprised and apologetic. 'It sure is good to see you home safe 'n' sound.'

Hank nodded. 'You OK?'

'Oh yes, sah.'

'I'm trying to work out what happened that day, the day the fire started. I only just got to hear about it. Were you actually here?'

'Yes, sah. Ah was here.'

'So what happened, Alfred?'

'Well . . .' Alfred looked over Hank's shoulder at Jimmy, wondering who he was but afraid to ask.

'This gentlemen is with me, Alfred,' Hank said. 'We'd like you to tell us what you saw, if you don't mind going through it all again.'

'Well, Mister Harvie an' the family been in Can'da since the fightin' start. Then Mister Harvie come back to see to the business. They was goin' off again. Real soon. To England.'

'Did he tell you this?'

'Missus Harvie told Vanessa. Sez they was going soon as Mister Harvie seen to the business. Missus Harvie sez Vanessa an' me was to stay at the house for the time being.'

'So what happened?'

'Mister Harvie go down to the office. Then Missus Harvie go down there. Then Missus Harvie come back and this big crowd is chasin' her. They come in the house an' she tell Miss Imelda to go upstairs an' lock herself in her room. But the crowd . . . they ran all over the place, stealin' things. Then the crazy man start the fire.'

'The crazy man? Who was he?'

'Just a crazy man, Mister Hank. He done it before. Always startin' fires. Been in the jail for burnin' down the fire station.'

'What happened to him?'

'He was one o' them died in the fire. He was just a crazy man.'

'So Mrs Harvie died in the fire. What happened to Imelda?'

Alfred hung his head. 'Ah only know what ah hear.'

'What was that? What did you hear?'

'Well, these men came an' they took Miss Imelda to the wood. But ah don't know, Mister Hank. Best ask Vanessa. Vanessa was there.'

'Who were these men?'

Alfred could sense the anger building up in Hank. 'Ah don' know, sah. But ah know one was Briggs, used to work for Mister Harvie.'

'Briggs.'

'Yes, sah. Best ask Vanessa, Mister Hank. She was there.'

'Where is Vanessa?'

'She gone stay with her brother. Down the shanty.'

Hank nodded and put a hand on Alfred's arm. He had suddenly noticed the pallet by the first stall, the little table and the kettle and he realized this must be where Alfred was living. He put his hand in his pocket and drew out several notes. 'Take care, Alfred.'

Alfred declined to take the money but Hank insisted.

'Poor old fellow living in the stables,' Hank said as they left.

'Better than some folk have,' Jimmy said.

That afternoon Hank and Jimmy saddled up and rode over to the cluster of houses known as 'the shanty' out Cambridge way. It was a small settlement of wooden shacks and wattle fencing mainly occupied by black families. Set along a lovely stretch of the Charles River it was constantly under the covetous gaze of property developers and land speculators.

Vanessa had a brother who lived here in what had been their family home for several generations. At fourteen Vanessa had gone into service with Max Harvie's mother and she had been with the Harvies' for the best part of forty years.

The two tall handsome horses, pick of the Blanchard stock, were at walking pace now. Hank steered his mount to a halt in the dried mud clearing at the heart of the settlement. Jimmy closed up behind him. Together they dismounted as a small group of onlookers gathered at a respectful distance.

Hank had been here before with Imelda when they were no more than fourteen years old. They had a message for Vanessa on that occasion and he was trying now to remember which of the shacks they visited. Most of them looked the same. Then he noticed a grassy path that looked somehow familiar. They went across and found there were three dwellings in a row. He knew it was one of these he wanted but he was not sure which.

Two small children went on playing on some well-worn steps as a long thin Negro came from the side of one of the shacks. He saw the watching crowd at the end of the pathway and turned to face the visitors with no smile, no greeting, nothing.

Hank guessed he was Vanessa's brother. He was about Vanessa's age, a little older perhaps. 'Hello there!' Hank said pleasantly. 'My name's Hank, Hank Blanchard, and this is my friend Jimmy.'

The Negro looked at Jimmy, who was still wearing his sergeant's stripes. Jimmy nodded and smiled but the man remained silent, wary.

'We are looking for a lady,' Hank offered. 'Lady called Vanessa. Do you know her? Vanessa . . .'

It was the only name he knew her by. If she had a surname he didn't know it. Still no response.

'Look,' he said, his patience waning. 'Do you know someone called Vanessa or not?'

'It OK, Sam,' a voice called and Vanessa came out on to the narrow porch. 'It sure is nice to see you, Mister Hank. Come on inside.' She laughed. 'Folk might think you is back from the dead.'

Still without expression Sam took the reins of the two horses from Hank and Jimmy as they followed Vanessa indoors.

'Don't have much to offer but ah can find you somethin'.'

'We don't want to put you to any trouble,' Hank said.

'No trouble,' Vanessa said cheerfully. 'Come on in and sit down.'

She bustled away through the back door and Hank and Jimmy looked around the small room. There was a low bed against one wall, a couple of pallets propped against the other. A table and three dining chairs made up the rest of the furniture on the bare wooden floor. On one wall hung a cloth sheet with what looked like an Indian design. In a corner were some carved wooden toys, a bear, a wolf, a mountain lion.

Vanessa came back with a tray and a jug of apple juice. 'This is ma brother's place now. He lives here with his little gran'children. Wife died a long time back. Then his two boys left home an' their sister had the babies an' did likewise. Left ma brother to care for them. That's five years back an' he ain't seen nor heard nothin' since.'

She looked at Jimmy.

'This is my friend Jimmy,' Hank said. 'Sergeant James Ray, C company, 1st Battalion, General Greene's Congressional Army.'

'It's a pleasure to meet you, ma'am,' Jimmy said, speaking carefully and precisely.

Vanessa smiled. 'Right. One o' them uppity Negras, huh?'

Jimmy laughed. 'You could say that.'

'Where d'you get to talk like that?'

'I learned to read,' Jimmy said. 'In fact, Hank and Tom taught me how to read and I'll be eternally grateful.'

'So you should be,' Vanessa told him. To Hank she said, 'You never taught me how to read.'

'You never asked,' Hank said with a grin.

'Nah, an' ah don't suppose ol' man Harvie would have liked it.'

'What happened to him, Vanessa? I mean, what really happened?'

'Well,' Vanessa said, 'you know what he was like. Mister Big Man. But he never deserved that.'

'What did they do to him?'

'They tar an' feather him then they throw him in the green dock.'

Hank screwed up his nose, recalling the stretch of stagnant dirty water he and his friends had always known as the green dock.

'He drowned,' Vanessa said. 'Turned out he couldn't swim.'

'But that's murder,' Hank said angrily. 'Was anyone charged?'

'No witness,' she said. 'Big mob there, but nobody saw nothin'.'

'Same mob that chased Mrs Harvie?'

'Ah guess so.'

'So what happened at the house?'

Vanessa heaved a big sigh. 'Ah was lucky to get outa there alive. That mob come burstin' in an' they beat me up an' left me on the floor. They trample all over me. An' ah got this big cut on ma head.' She pointed to a badly healed gash on her forehead. 'But ah guess ah was luckier than the missus.'

'Why didn't Mrs Harvie get out?'

'Well, she could've. The mob was not so much after her as the clothes on her back. There was a lot o' them rough women off the street. They just wanna steal anythin' they could get their hands on. Then Missus Harvie run upstairs. That was her mistake, ah guess. She was up there when the fire start. Couldn't get back down. Ah guess she musta gone up there lookin' for Miss 'melda.'

'So what happened to Imelda?' he asked, dreading the answer.

'Miss 'melda was upstairs sure enough. But those men was after her an' they was up to no good. Ah run out the back o' the house when the fire start an' ah see Miss 'melda sorta hobblin' along. Ah guess she musta jumped out the window.'

Hank knew that window. It was quite a drop. 'You sure? She jumped from the window?'

'Must have. Stairs was on fire. Some o' them men musta jumped, too. Anyway, she look' sorta dazed an' ah went to get her but these men come an' carry her off to the wood. Ah couldn't do nothin'.'

'How many men?'

'Five or six, ah guess.'

'Who were they, Vanessa?'

'Ah don't know . . .'

'Who were they?' Hank demanded.

Jimmy stepped forward to lay a restraining hand on Hank's arm. 'Easy, Hank.' To Vanessa, he said, 'He just wants to know what happened, ma'am.'

'He don't want to hear this,' she said.

'Tell me,' Hank insisted. 'What did they do to her?'

'They take her to the wood and they rape 'er. Four, five, six, ah don't know. Then Miss Mel'nie come with a rifle an' start shootin'.'

'Melanie Stokes?'

Vanessa nodded. 'Tough lady Miss Mel'nie. Shoot one o' them in the leg an' she says if he don't get outa town she gonna kill 'im.'

'She knew him? She knew who he was?'

'Oh yeah. Scum called Briggs.'

'Where is Imelda now?'

'Ah don't know. Ah guess Miss Mel'nie take her home to her place. Miss 'melda look' pretty bad. Look' to me she lost her mind.'

THIRTY-TWO

H<small>ANK</small> had not yet been to see Melanie. He was waiting until Tom came home. Then they could go to see her together. They had no real news about Ben and he didn't want to be the one to tell her that Ben was probably dead. Tom would be better at that. But now he couldn't wait. He had to find out what had happened to Imelda, where she was, *how* she was.

Jimmy was also waiting for Tom. Desperate to see Chrissie, he wanted to go and buy her freedom. He had the money but Tom had told him he needed to be a free man himself before he could go buying someone else's freedom. Tom had promised to bring a letter that would force old Mabbut to renounce any claim he might still think he had on him. Promise me you'll wait until I get home, Tom had said. And he had promised.

'I've got to see this girl Melanie,' Hank said.

'I'm coming with you,' Jimmy said.

'You don't have to.'

Jimmy felt his friend might be in need of some kind of help or protection. He didn't know any of these people but the girl Imelda, whoever she was, seemed to mean a lot to him. If he decided to go in search of the people who attacked her Hank was going to need some back up.

'I think maybe I do,' he said.

Hank had left Vanessa with a hug and a promise to keep in touch and they had taken their leave. They went directly to the small house where Melanie Stokes lived with her mother.

Melanie saw them riding up the narrow roadway and hitching their horses. She ran out the front door and threw her arms around Hank's neck. Jimmy smiled. They sure were a friendly bunch around these parts, he told himself.

Melanie pulled back, her arms still holding Hank, and looked at him fondly. 'You don't know how good it is to see you, Henry Blanchard. You were supposed to be dead. And Tom, too. How is he? Is he home yet?'

'End of the week,' Hank said with a smile. 'He had meetings to attend. Big shot now my brother. *Major* Thomas Blanchard.' He took her hands. 'But what you really want to know is . . . Ben.'

Melanie put her fist to her mouth.

'We don't know, Melanie. We were at a big battle, place called Cowpens in South Carolina. We were with General Greene. Ben was with General Morgan. Huge battle, lot of people injured. Lot of field hospitals. We've been searching through them. Still making enquiries. But nothing yet. If . . . well, we'll find him.'

'You mean if he's alive?'

'We have no reason to think he isn't.'

She looked at Jimmy, who was a little embarrassed by now.

'I'm sorry,' Hank said. 'This is Jimmy, my friend and brother-at-arms. Sergeant James Ray. Jimmy, this is Melanie, the girl we all love but she belongs to this fellow Ben.'

Melanie smiled and held out a hand.

'I'm very pleased to meet you, miss,' Jimmy said.

'Did you know Ben?'

Jimmy shook his head. 'I'm afraid I didn't. But I've heard a lot about him and I sure hope he's OK.'

'We've been to see Vanessa,' Hank said.

'Oh, Hank,' Melanie said. 'She told you about Imelda?'

He nodded. 'She said you sort of rescued her.'

'When it was too late, I'm afraid.'

'So what happened to her? Where is she?'

'She's here, Hank. She's been here with us since . . . well, since what happened. She has no family now. Father, mother dead, and it seems Edward was killed quite early somewhere in New Jersey. She only has her cousin Sarah and Sarah surprised us all by going off with a British officer called Handsome Jack.' She raised her eyebrows. 'I'll tell you about that later. Let's go inside.' She gripped his arm. 'But be prepared,' she told him. 'She's not exactly the Imelda you know.'

Hank followed her up the three steps to the porch and the front door. Jimmy felt that he shouldn't be there, that he was intruding in someone's private affairs.

He sat down on the steps. 'I'll wait here, Hank.'

'No, please,' Melanie said. 'Come in.'

Jimmy just smiled and indicated he would stay where he was.

Hank and Melanie went into the house and Mrs Stokes came forward to meet them and kiss Hank on both cheeks. 'So glad to see you're safe, dear,' she said. 'Imelda is in the garden.'

Imelda was sitting on a bench outside with her back to the house. She was dressed in a simple white smock and there was a sun hat on the bench beside her. Hank glanced at Melanie, put a finger to his lips and Melanie waited as he picked a wild flower and went forward alone.

'Who is this lovely lady sitting in the sunshine?' he asked.

He didn't know what to expect, what reaction there might be. But there was no reaction, nothing. Imelda simply looked back at him and smiled as if he had never been away.

'Come and sit down,' she said, patting the bench.

He sat beside her and looked into her eyes. She didn't look any different. She was as pretty as ever if a little pale. But he knew she *was* different. She looked tranquil, sitting quietly in the garden. But he felt that this was a fragile tranquillity, that terrors waiting to erupt lurked behind those blue eyes and that she was not always as calm as this.

'You were dead,' she said, mildly rebuking him as if he had played a practical joke.

'Not really,' he said quietly.

'Daddy said you were. Why would Daddy say you were dead?'

'I don't know,' Hank said, and he could see what it was, how she was different. She was a child again. Perhaps she had erased all recollection of that dreadful ordeal and was back living in a pure, unspoiled past.

'I'm glad you're not,' she said.

Hank went to touch her hand but she flinched and drew back. She stared straight ahead, dreamily. Then she said quietly, 'You must wait, Henry Blanchard. I need time, time on my own. Then I will marry you.'

Melanie came closer. To Hank she said, 'Mother wants to get you something to eat, a drink or something.' To Imelda she said, 'Isn't it wonderful to see Hank again?'

Imelda was still staring ahead. 'I knew he would come back,' she said. 'He had to. Hank and I are going to he married.'

Hank was still holding the wild flower. He placed it on the bench beside her and indicated to Melanie that they should go back into the house. Imelda didn't seem to notice they had gone.

'The doctor says it will take time,' Melanie said. 'A long time. She may get better but she will never really get over what happened.'

'She's like a child.'

Melanie nodded. 'She's like that most of the time. But sometimes, in the night she wakes up screaming. Her whole body shakes as if she's terrified and I have to sit with her and hold her together until she calms down. Then eventually she falls asleep.'

'This man you shot. I understand his name was Briggs. Vanessa said you told him he was to leave Boston. So did he?'

Melanie shook her head. 'I don't know. I don't think so. Alfred says he's seen him down at the market.'

'Right,' Hank said purposefully. 'If there's any news of Ben I'll come round right away, I promise. But I'll be back anyway to see Imelda, if that's all right.'

'You're welcome here any time. You know that,' she said, then she added, 'I don't know what's going to happen with Imelda in the future. But she'll stay here for now, for as long as she needs to. We'll take good care of her.' She smiled sadly. 'But the way she is you couldn't marry her, Hank, even if you wanted to.'

Hank took his leave of Mrs Stokes and Melanie on the steps and as they rode away Jimmy didn't like the look on his face. It quite clearly meant trouble.

'I know that face,' he said. 'Where are we going?'

Hank drew up his horse. 'You don't need to come, Jimmy. It could mean trouble and it's not your fight. It isn't fair to involve you in something like this. You go home. I'll see you later.'

'If it's your fight it's my fight,' Jimmy said.

Hank shrugged and they set off again. It hadn't been a market-day and the square was quiet. But it was getting dark. Already there were people in the tavern, silhouettes in the yellow light that spilled on to the grass outside. By the entrance a small boy was playing with a dog. Hank dismounted, handed his reins to Jimmy and walked over to the boy.

'Do you know a Mr Briggs?' he asked.

The boy drew the little dog closer to him.

'Fellow called Briggs?' Hank was tossing a coin and catching it with one hand. 'This – if you can tell me where he lives.'

The boy looked at the coin, wanting it. 'Briggs? Down there.' He pointed towards the dockside. 'Near the wharf.'

'Can you show me?'

The boy nodded, started walking, the dog at his feet. Hank signalled to Jimmy and Jimmy followed with the horses. It was quiet along the waterfront and poorly lit. A lodging house for sailors and merchant seamen, a run-down property with a red light over the entrance, two or three derelict buildings then a warren of hovels. The boy stopped at a narrow passageway and pointed a finger as if too scared to go any further. Hank gave him the coin and he ran off, the dog jumping beside him.

Jimmy tied the reins to a hitching post and followed Hank down the dirty passage. The smell was foul, a putrid mix of dog dirt and decay. There was just one door then the passage opened on to a back-yard of overgrown weeds and discarded rubbish. Hank knocked at the door and waited. He knocked again. Nothing. He pushed at the door and it opened inwards.

Hank went inside leaving Jimmy, his nose twitching, in the passage. A large man was asleep in an armchair. There was no fire in the grate just dead ashes. A table, a chair, not much else. A grimy window appeared to look out on to the yard.

The man's face was vaguely familiar. Hank felt he had seen him before somewhere. He kicked the man's leg. 'Briggs!'

The man jumped awake. 'What? What's. . . ?'

Hank looked down at him. 'You Briggs?'

The man looked up at him defiantly. 'Who wants to know?'

Hank hit him across the face with the back of his hand then gripped his shirt at the neck. 'Are you Briggs?'

'Yeah,' he said, his face stinging. 'What is this?'

Hank took a step back. 'Get up. I said get up!'

Briggs struggled warily to his feet and Hank hit him hard. He fell backwards into the table then to the floor.

'Get up,' Hank said quietly but Briggs stayed where he was.

Hank gripped him by his shirt front and pulled him to his feet, but Briggs clearly didn't want to fight.

'So you're a coward, too,' Hank said and hit him again. 'Rapists and men who hit women usually are.'

Briggs's nose was spurting blood. Hank dragged him up then knocked him down again, repeating this until the man's nose was broken, his few remaining teeth were knocked out and he was barely conscious.

'No, no,' he begged as Hank picked him up yet again.

'You're coming with me,' Hank told him quietly, menacingly.

'Where? What? What yer goin' t' do?'

'Throw you in the dock,' Hank said.

'I can't swim,' Briggs protested, his face covered in blood.

'Neither could Max Harvie,' Hank said.

'I didn't have nothin' t' do with that.'

'But it was you who raped his daughter.'

'It wasn't just me.'

'So that makes it all right, does it?'

Hank grabbed him by the scruff of his neck and threw him at the outside door. Jimmy had been waiting in the passage, wincing at every blow. Now he was shocked at the state of Briggs.

'Right,' he said. 'Looks like you got your man. Let's go.'

'Oh no,' Hank said. He hadn't finished yet. Gripping Briggs by his matted hair he dragged him along the passage and threw him out into the street. Briggs could barely stand but Hank forced him to his feet and pushed him, stumbling and falling towards the dock.

It was dark now. There was no one about. Disorientated, Briggs staggered ahead as Hank pushed him from behind. Jimmy brought the horses, not sure of Hank's intention. With the horses as cover he shielded the clearly distressed Briggs from view as two seamen appeared on the other side of the road and went into the building with the red light. Hank grabbed Briggs and thrust him towards the water's edge.

'What are you doing?' Jimmy asked in alarm. 'He's had enough.'

'Not for me, he hasn't,' Hank said.

'Leave him alone, for God's sake. The poor man's half dead.'

But this was a side of Hank that Jimmy hadn't seen before. 'He's going for a swim,' Hank said calmly.

At this Briggs seemed to realize where he was. He looked back at Hank, begging, pleading with his eyes. 'I tol' yer, I can't swim.'

'Too bad,' Hank said and with that he raised a foot and pushed Briggs over the edge.

'You're mad!' Jimmy cried, looking around for a rope, a lifeline, anything. There was nothing, nothing at the saddles, nothing lying around. He did an anxious dance at the water's edge, but there was no sign of Briggs in the swaying water. He thought he saw an arm break the surface and he pulled off his jerkin, preparing to go in. But the moon went behind a dark cloud and the darkness was almost total. The horses stirred uneasily. He looked at Hank, his eyes and teeth in the darkness, and he seemed to be smiling.

The moon emerged from the clouds but there was no sign of Briggs. Hank took the reins and mounted his horse.

'We can't just go.' Jimmy couldn't believe this was happening. 'If you leave now you're not the man I thought you were.'

'Then I'm not the man you thought I was.'

Jimmy scanned the water, appalled at Hank's behaviour. But he knew there was nothing he could do. He shook his head, reluctant to leave.

'Go in, if you must,' Hank said. 'You'll find him down there with all the mud and the shit and the slime – where he belongs.'

He turned his horse and moved off. Jimmy looked again at the dark water. A few seamen spilled out of the bawdy house, laughing and jostling each other. Jimmy hesitated. Perhaps he should enlist their help. But they looked drunk and he knew that he, a black man, wouldn't command much respect even if they were sober. Feeling like a criminal skulking away from the scene of a crime, he mounted his horse and followed Hank.

At a walking pace, they rode back to the Blanchard farm in silence. Hank glanced sidelong at Jimmy but made no comment then, as they dismounted, Jimmy said, 'You killed that man.'

'I've killed a lot of men lately,' Hank said, unrepentant. 'I've killed good men, men who didn't deserve to die, but they were soldiers in a war. This fellow didn't deserve to live.'

'It was murder, cold-blooded murder.'

'You didn't see Imelda.'

'So what are you going to do now? Find the rest and do the same to them? Are you going to murder them all?'

'If I find out for certain who else was involved, yes.'

'You're wrong, Hank. You can't go around killing people. The war is over.'

Hank turned and faced him. 'I hope it never happens, but if anybody treats someone you care about the way Briggs treated Imelda then let's see how you react.'

Three weeks later the newsletter published periodically from the print shop formerly owned by Max Harvie reported – *The body of a forty-two year old man has been dredged up by a fishing boat almost two miles beyond the harbour limits. He was William Briggs, well known locally as a regular customer at the Market Tavern. Briggs was* a heavy drinker and it was assumed he had fallen in the dock on his way home.

THIRTY-THREE

IN New York Tom Blanchard had been introduced to John Adams, the man destined to succeed George Washington and become the second President of the United States. Adams, a founder member of the First Continental Congress, was a Bostonian, a lawyer educated at Harvard, and he was much impressed with the young major. He recommended that Tom should spend some time at Harvard, perhaps study law.

The new America was in the throes of evolution and Tom wanted to play a part in that. But first a number of matters at home required his attention. He had not seen his parents for almost three years and he wanted to catch up on all the news. There was Melanie, too. Hank would have prepared her for the worst by now but Tom still had nothing new to tell her. He didn't want to say so but in all probability Ben was dead.

Tom wanted to spend some time with his father, time to explain that he wanted to leave the running of the farm and the stud business with Hank and pursue a diplomatic career in New York or Philadelphia. He hadn't told Hank this yet but he soon found that Hank had plenty to tell him. All this had to wait anyway when he arrived home that first evening. Hank had prepared an elaborate homecoming party for him and the Blanchard house was filled with relatives and guests.

Jimmy had persuaded Mr Blanchard he was an experienced groomsman. That was what he did when he worked at the Mabbut place, he said, and he'd had plenty more experience with horses in the army. He wanted to earn his keep. Now, at the party, he was serving drinks and generally helping out until Hank told him to relax, he was a guest. Tom gave him a bear hug and whispered, 'I've got it. I've got all we need.'

'It' was a signed letter from General Nathanael Greene. It read, *Sergeant James Ray has served his country with great distinction and has been a highly valued soldier of the Congressional Army. By order of our supreme commander, General George Washington, and in recognition of his outstanding contribution to our noble and victorious cause, the aforementioned Sergeant Ray is to be granted his freedom forthwith.* Attached was a form of release for signature.

When the guests had gone and Mr and Mrs Blanchard had gone to bed, Tom, Hank and Jimmy were out on the porch in the moonlight. There was so much to talk about they didn't want the evening to end. Tom produced the letter and Jimmy read it with tears in his eyes.

Hank took it from him, read it and laughed aloud. 'What a load of tripe!' he said. 'Who wrote this stuff?'

'It's beautiful,' Jimmy said, looking at Tom. 'How did you do it?'

'I wrote it out and asked the colonel to sign it but he went one better and got General Greene to do it.'

'Do you realize what this means?' Hank said, joking. 'This uppity Negra will believe all that stuff.'

Jimmy laughed. 'It's true. I was a top sergeant. The best!'

'All right,' Hank said, more seriously. 'It's fine. But we don't really need it. We don't recognize slavery in Boston any more.'

'*We* don't,' Tom agreed. 'But you can bet old goats like Mabbut still do. I'm going to see him tomorrow, going to make him sign it.'

Jimmy read the letter again and again, his eyes shining.

'You need to see Melanie,' Hank reminded him. 'She was invited tonight but she couldn't make it. I want you to see Imelda, too, see what they've done to her.'

'I can't believe what they did to the Harvies,' Tom said. 'Old Max, even he didn't deserve that. And Mrs Harvie.' He shook his head. 'And Imelda. She was just a silly girl. But she was a nice girl and a good friend, one of the gang.' He looked at Hank. 'We need to find those animals and do something about it.'

Hank nodded. 'But nobody has any names. It might all come out in time and when it does we'll have them.'

Jimmy looked up but Hank made no mention of Briggs.

'They should have gone to England,' Tom said. 'Big mistake to come back. I suppose old Max wanted to sell up, grab his money.'

Hank nodded. 'Typical of Harvie. Sheer greed.'

'Maybe he was short of cash,' Tom said more charitably. 'Good thing Sarah didn't come back with them. I suppose she was lucky, going off with her handsome bloodyback.'

'Come on, Tom,' Hank said. 'She thought you were dead.'

'Maybe it would be better if I was,' he said bitterly. 'Planning ahead for Sarah and me is what kept me going.'

'Well, it might not be too late. She might not be married yet.'

'And how do we find out? It would take months, even if we had an address to write to. We don't know where she is or who this bloodyback is.'

'Yes, we do. He's called Colonel Danvers.'

'You could write to Colonel Danvers, British Army Headquarters, London, England,' Jimmy suggested. 'It would get there eventually.'

'Yes,' Tom said. 'And by the time it did she'd probably be married with about ten children.'

'I'll ask Melanie to write to her,' Hank said. 'She knew Sarah well enough. She can tell her all the news. She needs to know that you're still very much alive. And she might not even know about Imelda and her Uncle Max and Aunt Mary. She may have property here herself, from the Dowling estate. She needs to know, Tom. We owe her that.'

'Maybe,' Tom acknowledged. 'But, as far as I'm concerned, all is lost. Not for you though, my little brother. Guess who I met at Colonel Putnam's funeral.'

Hank looked blank.

'Guess,' Tom insisted.

'I don't know. George the Third?'

'That doctor from Valley Forge, father of your one true love.'

'Kathleen? Kathleen's father?'

Tom nodded, amused at Hank's reaction. 'The schoolmistress. The one you went off to see when you should have been on duty. If it hadn't been for my timely intervention you would have been reduced to the ranks. Absent from post. Dereliction of duty.'

'All right, Mr Perfect Soldier, what did he say?'

'He said that Kathleen is crazy about you and you ought to go and see her as soon as possible.'

'What did he really say?'

'He said you would be very welcome to visit. But it's pretty obvious he doesn't know you.'

'Why do you say that?'

'Well, he said you were a fine young man.' Then seriously Tom said, 'I'd go and see her, Hank. I know it's a long way but I'll be here for a while. I can keep an eye on things until you get back. And we've got Jimmy now.'

Jimmy nodded. 'You thought she was pretty wonderful at the time. Girl like that won't wait around forever. You should go, Hank, and the sooner the better.'

'I can't,' Hank said, as if it was out of the question.

Tom knew that he was serious. 'What is it, Hank? Why can't you? I thought it was what you wanted.'

Hank shook his head and went inside. Tom raised his eyebrows at Jimmy but he didn't question Hank further. Hank would tell him, in his own time, if there was a problem.

Next morning, after an early breakfast, Tom and Hank appeared in their rather dull Congressional Army outfits of dark-blue shirts and long dark coats, their white sashes adding a touch of grandeur. The military insignia showed they were men of rank.

'Good sir,' Hank said, with a flourish and a bow, 'May I present Major Thomas Blanchard? And I, sir, am your humble servant, Lieutenant Henry Blanchard. We, of the victorious Congressional Army, defeaters of the British, liberators of our homeland.'

Their father looked amused but he was quietly proud of them. 'What're you two up to?' he asked. 'Who you going to fight now?'

'Mr Mabbut,' Tom said. 'He needs to be taught a lesson.'

Hank grinned. 'And we're the boys to teach him.'

Jimmy brought the horses. He was excited now. He had wanted to go with them, see old Mabbut's face when they handed him the letter. But Tom had said no, better not. 'Good luck,' he said and he waved them off, a huge smile lighting his face.

They rode out towards Boston Neck until Tom slowed down, turning his mount off the road and up a dirt track.

'You sure this is the right way?' Hank asked.

Tom nodded towards a small faded board in the undergrowth. 'That's what the sign says.'

The track looked familiar now, the shaded copse where they had left the horses and then the gateway. They had not passed beyond the gate that previous occasion but they rode through now at walking pace, tall and confident in the saddle.

'I'm going to enjoy this,' Tom said.

314

Chickens scuttled out of the way as they dismounted before a long low farmhouse. A young black woman was sweeping out the porch. She paused, her broom in mid-air. Tom doffed his hat as he approached. Hank took the reins of both horses and hitched them to the hitching post.

'We're here to see Mr Mabbut,' Tom said with a smile.

The young woman laid the broom aside and went indoors. Seconds later a young man dressed in rough work clothes emerged. He was covered from the waist down by a pigman's long black apron. He noted the army uniforms with a frown, his expression distinctly unfriendly.

'We're looking for Mr Mabbut,' Tom said pleasantly.

'Which one?' the young man asked with a hint of aggression.

'The only one that counts,' Hank said, equally aggressive.

Tom gave Hank a disapproving look and said, 'We'd like to see Mr Mabbut senior, if you don't mind.'

'Who wants him?' the young man demanded.

'Major Blanchard, Congressional Army.'

'What's it about?'

'We're here to see Mr Mabbut,' Tom said, his voice hardening. 'What it's about is his business. Will you tell him, please?'

The young man went back inside and they waited on the porch. The young black woman came out and smiled at them shyly as she picked up her broom ready to resume her sweeping.

It was Mr Mabbut who came to the door, the young man, his son, hovering behind him. Mabbut looked them up and down, his surly expression an older version of his son's. 'I'm Mabbut,' he said. 'This is my land. Uninvited visitors are not welcome.'

'There's something we need to discuss, Mr Mabbut,' Tom said.

'Like I said, this is my land. . . .'

'Nobody disputes that this is your land. And this is not a social call. We can discuss your business out here if you wish. In public.'

Mabbut hesitated, then with a reluctant twitch of his head he invited them into a sparsely furnished room. There was a moose head on one wall, a gun cabinet on another. A small drinks table and several wicker chairs were the only other furniture. But they were not offered a drink or invited to sit down. Tom glanced at the young man who was still hovering in support of his father.

'He's my son,' Mabbut said. 'You can say what you have to say in

315

front of him.'

'Good,' Tom said. 'My name is Tom Blanchard. This gentleman is my brother Hank.'

Mabbut nodded. 'I thought you looked familiar. You two have been here before.'

'Yes,' Hank said, unwilling to take time over formalities. 'We were here before, when you tried to tell us rebel soldiers were responsible for the massacre at the Dowling place.'

Mabbut was taken aback and clearly less sure of himself.

'We're not here about that,' Tom said, wishing Hank would let him do things his way. 'We're here on behalf of General Washington, Supreme Commander of the Congressional Army.' This seemed to disconcert Mabbut even more and Tom pressed home his advantage. 'We have a document for you to sign.'

'I ain't signing nothin',' Mabbut said and his son bristled.

'You're signing this,' Tom told him. Then he said, 'You had a young man here by the name of Jimmy.'

'Yeah,' Mabbut said, 'and I heard he joined the rebels. That means I'm entitled to half his bounty and half his pay.'

'You're entitled to nothing,' Hank said scornfully.

'Gentlemen, please,' Tom said. He turned to Hank. 'Lieutenant, read Mr Mabbut the document.'

Hank took out the letter from General Greene and read it with a flourish, dwelling on the words, '. . . *the aforementioned Sergeant Ray is to be granted his freedom forthwith.*'

'What about his bounty?' Mabbut demanded.

'Sure,' Hank said. 'You can have half of that. There wasn't one.'

'Then I will demand compensation.'

'In that case,' Tom said, 'John Richard Mabbut, with the powers vested in me as a Congressional Army officer, I'm arresting you for crimes against Congress.' Again he looked at Hank. 'Lieutenant.'

Hank stepped forward.

'Wait, wait, wait.' Mabbut put his hands up. 'What crimes?'

From the pocket of his apron, the young Mabbut produced a large knife. Tom ignored this and announced, 'Mr Mabbut, we have full and conclusive proof backed by witnesses that, in collusion with the county sheriff, you wilfully denigrated the good name of the Congressional Army by falsely claiming Congressional Army troops were responsible for the murder of several members of the Dowling

316

family and for the rape and murder of a young female employee. You will come with us, please. Or we will return with a detention squad and your home and farm will be confiscated.'

Hank looked at Mabbut's son. 'You can put your knife away, thickhead. If I remember rightly you joined the British. What did you do with your red coat? Burn it? I'd lie low, if I were you. We have vigilantes in Boston. They bury ex-redcoats.'

Mabbut senior was shaking. 'Look,' he said, 'this is all wrong.'

'Absolutely,' Tom agreed. 'We came here to secure the release of Sergeant Ray. If you refuse to sign the release we are fully authorized to invoke our powers of arrest. Which is it to be?'

Mabbut frowned. 'What do you want me to sign exactly?'

'This.' Hank held out the release note, pointing out the place. Mabbut squinted at it. 'What does it say?'

'If you can't read, don't worry, Mr Mabbut,' Hank said, taking pleasure in provoking him. 'You can just put your cross and we'll get your son to countersign it.'

'I can read, goddammit,' Mabbut said, angry at the implication. 'Where? Where do I sign?' He looked at his son. 'Get the quill.'

'It means,' Tom said, 'that Jimmy Ray is a free man and you have absolutely no claim on him whatsoever. Is that understood?'

'And that's the end of it?' Mabbut asked.

Tom nodded. 'Sign this and, you have my word, we'll leave you in peace. But you had better understand you're going to have to treat your people well in future. We don't have slaves any more.'

'I've always treated my people well,' he said indignantly.

'That's not we heard,' Hank said.

'Sign here,' Tom said and Mabbut hurriedly signed his name. Tom took back the letter and the form of release. 'We'll bid you good day then, Mr Mabbut. Lieutenant?'

Hank followed him to the door but couldn't resist a parting shot. 'Times are changing, Mr Mabbut. Things are different now.'

Outside they mounted the horses. Tom touched his hat and led the way, his horse at walking pace. Mabbut and his son stood on the porch, glowering as they watched them go.

Once through the gates Hank cracked up with laughter. 'Where the hell did you get all that stuff?' In a pompous caricature of his brother, he announced, 'We are fully authorized to invoke our powers of arrest. With the powers vested in me we will return with a detention squad.

317

Your home and farm will be confiscated. Where the hell did you get all that? You don't have any powers of arrest. And where do we get this detention squad?'

'It worked, didn't it?'

'It worked all right. Jimmy will think it's his birthday.'

'It is. Birth of a new life for Jimmy,' Tom said. 'He deserves it. He's a good man, Hank.'

'You don't have to tell me that.'

'We need to free Chrissie now. And they can start a new life together. Throw off those invisible chains they've been stuck with all their lives.'

Hank glanced fondly at his brother as they rode side by side. 'You're getting pretty eloquent these days, Thomas Blanchard. Might make a congressman yet.'

'A little eloquence and gentle persuasion are the right tools, Hank. Threats and violence are always wrong.'

This was something Hank would never accept, but he rode on in silence. He hadn't told Tom what he'd done to Briggs. He knew what his law-abiding brother's reaction would be. He would tell him one day, he decided. But not yet.

THIRTY-FOUR

T HE Congressional Army had been rapidly scaled down, not as a matter of policy but because most of those who volunteered left in droves to go back home to their families. Many were disillusioned at the poor treatment they had received and for some months there had been murmurings of mutiny over the lack of pay. This too rapid reduction in numbers rendered many small communities vulnerable to attacks by disaffected Indian tribes, a problem that was to fester for another ten years until the offending tribesmen were brutally crushed, divided and ruled.

To many Americans little seemed to be happening on the national front but then most of the would be administrators and political activists were busy delineating their territories and drawing up their own state constitutions at home. After Yorktown in October, 1781, the war was over yet it was not until April, 1783, an official cease-fire was declared. A mere formality, this was of little consequence to most Americans. The war was won. Now there was much to be done.

And so, as the war of the battlefields finally ended, the war of words began. The leaders of the new America, men like John Adams, Chief Justice John Jay and the worldly old charmer Benjamin Franklin, were negotiating from a position of strength. They were well aware that the British were anxious to maintain and strengthen commercial ties with their former subjects and bent on driving a wedge between them and their wartime allies the French.

Communications were difficult, at least on a national level, and negotiations of an international nature were conducted by a small self-appointed coterie of talented individuals, men who were little inclined to relay details of their often intricate negotiations abroad. The prospect of conducting diplomatic relations with other countries seemed wholly seductive to Tom Blanchard. It was what he wanted to do.

His mentor, John Adams, had told him, 'There are going to be lots of great opportunites for young men in our national government. You can go home to Boston. Of course you can. Be a farmer, a horse breeder, whatever it is your family does. You can stay home. Combine the two. Politics and farming. In time you could become Governor of Massachusetts. Or you could spend a year at Harvard then come back to New York, become a player on the world stage. It's up to you.'

Tom knew he was not going to stay home. Hank could do that. It was what Hank wanted. He could run things. Take over from Dad. Be his own boss. Hank had never been much good at taking orders or playing by the rules. But Tom wanted more. He wanted to travel, see something of the Old World. London, Paris, Rome. And now, especially, London. He had not yet fully acknowledged it to himself but he knew a notion had taken root at the back of his mind, a notion that one day he might travel to London as some kind of ambassador and by chance meet up with his one and only Sarah Dowling.

It was a matter of chance that he called to see Melanie Stokes that warm sunny afternoon. He was in the neighbourhood and he knew, as it was a Sunday, Melanie would not be at work at the school. He wanted to talk about Sarah. He rang the doorbell and nobody came but he could hear voices at the back of the house. He went down the side. Melanie was sitting on a hammock that hung between two trees. She jumped off and ran to meet him.

She searched his eyes and, a little embarrassed, he realized calling unexpectedly like this might have led her to assume he had news. 'It's nothing, Melanie,' he said. 'I was just passing.'

'Yes, of course,' she said. 'It's lovely to see you. Come and sit down.' She led him to the bench seat on the back porch, the porch where so often in the old days they had gathered just to sit around and be together and sample Mrs Stokes's apple juice. Melanie, Ben, Hank, Imelda, and sometimes Sarah.

Imelda was asleep in an armchair out of the sun.

'She looks pretty peaceful back there,' Tom said. 'How is she?'

'The same, I suppose,' Melanie said quietly. 'Calmer, I think.'

From a small arbor of trees Melanie's mother emerged. She was holding a baby girl by the hand as if helping her to walk. When she saw Tom she raised a hand and waved.

Tom raised his hand in response and guessed the baby was a neighbour's child or perhaps one of Melanie's charges from the nursery school. He saw that Melanie was watching him closely as if awaitng a reaction. Then a thought occurred to him. He looked at the sleeping Imelda. 'It's not . . . it's not Imelda's baby?'

'No, thank goodness,' Melanie said. 'She's mine. And Ben's.'

He looked at her, quietly astonished. Then he stood up, went down the steps and walked to where Mrs Stokes was doing her best to hold the baby upright. 'A little girl,' he said, incredulous as he went down on one knee. 'Hello. And what's your name?'

The baby looked up at him wide-eyed. 'She's called Sally,' Mrs Stokes said. 'It was Ben's mother's name.'

Tom took the baby's other hand and with Mrs Stokes walked her back to Melanie. 'She's beautiful,' he said, lifting her to her mother's arms. 'Just beautiful. Why didn't you tell us about this?'

Mrs Stokes shook her head as if she knew why but didn't approve. 'Can I get you something, Tom?' she said. 'A drink?'

'I'm fine, thanks,' Tom said.

She looked at Imelda. 'Don't let her sleep too long,' she told Melanie as she went indoors, 'or she won't sleep tonight.'

'Wait until I tell Hank,' Tom said, still thrilled at the baby.

'He knows,' Melanie said apologetically.

'He does?' Tom said with a frown. 'He hasn't said anything.'

'I asked him not to. I didn't want you to know. You see, if there was still a chance you might find Ben alive I didn't want you to tell him.'

'But why? He'd be delighted. You know he would.'

'I know. But I wanted him to come home because he wanted to, not because he felt he had to because there was a baby.'

'That's crazy. Of course he'd want to come home.'

'I'd want him to come home for me, not because he felt he was under some obligation.'

'I don't understand that,' Tom said.

'Well, maybe another woman would,' she said.

'You and Ben,' Tom said. 'Of course he'd come back. You were all he ever wanted. You know that.'

'Well.' She shrugged her shoulders. 'It doesn't matter now. We can be pretty sure he isn't coming back. But it would be nice to know what happened and where he's buried.' The baby had fallen asleep.

321

Melanie transferred her deftly to her lap. 'Sally and I will want to visit him one day.'

They were silent for a while, then Melanie said, 'What was it like, Tom? I mean, what was it really like in a battle? You must have been in many. How did it feel?'

'You don't need to know,' Tom said. 'In fact, it's better you don't know.'

'I do need to know. I need to know how Ben was feeling in those last days. I need to know what it was like, what he must have gone through. I want to live it, as if I was with him.'

'You can't do that. You'd have to be there to understand.'

'Tell me, Tom,' she insisted. 'Tell me what it was like.'

He looked at the baby, the sleeping innocence in Melanie's arms. It was all there to be lost. We all start out that way, he told himself, and gradually, day by day, it gets eroded. Every day of our lives we lose a little more until there's nothing left.

He looked out at the field that began where the short stretch of garden and the vegetable patch ended. The pale grass, the bracken, the gorse, the distant hills. And as he looked the crack and echo of gunfire, the cries and the screams of battle resounded at the back of his mind.

'Tell me,' she said again. 'Tell me what it was *really* like.'

'Sometimes,' he said, 'it was easy. Our big guns would open fire and they would run away before the battle began. Other times they would come on and on and you would see the red coats in the flash of gunfire, the swords held high, the whirl of a cutlass. And sometimes you would see a man, very close, as close as I am to you. He would be just a man, not a devil or a demon, just a man. But he would want to kill you. He would be determined to kill you. You didn't want to kill him. But you had no choice and no time to think about it. It was kill or be killed. Kill, kill, or be killed.'

Tom seemed to be transported, staring into the distance at something only he could see. 'There were men on both sides,' he went on quietly, 'good men, trying to kill, knowing that other men had to die for them to live. A neck gashed by a sword, an arm blown away, a decapitated head bouncing on a grassy bank. A severed leg in the mud and slime.

'Cannons and howitzers and mortars. Shells bursting all around. Legs, arms, bodies shattered by grapeshot. A man beside you is struck by a stream of musket fire. His leg is gone below the knee. And the dead lie everywhere, mounds of them all around. And from somewhere among the limp and the lifeless, the pitiful cries and the sad moans of the wounded. A boy with one foot crying for his mother. And nearby a horse writhing in agony, four legs in the air, and you do the only thing you can. The tears streaming down your cheeks, you put it out of its misery. A man, so badly wounded his stomach has spilled open and bloodied his legs, calls out and begs you to do the same for him. But he's a man. You can't do it. You walk away. Then you walk back and you look him in the eyes. He tries to smile. "Please, please", he whispers. And you shoot him, too.

'You remember the smoke and the noise, the blind fury of the desire to live. You want it to end and you want to survive and you know there are no heroes, just men, ordinary men who, for a few crazy moments, are touched by a kind of madness.'

Melanie had been very still, listening in awe. Tom had spoken quietly, gently, as if lost in the recollection. Now, as if coming out of a trance, he said, 'Oh, Melanie. I'm so sorry.'

'Don't be,' she said, her hand on his arm. 'I wanted to hear.'

They were silent again. Then Melanie asked, 'Why, Tom? Why did it happen? We've all lost so much.'

'It had to happen,' Tom said. 'If we hadn't fought this war, our children would have had to do it. It had to be fought sooner or later. And now it's over.' He smiled. 'But what about you? How do you survive, Mel? The baby, Imelda, your job?'

'My mother takes care of the baby and Imelda when I'm at the school. And when Sally gets a little older I'll be able to take her in with me. We're OK.'

'What's going to happen with Imelda?'

'Well, that's something I need to see you about,' she said. 'I'm a bit concerned about Hank, Tom. He's been here every day. He comes to see Imelda and that's fine. She expects him now. But I'm worried that he's getting too . . . too involved. Imelda acts as if he's her beau. And I think Hank feels he's sort of responsible for her. Well, of course, he isn't. None of this is his fault. If it hadn't happened Imelda would be in England with Sarah and her parents. But she says things like, "Hank is all I've got now".

'At first, he was just sort of helping out, caring for her. But she's become very possessive about him and it isn't fair to him. It isn't fair to either of them. There's no future for them.' She paused and looked at him in earnest. 'I think you will have to talk to him, let him see just what he's getting into. He can't throw his life away on Imelda. She will never be the girl she was. I think he needs to walk away. Before it gets any worse.'

Was this why he was so cool about Kathleen? Tom wondered. 'He met a girl and he was smitten with her,' he said. 'It was at this place called Valley Forge. I didn't meet her but Jimmy did. He said she was a lovely girl, a schoolteacher, but that day she was helping with the wounded. Her father was the doctor.'

'Well,' Melanie said, 'he told me he plans to settle down, find a wife. Then he should do that. Imelda could never be a wife.'

Hank and Jimmy had been working with the horses when Tom got back and Mrs Blanchard was serving supper. At the table it was much quieter than usual then Tom realized it was down to Hank. He seemed subdued, not saying much, which was not like him. He usually had more to say than anybody. Tom looked at Jimmy, but Jimmy merely raised his eyebrows as if to say yes, he'd noticed but he didn't know what, if anything, was bothering him.

It was much later when Tom got a chance to talk to his brother. He went out to the back porch and found him sitting there alone in the shadows. The night was still, no wind, not even a breeze and the quiet fields were bathed in a pale glow from the moon. From the woods the occasional hoot of an owl would punctuate the silence but otherwise there was not a sound. It was the kind of warm, comfortable peace a soldier far from home might dream of when lying in a cold, damp tent the night after some fierce battle.

Tom felt like an intruder. He indicated a seat as if asking for permission to sit down. Hank nodded but didn't speak.

'You all right?' Tom asked.

'Yeah,' Hank said, a little wearily. 'I'm all right.'

'What is it, Hank? What's going on?'

Hank shook his head dismissively but Tom was not convinced.

'I called to see Melanie today,' he said. 'You didn't tell me she has a baby.'

'She asked me not to.'

'Yes,' Tom said. 'She told me. Great little kid.'

'Yes,' Hank agreed. 'And it's good for Mel. It's what she wanted. Something of Ben's.'

They were quiet for a while, then Tom said, 'I saw Imelda, too. I didn't speak to her. She was sleeping.' He waited but there was no response. 'I guess something will have to be done about Imelda. Melanie can't have her forever. She's got to take care of the baby. Maybe Imelda should be taken to England to be with Sarah. Sarah's her only relative now, as far as we know. And it seems Sarah has done all right for herself. She should be able to make suitable arrangements.'

'Imelda is not going anywhere,' Hank said decisively.

'How do you mean?'

'I'm going to build a house out by the old barn. Two houses, in fact. One for Jimmy and Chrissie. One for me and Imelda.'

'What?' Tom almost laughed aloud. 'You're crazy. You can't take care of Imelda.'

'I'm going to bring Vanessa to live with us. She knows Imelda and Imelda knows her.'

'What makes you think Vanessa would come?'

'Sure she'd come. She's living in a hovel with her brother and his family. She deserves better than that and we can provide it.'

'Imelda can't live with you, Hank.'

'She can when we're married.'

'Married?' Tom exploded. 'Now I know you're crazy. You can't marry Imelda. She's not . . . Well, she's. . . .'

'She's not what? Not all there? She's been badly hurt. Broken, yes. Well, I'm going to put her back together again.'

'Hank,' Tom said seriously. 'I can't let you do this.'

Hank laughed. 'You can't stop me. You go off and play your game of politics. I'm going to stay here . . . with the real people.'

THIRTY-FIVE

T OM had an interview at Harvard that Monday morning. Hank had planned to go to the horse sales at Cambridge. But Jimmy was anxious to go to Lexington and bring back Chrissie.

'I can go on my own,' Jimmy said. 'I'm a big boy now.'

'I think you need to have one of us with you,' Hank told him.

'Why? I have the money.'

'The boss man might not want to sell.'

'He'll sell.' Jimmy was confident. 'You said yourself things were getting tough for slave owners. He'll take the money. In a few months he might have to let all his people go and for nothing.'

Hank laughed. 'You keep saying you've got the money. Where did you get it, I'd like to know? Or maybe, *how* did you get it?'

'You remember Cass? Casper? Tall, thin fellow played banjo? Old Cass got hit at Cowpens. He couldn't walk. I went out to help him but his right leg had gone and he was oozing blood. There was nothing I could do and the shells were popping off all around. But he grabbed my arm. He didn't want me to go. So I stayed with him.'

'Crazy,' Hank said. 'You should have got out of there.'

'I know,' Jimmy agreed. 'But I couldn't leave him, Hank. He was dying. He pulled me down and sort of whispered in my ear. He said he knew he was going to die and he wanted me to look in his shoe.' Jimmy's face creased at the recollection. 'His legs were covered in blood but one of his shoes was still hanging on. I went to take it off but he said no, the other shoe. This other shoe was lying in the grass with his leg and his right foot still in it. It was tough, not easy to deal with, but I closed my eyes and I reached out for it and took the shoe off. Old Cass just sort of nodded and I looked inside and there was this wad of money.

326

'He was fading fast and I had to get down real close to ask him what it was. He sort of whispered it was to buy his freedom. But he didn't need it now, he said. He'd soon be free anyway and he wanted me to have it. Buy your freedom, Jimmy, he said, and be happy.' Tears were rolling down Jimmy's cheeks. 'Then he died.'

They were silent for a moment then Jimmy said, 'I went back later and I dug a real grave and buried him right. That's where I was that time when you were looking for me. Do you remember? You wanted me to go with you to look for your friend Ben. Well, thanks to you and Tom I'm free now. I've got my freedom and I want to use this money to buy Chrissie hers.'

Hank nodded. 'I'm sure Cass would approve of that.'

'And I want to do it now, today.'

'Well look,' Hank said. 'Come with me to the show this morning. You need to see how these sales work. We won't be buying. I just want to check out a few things. Lunchtime we'll get something to eat then we'll call on Mister Slave Driver.'

They took the dray, the low cart Hank and Tom were riding the day they picked him up on the road to Roxbury. Jimmy remembered how much he struggled with that firebox. Mabbut was a monster to make him carry that old thing all the way to Roxbury on foot. But it seemed now as if it had happened to someone else. It was all such a long time ago. So much more had happened since that hot dusty day.

Without hesitation he climbed aboard, up front beside Hank. No sitting in the back these days. Not for Sergeant Ray. For Jimmy Mabbut, maybe. But Jimmy Mabbut was long gone. Jimmy Ray was not Jimmy Mabbut. Not any more. He was a war veteran, a new man, his own man, a man who could read, a *free* man.

The horse sales went on much longer than they expected but Hank wanted to stay to see all the business done. If they were going to bring stock here he wanted a clear idea of where they should set their prices. By the time they left Cambridge in the dray with Jimmy at the reins it was late afternoon.

'Could be pretty late when we get back,' Jimmy said.

'That's all right,' Hank said. 'You're not afraid of the dark, are you, Sergeant?'

Jimmy laughed. He was obviously excited, looking forward to seeing Chrissie again, hoping to sweep her into his arms. Hank could sense his high optimism. Everything was going to be fine, Jimmy had said. There would be no problems. But Hank was beginning to have his doubts. Perhaps he should try to contain Jimmy's enthusiasm, point out that things might not go as well as he expected. They'd been away a long time. Maybe things had changed. Jimmy had only known Chrissie very briefly yet all his hopes were pinned on those few moments in the whore tent. He could be in for a huge disappointment. Something, Hank knew, he would find hard to take.

'Do you know where this place is?' Hank asked.

'Chrissie said the Dixon place, Half Edge, Lex.'

'You know,' Hank said, 'you better not get your hopes up too high over this. Anything could have happened. I mean, it's been a long time. Things change.'

'This won't have changed, Hank,' Jimmy said confidently. 'I just know she'll be there, waiting for me. I'm all she has.'

The Dixon place was not hard to find. Jimmy turned the dray off the highway and along a caked mud road towards the house. A huge barn was off to the left and there were three rows of tumbledown shacks beyond and fields of corn all around. Looks like a lot of gathering in to be done, thought Hank when he saw the extent of the cornfields. Lots of labourers required. Slave labourers, no doubt.

Jimmy stepped down from the cart and Hank made to follow but Jimmy held up a hand apologetically. 'I'd like to do this on my own, Hank, if you don't mind.'

Hank wasn't sure about this. 'You don't know this Dixon. You don't know what he's like.'

Jimmy was confident. 'I'll soon find out.'

Hank nodded. 'Well, you know where I am if you need me.'

Jimmy felt the money in his breeches pocket and set off for the house. A cow bell hung in the front porch. He rang it and almost at once a small, wrinkled black lady came to the door. Already it was getting dark and she peered up at him, surprised that he was black and had come to the front door.

'You shouldn't be here,' she said, scolding him as if he ought to know better. 'You suppose to go round the back door.'

Jimmy smiled down at her. 'I wish to see Mr Dixon, ma'am,' he said. 'Would you please inform Mr Dixon that Sergeant Ray of the Congressional Army is here.'

She hesitated. His measured tone and the careful way he spoke his words had taken her by surprise. He was clearly an educated man but

Mr Dixon didn't allow black folk at the front door.

He raised his eyebrows at her pleasantly. 'Would you tell him, please? Sergeant Ray.'

It was her turn to raise her eyebrows. She invited him to step inside, held up her hand for him to wait there and come no further and went in search of her master.

Dixon was a smallish man with a lined face and thin sardonic lips. At first glance, thought Jimmy, not a pleasant character. The old lady had evidently not told him his unexpected visitor was a black man. He stopped dead in his tracks, hostile and affronted.

Jimmy held out a hand and smiled pleasantly. 'Sergeant Ray, sir. Sorry to call on you without prior notice. I hope this is not an inconvenient time.'

Dixon ignored Jimmy's outstretched hand. 'What do you mean by coming to my front door, boy?'

This was obviously an issue with Dixon. His front door was sacrosanct. Jimmy dropped any attempt at courtesy. He looked around and behind him. 'Were you addressing me, boy?'

Dixon's eyes flashed. 'Who's your master, damn you?'

'Master? Ah! Massah Dixon, sah! That what you want? Well, you won't get it from me. I'm free, boy. And so will all my brothers and sisters be when animals like you get into their thick heads that the old days are over.'

Dixon was almost apoplectic, spluttering with rage.

'You read the Declaration of Independence?' Jimmy went on. 'We hold these truths to be self-evident? All men are created equal? No? I'm sorry, maybe you can't read.'

'Of course I can read, damn you!' Dixon spluttered. 'It don't mean a thing! It's just words. Rubbish.'

'I see.' Jimmy nodded. 'I'll pass your comments on to Mr Jefferson. In the meantime, we get down to business.'

Dixon was unsure of himself. He had never met anyone like Jimmy before. But he had noted Jimmy's cultured voice, his self-assurance. This negra needed taking down, putting in his place with a good kicking and a few lashes. 'What business?'

Jimmy drew the wad of money from his pocket. 'I'm here to purchase the freedom of one of your . . . er . . . captives.'

Dixon laughed dismissively. 'I don't do business with Niggers, 'specially fancy talkin' ones like you.'

'You're living in the past, Mr Dixon,' Jimmy said mildly. 'They may not be moving too fast in the South, but here in Boston things are different. Slavery is on the way out. In a few months' time new legislation will force you to give the people you have lived off for so long their freedom. Just as well take the money. There may not be any later.'

Dixon looked at Jimmy with raw hatred, his lips twisted, his eyes venomous, as the rage built up inside him. He had never known a Negra with this kind of self-assurance before and he was not sure how to handle him. His foreman had gone home and the two white men he employed to manage the workforce would be down at the tavern. He was on his own. He turned on his heel and went through a door.

Jimmy waited calmly, glancing around the low beamed room. It was sparsely furnished, not unlike Mabbut's reception hall. A fire burned brightly in an open fireplace and the wood logs crackled merrily in the large grate giving the room a cosy glow. There was a chest of drawers and two or three easy chairs, a gun cabinet and a drinks table from which drinks were dispensed and offered to visitors. But not to unwelcome visitors like Jimmy. He smiled wryly. Why do people like Mabbut and Dixon hate us so much? Why do they have to treat us so badly? Because deep down, he concluded, they're scared of us. Scared stiff.

When Dixon returned he was brandishing a horsewhip. 'This is the only business you'll get from me, Nigger,' he said.

As Dixon raised the whip Jimmy didn't hesitate. He stepped forward and grabbed Dixon's whip hand. He was much stronger than Dixon and he had little trouble in forcing the older man's hand down, gripping his wrist in a tightening clamp until he let the whip go.

Jimmy picked it up and threw it on the fire. Then he stepped close to Dixon again and Dixon cowered back. 'Are we going to do business or not?'

Dixon was shaking with rage. 'Get out! Get out of my house! I'll call the sheriff.'

Jimmy gave him a look of total pity and contempt. 'No need for that, boy. I'm going. You can crawl back under your stone.'

The little black lady, standing in the kitchen, had heard it all. Filled with apprehension she knew from experience 'the massah' would take this out on her and on any of the black folk who happened to cross his path.

Jimmy walked out the front door the way he came. But he didn't go straight to the dray. He was here and he wanted to see Chrissie before he left, maybe even take her with him. He went down a narrow path towards the row of shacks in the moonlight. He could hear singing, several voices harmonizing a low tuneful lament, someone plucking softly at a banjo. A ring of shadowy figures sat around a small bonfire and as he drew close he saw the light from the fire flickering on their faces. Also, in the shadows, others were standing around or sitting in groups on the grass, listening and swaying gently to the music. Men, women, boys, girls, young and old alike.

He stood by some tall trees and watched the quiet, peaceful scene, fully aware of all the sorrow and all the sadness those assembled hearts contained, the sadness that saw only the weary monotony of a life ahead in the drab world created for them by unfeeling white men and the sorrow that mourned the loss of the lives they might have had.

And then he saw her. There was no doubt. Her silhouette, black in the dark blue night, took his breath away. He would know that lovely, delicate profile anywhere. He moved nearer to the small group where she was sitting on an upturned box. Others were standing but Chrissie was privileged. She had a seat.

'Chrissie!' he whispered and several heads turned towards him. 'Chrissie, over here!'

She looked back like a startled doe and their eyes met in the light from the fire. 'It's me,' he told her, still in a loud whisper. 'Jimmy. I've come to take you away – like I said.'

But there was no reaction. She looked away nervously, remained seated. He tried again. 'Chrissie? I want to talk to you.'

The people around her turned to confront him as the mood turned quietly hostile. A large man nearby looked at him quizzically and said, 'Maybe she don't wanna talk to you.'

'I don't understand,' he said, unwilling to leave. 'Chrissie!'

Three or four of the younger men were adopting a protective pose. Then, finally, Chrissie stood up. She turned towards him and as she turned he saw that she was heavily pregnant.

Jimmy's mouth fell open and he gazed at her with intense disbelief. 'Chrissie,' he murmured as if speaking her name might change things.

She turned, ran towards the shacks and several men moved in to prevent him from following. He backed away in shock. He had not expected this and his heart was heavy. She said she would wait but she

331

had not waited.

He stumbled and backed away, looking for the narrow path. There was no point in attempting to pursue her. He was too late. Someone else was involved now. He pounded his fist into the palm of his hand, tears pricked his eyes. All his plans, all his hopes, all his dreams were gone. He had waited. He had believed she would wait, too. But she had found someone else.

Half-blinded by tears he followed the path. Then he stopped, sensing there was someone behind him.

'Hey!' A woman's voice. 'You Jimmy? You that Jimmy?' He looked at her in the shadowy gloom. As far as he could tell she was small, thin, worn-out looking though she might have been pretty once, and she was a good ten years older than him, maybe more. 'What do you want?' he asked.

'Don't go feeling too bad 'bout Chrissie,' she said. 'That girl is heartbroke.'

'She didn't wait. She couldn't wait! She found someone else.'

The woman shook her head. 'You don't understand.'

'I understand all right,' he said angrily.

'No, you don't, you great lump. She didn't find someone else. Only babby Chrissie want was yours.'

His eyes narrowed. 'What are you saying? She was attacked?'

'Ah suppose you can call it that. That babby is the massa's babby. He do that to all the girls. All the pretty girls anyway. You come over in the daylight, boy, see all the little mulattoes.'

'He can't do that.'

'Oh, yes he can. That's what he do. That's what he always done.'

'What's your name?' Jimmy asked.

'Tilda,' she said. 'But don't you go gettin' me in no trouble.'

'I won't, Tilda,' he said, his rage growing. 'I promise.'

He hurried away, rage surging in his chest, in his whole being. He was going to kill that Dixon. He was going to kill that little weasel, blast him from the face of the earth. He burst out of the path and the shadow of the trees into the moonlight and ran to where Hank was waiting, half-asleep.

'Where the hell have you been?' Hank asked, but Jimmy had reached behind the driving seat and drawn out the rifle. Hank jumped down and tried to wrestle if from him. 'What's this, Jimmy? What's going on?'

'I'm going to kill that little bastard.'

'What little bastard?'

'Dixon!' Jimmy cried. 'Let go! Give me the goddamned rifle.'

But Hank wouldn't let go. 'Stop it! Stop it now! And tell me what this is all about.'

Jimmy leaned against the dray, breathing hard. 'I'm going to kill him, Hank,' he said, 'if it's the last thing I do.'

Hank had the rifle now and he could see Jimmy's tears in the pale light. Something had upset him pretty bad. 'Jimmy, Jimmy,' he said soothingly, 'just take your time. Tell me what happened.'

Jimmy was standing by the dray, his head in his hands. 'I saw Dixon,' he said. 'I offered him the money and he said he don't to business with Niggers. Threatened me with a whip but I took it off him and I left.' He looked back at Hank. 'I heard this sort of singing and I went down the path over there. I wanted to get Chrissie and bring her away. There was a bonfire. People all around, singing, listening, you know. Then I saw her. I saw her, Hank, and when she saw me she got up and ran away.' His face creased. 'She's with child, Hank. Baby nearly due.'

'Ah.' Hank nodded. 'Well, we've been away a long time, Jimmy. She couldn't be sure you would come back. I mean, to be fair, you barely knew the girl.'

'She did want to wait and she didn't find someone else,' Jimmy said quietly. 'She was raped. By Dixon.'

Hank's expression changed. 'How do you know this?'

'Lady told me. Lady called Tilda. She came after me. I guess she was a friend of Chrissie. She said Chrissie did want to wait. She was always true to me. But that little rat raped her. Seems he does it to all the girls there.'

'Can we prove that?'

'Tilda reckons the place is full of mulatto kids. He's been doing it for years. Well, I'm telling you, Hank, this time he's not going to get away with it. Rifle or no rifle, I'm going to go back there and I'm going to kill him. If I have to do it with my bare hands I'm going to kill him.'

'No, you're not,' Hank said. 'Get up front. We'll talk about this on the way home, work out what we're going to do.'

'Get off me.' Jimmy pulled away. 'I'm going back up to that house and I'm going to kill him. Now. Tonight.'

'You can't do that, Jimmy. You can't kill a man.'

'You did,' Jimmy said.

Hank nodded. 'That was different. Even if I was found out they wouldn't touch me. I had a good reason.'

'I have a good reason.'

'It's not the same. Briggs was a nobody, a drunk. This man Dixon is a farmer, probably has connections. He may be well respected in the community round here.'

Jimmy gave a hollow laugh. 'Well respected?'

'Yes, and that's what we have to think about. Let's go home, talk to Tom, see what he thinks.'

'So you can get away with murder but I can't. Now why is that?'

'All right,' Hank said. 'You know why but you want me to spell it out. Right. Fine. You can't get away with it because you're black.'

'Even if I have a good reason?'

'A black man can't kill a white man. It would never get to court. They'd come for you with a lynch mob. They'd hunt you down with dogs and then they'd string you up. You know that. And I'm not going to let that happen. We'll get Dixon one way or another. Just let's talk to Tom first. Come on. Get up.'

Hank took the reins and reluctantly Jimmy climbed up beside him. Subdued now, his anger still simmering, Jimmy was quiet for most of the slow trot home. The picture of Chrissie he had kept so vividly in his heart had been distorted, spoiled for him. He closed his eyes. He didn't want to see the beauty of the night.

There was no breeze and the trees, silver in the moonlight, stood quite still like sentinels. The road ahead was a pale ribbon laid out in the glow from above. The night was beautiful and where once he would have gloried in such tranquil beauty he didn't want to look. Nothing had changed, yet everything was different.

Hank glanced sidelong at him. 'You all right?'

Jimmy sat back. 'Can I ask you something?'

'Sure,' Hank said. 'Anything. You know that.'

'Why do you and Tom care about me?'

Hank laughed. 'We don't care about you, you no good Negra.'

'No, seriously, Hank,' Jimmy said quietly. 'Why did you pick me up that day? Why did you and Tom stop the dray and give me a lift all the way into Rox?'

'You had that big old firebox.'

'I was just a black kid taking a rest at the side of the road. You gave me a ride on the dray. You told me to sit up front with you. You offered me a drink from your own canteen. Why? White fellows don't do things like that.'

'It was Tom, not me.'

'No, it wasn't. It was you, too. Who got me to join the rebels? Who helped me win my stripes?'

'You got your stripes because you were the best man for the job.'

'A black sergeant in a white company? Must have been a word in the right direction. Anyway, who helped me to read? Who put me right when I got words wrong? Who still does? Who found books for me to read?'

'That was Tom.'

'It was you, too, Hank. And I'll always be grateful. But I'd like to know why? Why did you help me the way you did?'

'Because we're crazy.'

'Things have gone wrong with Chrissie and I don't know what I'm going to do now. But whatever happens I'd like you to know you're the best friend I ever had.'

'Listen,' Hank said seriously, 'you're not going to do anything right away. I don't want you to go looking for trouble. I need you at the stud, long term. We're going to breed thoroughbreds, the best horses in Massachusetts, and we're going to build houses. I'm home now and I'm staying home. And you're home, too, Jimmy.'

'I'd still like to know why you picked me up that day.'

Hank glanced at him again. 'All right, mulehead. It's simple really. Our gran'pa and gran'ma were Quakers. Gran'pa got himself into all kinds of trouble in the old days fighting slavery. Said it was evil, the way of the Devil himself. He'd get up at a public meeting and tell all the slave owners they were going straight to Hell. He'd call them parasites, bloodsuckers, living off the misery of others and he'd get into fights and get himself thrown out of places.'

'I thought Quakers were gentle, peace-loving folk.'

'And so they are. But not him. He was always fighting for the underdog, not just blacks. He insisted everyone was entitled to the same level of respect. Blacks, whites, whatever. Everyone is entitled to a little dignity, he'd say. And having to drag a firebox all the way to Roxbury is not exactly dignified.'

'So how come you and Tom are not Quakers?'

'Well, Dad hasn't made his mind up about all that stuff. I mean, he's the same as Gran'pa in his philosophy. He was living by the Declaration of Independence before Mr Jefferson wrote it. But he's sort of not sure about God. He says he can't make up his own mind about that so why should he try to influence us. We have to think that one through for ourselves.'

'And have you?'

'Not really. I talked to God once or twice when the British came at us with bayonets, especially that time on Long Island. Fellows getting run through all around us. I guess I spoke to Him then.' He laughed. 'I asked Him to promise me I wouldn't fill my breeches.'

THIRTY-SIX

THEY came to a halt, their horses in a ragged line, outside the Blanchard house, eight of them carrying sticks and a variety of blunt instruments as weapons. Mrs Blanchard had been sitting on the rocker on the front porch in the late afternoon sun. She hurried indoors to ask her husband in alarm, 'Who are these men? What do they want?'

Mr Blanchard went out to the porch, picking up his rifle on the way. 'You men are on my property,' he said mildly.

A heavily built man in the centre of the line told him, 'We've come for the Nigger.'

Mr Blanchard levelled his rifle at him. 'You get off my land now or I'll blast you off.'

Tom came hurrying through the house. 'Hey! What's going on here?' Several faces he recognized. Jobbing labourers, most of them. 'What is it, Jeb?' he asked one of the oldest of those present. 'What do you fellows want?'

The man called Jeb was normally a quiet, peace-loving fellow. He'd been bribed into this with a few drinks in the tavern at lunchtime and he was not sure what it was all about. All he'd been told was that they were going to teach some Negra a little respect. He hesitated, looking around for support.

'We want the Nigger,' a thin-faced fellow said.

Tom looked along the line, noting the nature of their ruefully inadequate weapons. Hank came out from the porch to join him and handed him a rifle. Together, rifles at the slant, they moved forward and most of the posse backed off. Then when Jimmy appeared on the steps they formed up again.

'There he is!' someone cried. 'Let's get him.'

337

They moved forward, back in line, but Mr Blanchard fired a shot in the air and brought them to a halt. 'You fellows tired of living?' he asked. All three had their rifles levelled at the riders. 'This young man' – Mr Blanchard turned and gestured towards Jimmy – 'this young man is a guest in my house. What is your business with him?'

'He's a Nigger,' the youngest, a callow youth, called out.

'And you, my little friend,' Mr Blanchard said calmly, looking directly at the youth, 'are as stupid and ignorant as you look.' He turned to the rest. 'I suppose you all feel pretty safe in a crowd. Makes you feel big and tough. Is that it?' He went forward to the man who looked as though he might be their leader. 'You responsible for this rabble?'

'What if I am?' the man answered defiantly.

'Well now, I don't normally approve of violence but in your case I'll gladly make an exception. Get down from there, put down that lump of wood and come face my man. One to one.'

The man on horseback didn't move.

Mr Blanchard glanced back at Jimmy who nodded to express his readiness. 'Why, my friend here would give you the hiding of your life and you would deserve it.'

The man in the saddle shifted uneasily. This was not working out the way he'd planned.

'Are you game?' Mr Blanchard persisted. 'No, of course you're not. You're all the same. Big men with a mob behind you but on your own' – he spat on the ground – 'you're not worth that.'

The men were waiting for a lead but none was forthcoming. Then a young man from the livery stable spoke up. 'He's just a Negra, Mr Blanchard.'

'He's a soldier, son. A soldier of the rebel army.'

'All right,' the man Mr Blanchard had singled out said. 'You got guns. So we'll leave it for now. But we'll be back. Not just eight of us. We'll have twenty eight. And we'll be armed, too.'

Tom said, 'You two.' He pointed out two of the men in the line-up. 'You were in the Congressional Army. You fought against the British.'

The two young men nodded proudly.

'Well,' Tom bluffed, 'you must have heard of my Company. Company C. The worst bunch of killers in General Greene's army. Well, I'm still in the army. Major Blanchard. My boys are only based over at the Neck. I can have them here in less than twenty minutes.

You know how it is. They're a bit short of action right now and they would enjoy this. Come back here looking for trouble and everyone of you is a dead man.'

The two former rebel soldiers looked at each other, turned their horses and rode away. The man called Jeb backed his horse out of the line and he, too, rode away. Then they all began to turn but Mr Blanchard levelled his rifle at the man who had threatened to return. 'Not you,' he said. 'You're not going anywhere.'

'Get down!' Tom ordered. 'Down!'

The man, scared now, dismounted. He looked around but the others had gone. 'What? What is this?'

They closed in on him. Mr Blanchard, Tom and Hank.

'Look,' the man said.

'No, you look,' Hank said angrily. 'What's your name?'

'Johnson.'

'Well listen, Mr Johnson,' Tom said mildly. 'Do you mind explaining what you thought you were doing?'

'I was told to come here and get him.' He pointed at Jimmy.

'And who told you to do that?' Tom asked.

'Mr Dixon.' Johnson was genuinely frightened now. 'This is none of my doing. Mr Dixon told me to come over here and bring the . . . him back to the farm.'

'Do you always do what Mr Dixon tells you?' Tom taunted.

'I work for him. I'm his farm manager. Not a man to cross.'

'Is that so?' Tom said. 'And did he say why he wanted this young man?'

'He said he was disrespectful.'

Tom looked back at Jimmy. 'Is this true?' he said with mock surprise. 'You were disrespectful to a dirty old rapist?'

Jimmy laughed and Johnson blinked, fully aware of how his boss treated the young women he kept in slavery on his farm.

'You go now, Mr Johnson,' Tom said quietly. 'And in future don't get involved in this sort of thing. It's not for you.'

'What shall I tell Dixon?'

'Tell him . . .' Hank began aggressively but Tom gave him a look.

'What you tell Mr Dixon is up to you,' Tom said.

Later that day Mr Blanchard called his two boys together. He was worried about Jimmy, he said. This business with the girl had changed him. The boy was heartbroken and it would take a long time for him to get over it. So what do we do? Hank asked.

'Well, the way I see it,' his father said, 'you two brought this girl into his life. Now it's up to you to put things right.'

'How?' Tom asked. 'How can we do that?'

'I talked to your mother,' Mr Blanchard said. 'She says she'd just love to have a little one running around the place again.'

Tom and Hank looked at each other.

'Would it work?' Hank asked.

'We'd make it work,' Tom said.

'Don't say anything to anyone just yet,' their father said. 'There are one or two things I need to sort out first.'

The following afternoon Mr Blanchard said he wanted Tom to look at some horses at a sale up by the Charles River. It was a job for Hank but Hank and Jimmy were busy clearing out one of the tack rooms to make it habitable. Hank had some vague idea he might share the tack room with Jimmy, bring Vanessa and Imelda over to the house and build a new house as fast as he could. Right now there were no British taxmen telling them what they could or couldn't do. It was true this idea of bringing Chrissie over had complicated things but that was something Mr Blanchard wanted to talk to them about.

It was a warm day, with just a gentle breeze, no more than a ripple on the unspoilt stretch of river where Mr Blanchard surprised Tom by bringing his horse to a halt and dismounting.

'Used to bring your mother up here when we were courting,' he explained, sitting down on the grassy bank. 'Lovely spot.'

Tom agreed as he sat alongside him. 'Sure is, day like today.'

'This is what you were fighting for, son. All those brave young fellows fighting for what was theirs anyway.'

'We didn't want to fight, Dad. We knew some good people who stayed with the British. And so did you. It was just the way it was.'

'I know. But it had to be done.'

'I wonder. Surely talking is best. And I don't know about brave. There were times when I ran away as fast as anyone.'

'I expect you did. But that's honourable, too. Man wants to live.'

'I don't know about that,' Tom said. 'But some fellows go crazy on the battlefield. And some fellows really are brave. Take Jimmy. He was always there, in the thick of the fighting. Standing firm, helping the wounded then going back in. He should have been an officer, Dad. But they wouldn't have it. I tried, but I think they'd decided he'd gone far enough. It wasn't fair.'

'Life isn't fair,' his father said. 'But he's a fine boy. He'll be all right with us.' They were silent for a moment then Mr Blanchard went on, 'There are no horses to see today, Tom. I wanted to talk to you away from the house. See, things look pretty complicated right now but I think they'll work out.'

Tom laughed. 'I don't know where you're going to put everybody.'

'Well, Hank and Jimmy in the tack room. Pretty warm in there in the winter and they're both used to the smell of fine horses. They'll be OK. So you go over to see this Dixon and somehow you get the girl and you bring her home.'

'Leave it to me,' Tom said confidently.

'But before you do we speak to Vanessa, persuade her to come.'

'Hank says she doesn't seem too happy where she is,' Tom said. 'She's used to living in a real house. I think she'll come.'

'She has to,' Mr Blanchard said, 'or I guess it's all off. Your mother can't take care of the girl without any help.'

'But what about Hank? He's got this crazy idea he wants to marry Imelda, have Vanessa look after her. I mean, to be fair, Vanessa is right for Imelda. She's known her all her life, since Imelda was born, in fact. If anyone can help her, Vanessa can.'

'Your ma says she would ask Mrs Stokes and Melanie to keep Imelda a little longer, until Hank builds his house. I'll tell him it wouldn't be proper for Imelda to move in until they're married.'

'You think we should let him marry Imelda?'

'You know Hank,' Mr Blanchard said. 'Try and stop him. He'll do whatever he wants. Thing is, even if he does marry Imelda, it don't look as though there'd be any little ones for a while. Maybe for a long while – if ever.'

Tom looked at his father fondly. His father rarely had much to say but what he did say usually made good sense.

'One other thing,' Mr Blanchard said. 'We don't really know how Jimmy feels about the girl now there's a baby on the way.'

'We'll talk to him,' Tom said. 'Tonight.'

Mr Blanchard nodded. 'And how about you? Looks like there'll be nowhere for you to lay your head.'

Tom laughed. 'I'm due in New York Friday. Be away a couple of weeks. Then I go to Harvard for a year, about nine months actually. I can live in at the college and I can help Hank and Jimmy with the house building at the weekend.'

'So all this could really work out,' his father said. 'And with you and Hank it's the right thing. I'm sure about that. Hank is a better horseman than you. He can go to the auctions and spot a winner. And Jimmy seems to know what he's doing, too. You, you're not a farmer or a horse breeder.'

'Good old Dad. Tells it like it is.'

'Well, you're not. You're a politician.'

Tom had been lying back, hands clasped behind his head as he gazed up at the buttermilk sky. Now he sat up straight, pretended to be hurt. 'Don't call me that!'

'All right,' Mr Blanchard said with a laugh. 'A diplomat. You're a diplomat, son. You belong up there with Mr John Adams and Mr Thomas Jefferson and Mr Benjamin Franklin.'

That evening after dinner Tom and Hank got Jimmy alone.

'No, no, no,' Jimmy said. 'Do that and I'm leaving.'

'She's still the same girl,' Hank said. 'She's still this Chrissie, the one you've been going on about all these months.'

'She isn't. She's different now.'

'She's having a baby,' Tom said reasonably, 'and it's not her fault. It wasn't her idea. But it's happened and she'll have to take care of it when it arrives. She's the baby's mother and if she's the kind of girl you say she is she'll want to keep it and take good care of it.'

'That's nothing to do with me,' Jimmy said.

'So you don't care about her? Something bad happens to her, something she could do nothing about and you don't want her.'

'That's not fair, Tom.'

'Well, it certainly isn't her fault,' Hank said, 'and it isn't that little baby's fault. We're going to expose Dixon for what he is, but first we're going to go over there and bring Chrissie back.'

'We don't want no little mulatto bastard running around here.'

'Mulatto bastard?' Hank said grimly. 'Is that what you think? That little kid has no one except Chrissie and already you're calling him names. Well, that's not right, Jimmy. I didn't expect that. Not from you.'

'I'm sorry,' Jimmy said.

'Children can't choose their parents,' Tom said. 'That baby's been dealt a rotten hand and he isn't even born yet.'

Hank made a face. 'Could get worse. Might look like Dixon.'

Jimmy almost smiled.

'Or he might be a she,' Tom said. 'Could be a little girl who looks like Chrissie.'

They were quiet for a moment then Tom said, 'We brought you here, Jimmy, because you're our friend. Dad and Ma accepted you right away and you know you can have a good life here as part of our family. That's what we want. But now we know what happened to Chrissie we want to take her away from that lecherous worm Dixon. We'd like to give her a decent life, too. And maybe, in time, you two could be friends.'

'We're going to do this, Jimmy,' Hank said. 'You don't have to get involved. You don't need to speak to her. You can keep out of her way, if that's what you want. But we're going to bring her here and she's going to stay. And so are you.'

The next morning Tom brought out the dray. It was a clear day, bright and sunny, and he didn't want to waste any time. Hank was already at work at the stables.

He came running over. 'Maybe I should come with you.'

'No need,' Tom said. He didn't want Hank there, starting fights. Hank was sure to be too abrasive. 'I can handle Dixon.'

'You don't know the man. You never met him. He may have his mob on hand. I'm coming with you.'

Hank climbed up on the dray and the coupled horses jogged out and across town. The shell of the Harvies' house and the shattered windows of the British Army recruiting office on North Street were still there, reminders of the conflict, but the streets were gradually being cleaned up and some semblance of normality was returning.

The Charles River looked as clean and clear and as beautiful as ever in the early morning. It was theirs, a part of their childhood and their youth and they loved it, aware that the gentle flow, the overhanging trees and the dappled sunlight would be with them always, wherever they were and for the rest of their lives.

The road rose above Half Edge and they could look down on the wide sprawl of Dixon's Farm, the stooping figures at work in the fields. The dray rumbled down a side track and in at the gates. From a distance the farm manager, Johnson, saw them coming and ran to inform his boss. When they drew up at the house Dixon's elderly housekeeper had the front door open and they followed her inside.

343

Dixon was ready for them. He was standing in the centre of the room with the big fireplace, empty and dead today, behind him. He was aiming a long-barrelled shotgun directly at them.

'Mr Dixon, I presume,' Tom said cheerfully. 'This is a novel way to welcome guests.'

'You're not welcome,' Dixon said sourly.

Hank didn't hesitate. He simply strode up to Dixon, snatched the shotgun, broke it open and emptied the breech. Then he threw the gun in a corner.

Dixon was defiant. 'What do you want?'

'No need to be uncivil, Mr Dixon,' Tom said and he turned to the elderly housekeeper who was hovering by the door. 'You, ma'am. Do you know a young lady by the name of Chrissie?' He made a curving gesture to indicate the girl was pregnant.

The old lady's eyes were wary and apprehensive.

'I think you do,' Tom said. 'Go get her, please. Tell her to bring whatever belongings she has.'

'I don't expect she has much,' Hank said.

The old lady's eyes appealed to her boss for guidance. Dixon nodded and she scurried away to the back door.

'You brought the money?' Dixon asked.

'What money would that be, Mr Dixon?' Tom asked.

'Your Nigger friend had the money to buy her.'

'Oh, we're not here to buy, Mr Dixon. We're here to take. To take her away from you and your dirty little habits. But come to think of it, now you mention money, you might as well know we will be applying for an enforcement order. An order for you to pay for the baby's upkeep.'

'What?' Dixon was scornful. 'She can live here with the brat. That's all the upkeep they need.'

'Along with all those other mulatto children of yours? Things are different now, Mr Dixon. We'll be notifying the Governor's office of your conduct, the way you've treated young women in your employ over the years.' Tom looked back at his brother. 'Looks like a few criminal acts been committed here.'

'Sure does,' Hank said. 'Rape and abuse long term. Sounds like a hefty jail sentence to me.'

Through a window Hank saw the housekeeper with Chrissie. He went out to the front and helped the frightened girl up on the dray.

Indoors Tom put his face close to Dixon's and said quietly, 'You start treating your people well from now on. Pay them right and quit dragging young girls into your bed. Start now. Before the investigators come. Good day, Mr Dixon.'

They were ready to go but when Tom came out Hank went back inside. 'Hey!' Tom cried. 'Leave it, Hank.'

Hank's reappearance startled Dixon and he cowered back.

'This is for our Nigger friend, Mr Dixon,' Hank said with a smile and he hit Dixon hard with the back of his hand and sent him sprawling into a corner.

THIRTY-SEVEN

A few days later Tom left for New York where he was to present himself at the office of John Adams to whom he had first been introduced by General Greene. Mr Adams, he soon discovered, was as interested to hear what was going on in his home state of Massachusetts as Tom was to learn of matters of national importance. He liked Adams and he felt he could talk openly and freely with him.

The popular feeling back home, Tom told him, was that little was happening. People felt that the year 1782 was becoming a disappointment with endless squabbles at the top and little real progress anywhere else. Adams listened carefully to what Tom had to say, neither agreeing nor disagreeing. There is much to be done, he said finally. We have won on the battlefield. There is a ceasefire. But the war is not officially over. A peace treaty is our priority now, then we can begin to build a new nation.

Later, on reflection, Tom was concerned that he may have been a little too forthright in expressing his opinions, a little presumptuous perhaps to think that Adams would care what he thought. He told the young man charged with showing him around, one of Adam's aides, a New Yorker called Smith. All Smith said was, 'Nah, he's all right. If he doesn't like it, he'll tell you. Stick with Mr Adams and he'll probably get you a job as the delegate from Massachusetts.'

'Well, fine,' Tom said, but he didn't want to be a delegate from anywhere just yet. He wanted to see the world he told Smith. Go to Europe. Paris, London.

Then you should work with Mr Franklin, Smith said. He's been everywhere, knows everyone. When you get to Harvard you should do French as well as Law. It was good advice.

Smith, whose first name was Sam, explained that because he had picked up a smattering of French in his schooldays he was promoted captain and seconded as liaison officer to one of the French generals, Major General le Marquis de Lafayette. Tom said he had met the marquis that winter at Valley Forge. He was an officer much respected by the men.

Sam said he wished now he had not resigned his commission quite so soon after Yorktown. He ought to have kept the title captain a little longer. It's a clear indication, he said, that one has played one's part in the war. He urged Tom not to resign just yet and allow himself to become known for a little while as Major Blanchard. It was another piece of sound advice.

Sam Smith and Tom Blanchard soon became firm friends. A couple of years older than Tom, Sam had qualified as a lawyer and was now finding his way along the lower reaches of the new administration. They saw each other most days the two weeks Tom was in New York and several evenings, as young men about town trawling the taverns and the bawdy-houses along the waterfront.

Of all the top men running the country, Sam told Tom when they were out on a spree, by far the most interesting and entertaining is the man from Philadelphia, Benjamin Franklin. He's an old man now, seventy at least, Sam said, but he's seen more of this world and done more than anyone I've ever known. In London he was a member of the Royal Society, Sam enthused, in Paris a member of the Royal Academy of Sciences. Sam, who had clearly had rather a lot to drink, was obviously a fan of the great man.

'He is highly respected in London,' he repeated, slurring his words now. 'And the French love him. He's been everywhere and he's done everything, including half the women in Paris.'

Tom laughed. 'You can't say things like that.'

'It's true,' Sam insisted. 'You want to go to Paris? Then I say, go with Uncle Ben. You'll have a great time.'

One man he really wanted to meet or, at least, hear in action, he told Sam, was Thomas Jefferson, the man who wrote most of the Declaration.

'You might be disappointed,' Sam said. 'Good man. Of course, he is. But I reckon he's a better writer than a speaker. Best at putting words on paper.'

Apart from the occasional hangover that followed a night out with Sam, Tom was loving every minute of his stay and he went out of his way to meet and make friends with as many people as possible in his allotted two weeks. Apart from Mr Adams, he reflected later, the most influential man he met was the New York lawyer, John Jay. In 1782, ten years younger than Adams, Jay had just come to the end of an appointment as Minister to Spain and was now involved, with John Adams and Benjamin Franklin, in negotiations with Britain and France.

Intoxicated by these priviliged glimpses of the powers-that-be Tom was reluctant to leave. But he was due at Harvard and so, after a farewell drink with his new pal Sam and armed with a letter of introduction to the Governor of Massachusetts, he left for home more determined than ever to qualify as a lawyer and make his way in this seductive new world of hope and promise.

Back home Vanessa had not been sure about moving to the Blanchard house. She knew Mrs Blanchard and she had known the boys most of their lives, especially Hank. She had always thought Hank was right for Imelda. He handled her with just the right amount of tolerance, calmly and quietly telling her to behave whenever she overstepped the mark which, in the old days, she often did. And, though she would never admit it, she usually did as he said. Despite this, Vanessa was not sure they should be married. She had visited Imelda at Melanie's house several times and she knew the girl was not right and was not making much progress. Imelda was nervous, jumpy, frightened of men. Apart from Hank, that is. She seemed to live for the times when Hank called.

That summer Hank spent almost every day until late evening building a house and it soon became obvious that the house had become an obsession, as if something was driving him on. The running of the farm and the stables had been left to Mr Blanchard and Jimmy, the young fellow they had brought back from the war. He seemed a good boy, shy and always polite, and Vanessa had the impression he had once known Chrissie, the girl in her care, as if there may well have been something between them. But it wasn't Jimmy's baby. She knew that for sure. From Mrs Blanchard she had heard all about Dixon the awful slave boss. Now it seemed a great shame that Jimmy and Chrissie never spoke to each other. Never a smile or a good morning passed between them. But there was something there, Vanessa told herself, and no doubt Chrissie would tell her all about it when she was ready.

Vanessa liked it here and she wanted to stay. Mrs Blanchard was another Aunt Mary, thoughtful and kind, and any doubts she may have had about Mr Blanchard had soon been dispelled. There was no doubt he was head of the household, but he was a quietly humorous man and he was certainly no Max Harvie.

It was not long before Chrissie's baby arrived and soon after Mrs Blanchard held a celebration. It was late one afternoon on a warm September day and the party spilled out on to the back porch. Hank and Tom, Melanie with her little girl, Mrs Stokes and Imelda and some of Mrs Blanchard's friends attended. But Jimmy busied himself at the stables.

The weeks went by and at the end of October the house was finished. Hank and the helpers he'd employed had done a fine job but the house was only small. It was not really big enough for Hank and Imelda and Vanessa and Chrissie and Chrissie's baby. 'But ideal for an old couple,' Mr Blanchard decided. 'It's my land and my choice. Ma and me are having the new house.'

Mr Blanchard knew there would be no objection but this meant that if Hank moved into the farmhouse with Imelda there would have to be a wedding. We could have a Christmas wedding, Mrs Blanchard said, and the preparations began.

That Christmas 1782 Hank Blanchard and Imelda Harvie were married. Imelda's doctor had advised against it but his wife had told him to shut up. She wanted an invitation. Some agreed with the doctor, fearing that Hank was making a big mistake. Others believed their marriage might aid Imelda's recovery. Whatever happened, Hank knew Imelda had a long way to go. It would take time, maybe a long time. He would have to be gentle and patient with her. Even now, on their wedding day, she flinched when he touched her arm and there was no question of anyone kissing the bride. But Hank firmly believed that one day she would start to recover.

The wedding was a grand affair with relatives and friends from near and far. Imelda, looking stunning in a white dress, revelled in the occasion and even at times seemed like her old self.

The church hall, already decked out with Christmas bunting, made a perfect setting for the reception, but sadly there was no one left to represent the Harvies. Melanie had written to Sarah, as Imelda's one remaining relative, in good time and in the vague hope she might find it possible to attend. But there had been no reply. And so, there was no one. No father, no mother, both of them victims of the conflict. Even Imelda's brother, Edward, had died in battle.

In Tom's eyes the curse of the war hung over the proceedings. It was supposed to be a time of great joy, a celebration, but he couldn't shake off the feeling of sadness that gripped him as he glanced around. Even as he danced with Melanie he was acutely aware of the loss that lay behind her smile. Ben was gone and there was no one, could never be anyone else. Thank goodness, he thought, for Sally. At least Melanie had something of Ben. A little girl who had never known her father. He cursed the war and what it had done to so many people.

'When you go back to New York,' Melanie said, 'maybe they'll send you off around the world. Maybe you'll get to London.'

Tom smiled. 'I'm afraid it's too late for Sarah and me.'

'She knows you're home and safe. You should write to her.'

'She has a new life now, Melanie.'

'Yes,' Melanie said. 'Very grand. Lady Danvers, no less.'

'I hope she's happy,' Tom said sincerely.

They laughed as Mr Blanchard lifted Sally and danced with her to a military two-step. Imelda clapped her hands in delight as the little girl stretched out her arm primly like all the other ladies. Hank smiled, wanting to dance with his bride, but he held back, aware that any move in that direction must come from her.

Vanessa had been on her feet for most of the day, helping out in all directions. Now she was content to sit quietly in a corner, Chrissie's baby sleeping in her lap, and watch Imelda, the little girl she had watched grow up. There was something there, some familiar traits, some semblance of the old Imelda. Perhaps it was only a matter of time. One day her girl might wake up and shake off the burden of fear and guilt and shame that still gripped her. Vanessa hoped so. She was still young, outwardly unravaged by the horrific nature of that brutal assault. And now she had a husband, a good man Vanessa knew would take care of her.

Imelda had enjoyed being the centre of attention but she had not danced all evening. Now, when an older man asked quite reasonably if he might dance with the bride, she turned at once to Hank for protection. Hank smiled at the man and said sorry, she was taken. Imelda allowed Hank to hold her in his arms and they danced away, a moment noted with approval by several of those who remained in the thinning crowd. For the short time that was left she danced only with

Hank, holding on to him as if fearful of letting him go.

With Vanessa nursing her baby, Chrissie was busy helping with the clearing up. Like Imelda she had not danced all evening but she had enjoyed every minute. There was a shortage of suitable cloth for finery but one of Mrs Blanchard's friends had produced a roll of white silk for the wedding gown and there was enough left over to make a simple dress for Chrissie, the one and only bridesmaid. Chrissie loved it. She felt like a princess but, though she attracted the attention of more than one of Hank's friends, she had been careful to stay out of the limelight.

Jimmy had been standing apart, on the fringe of activities, all evening. He was more like a spectator than a guest, but it was his own choice. He had tried not to look at Chrissie too often but he had found it difficult to take his eyes off her. He knew she was beautiful, but he had never seen her looking as lovely as this. He didn't want to leave. He was happy just to be there. But others were leaving now and he didn't want to be left with just the family and Chrissie. He was sure that would embarrass her. He paid his respects to Hank and Imelda and thanked Mrs Blanchard for inviting him. 'We couldn't have a party without you, Jimmy,' Mrs Blanchard, a little light-headed, told him. 'You're part of the family now.'

He smiled and as he turned he caught Chrissie's eye. Biting her lip, she gazed back at him doubtfully. But as he left he nodded and waved and Chrissie was thrilled.

One afternoon in January, returning to his room at the college, Tom found a folded paper pinned to his door. He unfolded it curiously and read: *Dear Major Blanchard, At your convenience please contact me at my office, Warren Simpson.* Tom looked at the letter heading. Warren Simpson. Surveyor, Valuer, agent for estates. And there was the address of an office near the dockside.

Tom knew of the man only vaguely and wondered what he could possibly want. The following afternoon, his lectures over for the day, he called to find out.

A rather distinguished-looking gentleman in a sober suit, Simpson was friendly and informal. He was in his early fifties, about Tom's father's age. He smiled and said, 'Good to have you back, son. And how are you finding things now the bullets have stopped flying?'

'Peaceful,' Tom said.

'I understand you're studying law.'

'Yes, sir,' Tom answered, wondering where this was leading.

'You plan to practise in Boston?'

'Well . . . I don't know yet.'

'No, no, of course. None of my business anyway. I asked you to call because I've had some correspondence with a gentleman by the name of Sir Jack Danvers. He was formerly a colonel in the British Army. Sir Jack married one of our own local girls. Sarah Dowling. Don't know if you are aware of what happened to the Dowling family. Dreadful business.'

'Yes, sir,' Tom said. 'I do know what happened.'

Simpson nodded. 'Well, the thing is, Jack Danvers – I'm afraid I never got used to "Sir" this and "Lord" that – I'll just call him Danvers. Well anyway, Danvers, in a letter to me, has asked if I will make an evaluation of the Dowling estate, the house, the farm, the land. Quite a valuable asset, I should think. In a state of disrepair right now, I expect. However, quite valuable I'm sure. And, of course, it now belongs to Danvers' wife.'

Tom had listened carefully but he failed to see how any of this could possibly concern him.

'Thing is, Major. . . .'

'Just call me Tom, Mr Simpson,' Tom said.

'Thank you,' Simpson said. 'The thing is, Tom, I told Danvers that if I am to give an evaluation I can't be his representative or sign documents on his behalf. Conflict of interests. He would have to nominate a representative over here. He suggests I ask you.'

Does he now? thought Tom. Steals my girl. Now he wants me to safeguard his interests. 'What's involved?' he asked.

'Well, I would put a current value on the property. You would assess the market. See if you think the price is fair and reasonable, and advise Danvers whether to sell or wait until things get better.'

'That all?'

'You would be authorized to sign the new Land Registry in the absence of the owner. The old Registry is to be replaced and the property now needs to be registered in Mrs Danvers' name. You would sign as her nominated signatory.'

'I don't see any problem,' Tom said. 'But why me?'

'You are from an established local family, a major in the war, a lawyer-to-be. Mr and Mrs Danvers must regard you as a friend.'

'Sounds fairly painless,' Tom said. 'Yes, I'll do it. I'm glad you asked, in fact, because this raises the question of my sister-in-law's claim to the Harvies' house, or at least the land it stands on.'

'Your sister-in-law?'

'Imelda Harvie married my brother at Christmas.'

'Oh, that's nice,' Simpson said, without a trace of irony. 'I'm sure old Max would have been pleased.'

'I don't think so,' Tom said. 'My brother was an officer in the Congressional Army.'

Simpson smiled. 'I see. Well, I'm sure Mary would have been happy for Imelda. She only ever wanted what was best for the girl.'

'You knew Mrs Harvie?'

'When I was your age I was crazy about her. But unfortunately, so was Max.' He laughed. 'But that was all a long time ago.'

'I think she made the wrong choice, if I may say so.'

'Thank you, son. Very diplomatic.'

'I mean it,' Tom said sincerely.

'Well anyway, Max Harvie was a client of mine so the same thing applies, if I give a valuation on the Harvie property I can't act on Imelda's behalf. Perhaps you could be a signatory in both cases.'

Tom agreed and Simpson said he would write to Danvers and to Imelda and he would confirm matters with Tom in due course.

'So it's to Mrs Imelda Blanchard now, I take it?'

'Yes,' Tom said with a smile. 'I guess we always knew they would end up together.'

'It's good to see things are getting back to normal. So many young people getting married right now with the boys home from the war.'

'Those who came home,' Tom said, thinking of Ben.

'Yes,' Simpson said soberly. 'You not married yet, Tom?'

'No, sir.'

'Well, there's plenty of time. And it's good to see relations with the British are not totally beyond repair,' he said as he accompanied Tom to the outer door.

Tom looked puzzled.

'You and Danvers,' Simpson said. 'A colonel in the British Army.'

'Actually, I don't know Danvers. I've never met the man.'

'Then you must know Mrs Danvers.'

'Yes,' Tom said quietly. 'I do.'

'I see,' Simpson said, intuitively picking up the implication.

'Forgive me, Mr Simpson,' Tom said, 'but . . . did you never marry?'

'After Mary Lowell, you mean? Of course, I did. I think of Mary from time to time. But that's all. I have a lovely wife and we have a lovely family. And so will you, son, I'm sure.'

THIRTY-EIGHT

LETTERS from Sam Smith in New York were what kept Tom Blanchard's aspirations alive during his time at Harvard. Keen political insights into the machinations of the contenders at the top kept him entertained and he always honoured the directive that ended each letter. *Burn this document now! Or its author may well be tried for sedition. PS: That is why I fail to append my signature. Yours Samuel Smith.*

The only person he knew who would be genuinely interested in what was going on in the capital was Dad. And he couldn't show Dad the letters anyway as Sam always included a salacious message from the entirely fictitious fan dancer, Bouncy Bertha, at the Crow's Nest, a dingy tavern on the seafront. This was a lady, Sam alleged, who was pining daily for Tom and couldn't wait for his return.

There were still British soldiers in New York. They seemed like a forgotten army, abandoned by their leaders, Sam reported. They were poorly paid and underfed and not surprisingly they tended to commit many minor crimes that antagonized the populace and the populace wanted them out. There were murmurings that the Congressional Army had been scaled down too fast and a much stronger force should have been retained. We may well be called back to arms, Major, Sam warned and he was only half-joking.

The main trouble since hostilities ceased, it seemed, was with the Indians. Most of the tribal chiefs had little understanding of what agreement the British and the Americans had reached and, where frontier communities were left exposed, they took full advantage. It was a problem that was to persist until the Indians were finally crushed by a force led by a Congressional Army Major General known as 'Mad' Anthony Wayne.

The war with the British was not yet officially over but by late November 1782 the Treaty of Paris had been drawn up. And it did not become apparent until later that the great skill of the old fox, Benjamin Franklin, had extracted extremely favourable concessions from the British who, he knew, were desperate to keep France and the new America apart. The French were not happy that he had concluded the negotiations without consulting them. Yet somehow, with his audacious charm, he succeeded in not completely alienating America's wartime allies. In April 1783 the Treaty was ratified by Congress. The war was finally at an end and later that year the remaining British soldiers left New York.

Tom Blanchard at Harvard was studying hard and he couldn't wait to qualify, get to the capital and start work. In the summer holidays he moved into the former tack room with Jimmy and worked at the farm and the stud, mending fences, exercising the horses, doing whatever job came to hand. He welcomed the fresh air and the sunlight after the cloistered life he'd been living the past few months. At the end of August, he had promised himself, he would spend a couple of weeks with Sam in New York.

It was late one afternoon as he was returning to the tack room that Sally, Melanie Stokes little four year old, came running to meet him. He picked her up, swung her round and she laughed and shrieked. 'Mommy wants you,' she told him.

Melanie waved to him from the back porch and he went to greet her, the little girl high on his shoulder. 'Tom,' Melanie said and her face was flushed. 'Come and sit down.'

Tom sat down in the back porch and Sally ran indoors to play with Chrissie's baby. 'What is it?' he asked. 'What's happened?'

'Oh Tom,' she said. 'I've had the most beautiful letter.'

He waited expectantly and she nodded. 'From Ben,' she said, then she realized she had given him the wrong impression. 'It doesn't say he's alive,' she added quickly. 'It's a letter from this lady and her husband on Long Island. Mr and Mrs Lowe. They say that Ben stayed with them for a while when he was on the run from the British. They're Americans, Tom, and they took him in and kept him safe until he could join the rebels.'

Tom waited, disappointed that her news was not more positive. Hank had arrived at the stables now on horseback. Tom waved and signalled to him. He dismounted, left the horse with Jimmy and came to join them.

Melanie went over her news again. 'And they enclosed a letter from Ben. He wrote it just before he left and asked them to send it on after the war. It's such a lovely letter. He says he's done what he set out to do and now he is about to join the rebel army.'

Tom recalled it was when Ben joined the rebels and was offered a commission that they were asked to vouch for him. So this was nothing new. But he smiled, not wanting to deflate Melanie's joy. The letter from Ben had obviously touched her deeply.

'What was it he set out to do?' Hank asked.

Melanie told them the story of Ben's encounter with the two redcoats in the woods when he was out with his dog. It seems one of them was dead now but the other a man named Duckett was still serving with the British. Ben was only twelve when it happened but he vowed from that day forward that when he was old enough he would find this man and kill him.

'Good for him,' Hank said.

'And did he find him?' Tom asked.

'Yes, he says John Foster helped him find out where the man's unit was stationed and even got him posted there.'

'So he got this fellow?' Hank asked.

'Yes,' Melanie said. 'It seems this man hadn't changed much. He was in trouble with the local people. They said he'd killed a boy from the village in some dispute. Anyhow, Ben got the man away from the camp and took him out to some quiet place. But he couldn't do it. He'd gone to all that trouble to get him and when he finally got him he couldn't do it. Killing a man on the battlefield is one thing, he says. It's kill or be killed. But killing a man in cold blood is something else. He just couldn't do it.'

'So what happened?' they asked.

'Well, it turned out he didn't have to. The people in the village had somehow got to know that this fellow was nearby and they arrived *en masse. They* killed him.'

'Good,' Hank said.

'Sounds horrible,' Tom said.

'Ben says in his letter he felt pretty bad about it. But the man deserved it.' She was quiet for a moment then she said, 'Trouble is I have to write to Mr and Mrs Lowe now and tell them Ben didn't come home.'

Sally came running out to the porch and jumped up into Hank's lap. Melanie's eyes had filled with tears. 'That little girl needs her Daddy,' she said quietly.

'Well,' Hank said expansively, 'she's always got two Daddys here, haven't you, smiler?' And he tickled Sally until she shrieked and wriggled away.

Another afternoon Tom came back to the house to find Vanessa standing in the doorway. 'You sit down here on the porch, Mister Tom. You look whacked out. Ah'll get you some o' that apple juice.'

'No,' Tom said and he waltzed her round. 'You sit down and I'll get *you* some apple juice.'

He sat Vanessa in the back porch and brought a jug of juice and two glasses from the kitchen. Vanessa was standing up again. 'For goodness sake,' he said, 'sit down and relax. I want to ask you something.'

'Well, that's strange,' Vanessa said, her ample frame filling the wicker chair, 'cos ah wanna ask you somethin', too.'

'All right,' Tom said. 'Ladies first.'

'It's that Jimmy,' she said. 'You know how Jimmy can read an' all? He reckons he wanna show us all how to read. Me an' Chrissie an' Chrissie's little babby when he's old enough. He reckons all of us black folk should learn to read.'

'Well, he's right.'

'You think so? Even me at ma age?'

'Doesn't matter how old you are. Think of all the fun you can get from books. Even newspapers, notices, little things.'

Vanessa looked at him, her eyes wide. 'Me? Read a book?'

'I don't see why not. I think everyone should be able to read. There's great pleasure to be found in books, stories, poems.'

'Black folks ain't suppose' to read.'

'Who says? Hank and I taught Jimmy how to read and if he wants to teach others that's fine, that's wonderful.'

'You think so?'

'I know so,' Tom said. 'You do it, Vanessa. Once you can read you'll love it. I promise you.'

Vanessa nodded. She loved this boy, she loved this family. She couldn't imagine Max Harvie urging her to learn to read. 'What did you wanna ask me, Mister Tom?'

'A couple of things,' Tom said. 'How are they getting along? Hank and Imelda. I mean, how is it *really* going.'

'Well,' Vanessa said carefully. 'Miss 'melda is a lot better. Not so jumpy now. An' she smiles a lot more these days.' She lowered her voice and leaned forward. 'An' ah think, well, ah'm pretty sure that one day soon she an' Mister Hank'll be all right.'

'How do you mean?' Tom asked.

'You watch Miss 'melda with Chrissie's babby, Mister Tom. She loves that little fella. An' ah reckon it won't be long before she want one for herself.'

'A baby?' Tom said. 'Hank would love that.'

'Ah think that'll happen. An' it won't be long. Miss 'melda got that baby look in her eyes all right.'

'Good,' Tom said. 'That would be great.'

'An' was there somethin' else?'

'Jimmy,' Tom said. 'What about Jimmy and Chrissie? How are they getting along these days?'

Vanessa sat back on her seat and laughed. 'Those two,' she said. 'They is like schoolkids, Mister Tom. They is crazy about each other but they won't admit it. Ever since the wedding they been dancing around each other. Wanting to get together but scared o' making the first move. You know what ah mean?'

'You reckon they'll be all right, too?'

'Oh, ah'm sure.'

'Well, Jimmy seems to get along fine with Chrissie's little boy.'

Vanessa nodded. 'That reminds me, Mister Tom. We just been calling that little boy 'babby' up to now but he gotta have a name. Chrissie wants to call him Joe after your Daddy.'

'I think Dad would love that,' Tom said. 'I really do.'

The officers and men left in General Washington's army were complaining bitterly about the lack of pay and the non-payment of the money they were owed. There were rumblings of mutiny and noisy airings of their fully justified grievances, a discontent that was only contained when Washington himself appealed to his officers in New York for calm and patience. He said he was old now, the war had taken its toll and he even hinted that he was going blind. He would do his best, he said, to speed things up. Soon after this he bade his loyal officers goodbye and went home to Virginia and Mount Vernon where he hoped to enjoy a long-awaited peaceful retirement. It was a forlorn hope, for his military career was soon to be replaced by his role as the new country's first president.

Tom Blanchard arrived in New York for a two-week holiday with Sam Smith late in August when the army unrest was at its height. It was time, he decided, to resign his commission and become plain 'mister' once again. Yet the people he knew in New York, to Sam's great amusement, persisted in calling him 'major'. Sam was delighted to see him and insisted on again showing him around town which meant that most mornings he woke up with a throbbing hangover.

'Tonight,' Sam announced, after more than a week of excess, 'we are to dine at the Champlain. Eight o'clock we meet up with Mr and Mrs Henry Holt. Mr Holt is the head of my department, a close colleague of John Jay and a man we do not wish to offend in any way. We must be on our best behaviour, Major. View him as a potential future employer. Charm his wife but not too much. Our Mr Holt can be a prickly character.'

'Sounds great!' Tom said ironically.

'Don't look so disheartened, Major. The Holts like to be in bed by ten-thirty, though I don't know why. Can't imagine anything much happens there.' He laughed. 'All you have to do is find out what's on at the theatre and pretend you know what it's all about. They're both crazy about the theatre. Then after dinner they might want to play a few hands of cards. Whatever you do, let 'em win.'

'As I said,' Tom told him. 'Sounds great!'

'No, listen. Plan is we see the Holts for an hour or so. They're nice people really. Then when they've gone our girls arrive.'

'Our girls?'

'Two young ladies wish to meet us later this evening and join us in a little carousing.'

'Oh yes?' Tom said. 'And what are they like these two?'

'Well, I'm afraid I couldn't get Bertha for you.'

'Why not? I thought she was pining for me.'

'She was. But she's got the pox.'

Tom laughed. 'How do we know these two haven't got the pox?'

'Wait 'til you see them. They're only young and they're lovely.'

They weren't lovely, but they weren't as awful as Tom expected and after a drink or two they looked quite acceptable. Several drinks later they looked even more so.

It was three o'clock in the morning when Tom and Sam staggered back to Sam's rooms. Sam was due at the office at nine. Nine-thirty, he said, at the latest. Tom slept until noon then jumped up with a start. He had no idea what time it was but Mr Holt was expecting him at three for afternoon tea at the Champlain Hotel.

The previous evening was a purely social occasion, Henry Holt explained. You don't know *how* social, thought Tom. Today, Mr Holt wanted to talk to Tom about his plans for after Harvard. There was a place for him in the congressional office but there were a few things he should know and understand. Tom nodded attentively as Mr Holt listened to himself speak. He was a short fat man, a little pompous. But Tom didn't dislike him.

It was an exciting time for our country, Holt told him, and Tom was lucky to be young and bright at a time when bright young men were in demand. If he came to New York he would be in at the beginning. Come back and see me as soon as you graduate, he said, and we'll see what we can do. Tom thanked him and said he would certainly do that. He didn't mention that John Adams had said much the same thing. The new leaders, it seemed, were collecting up-and-coming young men around them as insurance for the future. Mr Holt said he had to get back to his office but there was still coffee in the pot. 'You stay, son,' he said with a rosy-cheeked smile, 'and finish it off.'

The afternoon tea room at the Champlain Hotel – where, it occurred to Tom, everyone drank coffee and they would no doubt be put out if anyone asked for tea – was less than half full. Two old men, sitting alone, were reading newspapers. It was mostly old and middle-aged ladies in hats gossiping and rattling cups and saucers whenever they wanted something.

Coffee cup and saucer in hand, Tom ambled out on to the balcony in search of fresh air. The four or five tables there were empty. He chose to sit where he had a view of the busy street below. Still sleepy from the previous night's excesses, he sipped the lukewarm coffee, vowing to stay sober for the remainder of his holiday though he knew there was little chance of that with Sam in charge of proceedings.

Apart from a couple of official-looking stone buildings and in the distance, away down the avenue, the impressive edifice he guessed was the County Hall, most of the buildings, including the rather grand Champlain Hotel, were of a wooden structure.

The unmade road was dry, the traffic – men pushing handcarts, horses pulling overloaded drays, people going about their business – was sending up little clouds of dust, and the afternoon sun was filtered through a haze that seemed to hang lazily over the city.

Tom watched as a gang of children, poorly dressed urchins, boys and girls, scrabbled for something in the gutter then ran round a corner out of sight. He was tired and he was finding it difficult to keep his eyes open. Resolutely he studied the fronts of the shops opposite. A pawnbroker, an undertaker, a general store and, on the corner, a tavern.

He gazed sleepily through the haze and watched the figure of a man who was standing outside the tavern. The man was very tall and slim and he was reaching up to adjust the sign over the tavern entrance. Tom stood up, his chair scraping back as he almost dropped the coffee cup. He knew that outline, he knew that profile. There was no doubt, none whatsoever. He would know that man anywhere.

THIRTY-NINE

Tom hurried through the coffee room, his sudden haste startling the ladies in hats. He rushed down the wide stairway, through the reception area and out to the busy street. He was wideawake now but as he attempted to cross the road he was forced to jump back out of the path of a horse-drawn carriage. When he did get across and arrived at the tavern there was no sign of the man.

The double doors at the main entrance were closed. It was too early. The tavern didn't open until five o'clock. But just round the corner, he noticed, a side door was open. He went inside, blinking at the dark interior as slowly his eyes adjusted to the gloom. Chairs and stools, turned upside down, were stacked on tables. His face impassive, a young Negro mopping the floor looked up at him.

'There was a man,' Tom said. 'Just now. A tall man.'

The young Negro looked blank as if he hadn't understood.

From a door behind the bar at the end of the long room a small creased-looking man appeared. His little face was crumpled as if he had no teeth but his eyes were bright and alert. 'Sorry, sorr,' he said with a distinctive Irish brogue. 'We're not open, so we're not. Foive. Foive o'clock.'

Tom went down the room to the bar. 'I'm looking for someone,' he said hopefully. 'A gentleman. I saw him just now, outside.'

The little Irishman looked back at him doubtfully.

'He was here,' Tom said. 'Just a minute ago. He was outside the front door. Tall man. Very tall, slim.'

'An' what would ye be wantin' with this gentleman?'

'I know him,' Tom said. 'He's an old friend. Ben. Ben Withers.'

'An' 'e was here, ye say?'

Ben Withers appeared in the doorway behind the bar. 'It's all right, Paddy,' he said.

The Irishman, Paddy, withdrew as Tom rushed round the bar.

'Ben!' Tom gripped Ben in the Spanish-style *abrazo* they had employed since the days of their childhood gang. 'It *was* you!'

Tom realized that Ben was not responding, not sharing his joy. He drew back questioningly. Ben looked older. He was thinner and he was wearing a black eye patch over his left eye. But he hadn't changed all that much.

'It's good to see you, Ben,' he said quietly, but it was obvious something was wrong. Ben seemed unmoved. There was no warmth in his expression.

'Ben,' he said. 'It's me. Tom. What's going on?'

'Will I get ye a drink?' the Irishman asked, taking two chairs from a table top and setting them by the table.

Ben shook his head and Tom also declined. Then they sat down, facing each other.

'You got hit,' Tom said, referring to the eye patch.

'Cowpens,' Ben said. 'Walked into it.'

'We searched the field. Hank spent hours looking for you.'

He nodded. 'They put us in some church, left us for dead.'

'So what are you doing here? In a bar in New York.'

'I came to see Paddy. He's a good friend.'

Tom still didn't understand.

'He always said he would open a tavern in New York and he wanted me to join up with him. Well he has and after they sort of straightened me out I came looking for him.'

'Why didn't you come home?'

He laughed, a short bitter laugh. 'Home? Why would I?'

'Because Melanie is heartbroken. She thinks you're dead.'

'Good,' he said. 'I'd like to keep it that way.'

'But why? What's changed?'

'Me. I've changed. Look at me. I'm a wreck.'

'You're not the only one who was damaged in this war,' Tom told him, his voice hardening.

'Sure. And what use are we? We'd be better off dead.'

'How can you say that? You've got Melanie at home. And she wants you back. You know how it is with you two, how it's always been. She needs you.'

'She doesn't need me,' he said dismissively. 'Nobody needs a one-eyed wreck with a shattered leg.' He indicated his right leg. 'Look at that. Bone shattered, muscles torn. Useless. I can't run. I can't ride a horse. All it's good for is hobbling around. I'm finished.'

Tom was surprised and disappointed. This was purely self-pity, something he would not have expected from a man like Ben.

'Feeling sorry for yourself is no good,' he said. 'I thought you were better than that.

Ben reacted angrily. 'You did? Well, look at this.' He rolled up the leg of his breeches as far as the knee. 'Look at that!'

The leg was bent awkwardly, the skin lacerated and scarred, not fully healed even now. 'Might as well have taken it off for what use it is.' He snatched at the eye patch to reveal an empty socket. 'Not so good, eh? Well, I can get by with this.' He put the patch back in place. 'But not with a leg like that. Can't work. Can't hold down a job. Melanie doesn't need me. I'm a liability.'

'That's not true,' Tom said carefully. 'You're working now, aren't you? You're working here.'

'It's a tavern. And I'm not much use anyway, Paddy's taken me in for now but I can't stay here indefinitely. He needs a working partner not an invalid.'

'Come home, Ben. Come home with me. You know horses far better than I do. We can find something at the stud. And Dad'll love to see you again and Ma and Hank. They all think you're dead.'

'I don't want charity.'

'Come home for Melanie's sake.'

'No,' he said. 'I want her to forget me, find someone who can support her, give her a decent life.'

Tom was shaking his head but Ben leaned across the table and gripped his jacket. 'Promise me you won't tell her you've seen me.'

'No chance,' Tom said. 'I can't do that.'

'Then you'll be wasting your time and causing a lot of trouble for no good reason. Because, you know, the way things are, it's pretty easy to disappear these days. And that's what I'll do. Apart from Paddy, nobody knows me here. Sure everyone knew me when they needed me. I was Lieutenant Withers. What was that worth? Well, I'm not worth a bean now. So come looking for me again, Tom, and I'll just disappear. Leave it, eh? Forget you ever saw me.'

Tom sat back and regarded him coldly. 'Ben Withers, my old friend, I can't believe it. I thought you were a man.'

'I was once,' Ben said. He leaned forward again, looked at Tom earnestly. 'Please. If you are my friend, don't tell Melanie you've seen me. No good letting her think everything's all right because it isn't and it never can be now.'

Tom didn't know what to say.

'We open at five,' Ben told him. 'I got to sort these tables out.'

Tom nodded. 'Look,' he said. 'I'm leaving Friday. I want you to come home with me. I'll book another place on the coach. I'll ride shotgun if I have to. Just promise me you'll think about it. For old times' sake.'

'Tom, I know you mean well but it's over. Everything's over for me. I get depressed. I can be a moody bastard. I'm not going to saddle Melanie with any of that.'

He stood up and started to remove the chairs and stools from the table tops and set them upright, their meeting plainly over.

'I'll be back later,' Tom said. 'About eight. I'm out with a pal of mine tonight. We'll call in. If this really is the last time we see each other we can at least say goodbye with a drink.'

Ben looked doubtful.

'It's all right,' Tom told him. 'It's no one you know. Sam Smith. A lawyer. Works in the Congressional office. Good man. You'll like him. We're going out on the town. Join us if you like.'

Ben shook his head. 'I don't think so.'

Tom left the gloomy daytime interior of the tavern and went out into the dust-laden sunlight. He had not expected such a reaction from Ben and he didn't know what he could do about it. He knew how stubborn Ben could be. But he didn't have to go along with him. Ben couldn't expect him to go home and say nothing. He didn't agree with what Ben was doing and he wasn't going to help him do it. But then Ben was his oldest friend. Same school, same grade, same gang. No, he decided. It wouldn't be fair to Melanie. Ben had been badly wounded and he was partly disabled. But Melanie would still want him back and she would take good care of him. It was really his pride that was wounded.

That evening Tom told Sam Smith the whole story. 'I said we'd call in and see him. It's a bar opposite the Champlain.'

'I know it,' Sam said predictably. Sam seemed to know all the watering holes around town. 'It's called Hogan's. Hogan's Tavern. Run by a little Irish fellow. Paddy Hogan.'

'I just want to give it one more try and then that's it.'

'Did you tell your friend he has a little four year old?'

'No,' Tom said. 'I didn't. We don't want him to come home because he thinks he has to. And Melanie wouldn't want that, either. She would want him to come home because he wanted to, not because he felt he was under some obligation.'

'Right,' Sam said approvingly. 'You're not as dumb as you look, Major.'

By eight o'clock when Tom and Sam arrived the tavern was rapidly filling up. The clientele was mostly from what Sam described later as the lower end of the social scale and at a couple of tables there seemed to be a loud array of doubtful looking ladies. The level of noise in the place, Tom noted, would render any serious discussion impossible. He shrugged helplessly at Sam.

Paddy and the young man, who had earlier been mopping the floor, were behind the bar. But there was no sign of Ben.

'I hope he's still here,' Tom said tensely, as they made their way down the long room, fending off the over-familiarity of the ladies who, they saw, were hardly in the first flush of youth.

'He's probably taken to the hills,' Sam said, extricating himself with a charming smile from the arms that had somehow found their way around his neck.

Paddy Hogan was waving to them directing them to the end of the bar. 'Come on through,' he said. 'Through to the back.'

Beyond the door behind the bar was a kitchen and by the rear window Ben was sitting at a table with a bottle and three glasses. He stood up to greet them and Tom did the introductions. The three of them sat down and Paddy said, 'I'll leave you to it then.'

'I asked at the coach stop,' Tom said, 'and there is a seat for you. Friday morning. Seven thirty.'

Ben shook his head resignedly. 'I told you, Tom. This has got to be a farewell drink so don't spoil it. I haven't much time. I've got to help out in the bar. This place gets full later.'

'This isn't full?' Sam asked with a laugh.

'You wouldn't believe it,' Ben said. 'They're spilling out on to the street by nine o'clock. Temperance people are going crazy.'

'It's not your sort of thing, Ben,' Tom said.

'Like I said, old friend, we'll crack this bottle, say goodbye and no hard feelings.'

'So you're never going shooting again in Spring Meadow? Never going fishing on old Charlie, Sunday afternoons?'

'Stop it, Tom,' Ben said quietly. 'Those days are long gone. I'm not going back and I've told you why.'

Sam Smith was sitting there, saying nothing. Now Tom turned to him for help. 'What do you make of him, Sam?'

'Well,' Sam said carefully, 'I can see his point of view. But this is really none of my business. This is between you two.'

'But it's not,' Tom said. 'It's not just between us. It's between him and his lifelong girl, his poor old aunt who's taken care of him, my brother, his friends. He's turning his back on all of us.'

Sam shrugged. 'Like I said, none of my business.'

'No,' Tom insisted. 'What do you think?'

Sam shook his head but Ben said, 'Have your say. I don't mind. It won't make any difference.'

'You don't mind?' Sam put down his glass and a change seemed to come over him. 'You're inviting me to express an opinion?'

'Sure,' Ben said. 'Why not?'

'Well, I'll tell you,' Sam said. 'I think you're a disgrace. You're a coward. Running away because you can't face up to the way things are. You look to me as though you've had it pretty good up to now. You've got an education. You've got friends who care about you. You have a lot going for you. All you've lost is one eye and some of the use in a badly injured leg. You didn't run away from the British so why are you running away now? I'll tell you why. You're running away because you're vain, conceited, arrogant and sorry for yourself.'

This was strong stuff and Ben was bristling. Tom watched him warily, ready to restrain him if he suddenly erupted.

'Let me tell you something else,' Sam said. 'My brother-in-law was killed at Hobkirk Hill. My sister wouldn't care if he had no eyes and no legs if she could have him back. Your problems are nothing, pal. Why, your injuries could be an asset. You could travel around the country, raising money for the women who have been widowed and the kids who have lost their dads. You've still got your life. Use it, man.'

Ben sat quite still, taking it all.

Sam stood up suddenly. 'I'm not sitting here, drinking with this fellow,' he said. 'He's pathetic. I'll see you outside, Tom.' And with that he left.

Ben was clearly shaken. He put his glass down carefully.

'I'm sorry, Ben,' Tom said. 'I think that was a bit much. But you did ask him.'

Ben didn't speak. He just stared at the floor.

'I'd better go,' Tom said. 'If it's goodbye, then I'm sorry. I wish you well whatever you decide. You know that. But if you change your mind I'll be at the coach stop seven a.m Friday.'

Sam was waiting outside, apparently enjoying the provocative banter of the street women. Tom emerged and they left to a flurry of suggestive catcalls.

'That was a bit strong, Samuel,' Tom said. 'You left Ben in a state of shock in there.'

'Good,' he said. 'That was the idea.'

'You were lucky he didn't knock you down.'

'He wouldn't do that. He's bigger than me.'

'Sorry about your sister,' Tom said.

Sam looked at him sideways as they walked along. 'Sister?'

Tom drew him to a halt. 'The one who lost her husband.'

'I don't have a sister,' Sam said innocently.

'Sam Smith,' Tom said. 'You lying sod.'

Sam laughed. 'It wasn't a lie. I'm a diplomat, Tom. I bend the truth a bit. That's what we diplomats do.'

'You lied,' Tom insisted.

'Listen,' Sam said. 'Telling lies is all right if you do it to help someone. If you're trying to make things better and it doesn't hurt anyone else it's OK. What I said to your friend Ben might help him think straight.'

They knew that night would be Tom's last night in New York for some time and Sam was determined to make certain it was a memorable one. But next morning Tom couldn't remember a thing and he left in a daze at a few minutes to seven. He had to run all the way to the coach stop but when he arrived, breathless, his heart jumped for joy.

'I thought you weren't coming,' Ben said.

When they arrived in Cambridge they went to Tom's room in college.

369

The vacation porter was not happy about this. The college was closed for the holidays. The only students there were those who, long before the end of term, had obtained permission to stay. My friend's a war veteran, Tom told him and when the man saw Ben, his eye patch, his dragging leg, he weakened. Just for a couple of nights, Tom begged and the porter relented.

The plan was that Tom would bring Melanie from home and he would leave them alone in his room until they were ready to come out. Early next morning he hired a horse at the livery stable and arrived at Melanie's just after breakfast.

'Uncle Tom!' Sally came running out and jumped up into his arms. He put a finger to his lips and carried the little girl into the house.

Melanie and her mother were surprised and delighted to see him. 'When did you get back?' Melanie asked.

Tom looked at her with an extremely serious expression but he couldn't sustain it. With its own momentum a huge smile spread across his face and broke out like a sunburst.

Melanie laughed. 'What? What is it?'

She stared at him, her eyes wide. Mrs Stokes stopped what she was doing and looked up.

'I've found him!' Tom said. 'Ben!'

Melanie looked as though she had been struck dumb. Mrs Stokes, her mouth open, picked up Sally. Then Melanie ran, as Sally had, and jumped into his arms and hugged him. Tom swung her round in the small living room.

She pulled back and looked into his eyes. 'Where is he?'

Tom set her down and took her hands in his. 'In Cambridge. He stayed in my room at the college last night. He came home with me from New York and it was really late when we arrived.'

'You should have brought him here.'

'Sit down,' Tom said, serious now. 'I couldn't do that. I wanted to see you first.'

'He's all right, isn't he?'

'Well, no,' he said, 'not exactly. He was quite badly wounded in a battle in South Carolina. Place called Hannah's Cowpens. He lost an eye, Melanie.'

Her hand went to her mouth. It was his eyes she saw when she thought of him. First thing she remembered in the morning, his eyes were with her all day and last thing at night.

'And his leg was pretty badly damaged. He walks with a limp.'

'But he's all right?'

Tom grinned reassuringly. 'Oh, sure. He's still Ben. He's still the crazy, unpredictable Ben we all love.'

Sally was wriggling on her grandmother's knee. Mrs Stokes took the little girl by the hand. 'This is wonderful news, Tom. I'll take Sally in the garden, leave you two to talk.'

Tom had decided to tell Melanie the truth, the whole truth, that he had found Ben working in a tavern in New York, that he wasn't planning on coming home because he didn't want to be a burden. He told her about Sam, too, and how Sam told him she would still want him if he had no eyes and no legs.

Melanie was laughing through her tears. 'Of course,' she said. 'Of course I would.' Then, anxiously, she asked, 'Does he know about Sally?'

Tom shook his head. 'No, but he'll be thrilled, Melanie. He'll just love her.'

Melanie touched her hair. 'I must go to him. I have to get ready. My mother will take care of Sally.'

'I think your mother and Sally should go with us. When I take you to Ben they can wait in the garden. Then when you're ready you can bring him out to meet her.'

Melanie was in a hurry now, worrying about her appearance, wanting to look her best, wanting Sally to look her best.

'I'll hire a trap,' Tom said, thinking it might be a good idea to get out of the way for a while. He rode down to the carriage post opposite Warren Simpson's office and when he returned with a pony and trap they were ready and waiting. They climbed up eagerly and as Tom took the reins, his hired horse hitched to the rear, the excitement was almost tangible.

When they arrived Mrs Stokes took Sally to see the fishpond. Tom led Melanie as far as the corridor outside his room. He put a steadying hand on her arm. 'You go in,' he said. 'I'll be outside.'

Melanie was apprehensive now. It was almost five years since she and Ben had said goodbye. 'How do I look?'

'You look lovely,' Tom said. Then, with a smile, 'I almost wish he hadn't come home.'

She reached up and kissed him on the cheek, then she showed him her crossed fingers and went inside.

371

When they finally emerged Tom was chasing Sally round the ornamental pond. Ben embraced Mrs Stokes who was struggling to hide her tears then Melanie gripped his hand. 'Come on,' she said. 'There's someone I want you to meet.'

FORTY

B Y 1786 Tom Blanchard was a qualified lawyer based in New York, a rising star in the new administration with all the right connections. Though there was much unrest and disillusionment with the way things were five years after Yorktown, Tom's own family had prospered and many problems had been resolved.

Hank and Imelda had two children, a boy they named Tom, a girl they named Mary. Imelda was quieter, more inhibited than she had been in the old days but she had closed a door on the events that redefined her life. The door would always be there and just occasionally a word, a reference might nudge it open and she would have to fight to fend off a recollection of that dreadful ordeal and the day she lost both her mother and her father. But most of the time she was well, delighted by and devoted to her children, and safe with Hank.

Hank and Jimmy were busy developing the Blanchard business to include, among other things, housebuilding. After building the small house now occupied by his parents, Hank had built a similar house with Jimmy and Chrissie in mind. It had become increasingly obvious that those two would eventually get together and with the completion of the second house Hank declared it was time for Jimmy to move out of 'that old tack room'. It might also be time, he hinted, for Jimmy and Chrissie to get married and they did.

Ben Withers was ready to build a bigger house for his family on the land left him by his father's brother, the project British taxes had previously put out of his reach. But believing Ben to be dead an opportunist land speculator had erected a six-foot high fence around the five-acre plot with a view to development and was now refusing to leave.

Hank advocated tearing the fence down and threatening the

intruder with violence, starting a small war if necessary. Ben, instead, consulted Tom who simply sent the man a letter on Congressional office notepaper warning him of 'costly' court proceedings and his subsequent portrayal as a profiteer who was attempting to steal the rightful heritage of 'one of our local revolutionary heroes'. The man quietly withdrew.

In New York Sam Smith, aware of Tom's eagerness to see Europe, had suggested he should recommend Tom for a post that would soon become vacant in Paris, aide to the American ambassador. 'You could really live the good life there, Major,' he enthused. 'All those *mad'moiselles*! They'd go crazy over a handsome young buck like Tom Blanchard.'

'What about you?' Tom asked. 'Aren't you interested?'

'Last week, yes. This week, no. Such is the fickle grasshopper nature of my ambition.'

'So what's changed?'

'I have,' Sam said. 'Sunday I met this girl. I know she's the one. Father's a merchant banker, finger in all the pies.'

'You haven't told me anything about the girl.'

'She's gorgeous,' he said. 'Bright, intelligent, beautiful.'

'It's not Bertha then?'

Sam laughed. 'The Bouncy Bertha days are over, Tom. My girl's a real beauty. Her name's Caroline.'

'Does she know she's your girl?'

'Not yet, no. But she will. And that's why, right now, I need to stay in town.' He looked at Tom with his head on one side and his usual lopsided grin. 'So do I recommend you for Paris? It's a major opportunity, Major.'

Sam was right. It was a major opportunity and Tom was eager to take it. 'Too bad you and I were not there when Mr Franklin was in Paris,' Sam said. Like most of the young men skirting the foothills of the political heights, Sam was fascinated by the skilled and seasoned negotiator Benjamin Franklin. 'Mr Franklin is what I call a true man of the world. Been everywhere, done everything. Been to bed with some of the most beautiful women in Paris.'

'Only *some*?' Tom asked in amusement.

'You may scoff, Major. But he loves the ladies, rich or poor, humble or grand, and they love him. What a man! Just wait until you meet him!'

When Tom did finally meet him, Benjamin Franklin was eighty years old and racked by a painful sciatica that caused him to bend slightly on one hip but he had lost none of his natural charm and magnanimity. As Mr Franklin had returned from Paris and was no longer Minister to France Sam Smith had little or no excuse for introducing a young, inexperienced aide to the great man. Yet undeterred, though with cautious deference, he said, 'Mr Franklin sir, may I introduce my friend Tom Blanchard? Tom is shortly to take up a post in Paris.'

Franklin, leaning heavily on his walking stick, regarded Tom sternly. Then he smiled and said, 'What a lucky young man you are. Fine fellow like you, you will have the time of your life. I envy you. I really do. You will love Paris and Paris will love you.'

He turned painfully to go on his way but he paused. 'Even an ugly *Parisienne* knows how to look beautiful,' he said. Again he turned to go and again he paused, 'Always remember, my boy,' he said, 'if you want to make beautiful music you must first practise on an old fiddle.'

This time he did go, waving his stick above his head as he went.

'What does he mean, practise on an old fiddle?' Tom asked.

'Come on,' Sam said. 'What do you think he means?'

'Is that all you ever think about?'

'I guess so,' Sam admitted. 'Beautiful girls and old fiddles. Mr Franklin and me we're birds of a feather.'

The long voyage out seemed a great adventure. Tom had sailed the rivers in boats and on home-made rafts but he had never been to sea. As a boy he had watched the big ships leaving Boston dock and wondered if he would ever sail in one. Now it was happening. Paris, France! And who knows? Maybe London, England.

Tom arrived in Paris in July, 1786 and he soon found himself in exalted company. Thomas Jefferson had been in Paris as Minister to France for the past two years. Jefferson, though not himself a war veteran, was a good friend of the Marquis de Lafayette who Tom remembered from Valley Forge. Much admired at home and abroad the marquis had a distinguished war record. Now he had taken to lobbying for fair compensation for those of his fellow officers, Frenchmen, who had suffered severe injury in the fight for America. The Minister to France was sympathetic, promising to pursue the matter at home.

Mr Jefferson's senior aide had a censorious American wife who had insisted on accompanying him on his Paris posting. Now he was pleased to allow Tom to take over the social duties expected of an aide to a minister. Tom was young and fancy free and he was always a welcome guest. Almost every evening and on many afternoons there was something going on and he soon discovered there was a whole orchestra of old fiddles eager for him to play.

The parties and the soirées and the afternoon At Homes soon palled. To Tom they seemed trivial and pointless with silly guests playing endless word games, dressing up in extravagant costumes and extraordinary wigs piled high and powdered so heavily that the wearer left a trail of dust in his or her wake. He wondered what someone like Dan Morgan would make of them all.

Tom had never consciously worn a wig, ever since he was aged seven, in fact, when he refused point blank to be a page boy at someone's wedding. Now, as he watched the mincing and the prancing of the foppish young men, he vowed he never would. His thick brown hair was tied back by a black ribbon and that was all the adornment he needed.

These people seemed to have no work to attend and they were always available for even the most fatuous get-together. Yet both the marquis and Mr Jefferson attended many of these events and appeared to enjoy being there. Tom could not reconcile the waste, the unnecessary quantities of food, the free-flowing wine, with the desperation he saw in people's eyes as he walked the streets. It was the street life that drew him, pierced his heart. There was poverty at home in Boston. But this was not mere poverty. This was a gnawing hunger for basic food, a crust of bread, anything. It was a hunger that turns to anger, the raging anger of a man who has worked and not been paid; and panic, the abject panic of a mother who has no food to feed her children.

Once, in Montparnasse, a coach had stopped and an associate of the marquis had counselled him to come aboard. '*Mon Dieu!*' the man had cried. 'You cannot walk the streets alone, my boy. This is not New York!' He knew the man meant well and was probably right. He had been pinned in a doorway once as an angry mob with flaming torches roared by intent on burning and looting. Their country had been drained by the excesses of the upper crust and by costly excursions into conflicts abroad. 'No more foreign wars!' they chanted. To a detached observer like Tom it was obvious that a day of reckoning could not be far off. Yet the king and queen and those close to them, their courtiers and hangers-on, the empty-headed partygoers and parasites seemed blissfully unaware of how their desperately poor, fellow Parisians were obliged to live.

Mr Jefferson, like Paris itself, was an enigma. He was a likeable man and, to Tom, he seemed to have an aura about him, as if he was somehow 'special', a man of destiny. Yet Tom was troubled by the knowledge that this man, the man responsible for those lovely words and cadences of the Declaration of Independence still employed slaves. He had actually brought two of them with him to Paris. Mr Jefferson was a widower and he had allegedly vowed, in love and respect for his dead wife, he would never again marry. Now it was fairly common knowledge he was having an affair with a married woman, a Mrs Cosway. It was a little less known that he was sleeping with a young mulatto girl, one of the slaves he had brought with him to France ostensibly to take care of his youngest daughter. None of these private matters concerned Tom. What concerned and disturbed Tom Blanchard was the fact that the man who wrote the Declaration still owned slaves.

He was puzzled, too, that the Marquis de Lafayette, whom he regarded as a fine soldier and a gentleman, could waste his time on high society's low life when clearly his country and especially Paris, a city he professed to love, so urgently needed the help and guidance of a man like him.

It was at a soirée one evening at the home of the marquis that Tom was surprised when the marquis beckoned him to his side and offered him a glass of wine. 'I 'ave intended to speak with you,' the marquis told him in his measured English. 'I 'ave noted your presence on several occasions.'

'Sir?' Tom said.

'Your face,' the marquis said. 'I feel I 'ave seen it somewhere. We 'ave met?'

Tom nodded. 'Valley Forge, sir. With General Washington.'

'Ah yes! Valley Forge. 'Appy days, huh?' The marquis sipped his wine. 'You enjoy your time in Paris?'

'I find the city is fascinating.'

His head to one side the marquis smiled and suggested, 'But not, peut-être, nos frivolités, our . . . how you say . . . our parties.'

Tom remained silent, not sure how he should respond. A young man in an extraordinary wig, an elaborately fussy jacket and extra high buckled shoes flounced by. The marquis caught the look in Tom's eye and smiled. 'You do not approve?'

'I'm sorry, sir,' Tom said, 'if I give that impression. It is not my place to approve or otherwise.'

'Say what you will,' he said and, wine glass in one hand, he indicated the dance floor. 'What do you think of these fellows?'

Tom hesitated, but then he said, 'I don't think any of them would survive Valley Forge.'

He felt at once it was a mistake. These were his host's guests. He had been discourteous. Perhaps his tact and discretion were being tested? But the marquis laughed heartily and slapped him on the back. 'C'est vrai, Monsieur. . . ?'

'Blanchard, sir. Tom Blanchard.'

'Well, Monsieur Blanchard, you must enjoy Paris. Every man who sees Paris when 'e is young must leave with the memory of some exquisite moment, a moment to lighten 'is old age, a memory to live in 'is 'eart until the day 'e dies.'

He called over a member of his entourage, a quiet man more soberly dressed than most. The marquis whispered in the man's ear then turned to Tom. 'A bientôt, m'sieur. Bonne chance!'

The man drew Tom aside to hand him an elegantly printed card. La Comtesse Irena, he read. There was an address in Notre Dame des Champs. One of Ben Franklin's old fiddles?

'Did Mr Franklin know this lady?' he asked innocently.

The man nodded. 'C'est possible, m'sieur. C'est très possible.'

In her younger days, Tom discovered, the comtesse had been a beautiful and much sought after courtesan. Now in her late sixties she was an elegant and discreet provider of young ladies for the delectation of gentlemen of rank.

In a very short time at the house of the comtesse on the Rue Huysmans, Tom became fond of a young lady named Monique. He had visited the young lady so often in recent months the comtesse had warned him that 'to fall in love' with one of her girls was not allowed. He must cool his ardour or Monique must be sent away. But Tom believed he and Monique had discovered something special, a true rapport. Either she was genuinely fond of him or she was a superb actress. Whatever happened now he would have his exquisite memories to take with him when he left.

He had been in Paris almost two years when the opportunity arose for him to fulfil a long-cherished ambition. The senior aide had been called home some months before and Tom was now his successor. When it became necessary for an envoy to take a trip to London on behalf of the minister it fell to Tom.

That November, 1789, Mr Jefferson returned home to spend a holiday at Monticello, his estate in Virginia. He had intended to return to Paris early in spring but in December he was appointed Secretary of State in New York. This meant that Tom could either take up a new post with Mr Jefferson or stay in Paris. He decided he would make his choice when he got back from London.

Tom Blanchard had met his country's four greatest statesmen by then, three of whom in unbroken succession were to become the President of the United States and a fourth who, had he been twenty years younger, would almost certainly have joined them. Tom was quietly ambitious and well aware that his career could best be furthered in New York but, despite the tension and the turmoil in the streets, he was enjoying Paris.

On 14 July a raging mob had stormed the Bastille. On 5 October the women of Paris had marched on Versailles demanding bread for their children. The city was in the throes of revolution and the King and his close coterie of Royalists had been slow to respond. Now, as Tom boarded the coach for Calais the driver offered him a musket with an insulting smirk. 'Know how to use one of these?' Tom took the musket. 'Better than you, m'sieur,' he said.

The driver was right to be cautious. Leaving Les Invalides the coach was shaken and jostled by a marauding mob, breaking through only when the lead horses reared up and raced away. Sullen faces had glowered in at the occupants of the coach, warned off only when Tom brandished the musket. Thus it was that on his long awaited trip to London, Tom found his thoughts were centred on the way things were in Paris and his concern for what might happen to a girl like Monique rather than his long held preoccupation with the posssibility he might see Sarah.

In London Tom was a guest of a Lord and Lady Phillips who were great friends of John Adams and his wife Abigail. They were extremely well connected and more than willing to advise him socially but the meetings and talks he had to attend took much of his time and he had less than four days left when he found an opportunity to enquire about Jack Danvers. It turned out that both Lord Phillips and Jack Danvers

---

were members of the Royal Society.

'Danvers?' Phillips exclaimed. 'Fine fellow. Like to meet him?'

'Yes, sir,' Tom said, and he told them about Sarah's property in Boston. 'I really need to contact him before I leave.'

'I can arrange that,' Phillips said at once. 'Leave it to me.'

'You're very kind, sir,' Tom said.

The chambers of the Royal Society in Somerset House on the Strand were limited in space and there was no room for a restaurant. Members lunched at an excellent small restaurant nearby. Lord Phillips arranged for himself, Tom and Danvers to meet there.

Tom had never met Danvers but when he and Lord Phillips arrived at the restaurant he had little doubt that Danvers was the tall distinguished-looking fellow who was waving at them from a corner table. He was handsome all right, Tom conceded, and not in the foppish, bewigged way of so many of his fellow Englishmen. He greeted Tom with a grin and a firm handshake.

'Major Blanchard,' he said, 'we meet at last.'

At lunch the main topic of conversation was the situation in Paris. But towards the end of the meal Tom mentioned Sarah's property in Boston. Lord Phillips finished his coffee and cognac and said he had to go. He would leave them to discuss their private business.

'I've heard a lot about you, Major Blanchard,' Danvers said when they were alone.

'*Mister* Blanchard now,' Tom said with a smile, 'but I would rather you called me Tom.'

Danvers nodded. 'Thank you, then you must call me Jack.'

'So, Jack,' Tom said, 'how is Sarah?'

'I suppose I owe you an apology,' Danvers said. 'I took her away from you. But it wasn't easy, believe me. She was still totally smitten with this Tom Blanchard but the man was dead.'

Tom wondered how much Danvers knew at the time about what Max Harvie did but he didn't have to ask.

'According to Sarah,' Danvers said, 'her Uncle Max was responsible for that rumour.'

'It wasn't just a rumour,' Tom said. 'He added my name and my brother's name to an official list of rebel dead.'

'I hope you don't believe I had anything to do with that.'

Tom shook his head. 'No, of course not.'

'As far as I knew you were dead and Sarah was alone in the world.

I was free to ask for her hand in marriage and, thank God, she accepted. If she had returned to Boston with the Harvies she might have suffered the sort of fate they did.'

'You heard about all that?'

'Sarah writes to a young lady – *Melanie*?' He spread his hands. 'No hard feelings then?'

'No,' Tom said. 'Of course not.'

'Well, look. This Sunday we'd like you to come out to the house. Sunday lunch. Sarah would love to see you again.'

Tom looked doubtful.

'You must,' Danvers said. 'She would never forgive me if I didn't bring you home. You two must have lots to talk about.'

Tom nodded. Danvers clearly didn't see him as any kind of threat. 'Thank you,' he said. 'I'll look forward to it.'

That Sunday morning Danvers sent a liveried coachman and an enclosed carriage to bring Tom the few miles out of the city to his family seat in Buckinghamshire. Enchanted by the verdant views and the distant, dust-coloured hills, Tom felt that in many ways this old England was just like his own New England. They even had the same kind of rustic ensconced under the eaves of a tavern, a glass of ale on an upright barrel at his side, both hands resting on a knobbly walking stick as if he was presiding over the world's court. Then he remembered that all this was here long before his homeland existed.

The quietly trotting horses turned in now at a short drive and came to a halt. Unhurriedly the driver slid from his perch and methodically swung open two tall gates. Then, with infinite calm and patience, he climbed back into his seat, shook his reins and the horses lazily ambled through. Tom watched as, with time passing at a walking pace, the coachman climbed down again and closed the gates behind them.

The house was at the end of a 200 yard lane and, through a variety of trees, Tom caught glimpses of a large russet façade with many windows. At last the coach trundled to a halt before a wide impressive entrance.

Danvers, was standing in the porch. 'Tom! Good trip, I hope?'

'Lovely countryside,' Tom said, 'I enjoyed it.'

A butler hovered, his routine countermanded as Danvers led Tom through a large elegant hallway to a comfortable drawing-room where Sarah was waiting. A cradle with a sleeping baby was by her chair. A small boy played on the floor with a tiny terrier dog. Sarah stood up slowly and came to greet him.

'Tom,' she said softly. 'Is it really you?'

She held out her hands and Tom took them in his and they faced each other, smiling. She hadn't changed much. Same startlingly green eyes, a little thicker round the waist after bearing her two children, a woman now, no longer a girl.

At that moment they didn't know what to say, or what they wanted to say. Sarah introduced him to the little boy whose name was Jack and the little boy told him excitedly about the fights his little dog had with the cook's cat. Then a nursemaid took the boy's hand and, wheeling the cradle, led him away.

Lunch was a strange affair. Polite conversation, Jack asking about Parisian friends none of whom Tom knew, Tom and Sarah self-consciously catching each other's eye. They sat through coffee with the silences growing longer until Jack stood up and with one of his most charming smiles said, 'I'll leave you two to talk. I'm surplus to requirements here.'

'Oh, no, not at all,' Tom said.

'Don't be silly,' Sarah said.

But he waved away their protests and left them alone.

'Well, Lady Danvers,' Tom said.

'Well, Mr Blanchard,' Sarah said. 'You look, I don't know . . .'

'Older?' he suggested.

'Stronger, more mature.'

'And you look as lovely as ever.'

Sarah seemed to withdraw slightly. 'It's been such a long time.'

'Ten years,' Tom said.

'So much has happened.'

'Yes,' he said. 'You've acquired a husband.' He smiled. 'A man who's a pillar of the English establishment, a title for yourself, a lovely home and two lovely children. In fact, you have everything Max Harvie wanted for Imelda.'

'Imelda will be safe with your brother.'

'Absolutely,' Tom agreed.

'Uncle Max,' she said, 'tried to control the future but it can't be done. The future goes its own way.'

'And are you happy, Sarah?'

She shrugged. 'What is "happy"?'

'You have what many ladies would want. Your husband. . . .'

'Jack is a good man.'

'He treats you well?'

'Oh, yes. Very well. And he loves the children.'

'And you love him?'

She hesitated. 'I *like* him. He's a nice man. Oh, he has his "gels" in town. His dancers and his chorus girls. They all do.'

'And you don't mind?'

'That's the way it is, Tom. The *English* way. The men have their mistresses but nothing comes between them and their family. The family is everything. The home, the children and the complaisant wife. That's what I was told to expect and that's the way it is.'

'But do you love him?'

'Not in the way you mean. Not in the way I loved you. But we were young. It was different then.'

'And now it's too late?'

'Oh, Tom. You know it is. My life is here now. You and I could never be. Not now.'

He came round the table, took her hand and drew her to her feet. Then he took her in his arms and she responded eagerly but just as suddenly she withdrew, her face flushed.

She pleaded with her eyes. 'Don't do this to me, Tom. Please. My life has been torn apart – twice. I lost my whole family then I lost you. As far as I knew, you were dead. Gone forever. But I never forgot you and I never will.'

He nodded, knowing it was over.

The rest of the afternoon passed in inconsequential chat and though both Tom and Sarah were quiet and subdued Jack Danvers, at his amusing best, didn't seem to notice.

'Thank you for today, Jack,' Tom said as his coach arrived and, with Sarah out of earshot, he added, 'I wanted to see Sarah again. I wanted to know if there was still something between us.'

Danvers smiled. 'And was there?'

Tom shook his head. 'No,' he said. 'We're just old friends. Nothing more.'

'Then I hope you will remain friends – with both of us.'

Sarah came to join them. 'Tom was just saying,' Danvers said. 'Friendship is everything now.'

Tom nodded. 'Our two countries must stand together. We must put the past behind us.'

He kissed Sarah lightly on the cheek, shook hands warmly with Danvers and climbed into the carriage. Then, as Tom raised a hand in parting, Danvers put a protective arm around Sarah's shoulder and together they waved him goodbye.

At the end of the lane the coachman went through his usual unhurried routine, opening and closing the gates, and as the tall gates closed behind them it occurred to Tom that Sarah was like a caged bird here, safe behind these aristocratic ramparts. But caged. He thought of those green eyes and that lovely face and of the first time he ever saw her, knowing he would probably never see her again.

He looked out at the country road that stretched ahead. His business in England was over, both official and personal. He must return to the turmoil that was Paris. There he must determine his future. Paris or New York.

Sarah was gone now but she had a hold on a part of his heart and, like the bond that bound this old country to those lost colonies, it would always be there.